Praise for D

"A woman on the run, a grieving husband, a bereft sister, a brokenhearted lover, a determined detective—or are they? Nothing is as it seems in Kimberly Belle's knockout thriller *Dear Wife*. I tore through the pages of this clever, multi-layered stunner. Not even the most astute suspense fan will see what's coming until the final, jaw-dropping twist. Clear your calendar and put *Dear Wife* at the top of your to-be-read list. Five breathtaking stars!"

—**Heather Gudenkauf, *New York Times* bestselling author of *The Weight of Silence* and *Before She Was Found***

"Subtle, insidious, clever—*Dear Wife* is spellbinding. I was hooked from the first page. You're going to love Kimberly Belle's latest outing. And you aren't going to see it coming."

—**J.T. Ellison, *New York Times* bestselling author of *Tear Me Apart***

DEAR WIFE

KIMBERLY BELLE

PARK
ROW
BOOKS

PARK
ROW
BOOKS™

Recycling programs
for this product may
not exist in your area.

ISBN-13: 978-0-7783-0508-8

Dear Wife

First published in 2019. This edition published in 2020.

Copyright © 2019 by Kimberle S. Belle Books, LLC

This edition published by arrangement with Harlequin Books S.A.

Park Row Books
22 Adelaide St. West, 40th Floor
Toronto, Ontario M5H 4E3, Canada
ParkRowBooks.com
BookClubbish.com

Printed in U.S.A.

For the lovely ladies of Altitude—Angelique, Jen, Mandy, Marquette, Nancy and Tracy. I'm still not jumping out of that airplane.

Also by Kimberly Belle

The Last Breath
The Ones We Trust
The Marriage Lie
Three Days Missing

DEAR WIFE

BETH

I hit my blinker and merge onto the Muskogee Turnpike, and for the first time in seven long years, I take a breath. A real, full-body breath that blows up my lungs like a beach ball. So much breath that it burns.

It tastes like freedom.

Four hours on the road, two hundred and eighty-three miles of space between us, and it's nowhere near enough. I still hear the clink of your keys when you toss them on the table, still tense at the thud of your shoes when you come closer to the kitchen. Still feel the fear slithering, snake-like, just under the surface of my skin.

You have three moods lately: offensive, enraged or violent. That moment when you come around that corner and I see which one it is always inches bile up my throat. It's the worst part of my day.

I tell myself, no more. No more tiptoeing around your temper, no more dodging your blows.

Those days, like Arkansas, are in my rearview mirror.

For early afternoon on a Wednesday, the highway is busy, dusty semis rumbling by on both sides, and I hold my hands at ten and two and keep the tires between the lines.

Oklahoma is crisscrossed with turnpikes like this one, four-lane highways dotted with cameras for speeding and toll violations. It's too soon still for one of them to be clocking every black sedan with Arkansas plates that whizzes by, but I'm also not giving them any reason to. I use my blinkers and hold my speed well under the limit, even though what I'd really like to do is haul ass.

I hit the button for the windows, letting the highway air wash away the smell of you, of home. At sixty-four miles an hour, the wind is brutal, hot and steamy and oppressive. It reeks of pasture and exhaust, of nature and chemicals, none of it pleasant. It whips up a whirlwind in the car, blowing my hair and my clothes and the map on the passenger's seat, rocking it in the air like a paper plane. I reach down, shimmy out of a shoe and smack it to the seat as a paperweight. You're serious about holding on to me, which means I need to hold on to that map.

It may be old-school, but at least a map can't be traced. Not that you'd have already discovered the number for the burner phone charging in the cup holder, but still. Better to not take any chances. I took the phone out of the package but haven't powered it up—not yet. Not until I get where I'm going. I haven't made it this far into my new life only to be hauled back into the old one.

So far, this state looks exactly like the one I left

behind—fields and farms and endless belts of faded asphalt. Sounds the same, too. Local radio stations offer one of two choices, country music or preachers. I listen to a deep voice glorifying the power of forgiveness, but it's a subject I can no longer get behind. I toggle up the dial, stopping on a Miranda Lambert anthem that's much more my speed these days—gunpowder and lead—and give a hard twist to the volume dial.

For the record, I never wanted this. Running away. Leaving everything and everyone behind. I try not to think about all the things I'll miss, all the *faces* I'll miss, even if they won't miss mine. Part of the planning was putting some space between me and people I love most, not letting them in on the truth. It's the one thing I can't blame you for—the way I drove a wedge into those friendships all by myself so you wouldn't go after them, too. There's only one person who knows I'm gone, and everyone else... It'll be days, maybe weeks until they wonder where I am.

You're smart, so I have to be smarter. Cunning, so I have to be more cunning. Not exactly a skill I possessed when we walked down the aisle all those years ago, when I was so squishy in love. I looked into those eyes of yours and promised till death would we part, and I meant every word. Divorce was never an option—until it was.

But the first time I mentioned the word, you shoved me to the floor, jammed a gun into my mouth and dared me to say it again. Divorce. Divorce divorce divorce *divorce*. I never said the word out loud again, though I will admit it's been an awful lot on my mind.

I picture you walking through the door at home, looking for me. I see you going from room to room, hollering and cursing and finally, calling my cell. I see you following its muffled rings into the kitchen, scowling when you realize they're coming from the cabinet under the sink. I see you wrenching open the doors and dumping out the trash and digging through sludgy coffee grounds and the remains of last night's stir-fry until you find my old iPhone, and I smile. I smile so damn hard my cheeks try to tear in two.

I wasn't always this vindictive, but you weren't always this mean. When we met, you were charming, warming up my car on cold mornings or grilling up the most perfect strip steak for my birthday. You can still be sweet and charming when you want to be. You're like the cocaine they slip the dogs that patrol the cars at the border; you gave me just enough of what I craved to keep me searching for more. That's part of what took me so long to leave. The other part was the gun.

So no, I didn't want to do this, but I did plan for it. Oh, how I planned for this day.

My first day of freedom.

JEFFREY

When I pull into the driveway after four days on the road, I spot three things all at once.

First, the garbage bins are helter-skelter in front of the garage door two days after pickup, rather than where they belong, lined up neatly along the inside right wall. The living room curtains are drawn against the last of the afternoon light, which means they've probably been like that since last night, or maybe all the nights I've been gone. And despite the low-lying sun, the porch lights are on—correction: *one* of them is on. The left-side bulb is dead, its glass smoky and dark, making it seem like the people who live here couldn't be bothered with changing it, which is inaccurate. Only one of us couldn't be bothered, and her name is Sabine.

I stop. Shake it off. No more complaining—it's a promise I've made to myself. No more fighting.

I grab my suitcase from the trunk and head inside. "Sabine?"

I stand completely still, listening for sounds upstairs. A shower, a hair dryer, music or TV, but there's nothing. Only silence.

I toss my keys on the table next to a pile of mail three inches thick. "Sabine, you here?" I head farther into the house.

I think back to our phone conversation earlier this morning, trying to recall if she told me she'd be home late. Even on the best days, her schedule is a moving target, and Sabine doesn't always remember to update our shared calendar.

She'd prattled on for ten endless minutes about the open house she'd just held for her latest listing, some newly constructed monstrosity on the north side of town. She went on and on about the generous millwork and slate-tile roof, the pocket doors and oak-plank flooring and a whole bunch of other features I couldn't give a crap about because I was rushing through the Atlanta airport to make a tight connection, and it's quite possible that by then I wasn't really listening. Sabine's rambling is something I found adorable when we first started dating, but lately sparks an urge to chuck my phone into the Arkansas River, just to cut off one of her eternal, run-on sentences. When I got to my gate and saw my plane was already boarding, I hung up.

I peek out the window into the garage. Sabine's black Mercedes isn't there. Looks like I beat her home.

I head into the kitchen, which is a disaster. A pile of dirty dishes crawling up the sink and onto the countertop. A week's worth of newspapers spread across the table like a card trick. Dead, drooping roses marinating in a vase of murky green water. Sabine *knows* how much I hate coming home to a dirty kitchen. I pick up this morning's cereal bowl, where the dregs of her breakfast have fused to the porcelain like nuclear waste, putrefied and solid. I fill it with water at the sink and fume.

The trash bins, the kitchen, not leaving me a note telling me where she is—it's all punishment for something. Sabine's passive-aggressive way of telling me she's still pissed. I don't even remember what we were arguing about. Something trivial, probably, like all the arguments seem to be these days. Crumbs on the couch, hairs in the drain, who forgot to pick up the dry cleaning or drank the last of the orange juice. Stupid stuff. Shit that shouldn't matter, but in that hot, quicksilver moment, somehow always does.

I slide my cell phone from my pocket and scroll through our messages, dispatches of a mundane married life.

Did you remember to pay the light bill?

The microwave is on the fritz again.

I'm placing an order for office supplies, need anything?

I land on the last one to me and bingo, it's the message I'm looking for.

Showing tonight. Be home by 9.

I spend the next half hour righting Sabine's mess. What doesn't go into the dishwasher I pitch in the trash, then toss the bags into the garbage bins I line up. And then I haul my suitcase upstairs.

The bed is unmade, Sabine's side of the closet a pigsty. I try to ignore the chaos she left everywhere: kicked-off shoes and shirts with inside-out sleeves, shoved on lopsided hangers. Nothing like the neat, exacting lines on my side. How difficult is it to put things back where they belong? To line the clothes up by color?

Ten minutes later I'm in shorts and a T-shirt, sneakers pounding up the path in an angry sprint west along the river. The truth is, I am perfectly aware I'm not the easiest person to live with. Sabine has told me more times than I'd care to admit. I can't help that I like things the way I like them—the cars washed, the house clean, dinner hot and waiting when I get home from work. Sabine is a great cook when she wants to be, when her job isn't sucking up most of her day, which lately seems like all the time. I can't remember the last night I came home to one of her home-cooked meals, the ones that take all day to prepare. Once upon a time, she would serve them to me in an apron and nothing else.

I've spent a lot of hours thinking about how to bring us back to the way we used to be. Easy. Sexy. Surprising. Before my job dead-ended at a human resources company that sells buggy, overpriced software nobody wants to buy. Before Sabine got her broker's license, which I used to laugh off as a hobby. Now, on a good month, her salary is more than double mine. I'd tell her to quit, but honestly, we've gotten used to the money. It's like moving into a house with extra closet space—you always use it up.

In our case, the money made us cocky, and we sank far too much of it into our house, a split-level eyesore with too-tiny windows and crumbling siding. The inside was even worse. Cheap paneling and shaggy carpet on the floors, climbing the walls, creeping up the staircase.

"You have *got* to be shitting me," I said as she led me through the cramped, musty rooms. It looked like a seventies porn set. It looked like the destitute version of Hugh Hefner would be coming around the corner in his tattered bathrobe any second. No way were we going to live here.

But then she took me to the back porch and I got a load of the view, a sweeping panorama of the Arkansas River. She'd already done the math: a thirty-year mortgage based on the estimated value after a head-to-toe renovation, an amount that made my eyes bulge. We bought it on the spot.

So now we're proud owners of a beautiful Craftsman-style bungalow on the river, even though as children of Pine Bluff, a working-class town wedged between farms and factories, we should have known better. The house is on the wrong side of town, a castle compared to the split-level shacks on either side of the street, and no renovation, no matter how extensive, could change the fact that there aren't many people in town who can afford to buy the thing. Not that we'll ever be able to sell. Our house doesn't just overlook the river, it is *on* the river, the ropy currents so close they swell up the back steps every time there's a sudden rain.

But the point is, Sabine's job, which began as a fun little way to provide some extra income, is now a necessity.

My cell phone buzzes against my hip, and I slow to a stop on the trail. I check the screen, and my gut burns with irritation when I see it's not Sabine but her sister. I pick up, my breath coming in sharp, sweat-humid puffs.

"Hello, Ingrid."

My greeting is cool and formal, because my relationship with Ingrid is cool and formal. All those things I admire about my wife—her golden chestnut hair, her thin thighs and tiny waist, the way her skin smells of vanilla and sugar—are glaring deficiencies in her twin. Ingrid is shorter, sturdier, less polished. The wallflower to Sabine's prom queen. The heifer to her blue-ribbon cow. Ingrid has never resented Sabine for being the prettier sister, but she sure as hell blames the rest of us for noticing.

"I'm trying to reach Sabine," Ingrid says, her Midwestern twang testy with hurry. "Have you talked to her today?"

A speedboat roars by on the river, and I wait for it to pass.

"I'm fine, Ingrid, thank you. And yes, though it was a quick conversation because I've been in Florida all week for a conference. I just got home, and she's got a showing. Have you tried her cell?"

Ingrid makes a sound low in her throat, the kind of sound that comes right before an eye roll. "Of course

I've tried her cell, at least a million times. When's the last time you talked to her?"

"About an hour ago." The lie is instant and automatic. Ingrid might already know I hung up on her sister this morning and she might not, but one thing is certain: she's not going to hear it from me. "Sabine said she'd be home by nine, so you might want to try her then. Either way, I'll make sure to tell her you called."

And with that I hit End, dial up the music on my headphones to deafening and take off running into the setting sun.

BETH

The District at River Bend is an uninspired apartment community on the banks of Tulsa's Arkansas River, the kind that's generically appealing and instantly familiar. Tan stone, beige siding, indistinguishable buildings of three and four stories clustered around an amoeba-shaped pool. There are a million complexes like it, in a million cities and towns across America, which is exactly why I chose this one.

I pull into an empty spot by the main building, grab my bag—along with the clothes on my back, my only earthly possessions—and head to the door.

People barely out of college are scattered around the massive indoor space, clutching paper coffee cups or ticking away on their MacBooks. Everybody ignores me, which is an unexpected but welcome development. I make a mental note that a complex like this one would be a good place to hide. In the land of self-absorbed millennials, anybody over thirty might as well be invisible.

I spot a sign for the leasing office and head down the hallway.

The woman perched behind the sleek glass desk is one of them. Young. Blonde. Pretty. The kind with a carefully curated Instagram feed of duck-face selfies and hand-on-hip glamour shots. I pause at the edge of her desk, and she looks up with a blinding smile.

"Hi, there. Are you looking for a home in *the* premier apartment community in Tulsa? Because if so, you've come to the right place."

Good Lord. Her Midwestern drawl, her Kardashian whine, her unnaturally white teeth. This girl can't be for real.

"Um, right. So I was looking at the one-bedroom units on your website and—"

"Omigosh! Then this is your lucky day. I literally just learned there's a Vogue unit available starting next week. How does eight hundred square feet and a balcony overlooking the pool sound?"

I hike my bag higher on a shoulder. "Sounds great, but I was hoping to find something that's available a little sooner."

"Like, how much sooner?"

"Like, immediately."

Her collegiate smile falls off her face. "Oh. Well, I have a couple of one-bedroom units available now, but they're all smaller, and they don't offer that same stunning view."

I shrug. "I'm okay with that."

She motions to one of the upholstered chairs behind me. "Then have a seat, and I'll see about getting you into one of our Alpha units. When were you thinking of moving in?"

I sink onto the chair, dragging my bag into my lap. "Today, if possible."

Her eyes go wide, and she shakes her head. "It's not. Possible, I mean. The application process takes a good twenty-four hours, at *least*."

My heart gives an ominous thud. "Application process?"

I know about the application process. I've already scoured the website, and know exactly what it takes to get into this place. I also know that this is where things can get sticky.

The woman nods. "I'll need two month's worth of pay stubs, either that or proof of salary on your bank statements, a government-issued ID like a driver's license or passport, and your social security number. The background check is pretty standard, but it takes a day or two depending on what time of day I submit."

I have all the items she requested, right here in an envelope in my bag, but as soon as this woman plugs them into her computer, one little click of her mouse will propel all my information into the ether. Background checks mean paper trails, clues, visibility. Once you spot me in the system, and you will, I'll have only a few precious hours before you show up here, looking for me.

She checks the time on her cell. "If we hurry, I could get everything through the system by close of business tomorrow."

By then I'll be long gone.

I push the envelope across the desk. "Then let's hurry. I start my new job in two days, and I'd really like to be settled before then."

She flips through the packet of papers. Her fingers pause on my bank statement, and the air in the room thickens into a soupy sludge. Apartment complexes require a minimum salary of three times the rent, which is why I added a couple of zeros to that statement in lieu of proof of salary. Part of the preparations for Day One included learning Photoshop.

It's not the amount she's focused on, but my former address. "Arkansas, huh? So what brings you to town?"

I relax in the chair. "I got a job at QuikTrip."

It's a lie, but judging by the way her face brightens, she buys it. "A friend of mine works there. She loves it. *Great* benefits. Way better than this place, though if you ever repeat that I'll deny ever saying it." She grins like we're in on the same joke, and so do I.

I gesture to the packet in her hand. "I don't have pay stubs yet, which is why I've included a copy of my contract." Forged, but still. It looks real enough. As long as her friend doesn't work in human resources, nobody but me and the Pine Bluff Public Library printer will ever know it's a fake.

I give her time to flip through the rest of the documents, which are real. My real driver's license. My real social security number. My real address—scratch that, *former* address. This entire plan rests on her accepting the papers in her hands, on me laying this decoy trail, then disappearing.

She looks up with a wide smile. "It's not often that I get a prospective tenant with a record this spotless. Unless the system catches something I've missed, this is going to be a piece of cake."

I can't tell if her words are a question or a warning. I smile like I assume they're neither.

She drops the papers on her desk and reaches for the mouse. "Let's get you in the system, then, why don't we?"

You and I met at a McDonald's, under the haze of deep-fried potatoes and a brain-splitting migraine. The headache is what lured me there, actually, what gave my body a desperate craving for a Happy Meal. A magical, medicinal combination of starch and salt and fructose that works better than any pill I've ever poked down, the only thing that will loosen the vise clamping down on my skull and settle my churning stomach.

But good, so there I sat in my sunglasses, nibbling french fries while tiny monsters pounded nail after nail into my brain, when you leaned into the space between our tables.

"What'd you get?"

I didn't respond. Speaking was excruciating and besides, I had no clue what you were talking about.

You pointed to the box by my elbow. "Don't those things come with a toy? What is it?"

I pushed my sunglasses onto my head and peered inside. "It's a plastic yellow car." I pulled it out and showed it to you.

"That's a Hot Wheels."

I settled it on the edge of my tray. "A what?"

"Pretty sure that one's a Dodge Charger. Every boy on the planet has had a Hot Wheels at some point in their lives. My nephew has about a billion of them."

You were distractingly gorgeous, the kind of gorgeous that didn't belong in a fast-food joint, chatting up a stranger about kids and their toys. Tall and dark and broad-boned, with thick lashes and a strong, square chin. Italian, I remember thinking, or maybe Greek, some long-lost relative with stubborn genes.

I held the car across the aisle. "Take it. Give it to your nephew."

Your lips sneaked into a smile, and maybe it was the carbs finally hitting my bloodstream, but you aimed it at me that day, and the pain lifted just a little.

Three days later, I was in love.

So now, when I push through the glass door to the restaurant, I am of course thinking of you. Different state, different McDonald's, but still. It feels fitting, almost poetic. You and I ending in the same spot we began.

The smell hits me, french fries and sizzling meat, and it prompts a wave of nausea, a faint throbbing somewhere deep in my skull, even though I haven't had a migraine in months. I guess it's true what they say, that scent is the greatest memory trigger, so I shouldn't be surprised that one whiff of McDonald's can summon the beginnings of a migraine. I swallow a preventative Excedrin with a bottle of water I purchase at the register.

For a fast-food restaurant at the mouth of a major interstate, the place is pretty deserted. I weave through the mostly empty tables, taking note of the customers scattered around the dining area. A mother flipping through a magazine while her kids pelt each other with chicken nuggets, a pimply teenager watching a YouTube video on his phone, an elderly couple slurping brown sludge up their straws. Not one of them looks up as I pass.

I select a table by the window with a view of the parking lot. A row of pickup trucks glitter in the late afternoon sun, competing for most obnoxious. Super-sized tires with spit-shined rims, roll bars and gun racks, wavy flag decals on the rear window. People of God, guns and Trump, according to the bumper stickers, a common Midwestern stereotype that I've found to be one hundred percent true.

Another stereotype: the lone woman in sunglasses, sitting at a fast-food restaurant with no food is up to no good. I consider buying a dollar meal as cover, but I'm too nervous to eat. I check my watch and try not to fidget. Three minutes to five.

This Nick guy better not be late. He is a crucial part of my plan, and I don't have time to wait around. You'll be getting home from work in an hour. You'll walk through the door and expect to find me in the kitchen, waiting for you with dinner, with the end-less fetching of newspapers and remote controls and beer, with sex—though whether your desire will be fueled by passion or fury is always a toss-up. The thought makes me hot and twitchy, my muscles itch-ing with an immediate, intense need to race to my car and flee. An hour from now, a couple hundred miles from here, you'll be looking for me.

"How will I know you?" I asked Nick two days ago during our one and only phone call, made from the customer service phone at Walmart, after I lied and said my car battery was dead. Nick and I have never actually met. We've not exchanged photographs or even the most basic of physical descriptions. I didn't know he existed until a week ago.

Nick laughed. "What do you suggest I do, carry a rose between my teeth? Don't worry. You'll know me."

I cast a sneaky glance at the teenager, laughing at

something on his screen. Surely not. When we spoke on the phone, Nick didn't seem nearly so oblivious. My gaze shifts to the elderly man, offering the rest of his milkshake to his wife. Not him, either.

When Nick rolls up at thirty seconds to five, I blow out a relieved breath because he was right. I *do* know it's him, because any other day, at any other McDonald's, he's the type of guy I wouldn't have noticed at all.

It begins with his car, a nondescript four-door he squeezes between a souped-up Ford F-250 and an extended-bed Dodge Ram. His clothes are just as unexceptional—generic khakis and a plain white shirt over mud-brown shoes. He looks like a math professor on his day off, or maybe an engineer. He walks to the door, and his eyes, shaded under a navy baseball cap, don't even glance my way.

He orders a cup of coffee at the counter, then carries it over to my table and sinks onto the chair across from me.

"Nick, I assume?"

From the look he gives me, there's no way Nick is his real name. "And you must be Beth."

Touché. Not my real name, either.

Up close he's better looking than I thought he'd be. Wide-set eyes, angled chin, thick hair poking out the rim of his cap. In a normal world, in jeans and a rumpled T-shirt, Nick might not be half-bad.

He dumps three packets of artificial sweetener into his coffee and swirls it around with a red plastic straw. "It's the only way I can stomach this stuff, by masking it with something that tastes like it was imported straight from Chernobyl. If I grow an extra ear, I'm blaming you."

It's a little dig because Nick here wanted to meet at the Dunkin' across the street. He wasn't the least bit subtle about it, either. "If you don't mind, I'd really rather meet at the Dunkin'," he said, not once, but enough times that the old me almost caved, even though I *did* mind. Because what I called Nick here to discuss has to be done in a McDonald's. The universe demands it. Symmetry demands it.

"This place has special memories for me," I tell him now, not so much an apology as an explanation, an olive branch for the Chernobyl coffee. "Not good memories, but memories nonetheless. Let's just say it's karma that we do this here."

Nick shrugs, letting it go. "Karma's a bitch. Best not to piss her off, I always say." He takes a sip of his coffee, then puts it down with a grimace. Clasps his hands on the Formica table. Waits.

"I understand you travel extensively for business."

Nick came highly recommended to me exactly because of this qualification—*must travel extensively for business*. The other qualifications, *must be dependable and discreet*, were something I mentally checked off as soon as I clocked him walking through the door, on time and in clothing that might as well make him invisible.

"I'm on the road more often than not, yes."

"Long trips?"

"It varies. Sometimes I need to stay put for a day or two, but even then, I'm never sleeping in the same bed two nights in a row. I like to move around just in case."

He leaves it at that, *just in case*, and I don't ask. Whatever he means by it, I honestly don't care to know. For the job I called him here to do, it makes zero difference.

"But sure," he continues, shrugging again, "in a typical month, I'll log three to four thousand miles so I guess that qualifies as long trips."

"Do you have a home base?"

"Multiple home bases. But like I said, I'm hardly ever there."

"Perfect."

He grins. "Tell that to the missus."

I'm pretty sure he's joking, or maybe he's saying it to try to throw me off his tail. Men like Nick aren't the marrying type—or if they do marry it's more for convenience or cover than for love. Never for love.

"That's funny," I say, twisting the cap on my water. "I always liked it when my husband traveled for work."

As soon as I say the words, I want to swallow them back down. The skin around Nick's eyes tightens, just for an instant, but long enough I catch it. Unlike his joke, harmless words about a wife that doesn't exist, mine revealed too much—that the husband is real, that life was better when he was gone. Nick is not my friend. He's not someone I should be joking with over a cup of crappy coffee. This is a business meeting, and the less he knows about me, the better.

I slide a shiny Wells Fargo card from the side pocket of my bag and push it across the table. "I want you to spend my money."

He doesn't say anything, but he picks up the card, running a thumb over the shiny gold letters across the front—my real name, definitely not *Beth*. When he looks back up, his expression is unreadable.

"For the record, I don't mean spend it as in booking a first-class ticket to Vegas and going nuts at the roulette wheel, but spend it as in ten dollars here, twenty there. I want you to move around a *lot*. Never the same ATM, or even the same city, twice. The farther away the withdrawals are from each other, the more varied the locations, the better. Think of me as your ATM fairy godmother."

"You want me to lay a trail."

I tip my head, a silent confirmation. "Assuming you don't withdraw more than a hundred dollars a week, which you can't because I've set up the card with a weekly limit, you'll get five weeks of money off that card."

"And my fee?"

His fee is five hundred dollars, an amount he made very clear on the phone is nonnegotiable. Whatever it is I'm hiring him to do comes on top of that, which means this is a job that comes with a hefty cash bonus, one that's double his fee. Probably the easiest money he's ever made.

"Your fee is on there, too. You can withdraw that today. The weekly limits kick in as soon as you do."

He hikes up on a hip and slips the card into the front pocket of his pants. "You want me to go east or west?"

I know why he's asking, because he assumes I'd want him to head in the opposite direction. Or at least, I *think* that's why he's asking. But I'm still stinging from my slip-up, and thanks to the card in his pocket, Nick now knows my real name. No way I'm telling him—a criminal, a stranger—where I'm planning to land. Not that I think he'd come after me, but still. If there's one thing I've learned these past ten years, it's to trust no one, not even the people you're supposed to trust the most.

"East, west, north, south. I don't care, as long as your withdrawals are erratic and your stops unpredictable. I'll be watching the transactions online, and if I don't like what I see, I'll put the brakes on the account."

"You do know there are cameras at every ATM, right?"

I roll my eyes. Of course I know. I didn't spend the past ten months planning this thing to have not thought about something as basic as security cameras. But it'll be days, maybe even weeks before you find the withdrawals, longer before you see Nick's face on the tapes instead of mine. I'm not worried about the stupid cameras.

"Make sure to smile pretty." I pull my bag onto my shoulder, a sign that this conversation, an interview and marching orders at the same time, is over. "The pin is 2764."

Nick reaches for his coffee cup, still full but no longer steaming, then thinks better of it. He leaves it on the table and stands. "I bet that happens a lot, doesn't it?"

"What does?"

"That people underestimate you. That they think you're greener than you actually are. And before you roll your eyes at me again, you should know that's not a bad thing. If things get hairy, you can use it to your advantage."

Now, finally, he gets a grin from me. "I'm counting on it."

JEFFREY

I jerk awake on the couch, and the crystal tumbler balancing on my stomach pitches over a hip. I roll away from the spill, shifting to one side, but I'm too late. The liquid has already seeped through my jeans, dripping a good two fingers of expensive bourbon down my leg and into the fabric of the cushion. With a groan, I plunk the glass on the floor, push myself upright and try to get my bearings.

The half-eaten pizza I ordered for dinner sits cold and congealed on the coffee table, and I flip the box closed. Images of a house fire flicker on the television on the wall, a handful of figures in slick yellow gear under a dripping arc of water. I reach for the remote and hit the button for the guide. Tiny numbers at the top of the screen tell me it's 11:17 p.m.

Shit. When I stretched out on the couch, it was quarter to nine. The four days of travel, of being 'on' all day at the conference, must have worn me out more than I thought.

"Sabine?"

No answer, but then again, she's probably sound asleep. I picture her upstairs in bed, her long hair like silk across the pillow, and a familiar fire burns in my chest. Why didn't she come in to say hi? Why didn't she wake me?

I click off the TV and stand.

The downstairs is quiet, the lights still burning bright in the hallway. I flip them off on my way to the stairs, pausing at the doorway to the kitchen. The counter is still spotless, and the three matching pendants over the island light the air with a golden glow. Sabine might be a slob, but she hates wasting money as much as I do. If she were here, if she'd sneaked past me on her way upstairs, she would have turned off the lights.

Unease tightens the skin of my chest.

I jog across the kitchen tiles and yank open the door to the garage, getting a faint, heady whiff of gasoline. My car, right where I parked it. In Sabine's spot, nothing but an oil stain on the concrete. My heart gives a painful kick.

I take the stairs by twos and threes, sprinting down the hallway runner and into the bedroom, even though I already know what I'll find. The comforter, still unturned from where I'd made it. The pillows, still stacked and fluffed.

The bed, empty.

BETH

I stand at the bathroom sink of room seventeen in a grubby motor lodge on the outskirts of Tulsa and take inventory in the mirror. Chalky skin. Eyes shaded with purple circles. Hair too long, too thick to style.

You're always telling me never to cut my hair. You say you like it long—dark, thick strands streaked with shiny ribbons of bronze, with just the right amount of curl. It's the kind of hair you see on commercials, the kind women pay hundreds of dollars a month for. But it's more than just hair to you. It's a plaything, a turn-on, something to plow your fingers through or moan your orgasms in whenever we have sex.

But this hair you claim to love so much? You also love to use it as a weapon. To drag me by it from room to room. To pin me down. Hair is so much stronger than you think it'd be, the roots like barbed hooks in your skin. The scalp will rip open sooner than a hank of hair will break. I know this from experience.

I pick up a handful and a pair of shears and slice it in an uneven, stubby line.

It's a lot easier than I thought it would be. A hell of a lot less painful than when you grab me by the ponytail and lift me clear off the bed. The strands tumble down my chest, sticking to the white cotton of my shirt. I feel lighter. Unencumbered. Free.

I keep chopping, brushing the strands into the sink to toss later, not because I think you'll track me here, but because I believe in karma. One day very soon I'll need a job, and it's not unthinkable I'll end up in a hotel room like this one, scrubbing someone else's hairs from the drain. Not exactly what my parents were hoping for when they paid for my college, but a better paying job, a job I'm actually qualified for, would send up a smoke signal you might spot.

I've never cut my own hair before, and I don't do a particularly good job of it. I was going for a pixie cut, but it's more of a walk-in salon hack job, or maybe a sloppy bowl cut from the seventies. I pick up random chunks, pull them between my fingers like a hairstylist would, and slice in asymmetrical layers. When I'm done, I fluff it with my fingers and study myself in the mirror. With a bit of hair gel, it might not be half-bad.

You are not who you used to be. You are Beth Murphy now.

"I'm Beth," I say, trying on the name like a questionable shade of lipstick. It's the name I gave Nick, the one I signed on the hotel register, but only after forking over two twenties so the man behind the counter didn't ask for my ID again. "My name's Beth Murphy."

Beth with the crappy haircut.

I dig the box of hair dye from the CVS bag and mix up the color. In my previous life, I was one of those brunettes who never longed to be a blonde. Blondes are louder, bolder, more conspicuous. Flashy and competitive, like sorority girls and cheerleaders. Not good traits when your goal is to disappear.

The picture on the box advertises an ashy blond, the least in-your-face blond of the blonder shades. Blond for beginners. I paint it in lines across my scalp with the plastic bottle, then slip off the gloves and check my watch. Ten minutes until we find out if what they say is really true, that blondes have more fun.

While I wait for the color to set, I flip on the television. It's past midnight, and I'm three hundred miles away from Pine Bluff—too late for a local broadcast, and too soon for news of my disappearance to have spread across state lines and made it to cable. Still, I sit on the edge of the bed and flip between CNN and Fox, watching for the tiniest sliver of my story. An empty house. A missing woman. My face hidden behind dark sunglasses, spotted heading west. But there's nothing, and I'm torn between relief and dread. You'll be looking for me by now.

I shower and dress in the clothes I bought earlier at Walmart, a dowdy denim skirt and a shirt two sizes too big. The duffel on the bed is stuffed with clothes just like them, synthetic fabrics in Easter egg colors, cheap and outdated items I'd normally turn up my nose at. In my former life, I would have turned up my nose at Beth, too. With her baggy clothes and dollar-store hair, Beth is a frump.

I leave the key on the nightstand, gather up my things and step outside.

Sometime in the past few hours, clouds have rolled in, a dark and threatening blanket hanging over muggy, electrically charged air. The wind is still, but it won't be for long. I've lived in these parts long enough to know what a wall cloud looks like, and that they often swirl into tornadoes. A bolt of lightning rips the sky in two, clean as a knife slash. Time to either hunker down or get the hell out of Dodge. I choose door number two.

My car is exactly where I left it, at the far edge of the lot next to the dumpster, though "my" is a relative term since the car doesn't officially belong to me. It belongs to a Marsha Anne Norwood of Little Rock, Arkansas, a woman who seemed as eager for a discreet, all-cash transaction as I was. I bought it two weeks ago, then moved it from lot to lot in a neighboring town, but I never transferred the title to my name.

I peek inside and things are exactly as I left them. The keys, dropped in the cup holder. The title, folded on the front seat. The doors, unlocked. I cast a quick glance up the asphalt, taking in the other cars, jalopies like this one. My car is no prize, but it's an easy target. A jackpot for any wannabe thief. No, Marsha Anne's car won't be here for long.

I turn, head to Dill's Auto Repairs & Sales across the road.

"You can't buy a car," you told me once, when it was time for me to trade up. "Just keep your mouth shut and let me handle it."

Dill might disagree, seeing as I'm able to sweet-talk more than 10 percent off a 1996 Buick Regal. It's a rusty old pile of junk, but the motor runs and the price is right, especially once I discover that Dill likes it when I call him "Sugar." He forks over the paperwork and the address for the nearest Oklahoma DMV, which I promise to visit first thing in the morning. If I hurry, I'll be in the next state by the time the office doors open.

He hands me the keys and I fall inside and crank the engine, right as the skies open up.

JEFFREY

The first number I call is Sabine's, even though I know before I dial the first digit it's a waste of time. If Sabine is pissed, if she's punishing me for something, she's not going to pick up.

And if something's happened… My stomach twitches, and I push the thought aside.

Her phone rings, four eternal beeps, then flips me to voice mail.

"Sabine, it's me. Did I forget you were going somewhere tonight? Because I got the message where you said you'd be home by nine, but now it's almost midnight and you're still not here. Call me back, will you? I'm at home, and I'm starting to get a little worried. Okay, bye."

I hang up, think about calling 9-1-1, but she's what, less than three hours late? Not long enough to be an emergency. And don't the police require a minimum of twenty-four hours before you can report a person missing? What am I going to tell them, that my wife missed her curfew?

I slip my cell in my pocket and pace the length of the upstairs hallway. Okay, so I know she had a showing. A *late* showing. Even if it ran over, even if it were all the way on the other side of town and she decided to grab a bite to eat before coming home, she would have been here by now.

And it's not like Sabine to ignore her phone. It's one of her least desirable job requirements, that she's always, *always* available. From the moment she wakes up until the time she goes to sleep, there's a device either in her palm or pressed to one of her ears. If her car broke down on the way home, if she's sitting on the edge of a highway with a flat tire and no clue how to switch it for the spare, she would have called roadside assistance, and then she would have called me.

Assuming she's conscious.

My skin snaps tight at the thought of her bleeding on the side of the road or worse, floating facedown in the Arkansas River. I picture her bobbing in the currents or caught in the reeds that line our backyard. I see some sicko dragging her into the show house, her heels digging into the brand-new hardwood floor. Screaming into the empty house.

I've never loved the thought of her showing houses to complete strangers. It was one of the sticking points between us when she took this job, the idea that anyone could come by pretending to be a prospective client. What if a prisoner escaped from Randall Williams? What if he had a knife or a gun? She might as well put a sign out front and a target on her back. *Pretty broker, here for the taking.*

I pull out my phone and call her again.

"Sabine, seriously. This isn't funny. Where are you? I get that you're still mad at me, but at least shoot me a text so I know you're breathing. I'm really worried here. I'm giving you one more hour, and then I'm calling the police."

I hang up and haul in a deep, calming breath, but it doesn't help. Something's wrong. I don't know what it is yet. I just know that something is very, very wrong.

I pull up the number for her sister.

Ingrid picks up on the first ring, like she'd been lying there with her finger hovering above the screen, waiting for it to light up with a call. Her voice is gruff and insistent: "Hullo!" Not a question, said with an upward lilt at the end, like how a normal person answers the phone, but a demand. More grunt than word. How these two women share the same DNA is one of God's great mysteries.

"Ingrid, it's Jeffrey. Sorry to call at this hour, but—"

"I have caller ID, Jeffrey. Put Sabine on the phone."

I close my eyes and inhale, long and steady. "That's the reason I'm calling you in the middle of the night. I don't know where she is."

"What do you mean you don't know where she is? She's not with you?"

"She didn't come home after her showing, and she's not answering her phone."

"Jesus, Jeffrey. And you're just calling me now? What the hell have you been doing all this time?" I hear a rustling of fabric, the high-pitched squeal of bedsprings. Ingrid lives alone, in a condo a couple of miles from here, I'm sure because nobody else can stand to share a roof with her. "Who else have you called?"

"Nobody. You're the first." And already, I'm regretting it. Talking to Ingrid is like chewing on glass—you just know it's going to be painful.

"Do you know the number for her boss?" I say. "She had that late showing tonight, so maybe Russ will know what's going on."

"Russ?" Ingrid's voice is clipped with exasperation. "Russ moved to Little Rock in December. You should try Lisa."

"Who?"

"Lisa O'Brien. Sabine's boss?" She pauses for my reply, but I don't know what to say. Sabine has a new boss? Since when? "Oh my God, do the two of you even talk? This all happened months ago."

I huff a sigh into the phone, done pussyfooting around Ingrid's shitty attitude. "Do you have Lisa's phone number or not?"

"Not." A door slams. A car engine starts. "Call the police, Jeffrey. I'm on my way."

When early on in our relationship Sabine told me she had a twin, I remember thinking how lucky she was, how lucky *I* was. Somewhere out there was a carbon copy of this woman, the yin to her lovely yang. The idea felt like a novelty. Two Sabines for the price of one.

And then I met Ingrid, and the dislike was both instant and mutual. This was right around the time they buried their father, and their mom was starting to repeat the same tired stories often enough that the sisters noticed. In those first few weeks, I attributed Ingrid's testiness to grief, to worry. I gave her a pass.

But Ingrid was accustomed to being the most important person in her sister's life, and she made it clear she wasn't about to hand over the reins. Ingrid was fiercely territorial, and she treated me like a phase, an unwelcome but temporary intruder in their codependent lives. I accused Ingrid of loving her sister too much, and she accused me of not loving Sabine enough. Sabine felt caught in the middle, and from then on out, planned our lives so Ingrid and I were rarely in the same room. I've become a master at avoiding the woman, driving on at the first sight of her car when I'm out running errands, ducking into the next room at parties when she walks through the door.

I eye her now across the kitchen table, taking in her dust-bunny hair and shiny, rosacea-covered cheeks as she makes notes on a yellow pad of paper. Fat, black pen strokes scratching out the name of Sabine's firm, her height and hair color, the number for her cell. This woman looks nothing like my wife. She is the angry, ogre version of Sabine, the kind that bathes in swamp water and gnaws on bones under a bridge. Her face is scored with pillow marks, angry purple lines in the shape of a cross.

I sigh, wishing I was the one with a pen and paper, wishing there was something I could *do*. My legs bounce under the table. We are sitting here, waiting for the police to arrive, and I don't have any patience. I want somebody to go out there and find my wife.

"There's got to be an explanation," I say.

Ingrid shushes me. Actually flicks her fingers in my direction and hisses *shh*, never once looking up from her scribbles. Upside down, her handwriting looks just like Sabine's big, messy loops.

"Answer me, will you? I said there's got to be an explanation for wherever Sabine is. Where she went. I'm terrified something happened to her."

Ingrid grunts, and the sound sparks like flint in my gut.

"What is that supposed to mean?"

"I didn't say anything."

"Yes, you did. You grunted. If you have something to say to me, just say it. Don't grunt at me from the other side of the table." The words come out just as angry, just as venomous as I feel. It's the middle of the night, my wife is unaccounted for and the sloppier version of Sabine is sitting across from me, looking to start a fight. I don't know what it is about these Stanfield sisters, but they sure know how to scratch and pluck at my nerves.

"Jeffrey, I didn't *say* anything."

"No, but you wanted to. So go for it. This is your big chance. Say what you wanted to say."

"Fine. You want me to say it?" She slaps down the pen, pressing it under her fingers. "Where's Sabine?"

"I'm the one who called you, remember? Why are you asking me?"

Ingrid rolls her beady snake eyes. "Come *on*, Jeffrey. My sister and I talk every day. We tell each other *everything*."

This isn't exactly news. On a good day, Ingrid and Sabine will spend hours on the phone, discussing the minutia of everything from the tacos they ate for lunch to their favorite brand of tampons. Last weekend they killed an entire afternoon deliberating on the consistency of their mother's latest bowel movements, and whether changing her diet might slow down the dementia that's eating up her brain. I *know* they talk ten times a day. Most of the time, I'm witness to it.

"Well, clearly she didn't tell you where she was going tonight."

"Or maybe she was unable to."

For a second I don't understand, a fleeting moment of *she thinks something bad happened, too*, and then I go completely still. Ingrid thinks something bad happened all right, but she also thinks I had something to do with it.

"Careful." I say the word like an order, sharp and commanding. "If I didn't know better, I'd think you were accusing me of something."

"Why, do you feel guilty?"

"No."

"Because I know about your fights. Sabine calls me after every one."

Of course she does. The two are always on the same page, always, *always* of the same mind. They use the other both as a sounding board and a tuning fork. As long as the other sister agrees, then their opinions are vindicated. Two like-minded twins can't be wrong.

And then there's that weird twin telepathy Sabine and Ingrid share, that creepy ability to know what the other is about to say before they even say it. Last year for Christmas, they bought each other the exact same gift, a hideous beige purse in the shape of a take-out bag. The two of them squealed like they'd both won the lottery. I don't know how to compete with that.

"So? All couples argue, which you would know if you could ever hold on to a man long enough to be in a relationship. Wherever Sabine is tonight has nothing to do with our arguments."

She cocks an unplucked brow. "You didn't even know she had a new boss, and that happened ages ago. When is the last time the two of you actually talked? When is the last time you had sex?"

"None of your fucking business, that's when. And don't you *ever* ask me that again. Not while you're in *my* house."

She folds her hands atop the pad of paper, and I'd think she was calm if it weren't for her paper-white knuckles. "Really? Because I'm pretty sure this house belongs to Sabine."

It's the most hateful thing she could say to me, and as much as I hate her for it, the person I really blame for her words is Sabine. Sabine knows the name listed on the mortgage is like the drunk relative trying to talk politics at a dinner party, better just to ignore. It's always been a touchy subject between us, but like Ingrid said, Sabine tells her sister *everything*.

"My wife needs to keep her mouth shut. Our personal business is just that—personal. Sabine shouldn't be sharing every little thing that happens with you, just like I shouldn't have to tell you that wherever she is right now, *I had nothing to do with it*."

Ingrid goes silent, and I can tell she has more to say. She stares at me, chewing her lip, weighing her options. I see the exact instant the decision is made. Her eyes—Sabine's eyes—ice over.

"She told me what you did to her."

She says it just like that, her voice low and deceptively calm, like I'll know what she's talking about.

I *do* know, and the fury that rises in me is as familiar as the woman sitting across the table. Sabine told Ingrid what I did, and I want to leap across the table, wrap my fingers around Ingrid's throat and squeeze until she wipes those awful, horrible words from her brain.

"Did Sabine tell you what *she* did?"

"I already told you. Sabine tells me everything."

"Then you know that she pushed me first."

"That's not an excuse! A man should never lay his hands on a woman, Jeffrey. I shouldn't have to tell you this."

Ingrid's condescending tone burrows under my skin like a tick. Sabine told me I was forgiven. She *promised* we would never speak of it again, and then she went blabbing it to her sister. Of course Ingrid thinks the worst of me now. She only heard one side of the story.

"Sabine accused me of checking out of our marriage. She said I was emotionally and physically disengaged. She kept harping on about her love tank being empty, whatever the hell that means. You know what? I shouldn't have to explain myself to you. The point is, we had a fight, it was bad, we both apologized and we moved on. That's what successful couples do—they forgive each other and move on."

I hear the words coming out of my mouth, and I

wonder if they're true. Not the part about Sabine's complaints—she's never been shy about voicing those—but the part about us as a couple. Forgiving each other. Being successful.

Are Sabine and I a successful couple? Once upon a time, we were. For the first few years, we were *that* couple—the one every other couple wanted to be. Happy. In love and in lust, both of them at the same time. The kind of couple that shoulders major life disappointments together. Her mother's sudden forgetfulness. My low sperm count, and their decided lack of mobility to reach Sabine's wonky uterus. "We will get the very best care for your mother," I would murmur to a sobbing Sabine. "We'll adopt." That was back when everything, even the most impossible, felt possible. I was a champion, a supportive husband, a fixer. I could fix everything.

And then something happened that I couldn't fix: my career stalled out halfway up the ladder at PDK Workforce Solutions. "Account Executive" may sound impressive, but it's a midlevel slog that entails sucking up to needy, curmudgeonly customers so they'll buy crap they don't actually need.

But even more limiting, there's nowhere for me to go. The next rung is my boss's job, and he's blocking the ladder like a king-of-the-hill linebacker, with no plans to retire, change industries, or move to Toledo. I've put out some feelers, even talked to a couple of headhunters, but the only companies hiring are all the way in Little Rock, and Sabine wouldn't hear of moving.

So yes, I may be bitter but I'm not oblivious. I am

fully aware how unfair it is to blame Sabine, but her success makes it so easy. I'm forty and washed up, and she's just getting started. I come home beaten and burning with rejection to find Sabine glowing with the high of yet another sale. Lately, I've begun eating dinner alone in the den, mostly because I can't stomach her hum of satisfaction.

And so, late last year, after a particularly shitty day at work, when I got home and Sabine wouldn't stop nagging, when she kept pick-pick-picking at every little flaw, when she accused me of checking out of our marriage, of sitting back and letting her do all the hard hitting for our house, our bank account, our *sex life*, her words filled me with a pure, inarticulate rage. She shoved me, and I hit her. I didn't plan to. I didn't mean to. It just happened.

I know how this looks, believe me. I lost my temper with my wife, and now she's gone. Maybe she's trying to punish me for what I did, or maybe my earlier hunch is right, maybe something is really, really wrong. Either way, you don't have to tell me. I am the husband with a history of violence, the man living for free in the house his wife owns, the person with the most to lose or to gain.

This doesn't look good for me.

BETH

The storm blows north so I point the Buick south, aiming the nose toward Dallas. It's not the most efficient way to get to the East Coast, but I'm not in any sort of hurry, and it's an easy, roundabout route that circumvents my home state of Arkansas entirely. Even though you are hours, hopefully days behind me. Even though you'll be on the lookout for a brunette in Marsha Anne's black sedan, not a blonde in a gas-guzzling Regal, already down to a quarter tank, now is not the time to take any chances. I flip off the air-conditioning and roll down the windows, letting in the humid highway air. One advantage of this stupid new hair, it doesn't blow into my eyes while I drive.

My eyelids are dangerously heavy, and I stop often. To grab another coffee and some snacks, to splash cold water on my face, to load up on gas and an IHOP breakfast platter. Eggs, biscuits, sausage, the works. It's not my normal kind of meal—you like me thin and waiflike—but ever since leaving Pine Bluff, I've been ravenous. Maybe it's the relief of finally breaking free, or maybe it's that I'm no longer my normal self. I'm Beth now, and Beth eats whatever the hell she wants.

I'm nearing Atlanta when the sun comes up, streaking the sky with a spectacular orange and pink, so psychedelic bright that I reach for my sunglasses. My heart skitters in anticipation of my final-for-now destination. A city I visited for the first and only time with you, ages ago, for a college buddy's booze-fueled wedding. The reception was loud and rowdy and at the rotating restaurant atop the Westin downtown, where you twirled me around the dance floor until we were dizzy—me from the shifting skyline, you from the cheap Russian vodka. When we stumbled downstairs to our room, I asked if you were drunk and your answer was to shove me into a wall. Atlanta was the first time you hurt me that way, and the last place you'll think to look for me now.

I know I'm close when a giant Delta jet lumbers over my head, its belly white and shiny, its wheels braced for landing. I catch a whiff of jet fuel, brace for the roar of its engines, a sound somewhere between an explosion and a NASCAR race. It rattles the steering wheel, the windows of my car, my teeth. All around me, people slam their brakes, and traffic grinds to a halt. Six lanes of bumper-to-bumper traffic, red taillights as far as I can see.

I've studied the map, so I know where I'm going. Merge onto the downtown connector, follow it to I-20 east, then take a left on Boulevard to Cabbagetown. "Eclectic" and "edgy" is how the internet describes the east-Atlanta neighborhood, but what sold me on it is its affordability. Especially the Wylie Street Lodge, where one can rent a small but fully furnished room for a whopping twenty-two dollars a night. I'll have to share a bathroom and kitchen, but still. I've already prepaid for the first week.

An eternity later, I pull to a stop on Wylie Street and climb out. The road under me might as well be on fire, a steaming, sizzling furnace melting my tires and the soles of my sneakers, but it's the house I'm looking at, my stomach sinking at the sight. The yard is a foul-looking patch of dirt and scraggly branches that has seen neither fertilizer nor lawn mower since sometime last century. Front steps, rickety and rotting, lead to a porch littered with trash and a ripped brown sofa, where three raggedy men drink from paper bags. If it weren't for them and the hooker advertising her wares from a second-story balcony, I'd think the place was abandoned.

I stand on the sidewalk, thinking through my options.

I could cut my losses and leave.

I could march to the door and demand my money back.

I could suck it up and stay.

The men eye me from the front porch, and I know how they see me. The rusty Buick with Oklahoma plates, the soccer-mom shirt, my fried hair. I'm the naive country girl come to the big city. I'm an easy target.

The hooker calls down to me. "Hey, blondie. You looking for this?" She pulls her tube top down to reveal breasts as enormous as the fat rolls holding them up. She jiggles them back and forth like a bowl of caramel pudding.

"Uh, no thanks," I say. "I'm good."

She barks a phlegmy laugh, and she's not wrong. Beth is going to have to work on her one-liners.

I drop into my car and motor away.

Around the corner, I squeeze my car into a spot at the edge of a crowded parking lot. After the car, the hotels, the food, Nick's fee and debit card, I have just over two thousand dollars in cash left. Tens and twenties mostly, siphoned from grocery funds, birthday and Christmas money, forgotten bills swiped from your pockets when you were passed out. Saving was a long, laborious process that took me almost a year to do in a way that you wouldn't notice. I bought things on discount and shopped sales. I switched to cheaper toilet paper, coffee, washing powder. Ironically, I stopped cutting my hair. My stash of money grew slowly, deliberately. Anything else would have gotten me killed.

But two thousand dollars won't last long, not even with a strict budget. Hotels are expensive, and most require ID. Even if I got a job tomorrow, staying in one would blow through my cash.

For a city of six million souls, Atlanta has an astonishing lack of beds for abused or homeless women, of which I am both. I could sleep in my car, but it doesn't feel safe, and I probably wouldn't do much sleeping. A better option would be to find another lodge, one that is cheap and won't ask for identification. Like the ones I found before settling on Wylie—rooming and boardinghouses, a hostel or two, some seriously sketchy motels—if only I remembered their names.

And no, I didn't write any of them down. I couldn't. If you'd found anything even remotely suspicious—the search parameters on my laptop, a new number on my phone log, a faraway address scribbled on the back of a receipt—you would have confronted me. That was the hardest part of this past year, staying one step ahead of you.

I'm reaching for the burner phone to start my new search when I spot a sign at the far end of the lot for a Best Buy. Best Buy means computers, banks and banks of computers. The internet at my fingers, free and with no tracking, unlike the data on this piece-of-crap prepaid phone. I crank the key and head farther up the lot.

The store is packed for a Thursday morning. People everywhere, jamming the aisles and forming lines a dozen people deep at the MacBooks display. I push past them to a lonely, unmanned Dell at the end of the counter.

I navigate to the internet and pause. Stare at the blinking cursor. Check behind me to make sure no one is watching. Old habits are hard to break.

Two seconds later, I'm typing in the address for Pine Bluff's local news website. I hold my breath and scroll through the headlines. *Arkansas man accused of killing wife for changing TV channel. State police investigate Monticello murder. Pine Bluff officer shot in "ambush" attack.* Nothing about a missing woman. Nothing about me.

And yet, I've been gone for almost twenty-four hours now. Why is there nothing on the internet? Is the police department sitting on the story? Are they holding out on the press? Or has the media just not sniffed it out yet?

The Pine Bluff Police Department website doesn't make me any wiser. Their home page is as generic as ever, the last item on a long list of to-dos for the department, updated almost as an afterthought. The most recent post on their newsroom page is from 2016.

On a whim, I surf to Facebook, and I'm in luck. Gary Minoff, a middle-aged man from Conyers, Georgia, forgot to sign out. No one will think anything of him nosing around on the Pine Bluff Police Department Facebook page, which is much more current than their website. I scroll down their wall, past posts about robberies, murders, a deadly hit-and-run, and the knot between my shoulder blades tightens. Maybe something happened, and you haven't yet figured out I'm gone. Maybe I have more of a head start than I think. I can't decide if the old adage applies here: Is no news really good news?

"Best priced laptop in the place," a voice says from right behind me, a ginger with facial hair and a Best Buy polo. He gestures to the Dell. "Intel Pentium duel core processor, two megabyte cache, up to 2.3 gigahertz performance. All that and more for only $349."

I have no idea what any of that means. I give him a smile that is polite but perfunctory. "I'm just looking, thanks."

"For a few bucks more, you can upgrade. Tack on some more memory, or some cloud-based backup storage."

"I just want to play around a little more, try things

out. Maybe if you come back in ten minutes or so, I'll be ready to decide."

Or maybe, by the time you come back, I'll be gone.

He wanders off to bother another customer, and I exit out of Facebook. Time to get busy.

I Google *cheapest boarding houses Atlanta* and take a picture of the results with my burner phone, then do the same for area hostels. Just in case, I find five hotels advertising rooms under fifty dollars a night and take a picture of those, as well. The rest of the time I use for poking around on Craigslist.

Most of the housing listings are either too expensive or too creepy. A dollar for a live-in girlfriend? Pass. I click on one of the cheapest listings, a furnished basement bedroom in a house in Collier Heights, then back out of the page when I see the field labeled "driver's license number." I click on the next one, "for professional ladies only."

"My girlfriend got totally shafted on Craigslist." It's the ginger salesclerk again, hovering behind me even though it's been nowhere near ten minutes. "She'd booked a room with what she thought was a nice family, but it was a scam. She gets there and some crazy dude pulls a gun on her and next thing she knows, she's got no money, no wallet, no car, no nothing."

"That's…awful."

He shoves his hands in his pockets and grins, revealing a row of neat white teeth. "I'll say. Three months later she's at the courthouse, declaring herself bankrupt. Bastard stole her identity, then took out all sorts of loans and credit cards in her name. By the time she figured out what was happening, he'd racked up over fifty thousand dollars of debt in her name. It's going to take her years to get her credit back on track. Anyway, all that goes to say, you might want to be careful."

His gaze wanders to the picture on the laptop screen, and he's not wrong. This place is a dump. I click the X to close the screen.

He starts in on his sales pitch again, something about a LED-backlit screen and HD camera, and I'm about to tell him to back off when something occurs to me. His girlfriend's wallet was stolen. Some asshole took her credit cards, her driver's license, everything. Even if she went to the DMV that very same day, it would have taken her a couple of days, maybe a week, to get her new plastic.

My voice is a lot more friendly when I turn back to the salesman. "Where did your girlfriend stay in the meantime? After that guy took off with her wallet, I mean."

"Oh. Well, she couch surfed and stayed with me for a while until she found this sweet boardinghouse over on the Westside. Most places want some kind of credit card number as a guarantee, but this boardinghouse was cool with her paying cash, especially after she told them her sob story."

I realize this is only the first hurdle of many. I have no home, no ID, no more than a couple grand to my name. But I have a sob story, one that's so much sadder than this guy's girlfriend's, and I have something even better. Determination.

The smile that sneaks up my cheeks is genuine. "Do you remember the boardinghouse name?"

JEFFREY

The man on the other side of my door is not in uniform, but everything about him screams cop—dark pants, pressed button-down shirt, his soldier's stance and the gun strapped to a hip. Behind him on the driveway, an unmarked sedan ticks off the heat.

He flashes a badge. "Detective Marcus Durand, Pine Bluff PD. I understand you have some concerns about your wife?" His voice is low, his words businesslike. I search him for even a hint of concern, but I can't find anything beyond a weary intensity.

I swing the door wide and step back. "Thanks for coming."

My tone is thick with sarcasm, because I've been waiting for hours. Six of them, at least, trying to get some rest on the couch despite Ingrid standing above me, huffing like an angry dragon. The longer he kept us waiting, the harder she stomped on the floor, poking me on the shoulder every half hour to ask how it was possible for me to sleep. "I just lie down and close my eyes," I told her. "Maybe you should try it."

If the detective hears the snark in my voice, he doesn't acknowledge it. He's younger than me, midthirties maybe, and half a foot taller. He fills my foyer with his presence and size, making me feel small in my jeans and bare feet. I wish I'd changed into something nicer. I wish I had on some shoes. His jaw is set with the gravity of the situation. A missing woman, an after-hours house call means he's taking this seriously.

But not seriously enough to show up on time.

He looks around, his gaze pausing on the curved staircase, the custom newels with vertical slats, the antique Turkish rug under his feet—none of which he can afford on a detective's salary. None of which I could have afforded, either, were it not for Sabine. I consider telling him my wife made the million-dollar club four years running, that when it comes to decor she knows how to get the best bang for your buck, but then his gaze lands on Ingrid, standing at the doorway to the kitchen.

"Something's wrong," she says, her voice high and tight. In the light of day, I notice her sneakers are mismatched, one black, the other blue, both of them untied. "Something is terribly wrong, I just know it."

"And you are?"

"Ingrid Stanfield. Sabine's sister." She juts a thumb into the next room. "I've made some notes. They're in the kitchen."

Detective Durand shifts his weight, but his shoes stay planted to the hardwood. He turns to me, pulling a notepad from the front pocket of his pants. "I understand your wife didn't return home last night?"

I give him a perfunctory nod. "Sabine had a late showing, something that happens fairly often these days. She's a real estate broker, a really good one. She texted me earlier in the day that she would be home by nine, but she never showed up. I've called her multiple times. Her phone rings, but it keeps sending me to voice mail."

"I've called her, too," Ingrid says, nodding. "I've been calling her all night. Can you maybe trace her cell phone? I'm worried she's had an accident, that she's hurt somewhere and needs help."

Detective Marcus checks the time, by now closing in on nine in the morning, and he looks as exhausted as I feel. Drooping shoulders and pale, lined face. I'm guessing this is the end of his shift, and not the beginning.

"Could she have gone anywhere else?" he says, in a tone that's a tad too calm. He sounds like he's holding back a sigh, or maybe a yawn. Maybe both. "To a friend's or family member's house, or maybe grabbed a drink with someone and forgotten to tell you?"

I open my mouth to tell him no, but yet again, Ingrid beats me to it. "Sabine is too responsible to stay out all night without calling, and she *always* calls me back. Always. It's how I know something has happened to her. Something bad."

I turn to the detective with a pained smile. "Ingrid is right to be worried, I'm afraid. It's unlike Sabine to not let one of us know where she is. Their father is dead, and their mother is in assisted living over at Oakmont. The only other place she would have gone is to her sister's."

"Have one of you called over to Oakmont just to be sure?"

"I have," Ingrid says. "One of the nurses spoke to her on the phone yesterday, but the others haven't seen or heard from her in days."

The detective flips to a fresh sheet in his pad, writes OAKMONT across the top in all caps. He points to the kitchen, where the lights are still burning despite the early morning sunshine. "Maybe we could sit down?"

"Of course, of course." I sweep an arm toward the doorway like Vanna fucking White.

In the kitchen, Ingrid makes a beeline to the table, parking herself on the same chair as before, her back to the wall, her hands folded on her notepad. Detective Durand chooses my chair, the one at the head. A man used to being in charge.

"Detective, can I offer you something to drink? I think I have some Coke in the fridge, or I can make a pot of coffee if you'd like." I'll admit the offer is not entirely unselfish. Last night's pizza has resulted in a ferocious thirst, and it's probably not a bad idea to demonstrate I am both helpful and forthcoming. So far he hasn't said anything to indicate he might suspect me, but he's also not said very much.

"I'll have a water," Ingrid says, and I glare at her over the detective's head.

"Did either of you call any of your wife's friends before you called the police?" he says. "Her colleagues?"

I pull three glasses from the cabinet by the sink. "It was the middle of the night. I didn't want to wake anyone up. And I am certain my wife wouldn't go to their houses anyway. She'd go to her sister's."

"Jeffrey and I don't agree on much, but he's right. Sabine and I talk multiple times a day. I know her schedule. She would have come to me, and she would have told me if she was going anywhere else. That's why this is so urgent."

The detective looks at her with new interest. Not, I sense, because of her conviction some awful disaster has overcome her sister, but because of her first words. The ones that imply she and I don't get along.

She rips the top few pages from the notepad and holds them across the table. "The names and numbers of everybody I could think of who might know Sabine's schedule yesterday. I left messages with everyone I got through to. I also wrote down Sabine's description, the make and model of her car, her email and cell phone number. If you give me your number, I can text you her picture."

Detective Durand takes a few seconds to scan the pages, then looks up with a nod. "This is all very helpful, ma'am. A great start."

His voice is as earnest as his expression, and I get the sudden and sinking feeling that Ingrid is showing me up, making me look unprepared. That I'm uncaring, when I'm anything but. I'm the one who sounded the alarm in the first place. Leave it to Ingrid to make me feel defensive in my own house—which she so kindly pointed out is actually Sabine's. Leave it to her to make me feel like a bum, a mooch.

It's always the husband. Especially one like me—sexually frustrated and financially dependent. It wouldn't take much digging to uncover our marital issues. Ingrid knows. How long until she tells the detective?

I fill the glasses with water from the tap, a sudden surge to seem cooperative. "So what now? What's next?"

"You mentioned she had a showing. Where was it? What time?"

"I don't know," I say, "only that she said she'd be home by nine."

Ingrid's eyes hold mine for a second too long. "The showing was at seven thirty." She turns to the detective. "Sabine is the lead broker at that new development on Linden Street. You know, the one with the stone columns at the entrance and the big, colorful sign. I don't have the address for the house she was showing, but it was in that development—her boss Lisa can tell you which one. Lisa's name is at the top of the second page, but you'll have to track down her number. Unfortunately, I don't have it."

I pass out the glasses of water, and the detective doesn't look at me, but I can sense his judgment. The husband and sister are not friends. The sister is better informed than the husband. Neither reflects well on our marriage.

"When is the last time either of you talked to Sabine?" he says.

"I talked to her twice yesterday morning," Ingrid says. "The last time was at just before eleven. She was on her way to the office. But Jeffrey spoke to her later in the day, in the afternoon."

The lie comes back to me in a flash of icy hot. Ingrid, interrupting my jog, asking to speak to Sabine. Me, telling Ingrid I'd spoken to Sabine only an hour earlier so I could get back to my run. If I repeat the lie now, it would take the detective all of two seconds to catch me in it. One look at my call log would prove me wrong.

I sink onto the chair across from Ingrid and shake my head. "No, I didn't. I said I talked to Sabine yesterday *morning*, right before I boarded my connection in Atlanta." I turn to the detective, explaining, "I've been in Florida all week, at a sales conference."

Ingrid's head whips in my direction, and she glares across the table. "When I called you, at just before five, you said you'd talked to her an hour ago. So around four."

"You must have misunderstood."

She presses both hands to the wooden table, and they're shaking. "I heard you loud and clear, Jeffrey. I asked when did you talk to her last, and you said an hour ago."

"Do you want to see my call log? I didn't say that, and I didn't talk to her."

The detective raises both brows, taking a long breath through his nose like a parent might, when he's had it with his two squabbling toddlers. "Okay, okay, let's just back up here for a second. Am I to understand that neither of you talked to her since yesterday morning, is that correct?"

I nod. "Yes. That's correct."

"Apparently so," Ingrid mumbles.

"And when you talked to her, did she mention anything out of the ordinary? Maybe that her car was acting funny, or that she had an errand to run in another town, anything like that?"

Ingrid and I shake our heads. Finally, something we agree on.

"And this showing last night. Any idea who it was with?"

She waits until I shake my head again, then juts a triumphant chin. "I don't know his name, but he was from out of town. Some executive who's just started at the Tyson plant. Sabine had found him temporary housing while he searched for a house—an apartment just off 530, but now his wife was coming to town. This showing was more for her than for him. He already loved the house."

I'm silent, and also a little shocked. Ingrid's knowledge of her sister's business, all the particulars and detail. Sabine didn't tell me any of this—or maybe she did. Maybe I just wasn't listening. What else have I missed?

Detective Durand consults Ingrid's notes, taps the page with his pen. "This Lisa O'Brien will be able to tell me his name?" He's no longer directing his questions at me.

"I'm sure she can," Ingrid says. "In fact, if I had her number, I would have already called to ask. Can you, I don't know, look her up in your system or something?"

"I'll contact Ms. O'Brien, absolutely. I'll also drive by the development and see if anything looks out of the ordinary. I'm not saying it will be—I just want to be sure, to cover all the bases. If I do find any signs of foul play—" the words make me twitch like a spider "—I'll put a trace on her phone and contact you immediately."

"Can't you do that now? Trace her phone, I mean.

Because if something's happened, if she's hurt or..." Ingrid shakes her head, swallowing. "I just don't think we should waste any more time."

"I'm not going to waste any time, I assure you. A missing person is about as high priority as you can get. And I'm sorry to have to ask this, but has your wife been receiving any threats? Is there anyone out there who might have wanted to hurt her?"

"No!" I beat Ingrid to the answer this time, but I can't look at her. I keep my gaze, sure and steady, on the detective. "Absolutely not. Everyone loves Sabine. She goes out of her way to be friendly to everyone. Partly because that's her job, but mostly because that's just how she is. Friendly and helpful. She's never met a stranger."

Ingrid clears her throat. "It's true. Sabine is a lovely, lovely person."

The detective offers up a smile, but it's neither friendly nor comforting. "Okay. I'm going to start by checking the standard places—hospitals, medical centers, jails. I want the two of you to take a look at anything that might give us some insight as to her movements yesterday. Emails, texts, social media pages, mutual bank statements and credit cards, things like that. Compile a list of everything you find and send it to me."

Detective Durand slaps a card to the table, pointing to the number at the bottom. "Call me the second Sabine shows up, or if you think of anything else that might be relevant to where she could be. We'll regroup later today."

I nod, mainly because I don't know what else to

do. That's it. Interview over. The detective lets himself out and the two of us sit stunned, staring at each other with wide, horrified eyes.

Across from me, Ingrid starts to cry.

Now that the detective is gone, I shove Ingrid out the door and put on a pot of coffee. I make it extra strong, the kind that bubbles out opaque and is thick as molasses. Not that I think I'll need the caffeine. Despite my sleepless night, I'm not the least bit drowsy, my veins humming with adrenaline and purpose. If Sabine doesn't show up soon, if somebody doesn't figure out where she went and what happened to her, Ingrid won't be the only one who thinks I had something to do with my wife's disappearance.

The detective told me to comb through Sabine's social media and bank accounts, but I was one step ahead of him, already thinking about where Sabine left her laptop. It's an ancient Acer, a thick chunk of plastic and metal as manageable as a cinder block, and just as heavy. Its bulk is a big part of the reason why she doesn't usually lug it to work. The other part is that she's got a slick new desk computer at the office, and her iPhone is permanently attached to her palm.

But in order to see what she's been up to, I need her log-in credentials, the ones she keeps in an unprotected Excel file on her desktop. Usernames and passwords for pretty much anything you need a username and password for. Email accounts. Bank records. Credit card statements. Things that will give me a road map to wherever she is, or at the very least, which way she's gone.

I start upstairs and work my way down, moving from room to room looking for her computer, double-and triple-checking everywhere I can think of. The problem is, Sabine is not logical. She treats her laptop like an old sweater or pair of shoes—as an afterthought, an item to leave lying around wherever she pleases, half-hidden under the bed or the couch. I concentrate my search around the places where Sabine tends to sit. On our bed, the laptop resting on her stretched-out thighs. The left end of the couch, her legs curled under her like a cat. The desk in the study and the chaise by the window in the den. I peer on shelves and under tables, sift through stacks of papers and books, lift bed skirts and blankets. No laptop.

Typical.

In each room, before moving on to the next one, I stand in the middle of the floor and call her cell. Even though wherever she is, chances are her phone is with her and not here at home. I hit her number and then I hold my breath and listen for the familiar melody, or if it's on silent, the muffled buzzing of it vibrating under a pile of pillows or some clothes. But the only sound is the four lazy beeps, right before it goes to voice mail. I hang up and move to the next room.

After an hour, I end up back where I started, in the kitchen, empty-handed.

I pour myself a cup of thick, black sludge and sink onto a bar stool.

Maybe I'm wrong. Maybe yesterday was one of the rare workdays that Sabine needed her computer, to search the MLS system or draw up a contract from a coffee shop between showings, in which case I'll have to go to her office to fetch it. That is, assuming she left it there, and it's not sliding around her trunk or on the floorboards of her car. I often see it sticking out of that canvas tote she lugs around, the one I'm forever tripping over when she chucks it by the garage door to search for her keys.

I pop off the stool, race to the garage, and there it is. The tote, on the cool cement floor. I snatch it by a handle and carry it inside.

The laptop is completely dead. No surprise there. Sabine has needed to replace the battery for ages now, though what she really needs is a new laptop. One that doesn't require almost-constant charging.

I plug it in under the island counter and turn it on, topping up my coffee while I wait for the thing to power up, which takes forever. I think about Ingrid across town, doing much the same thing—hunched over a laptop in her lonely kitchen, combing her files in search of her twin. I see her red and swollen nose, her hair still frizzy from the pillow, her squinty eyes when she said those ugly words to me—*I know what you did to Sabine*—and I feel a momentary spurt of fury. Ingrid thinks I had something to do with this, that I am behind my own wife's disappearance somehow, and the idea makes me want to strangle her.

The Acer gives a metallic beep, then lights up with a log-in screen. A blinking cursor, but there are only so many things her password could be. Sabine's birthday, or mine. Our anniversary. Combinations of the dates with our names. With every try, the password dock shimmies, but it doesn't let me in.

She would choose something that's easy to remember. She doesn't have hobbies, and we don't have pets or children. I try the other people in her life, her mother, followed by her dead father. Still nothing. And then I sigh and type Ingrid's name and birthdate into the bar—the one I should have started with, honestly—and voilà. The screen dissolves into her desktop.

I email myself the password file, from Sabine's email program that is a giant, honking mess. More than twenty thousand unread messages, everything from stores to spam to requests for a viewing, automatically generated emails from the MLS and RE/MAX systems. It would take days to search through the chaos for anything remotely relevant, especially since I'm not even sure what I'm looking for. Instead, I flip to the sent messages and start at the top. Contracts, sales pitches, the usual stuff. After the one I just sent, the most recent message is from Tuesday, now two days ago.

I exit and head to Facebook.

Sabine has some three thousand friends, most of whom aren't friends at all. Clients, colleagues, people from Rotary and business clubs. I go to her profile page, scrolling through post after post boasting sales numbers and pictures of homes listed and sold. No wonder she's always on her phone, her pretty thumbs flying across the keyboard like a teenager's. Her Facebook page is a walking advertisement for her services, her success.

Halfway down, I pause on a video from last week, a Facebook Live clip featuring a newly built house on Longmeadow Street. I'm shocked at the number below it, a counter boasting 758 views. Sabine is one of the top brokers, but still. That many?

I click on the video, and the counter ticks to 759.

The video loads, and there she is. My AWOL wife. She's wearing her favorite summer dress, the yellow one with the ruffles around the hem, and the gold locket I gave her last Christmas, dangling from a chain around her neck. Her hair, pulled high into a ponytail, flicks cheerfully when she talks, bobbing over a tanned shoulder.

"Hey, y'all, Sabine Hardison here with the most fabulous house on the block." She laughs. "Okay, so I know I say that about every house, but this one really is the most fabulous I've seen in like, ever. Four humongous bedrooms, five and a half baths—yes, people, you heard that right, a full bath for every bedroom—and a master suite you have to see to believe. Let's take a look, shall we?"

She looks happy. Her skin is flushed, her cheeks pink with excitement as she backward-walks the camera through the house, pointing out the features. When she signed up for the real estate course in Little Rock, I bitched about the time commitment, didn't hold back about how the house and our social life and our marriage would suffer, but I knew she'd be good at it. The truth is, that's what I was more worried about. I lean forward on my chair, remembering when she used to smile like this at me. When I was the one to make her glow.

The computer beeps, and at the bottom of the screen, a window opens. A message from someone named Bella.

Hey you. I ran into Trevor last night at the grocery store, and he was asking about you. Like, really asking. If I've seen you lately, if we've talked, what we talked about. He wouldn't tell me why, just gave me this big-ass smile like a canary would pop out any second. Are you the canary? I'm here for you whenever you have something to tell me. XO

I sit back on my stool.

Trevor. Who the fuck is Trevor?

I click on the list of Sabine's friends and type the name in the search bar, with zero results. I repeat the search in her email program, and this time I get a hit. Multiple hits, actually, messages sent and received with Dr. Trevor McAdams, an ob-gyn at Jefferson Regional. Apparently, Sabine sold him a house last fall.

The most recent string is a boring exchange from November, setting up a meeting for the signing of papers, the official exchange of keys. I scan their back-and-forth, but there's nothing out of the ordinary. No flirtatious innuendo, nothing that implies a swallow-the-canary kind of outcome. The only thing Trevor says that is even remotely personal is that he wishes her a nice Thanksgiving. She thanks him, says she hopes he and his family will be happy in their new home.

His *family.*

Maybe I'm overthinking this. Trevor is an ob-gyn, so it's not entirely impossible he could be Sabine's doctor. Not because she's pregnant, something that's impossible when you haven't had sex in five—that's right, count 'em—five months. But women go to the gynecologist for other reasons. Maybe Sabine goes to this guy.

I scroll down to his signature, click through to his bio on the hospital website. Trevor McAdams is a decent-looking guy, probably somewhere in his early forties. Clear skin, bright eyes, full head of hair swept off a broad forehead. The type of face that plenty of women wouldn't mind having between their legs.

Is my wife one of them?

I return to the emails and open one of the attachments. Eight months ago, Trevor plunked down just over three hundred thousand dollars for 4572 square feet of newly renovated house on a quiet street overlooking Pine Bluff Country Club. That's a lot of square footage, and an address in the swankiest area of town. No mortgage, which means he earns a hell of a lot more than Sabine and I do added together. I jot his address on a sticky note, 1600 Country Club Lane.

I open Sabine's calendar, in search of the address for last night's showing, but it's empty. She hasn't synced it in ages, maybe never. I click the icon for the internet instead and surf to Google, where Sabine is already signed in. I pause, the cursor hovering over the symbol for Gmail.

Sabine has a Gmail account?

I stop. Stare at the screen. Breathe hard and fast through my nose. My finger lingers over the track pad because I know, I know, I goddamnitalltohell *know* what I'll find once I click it.

Hundreds of IM chats, all with Trevor McFuckingAdams.

I need to see you. Even if it's only for a minute.

I'm sitting next to him, thinking about you.

Meet me at our place in half an hour.

You said we wouldn't fall in love. You lied. (I'm glad)

I'm ready to tell them, Sabine. I'm ready to take that step whenever you are.

OMG, are we really going to do this? Can we?

Yes, dammit. All you have to do is say the word.

I love you. Let's tell them this weekend.

The coffee turns to oil in my stomach, and I shove the cup away. It skids across the counter and into the sink, and it's a good thing Sabine is not here, because if she were, I would fucking kill her. No, first I would hurt her, and then I would hurt Trevor, and *then* I would kill them both. No wonder he swallowed the fucking canary. For the past however many months, he's been having secret sexcapades with my wife while I played the role of clueless, foolish, idiot, ignorant husband. Somewhere across town, a bitch named Bella is laughing. At *me*.

Is that where Sabine is right now? In a bed somewhere, with *him*?

My gaze lands on the sticky note. 1600 Country Club Lane.

Ten minutes later, I'm death-gripping the wheel of my car, the pedal punched to the floor.

MARCUS

This case, I handle by the book.

I start at the show house, walking the grounds and studying the dirt for imprints—both shoes and tires. I press my face to the windows and peer into all the rooms. This place is a "show house" all right, every room packed with complicated, flashy furniture, every horizontal surface crammed with bowls and candles and crap. I try the doors, the latches on the windows, but the place is locked up tight. No sign anyone but a decorator has been here.

From there, I go to the office for a face-to-face with Sabine's boss, Lisa, a perfumed blonde in a ruby-red suit with lips to match. According to her, not only was Sabine a no-show for last night's showing, she also missed a company-wide training yesterday afternoon, where she was supposed to present on building a social media platform.

"You don't understand," Lisa tells me, a frown pulling on her Botoxed brow. "Sabine is my hardest worker, and she's always on time for everything, especially showings. Honestly, Detective, this is very worrisome. This isn't like her at *all*."

The other brokers I talk to say much the same. Sabine is responsible, considerate, punctual. Like Lisa, they're worried something happened. An accident, maybe, or worse.

"Could she have booked a last-minute vacation?" I ask every one of them. "Maybe she needed to get away for a day or two."

Head shakes all around.

I'm on my way to the station to write up a report when my phone rings. Bryn. My reaction is both instant and physical. I wince. My lungs deflate like an unleashed balloon. Three years since her husband passed—my former partner—and her calls still hit me like a punch to the gut.

Stifling a groan, I pick up on the handsfree system. "Hey, Bryn."

"Hi, Marcus. Do you have a minute?"

She sniffs, and I know it's not going to be a minute—pretty much the last thing I have time for right now. I need to get my ass to the department. I need to plug Sabine's name through all the available databases, make sure Chief Eubanks sees my hardworking face. I need to make it known around the department that I met the missing woman once, when she showed my wife and me a house, so there's no uncomfortable questions down the road. I need to get every cop on the street watching for her car.

But once upon a time, I made a promise to Brian and to God—to watch over his sons, to be there for their birthdays and school graduations, to make sure they go to church and stay out of trouble. They're two little hellions, but I love them like they're my own. The only problem is I'm not so crazy about his widow, Bryn.

Scratch that. It's not that I don't *like* Bryn, it's that I don't always agree with her parenting methods. She babies those boys, lets them get away with far too much, and without a man in the house to counteract her coddling, her boys have the run of the place. She's constantly calling me to bellyache— how they're walking all over her, how they could use a good talking-to. My wife, Emma, says it's a cry for adult male interaction—in this case, mine. For someone to shoulder the burden like Brian used to. Emma's not the best armchair psychologist, but in this case, I think she might be right.

Bryn sighs into the phone. "I was cleaning up Timmy's room just now, and I found a whole bunch of toys I've never seen before. Those spinners, you know the ones all the kids are flinging around these days, and a whole bunch of other stuff that's not his. The problem is, I didn't buy it, and there's no way he could have bought it all himself. First of all, he'd need me to drive him to the store, which I didn't do. And toys are expensive. How'd he afford so many on a dollar-a-week allowance?"

"You think he stole them?"

"I hate thinking that about my own son, but I don't know what else it could be. He didn't get them from me, that's for sure." She pauses, giving me time to make the offer. To tell her I'm on my way. "He talks to you, Marcus. He tells you things he won't say to me."

I don't have time for this. I'm almost to the station, and backtracking to her house will tack on a half hour, maybe more, of driving time alone. And visits to Bryn are never quick. They involve tearful conversations and awkward hugs, endless pep talks and bottomless glasses of sweet tea. I do not have time.

But I think of Brian and I can't say no.

I beat a fist on the wheel, then jerk it hard to the left, making a U-turn in the middle of the road. "I'll be right over."

Twelve minutes later, I skid to a stop in front of the house, a squat ranch that's seen better days. The grass needs mowing, the window frames could use a fresh coat of paint, and I count at least a half dozen shingles missing on the roof. I shake my head, shake it off. Not my responsibility. No time.

I'm coming up the walkway when the front door opens, and Bryn steps outside. She's lost more weight since the last time she called me here, less than a month ago, and it looks like she's gotten even less sleep than I did. Pale skin, eye bags, the works. She likes to joke that her kids are trying to kill her, and not for the first time, I wonder if it might be true.

"Thanks for coming," she says. "I didn't know what to do, who else to call."

How about her father, who lives just up the road? Brian's brother in the next town, or any one of the other fifteen detectives who stood behind her when she buried her husband? I'm not just her first resort, as far as I can tell I'm the only one. I meant my promise to Brian, but in moments like these, I sure wish she'd let the other men in her life help, too.

I drop a kiss on her cheek, which is cold and pasty. "How's he doing?"

"Pouting. Upstairs in his room."

I pat her shoulder and step inside, taking the stairs by twos. Timmy's door, the last at the end of the hall, is closed, but I'm pretty sure he's not pouting. Video game sounds are coming through the wood—a car race, by the sound of it. I rap the door with a knuckle. "Yo, Timmy. It's me, Marcus."

Timmy is the oldest boy, a wiry kid with his father's cowlick and a half-decent jump shot. He was only four when his father died, a bullet to the chest at a routine traffic stop. I heard the *pop*, looked up and Brian was on the ground, the kid who shot him running away. He's currently serving life in prison, but the point is, Timmy barely remembers his father. He only remembers me, stepping into his father's shoes.

When he doesn't answer, I open the door, lean my head inside. "I take it you know why I'm here."

Timmy is sprawled on his bed in sweatpants and bare feet, and he looks up with a sheepish expression—in my mind, another strike against his mother. She only calls when one of her kids need disciplining, which is all the damn time. If she's the pushover, I'm the bad guy, the strict—well, not parent, but certainly disciplinarian. I'd much prefer the role of cool godfather.

"Yeah. I know why." Timmy's gaze goes back to the TV, and his thumb works the joystick in his hands. On the television screen, his car, a bright green Mustang, is tearing up a dirt track.

I step inside, shut the door behind me. "You want to explain it to me then?"

He shakes his head. "Uh-uh."

"Come on, Timmy. Either you turn the game off, or I will."

Timmy sighs, but he hits Pause. He stares at his lap as the room falls into silence.

I sink onto the edge of his bed. "So, here's the thing. There's a woman missing, and for about—" I check my watch, do the math "—twenty hours now. The most crucial hours in an investigation, and the farther out we get from the time of disappearance, the less likely it is I'll find this woman in time. I shouldn't even be here right now, but I am because you're important to me, too."

He looks up, a lightning-quick glance. "You think the woman's dead?"

I should have known he'd latch on to that part. That's what happens when you lose a parent at such an early age. You have an unnatural preoccupation with death and dying.

But Timmy is smart, and he knows when someone is lying to him. "I'll tell you what, buddy, it's not looking good."

"Oh."

"Yeah, oh." I drape a hand over his scrawny leg, give it a jiggle. "So help me out here, will you? Tell me where you got the toys."

Timmy tosses the joystick on the bed and reaches over, pulling a notebook from his bedside table. He flips it to a page smothered in writing—big, sloppy letters and numbers lined up in crooked columns. I scan the page, taking in the list of names and toys. A logbook.

"You've been trading your toys and games?"

"Yeah. But only for a little while. We were gonna trade back after we're done playing with them, only Mom took everything and now I can't. That's why I kept a list, so I wouldn't forget where all my stuff went."

I toss the notebook to the bed, biting down on a grin. This kid may be a hellion, but he's not a thief. In fact, he's actually kind of brilliant. Whether he realizes it or not, this kid just created a co-op. "Okay. But you do realize if you'd just told your mom all of this, you could have saved me a trip."

Timmy frowns, folding his scrawny arms across his chest like I said something wrong.

I'm trying to figure out what when my cell buzzes, and I check the screen. A text from Rick, another detective on the force.

Hospitals, med centers, jails and morgues all clean. No sign of car, no activity on phone, either.

I type out a reply—On my way, be there in 15— and slide it back into my pocket.

"Listen, I need you to promise me two things. Timmy, look at me." I wait for him to meet my gaze, then I stick a thumb in the air. "First, that you'll tell your mom the truth about the toys. Explain it to her like you did me. Show her the list. Your mom's a smart woman, and she loves you. She'll think you're as smart as I do for coming up with such a plan. Do you think you can do that?"

He gives me a reluctant nod.

I uncurl a finger, hold it alongside my thumb. "And second, next time you want to see me, just pick up the phone and call. It's a hell of a lot easier for everybody involved. Way better than getting yourself in trouble just so I'll come over."

The look he gives me tells me I was right. His mother is not the only one in this family looking for a little male influence. The boys need it just as much. I resolve to be better, to *do* better.

I ruffle his hair and stand. "As soon as this case is behind me, we'll do something fun, just you and me, okay? A movie. A ballgame. You pick. Does that sound all right to you?"

Timmy looks up from his bed and smiles. "That sounds awesome."

"Now get up here and gimme a hug so I can go."

It's the fastest hug on record, as is my trek down the stairs. Bryn is waiting for me at the bottom, her expression hopeful and disappointed at the same time. I'm not staying. That much is clear from the way I hit the floor and keep going, heading in long strides to the door.

"Talk to Timmy. He promised to explain." My phone buzzes. Rick again, with a possible sighting of Sabine's car. *Shit.*

"Are you sure you can't stay?" Bryn says.

"Call you later," I say, and then I'm off like a shot, jogging across the front yard to my car.

BETH

I roll up at a two-story cottage on the Westside and double-check the address—1071 English Street. I take in the salmon-painted siding, white picket fencing, the neat, manicured front lawn lined with a cheerful border of impatiens. On the outside at least, Morgan House is a dream. A hundred times better than the shithole on Wylie Street, and that's without even taking into account the hooker.

I park at the curb, sling my bag over my shoulder and head for the door.

The woman who pulls it open is large. Amazonian large, with a stretched-out frame and limbs like a panther, lean and miles and miles long. The tallest woman I've ever seen, though… My gaze lands on her throat. Not even a shadow of Adam's apple.

She steps onto the porch in four-inch heels, and I have to tip my head all the way back to look at her.

"Can I help you?" Her voice is round and resonant, like she's talking into an empty jug.

I clear my throat and smile. "Yes. I'm looking for whoever's in charge of this place."

"Well, then, you're in luck, 'cause you found her." She sticks out a hand the size of a skillet. Her nails are pointy and sharp, painted a shiny hot pink. "My name's Miss Sally. And you are?"

Her makeup is immaculate, if a little heavy. Fuchsia lips, lined and shaded lids, a pinkish bronze lining her cheekbones. I search her chin for tiny pinpricks of whiskers—it's too early to have a shadow, but still—and find nothing. Her foundation looks spray painted on, dense but flawless.

"Beth Murphy," I say, shaking her hand. "A friend gave me this address because I'm looking for—"

"You don't look like a Beth." She leans back and studies me, her gaze exploring my face, my hair, my suspiciously dark eyebrows, which I didn't think to color until it was too late. "You look more like a Haley, or maybe a Madeline."

I go ice cold and overheated all at once. I don't look like a Beth. I don't feel like one, either. My baggy clothes, my dollar-store hair are all wrong. I've only been Beth for a day, and already I can feel her slipping away.

Miss Sally laughs, slapping me playfully on an arm. "I'm just playing around with you, sugar. In my house you can be whoever you want to be. Now come on in and I'll show you around."

I step inside the tiny foyer, and she shuts the door behind me. A TV blares from the room to my left, a square space crammed with mismatched couches and chairs, a table, some bookshelves. The only occupant is a man, in dusty jeans and a yellow hard hat. He looks over from his perch on the couch and lifts his chin in a greeting.

"Living room, TV room and study, all in one," Miss Sally says. "Those books there are loaners, meaning don't go leaving them all over town or selling them off to Goodwill. There's cards, darts and board games in the cupboard. The Wi-Fi is free, but the vending machines aren't. Parking is out back."

"Looks great," I say, but I'm talking to air. Miss Sally is already halfway down a long, narrow hallway. I hustle to catch up, peeking into the bedrooms as we pass. Tiny but neat—a single bed, a dresser and not much else.

"So, Beth," she says, stopping, turning on the hallway runner to face me. "Did you just get to town?"

"Yes. Today, in fact."

"How are you liking Atlanta so far?"

"It's okay. There's a lot of traffic."

She laughs, though it's not even remotely funny. "It's also jungle-hot, sprawled halfway to Tennessee and has entirely too many Republicans. But it's not all that bad, you'll see. You on your own?"

"Very."

"Where from?"

"Out west."

She twitches a brow that says she wants more.

You're a great liar. For years I've watched you tell the truth whenever possible, and not embellish with too much detail you'll only forget later. Lies multiply, contradict, proliferate. Sticking to something close to the truth is the only way for you to keep track of all your lies, to keep them from piling up and you from stumbling over the simplest answers.

I follow your example now. "I'm not really *from* anywhere. Not anymore, anyway. I move around a lot."

It's enough for Miss Sally. She turns on her heels, raps on a door with a knuckle. "We've got three bathrooms," she says, shoving the door open, "one for every four bedrooms, and they pretty much all look like this one."

She steps aside so I can see. Two pedestal sinks, a toilet and at the far end, a glass-enclosed shower, utilitarian and blinding white. The room smells clean, like Old Spice and bleach.

"Shower time is three minutes. Seems short, I know, but you can get everything you need to get done in that time if you're efficient, and if you're not…well, we know what you're doing in there. And you do *not* want to be going over. People start pounding on the door at two minutes, fifty-nine seconds, and they won't be polite about it, either. Bitches who hog the hot water aren't so popular around here, I can promise you that."

"It's very neat." No toothbrushes, no sticky tubes of cream or paste, no forgotten towels on the floor. The place is spotless.

Miss Sally gives me a nod that says she's pleased I noticed. "That's because anything you leave behind gets confiscated, if not by me, then by whoever goes in after you. Don't leave your shit lying around— that's one of the house rules."

"What are the others?"

She ticks them off on Jolly Green Giant fingers. "No smoking, no drugs, no sleepovers, and if you're not in the door by midnight you'll be sleeping on the lawn. Other than that, just don't be an asshole and you'll do fine."

"Does that mean I'm in?"

In lieu of an answer, she turns and moves farther down the hall. "Kitchen's down there, and the laundry room is in the basement. A buck a load, drop it in the lockbox on the wall. We live by the honor code here, and don't even think of stiffing me. I'm not saying I have cameras everywhere, but it's best to assume I have cameras everywhere."

I start at the word *cameras*, and my gaze wanders to the ceiling, searching out the corners.

Miss Sally laughs, a big sound that fills the hallway like a cello chorus. "Well, I'm not going to be that obvious about it, now, am I?"

I can't tell if she's fucking with me or not.

"And the price?"

"Single rooms are twenty-four dollars a night. Rent is due in cash on Sundays at noon. No exceptions. Come to me either short or late, and you're out."

A few bucks more than Wylie Street, but also a million times nicer. I nod.

She looks down her nose at me, and the silence that fills the hallway tightens the skin of my stomach. She's waiting for something, and so am I—for her to pose the question I've been dreading since I walked through the door: *Can you prove you are who you say you are?*

She opens her mouth, and my heart gives a sudden kick. "Who is this friend you mentioned earlier?"

I shake my head, confused. "I'm sorry, what?"

"When you knocked on my door, you said a friend gave you the address. Who? Tell me his or her name."

I think about how Beth should answer, if she's the type of person to lie easily and effortlessly, like you. The opposite of Old Me, who's never been a natural liar, though I've certainly sharpened my skills some. Don't change your voice. Don't fidget or become too still. Hold a steady, confident gaze, and whatever you do, don't look up and to the left.

But now I've waited too long to answer—the dreaded, too-telling pause. It's too late to blurt out a name and hope for the best, and my gut tells me this is some kind of test. That Miss Sally, with her third-degree tone and squinty eyes, would see straight through me.

"So maybe 'friend' was too big a word," I say, lifting an apologetic shoulder. "Maybe it was more like some random person I met at Best Buy."

Miss Sally's shiny lips spread in a grin. "Girl, welcome to Morgan House."

I celebrate securing a new room by falling onto the bed fully clothed and conking out for five hours straight. It's still light when I awaken, but the sun has dipped below the trees, giant pines that sway in the air above my window. My few belongings are tucked in the drawer to my right, an easy arm's reach from my bed. When Miss Sally shoved open my door, she handed me two keys—one for the door and the second for the drawer—but if she's the type to spy with secret, hidden cameras, then she's also the type to have a master key. My dwindling wad of cash is strapped to a belt inside my shirt.

Somewhere below me, people are starting to trickle in. The front door opens and closes, opens and closes, and voices worm up through the floor like distant waves. I wonder about the proper etiquette here. Do I go down and say hello? Stay in my room? I hear a sudden burst of laughter, and I am overcome with uncertainty. Venturing downstairs means talking to people. Introducing myself as Beth. Answering questions like the ones Miss Sally asked. Up here in my room, behind my closed door, I am invisible.

My stomach growls, and I unlock the drawer and dig out a small bag of peanuts, the last one. I rip off the corner and think what I really want is a burger, dripping in grease and draped in bacon, smothered in mayonnaise and ketchup and a thick layer of pickles. My mouth waters, and I remember all those times I ate pickles at the fair, giant, foil-wrapped mammoths my sister and I had to hold in both hands. We'd wander among the bumper cars and farm stalls, eating them until our stomachs ached. You say pickles make my breath stink. Tomorrow I'm going to buy a jar of Vlasics and eat every single one.

For someone who is trying to shed herself of a husband, I sure do think of you a lot. Part of it is habit—all those years of tiptoeing around your moods and catering to your every whim are hard to unlearn, like a Charles Manson brainwashing. And it's still a necessary measure to keep myself safe. I *have* to think of you, to imagine the steps you're taking to find me in order to stay one step in front of you.

But I can't stay up here, hiding in my room forever.

I reach for my phone, pull up the calculator. At twenty-four dollars a night, my two-thousand-dollar stash will last me only a couple of months, and that's assuming the pile of crap car Dill sold me doesn't blow a fuse or a tire. And Beth has to eat, which means Beth needs to do some seriously creative thinking. Even a job slinging burgers requires some sort of identification.

I turn the peanut bag upside down over my mouth, but all I get is crumbs. I toss the bag on the bed. Groceries and a job, that's on the agenda for tomorrow.

I think about what you're doing now, some thirty hours into my disappearing trick. I wonder if you've found my car, my cell phone, the clues that will lead you to Tulsa—the opposite direction of here. I picture you searching through my things, calling my sister and my friends, combing through the files on my computer, and my senses go on high alert. I listen for the rumble of your car, the scrape of your key in the door, the tremor of your heavy shoes coming down the hallway floor. I shoot a glance to the window, half expecting to see the pale moon of your face peering in, the flash of your *gotcha* smile before you point your gun at my head. My heart taps a double time, and I take deep, belly breaths, trying to calm my nervous system. Post-traumatic stress is no joke—flashbacks and nightmares and anxiety attacks like this one are the product of years of abuse. It'll take more than a couple days of freedom for my body to uncoil.

Freedom.

I'm not there yet, not even close. I'm more in danger now than that time the waiter accidentally brushed his fingers against mine when refilling my water, or any one of the times you came home after a particularly bad day at work. Leaving does not stop the violence, and it doesn't guarantee freedom. *Why doesn't she just leave?* gets asked in living rooms and courtrooms across the country, when a better question would be, *Why doesn't he let her go?*

It took me a while, but I've finally figured out the answer.

You'd sooner kill me than let me go.

JEFFREY

On a long stretch of stick-straight road, 1600 Country Club Lane is tucked behind a thick tuft of trees and bushes. I don't see it until I've already blown past, and then I slam the brakes and screech to a stop in the middle of the road, because what the hell. Nobody's on this street but me, and with any luck, the squealing of my tires lets them know I'm here, that I'm coming in.

I throw the car into Reverse, pulling into the driveway in a sloppy arc, my gaze lighting on an upstairs window. I picture the two of them popping up in bed behind the shiny glass, sheets pressed to their naked, panting chests. *I'm here, bitches.* Just in case, I lean on the horn.

The house is a renovated bungalow, sprawling and ivy-covered, the kind of place Sabine would go gaga over. A pompous thing that belongs in the rolling hills of Tuscany, not pressed up against the faded greens of the Pine Bluff Country Club. An easy sale, a house she'd already be in love with before Trevor walked through the door.

I climb out of the car and slam my door with a sharp clap that echoes down the street. Inside the house, a little dog barks, high-pitched and frantic. Good, at least somebody knows I'm here.

I stomp up the walkway and bang on the front door with a fist. "Sabine! I know you're in there so open up. Open this door right goddamn now!"

The fury fills me like a furnace, bathing my body in a thin layer of sweat. Somewhere inside this stupid, pretentious house, my wife's body is wrapped around her lover's, and if one of them doesn't open this door *right fucking now*, I'm going to bust it down with my bare hands. I cup my hands around my face and lean into the glass, searching for movement, but all I see is an empty foyer. I haul back a fist and bang some more. On either side of me, two gas-fueled porch lights flicker in the fading light.

Two feet appear at the top of the stairs—male feet, sticking out from under blue scrubs. The man comes down trailed by a tiny white dog that is losing its shit. Each frantic bark pops all four of his paws off the ground, a fluffy jumping bean bouncing down the stairs.

But it's Trevor, all right. A shirtless Trevor. I recognize him from his headshot—full head of hair, strong shoulders that taper down into the abs of a movie star, not an ounce of fat or love handles on him. Not that I would normally notice such a thing, but Sabine would. She'd notice, and then she'd want to trace all those sculpted muscles with her finger-tips, and maybe her tongue.

"It's you," he says, studying me through the door's paned windows. All those years of hospital training, of on-call shifts and middle-of-the-night births are working now like a Xanax, making him look almost bored at the prospect of his lover's husband banging on his front door.

I beat on the wood hard enough to crack it. "Where's Sabine? Tell that little bitch to stop hiding and get her ass down here!"

On the other side of the glass, the dog is going ballistic. Trevor scoops it up and cradles it to his chest like a football. His mouth is moving, but I can't hear his words over the barking and the doorbell, which I'm mashing over and over and over again with a thumb.

He opens the door with a whoosh of cool air and moneyed manliness. "I'm sorry, Jeffrey, but Sabine's not here."

Jeffrey. I've known about this motherfucker's existence for less than half an hour, and now he's calling me by my first name. Did Sabine show him my picture? Did they laugh about poor, clueless Jeffrey and talk about the best way to make me look like a fool?

I shove him out of the way, marching to the stairs and hollering up them. "Sabine! You can come out now. I saw the emails. I *know*."

"Jeffrey." A hand lands on my shoulder. "Calm down. She's not here."

I shrug him off, swinging my arm through the air. "You touch me again, *Trevor*, and I will shove my fist down your throat hard enough to come out the other side. Do you understand what I'm telling you?"

The dog kicks things up a notch or ten, barking so hard he's starting to foam at the mouth. Jeffrey holds a chill-out hand in my direction, then wraps his fingers around the dog's snoot like a muzzle. Finally, thankfully, the beast stops barking.

"Where is she?" I'm not looking at him, but beyond him into the foyer. A family's foyer. Kids' shoes, a soccer ball, forgotten jackets and book bags. I wonder if Sabine has met them yet, if they hate her for blowing their happy home to bits.

Trevor shuts the door. "I already told you. She's not here."

"Why should I believe you?"

"You shouldn't. But I'm telling you the God's honest truth that she's not upstairs. I'd let you look, but my kids are up there." He winces. "Jesus, I'm going to have to explain this to them, aren't I? They're only six and four. They're never going to understand."

If that was an attempt to make me feel sorry for him, it gets him nowhere. I don't give a shit about his kids, or the fissure in his family. I only care about mine.

"You fucked my wife."

A normal person would deny it, especially one who's just been threatened with a fist down his throat, but not Trevor. His shoulders slump and he sighs, and his body language just lays it all out there. *Yes. Yes, now that you mention it, I did fuck your wife.* He even has the balls to look apologetic.

"Look, if it makes you feel any better, we didn't

want you to find out like this. Sabine was going to tell you to your face this weekend. Ask her—she'll tell you we had it all planned out. She was going to tell you the right way."

"The right way. What in the fucking hell could possibly be the right way?"

Now that the dog's calm, he settles the thing on the floor. "By telling you that we're in love. That we want to be together. I know that hurts to hear, and believe me, we've struggled with it ourselves, but—"

I throw back my head and shout hard enough to burn the back of my throat, "She's married, you asshole!" The words bounce around the house, then fall into a silence so absolute it rings in my ears.

"I understand that, Jeffrey, and I'm sorry. Truly. You can't even imagine how sorry. But swear to God, Sabine and I didn't set out intending to break up two families. It just happened, and this isn't just some fling. This is the realest, most genuine thing I've ever felt. Sabine is my soul mate. I *love* her. I *adore* her. She's the best thing that's ever happened to me."

His speech might have worked on another man. His words might have been a balm on a brittle, broken heart. Sabine will be loved, cared for, cherished. He's not stealing her out of greed or spite, but because he has no choice, because their connection is too great to ignore. Only an asshole stands in the way of soul mates.

But we've already established that I am a bitter, bitter man.

"Well then, *Trevor*, I feel obliged to tell you that this woman you cherish so much? Your soul mate?"

The fur bag sniffs at my shoe, and I push it away with a foot. "She's missing."

Trevor makes a face like I punched him in his perfectly sculpted abs. "What do you mean, Sabine is missing? *Missing*, missing?"

I nod. "She had a showing last night—"

"With Corey Porter and his family, I know."

The doctor stops, waiting for me to continue, but I'm still processing the fact that he knows more about my wife's business than I do, than even Ingrid does. As much as I'd love to leave him hanging, I need to know what he knows. I fix him with a defiant stare. "She never came home."

"She never..." He swallows the rest, but his expression is screaming the words.

"Came home. Sabine never came home. She didn't show up, and neither did her car."

"Okay, okay. Let's think about this logically. I mean, she was pretty sure Corey would pull the trigger on the house. Maybe he did. Maybe they went out after to celebrate."

"Maybe. But now it's the next day."

"Did you call her?"

I sigh. Roll my eyes.

"Of course you called her. But, but..." Trevor runs a shaking hand through his hair. "What about Ingrid—did you call her? Did you call the police?"

"Yes to both. Ingrid was at my house when the detective got there. He was going to check out the show house, see if he saw anything out of the ordinary. That was hours ago."

Trevor's eyes go wide with fear, with horror.

"Oh my God. Oh my *God*." He stumbles into the kitchen, and I follow behind. I step on one of the dog's squeaky toys, and the beast comes running.

Trevor leans against the kitchen counter, tapping numbers into a cordless phone with his thumb. He presses the phone to his ear, muttering, "Come on, come on, come on." And then his shoulders slump, and he curses. "Babe, it's me. Jeffrey's here, and he said you never came home last night. Wherever you are, please call me, okay? The very second you get this. I need to know you're okay, that you're... I'm scared shitless. I love you. Call me."

He hangs up, and I almost feel sorry for the bastard.

He begins pacing, his bare feet slapping the hardwood floor. "Now what?" Under the kitchen can lights, his face is green and shiny, sweating despite the air-conditioning. "What are we going to do now?"

I shake my head, battling a rush of disgust at his use of the word *we*. "You and I are not on the same team here. We do not share Sabine. She's *my* wife. She's nothing to you."

He stops, takes a long, slow breath. "When is the last time you talked to your wife?"

"Yesterday morning. And then she texted me later in the day that she had a showing but she'd be home by nine. When's the last time *you* talked to my wife?"

"Has anybody confirmed that she actually made it to the showing? Did she meet Corey and his wife at the house?"

I shrug. "Like I said, I haven't heard anything from the detective, so I'm guessing so. What time—"

"Did anybody call Corey to ask?"

"You're the first person I've talked to who knows who the showing was with. The most I could tell the detective was the name of Sabine's boss."

He turns and races from the room, his footsteps crashing up the stairs. While he's gone, I take a look around, try to see the place like Sabine would, like she *did* when she showed it to her soon-to-be lover. I picture her leading him through the empty house, pointing out all the features. Open, rambling rooms with French doors and generous windows. A spacious kitchen with new stainless appliances. Custom molding and hardwood floors throughout. Was their first kiss under the arched doorway? Did he push her up against these granite countertops? The visions burn like acid in my eyes, and I rub them away.

The floor creaks above my head.

I open the fridge and study the contents. Definitely a doctor's refrigerator. Milk, fruit, yogurt, enough vegetables to stock a produce department. Nothing even remotely unhealthy except a lone IPA, shoved to the very back behind a container of organic pineapple. I'm digging it out when Trevor returns with a shirt, thank God, and his cell.

"Corey's not answering his phone," he tells me, "and neither is Lisa."

I shut the refrigerator and wave the beer in the air by my head. "Where do you keep your opener?"

Trevor ignores me, staring at the phone in his hand.

The first drawer I try is stuffed with pencils and Post-its, so I close it and keep going, moving down the island, opening and closing the drawers in search of a bottle opener. On the third try, I find one, a golf-themed piece of plastic that makes a cheering sound when I open the cap. I toss it back into the drawer mid-hurrah.

"You never answered my question," I say. "When is the last time you talked to Sabine?"

He looks up, and his eyes are liquid. "She came by the hospital yesterday afternoon. She wasn't there very long, only fifteen minutes or so. She left around one thirty."

I stare at him across the island. At one thirty yesterday afternoon, I was in Little Rock, fretting about the canyon that's cracked down the middle of my marriage and plotting the steps I can take to win my wife back, oblivious to the fact that she was more than likely being fucked by her lover in a hospital supply closet.

"Would you stop looking at me like that?" he says. "Sabine is *missing*."

"It's just that I'm having trouble letting go of the fact that she made time in her day to go to the hospital for fifteen minutes with you, when she can never squeeze in a lunch with me. She's hardly ever home for dinner!"

Trevor sinks onto a stool at the counter, shoving aside a coloring book and a Solo cup packed with colorful markers. "What about her car? Has anyone seen it?"

"Not that I know of. Ingrid gave the detective her license plate number, though, so I'm assuming he's on the lookout." I take a long pull from the bottle, then make a face. It's one of those snobby IPAs, bitter and aggressively hoppy. I check the label and see it's also organic. "Do you have any normal beer?"

Trevor plucks a blue marker from the cup. "What's his name?"

"Whose name?"

"The detective. What's his name?"

"Oh. Something Durand. Mike or Mark or something like that."

I pour the rest of the IPA down the drain while Trevor calls 9-1-1 and demands to be put through to the detective. He uses his doctor's voice, polite but overly self-important, each word delivered in a tone that commands attention. He introduces himself—Dr. Trevor McAdams, Chief Obstetrician at Jefferson Regional, romantically involved with Sabine for the past five months—then rattles off Corey's name and number. Sabine's schedule until the moment she left the hospital, at sometime around one thirty. Her cell plus another number I didn't know existed, for a phone I didn't know she had. The entire conversation lasts no longer than five minutes. He thanks the person and hangs up.

I slam the bottle onto the counter with a clap, and the dog, who'd curled into a sleepy ball on its bed by the table, looks up with a start. "Five months?"

Trevor frowns.

"You told the detective just now that you and Sabine have been romantically involved for five fucking months." Those were his words, "romantically involved." The beer turns to acid in my throat.

"Like I said, this isn't the way we wanted you to

find out, but can we drop the guilt trip for a minute? At least until Sabine is found."

I grip the granite with both hands. "Five months ago, Sabine started to cringe whenever I'd touch her. She started turning her head when I kissed her and complaining about headaches any time I reached for her in bed. I thought it was me, but it was *you*, wasn't it?"

Trevor sighs, and he lifts a hand from the counter. "I don't know what to tell you, Jeffrey."

"That phone number you gave the detective just now. Let me guess. Sabine got it when she started seeing you, didn't she?"

He doesn't answer, but his expression tells me it's a yes. Sabine has a secret phone. She got a separate device so she can talk to Trevor without me knowing. A Trevor hotline.

He opens the coloring book, scribbles across a smiling Dumbo in bright purple marker. "Corey lives in those gated condos on Old Warren Road. He must know something. I need to know what it is." He rips out the sheet and holds it across the counter to me, waiting for me to take it. "Please, Jeffrey. My kids are upstairs. I can't leave them. My wife…" He shakes his head. "She's already taking me to the cleaners. I can't have her taking them, too. *Please*."

I sigh, a hard huff filled with resentment and something sharper, something that gnaws at me like hunger—but for revenge. When I get home, I'm going to look up the number for this guy's wife and volunteer as a witness.

"You do realize that Sabine leaves her shit all over

the house, right? If you actually lived with her, if you spent time with her on a regular basis, you'd know she's demanding and forgetful and selfish. That she pees with the door open and she hogs the couch and she never bothers cleaning up her own dishes. You don't want her because she's your soul mate. You only want her because she's not yours."

He gives the paper a shake. "Please, talk to Corey. Don't do it for me. Do it for Sabine. For our—" He stops himself just in time, but it's too late. I already understand. I heard the words he didn't want to say.

"You motherfucking fucker." I pause, the realization lighting me up from inside—hot, smoldering coals that seethe in my stomach and spread outward until my limbs feel like they're on fire. One good spark, and I'll blow. "She's pregnant, isn't she?"

He doesn't nod, but his eyes are glassy in the dim light.

Finally, after all these years of wishing and wanting and eventually giving up entirely, Sabine is pregnant. With *Trevor's* child.

His gaze dips to the paper. "Please," he says, and his voice breaks on the word.

I take the paper, but then I stalk around the island and punch him in the face.

BETH

That night, you come to me in my sleep, a blur of lightning limbs and shouted curses, tearing through the house. Opening and slamming doors, whipping off pillows and bedcovers, flipping couches and tables, ripping pictures off the wall. You are searching for something, for me.

I teeter on the edge of awake.

I see you gaining speed, moving closer, and my stomach clenches into a spiky knot. You puff your big chest and scream, and that lock of hair I used to love to run my fingers through falls flat on your sweaty forehead. You push it off with the back of a fist, and that's when I see the gun.

Wake up! I pinch the skin of my arms, smack myself on the cheeks. But my legs, tangled in the sheets, are like lead. They won't move.

Suddenly, you're here, stomping down the hallway at Morgan House. The hollow thud of your footsteps trembles the floor, the walls, the lining around my heart. The noise stops in front of my door, and I am frozen with fear, with pure terror.

My doorknob rattles, then goes still.

I hold my breath, wait for the gun to go off.

The door explodes, wood splinters showering down on me like a million deadly spikes. The hallway sconces light you up from behind, glowing underneath your skin like blood.

I scream.

You grin and aim the gun.

I shoot upright in my bed, the scream ringing in my ears. I clamp a hand over my mouth and stare into the dark room, trying to get my bearings. My room, my bed at Morgan House. I'm safe. You're not here. It was only a dream.

And yet… Was it? The back of my throat burns in a way that tells me the scream might have been real, but the ache could also be from the sobbing. My cheeks are slick, the hair at my temples damp with sweat or tears.

I mop my face with the sheet and take several deep breaths, willing my hammering heart to slow. I check the time on my cell phone: 4:00 a.m.

Somewhere above me, a male body is snoring loud enough to rattle the floorboards, and I wonder what this says about my housemates. That they are either deaf or sleep like the dead… Or maybe they are immune to a stranger's scream ripping through their slumber. Miss Sally runs a tight ship, but this place is an oasis in a questionable neighborhood, one where the houses sport bars on the windows. This doesn't bode well for me if my nightmare turns to reality. What will they do if you find me here? Sleep through the screams? Hide behind the locked doors of their bedrooms?

Suddenly, the room is too hot, the four walls shrinking around me. I kick off the twisted sheets and reach for my shorts, in a wadded pile on the floor. I need a glass of water, or maybe a cup of tea if I can swipe a tea bag from somebody's supply. Mostly, I need to get out of this room. I strap my money belt around my waist, pluck my keys and phone from the nightstand, and creep into the hall, locking the door behind me.

The hallway is dark, lit only at the far end by a streetlamp somewhere outside the window. I move, breathless and on tiptoe toward its golden gleam, the pads of my bare feet silent on the polyester runner. The stairs are trickier, sagging and creaky in the middle. I hug the side instead, my fingertips skimming the walls, following them to the kitchen.

A single bulb above the stove casts faint light on the scuffed linoleum floor, but otherwise the room is a black hole. I power on my cell, use the light of the screen to guide the way to the cabinets on the far wall.

The first one is dinnerware, neat stacks of plates and bowls and plastic cups. I shut it and move down the line. Cleaning supplies, pots and pans, but not a single crumb of food, no box of dusty tea bags.

"You must be the new girl," a female voice says from behind me.

A grenade erupts in my chest, and I whirl around, searching for her face in the darkness.

The shadows shift, and the ceiling lamp buzzes to life, blinding me with sudden light. I cover my eyes, squinting through my fingers at the woman sitting cross-legged atop the kitchen table. Caramel skin and big brown eyes and the body of a fifties film star, petite but curvy.

She watches me with barefaced curiosity. "What are you looking for? Maybe I can help you find it."

She's as pretty as her accent, a South American cadence slowed with a Southern drawl. Two silver discs hang on delicate chains from her neck, each of them engraved with something I can't quite make out from this distance. Names, I'm guessing.

I wasn't expecting to find anyone here, not when the money belt hanging from my middle is about as subtle as a third breast. I pull on my too-tight T-shirt, fold my arms across my waist. "You scared the shit out of me."

"Was that you upstairs?" She pauses. "I heard somebody scream just now. Was that you?"

Shit. So that part wasn't a dream.

My face goes hot, thinking of all the sleeping bodies upstairs. "Sorry. Did I wake you?" How many others did I rouse from their slumber?

"No. My room is right next to Ned's." She points to the ceiling, the boards above our head rumbling like a faraway train. Ned, I assume. "Anyway, tell me what you came down here looking for, and I'll tell you where you can find it. Though I will warn you— Miss Sally keeps the good stuff locked in the pantry."

"Oh." Miss Sally's warnings ring in my ear—her honor code, and the hidden cameras everywhere. But surely a tea bag doesn't count as stealing, especially if I replace it first thing tomorrow. "I was hoping to borrow a tea bag, actually."

"Well, that's easy enough." She hops off the table and pads on bare feet across the room. Her shorts are the kind a cheerleader would wear, skintight and Daisy Duke short. "I've got a box of Lipton—hope that's okay."

You once hurled a full cup of piping hot tea at my head because it was Lipton. You said if you'd wanted a cup of hot piss, you would have asked for some.

I smile. "Lipton is perfect, thank you."

She pulls a yellow box from a drawer by the microwave, flips on the electric kettle, drops the bags in two mugs she finds in a cabinet.

"So, what were you doing down here?" I say, gesturing to the table. "Why were you sitting here in the dark?"

"I was meditating."

"Seriously?" It's not at all what I was expecting. She doesn't seem like the type—too fidgety, too *va-va-voom* to be that grounded. "In the middle of the night?"

"Why not? Meditation relieves stress, increases concentration, clears your mind and calms your nerves." She closes her eyes, holds her hands in the air, palms to the sky, in a classic meditation pose. I notice a tattoo that pokes out from the collar of her white tank top, winding down the skin of one arm. The other is covered in bracelets, leather and bright, colorful beads. "Ommmmmm." Her eyes pop open, her gaze finding mine. "I'll teach you sometime. Honestly, I'm glad to have another one of us here. Another female, I mean. We're the only ones, if you don't count Miss Sally. I don't know if you've noticed yet, but this place is boiling over with testosterone."

Her rapid-fire change of subjects is dizzying to my sleep-deprived brain, and I sink onto a chair at the table. I consider which part of her monologue to latch on to—the meditation, the proffer of friendship, the gender imbalance in this place—but she's already moved on.

"I take it you're new to town," she says.

"Just got here, actually. How long have you lived here?"

"Atlanta or Morgan House?"

I shrug. "Both, I guess."

"I'm a Grady baby, born and raised." She leans a hip against the counter, taking in my frown. "Oh, sorry. Grady's the hospital downtown, where they take all the gunshot patients and moms too strung out to know they're pushing out a baby. I spent six weeks in one of those heated bubbles, sweating the crack and Lord knows what else out of my system. By the time I was clean, my mom was long gone. They handed me over to foster care."

Her story has a few holes. Her accent, for one. Even if her foster parents were Latino, even if she grew up speaking Spanish at home, would her accent really be that strong? And why would someone born and raised in this city end up here, in a boardinghouse that caters to transients? Still, no way I'm planning to ask. The less she tells me about her life, the less she'll expect me to tell her about mine.

"I'm sorry," I say instead. "The foster system is tough."

She shrugs, a what-can-you-do gesture. "The worst part is not being wanted by anyone. That really messes with your head, you know? It can make you feel worthless if you let it." She pulls a bear-shaped bottle from the cabinet by the fridge and waves it next to her face. "Honey?"

I nod, even though I don't usually take my tea sweet. My stomach is sharp with hunger, and honey will help.

She squirts a generous blob in each mug, reaches in a drawer for two spoons. "I'm Martina, by the way."

A first name, nothing else. I follow her lead. "I'm Beth."

"Nice to meet you, Beth." She grins at me over her shoulder. "How you liking it here at Morgan House?"

"I haven't really been here long enough to know, and you're the only other person I've met besides Miss Sally." I lower my voice to a whisper. "She scares me a little."

Martina turns, swiping a hand through the air, her bracelets jangling. "Oh, don't you worry about Miss Sally. As long as you're cool, she's cool. Ditto for most of the people staying here. They might need more than a three-minute shower, but they keep to themselves, mostly, and they won't grab your ass or try to steal your shit, because they know Miss Sally would eat them for supper. Keep your head down and don't ruffle any feathers, and you'll do fine. How long will you be staying?"

"I don't know. It depends on how quickly I can get a job."

The kettle clicks off, the water gurgling in a rolling boil, and she pours it into the mugs. "The place I work for is always looking for some new help. Nothing fancy, just mopping floors and scrubbing sinks, but still. The work is steady and it pays enough to afford the rent here."

Your voice bubbles up in my head, as clearly as if you were sitting at the table across from me. *No such thing as a free lunch. Somebody offers you something, you best be thinking about what they want in return, because they always want something.* I study Martina's back as she dunks the tea bags up and down, up and down, and I wonder what she wants from me. The money strapped to my belly, most likely.

She glances over a shoulder. "Don't like cleaning toilets, huh?"

I push your words aside and flip the script. Tell myself this isn't about what this girl wants from me but what *I* want from *her*. The thing is, I already know that becoming Beth Murphy, *really* becoming her, is a pain in the ass, and maybe an impossible one. I need a Georgia driver's license, and for that I need documents that seem as elusive to me as sprouting fairy wings or finding a flying unicorn. A birth certificate, a social security card and not one but two documents proving residency, something like a utility or credit card bill. Miss Sally doesn't seem like the type who could be persuaded into slapping my name onto a rental agreement for a couple of crisp bills; I'm pretty sure she'd toss me onto the street if

I even asked. And what about the other documents? The utility bills, the birth certificate and social security card? My Photoshop skills are nowhere near good enough, and I'm pretty sure forging a government-issued document is a felony.

"It's not that I mind cleaning toilets," I say. "It's just that I lost my ID."

Martina gives me a look. "You lost it, huh? That happens a lot around here." She carries the mugs to the table and holds one out to me. "You don't have anything? Not even an old, expired one?"

Especially not that. My Arkansas license is a charred lump at the bottom of a hotel trash can four states away. I take the tea and shake my head.

But according to the internet, this city has more than three hundred thousand undocumented workers. The question isn't *if* there are jobs here, but where to find them.

"I can still get a job without one, right?"

She sinks onto the table, swinging her legs onto the wooden surface and crossing them underneath her, resuming her old position. "Sure, if you don't mind working construction or cleaning rich ladies' houses. Know any Buckhead Betties?"

I open my mouth to answer, but she waves me off.

"Never mind. You do *not* want to work for one of those bitches, I can promise you that. What I meant was, you'll need a roster of regular customers, people with big houses who don't mind paying you cash under the table."

My stomach sinks. "The only people I know in this city are you and Miss Sally."

"Miss Sally can maybe help you, but I can't. I try to stay out of the northern suburbs." She blows over the surface of her tea, regarding me with a thoughtful expression. "How much money you got in that bag strapped to your waist?"

The hand I press to the bag is automatic, as is the expression on my face, a mixture of distrust and defiance. *Don't even fucking try it.*

Martina laughs. "Come *on*, chica. I already told you people here don't try to steal your shit, and that includes me, though it's probably not a bad idea to keep your cash on your person at all times. What I'm asking is if you would be willing to part with some of it. Because if you are, I might know where you could find an ID."

I lean back on my chair, eyeing her with suspicion. My hand is still on my money belt, my legs still ready to pounce. I'm bigger than Martina, and thanks to you, I know the most effective places to land a punch. Kneecap, face, solar plexus, throat, temple. I'll be back upstairs, barricaded behind the door of my room before she stops writhing on the floor.

But an ID would solve a lot of problems.

"How much?" I say warily.

"Last I heard, Jorge charges somewhere in the neighborhood of three hundred dollars. You can probably talk him down some if you find him in a good mood. The hard part is finding him in a good mood."

"Is he any good?"

"The best. The Rolls-Royce of fake IDs. That's why he's so expensive."

I sip my tea and do the math. Three hundred dollars is a lot of cash, almost two weeks' worth of rent and 15 percent of my rapidly dwindling stash. But if Jorge is as good as Martina says he is, it might be worth the money. Finding a job will be so much faster and easier if Beth is legit.

"And you?"

Martina looks up from her mug, her brows sliding into a frown. "And me, what?"

"How much do you charge for telling me where to find this Jorge person?"

Martina looks at me for a moment, letting the silence linger. Her expression is that of someone making a hard decision, and I know what she's thinking. How much is the information worth to me? How much is too much? Your words run through my head—*no such thing as a free lunch*—and I hate you even more for being right.

"Las Tortas Locas on Jimmy Carter Boulevard," she says finally, unfolding her legs and pushing to a stand, walking with her mug to the door. "Consider it your housewarming gift."

JEFFREY

A pounding on the front door lurches me out of a dead sleep. I sit up on the couch and rub my face, blinking into the room. The only light comes from a thin slice of morning sunshine where the curtains don't quite meet, blanching a strip of carpet. I check my watch—11:00 a.m. I've been asleep for all of two hours.

The past two days have been a shit show. Coming home to find Sabine missing, discovering she's been screwing around, my surprise rendezvous with her lover, Trevor accidentally spilling the beans about the pregnancy. By the time I drove across town to Sabine's client, then did the same with her boss, every muscle in my body was knotted up, my skin vibrating with fury. Corey and Lisa told me exactly what they told the detective: that Sabine never showed up for the showing.

There's another pounding at the door, followed by three rapid-fire rings of the doorbell. I push off the couch and stumble to the door.

Ingrid doesn't look like she's slept much, either, but she's cleaned up since the last time I saw her. She's fresh from the shower; her hair is still damp, the ends gathered in wet clumps, dripping onto her dress, some awful blue-and-white thing. She barrels into my foyer, and I catch a whiff of her perfume, cloying and sweet.

She takes in my T-shirt and rumpled sweats, the same ones I was wearing the last time she was here, and frowns. "Why aren't you dressed? Didn't you get my messages?"

I wince, pressing down on my throbbing temples with a thumb and middle finger. Ingrid's volume, louder than usual, isn't helping what's pounding in my head like a hangover. And then there's that constant edge to her voice. I can't take much of her on a good day; now, after two bad days in a row, she's chipping away at my last threads of civility.

"Clearly not."

"Well, go upstairs and change. We're due at the police department in thirty minutes. The detective has an update."

My heart bangs a slow, heavy beat. An update could be anything. Her car, found wrapped around a tree. Her body, found rotting in a field of soybeans. Her killer, on the loose or locked behind bars.

"What kind of update?"

"I don't *know*, Jeffrey. He wouldn't tell me anything other than he had some news." She chews on a corner of her lips, which are already red and cracked. Her eyes are fat pink pillows. "What if he—"

She stops herself before she can finish, and I don't

touch it. A detective calling with news he wouldn't share over the phone can't be good. I turn and head upstairs for a quick shower.

Nine and a half minutes later I'm crammed into the passenger's seat of Ingrid's Acura, barreling south toward the police station. Traffic is light, but on the other side of her windshield, it's gearing up to be another blistering day. I turn the air-conditioning to high and aim the vents at my face. Trevor's news last night lit me on fire, and I've been burning up ever since.

"I suppose you knew about the baby."

Ingrid stares straight ahead, hands at ten and two, but she nods. "Sabine and I—"

"Tell each other everything. I know." I glare out the side window at the storefronts flashing by and wish I'd thought to bring sunglasses. "What else have the two of you been keeping from me?"

"She's been talking to a lawyer. She was going to ask you for a divorce this weekend."

The news hits me like an anvil; not that Sabine was planning to leave me—Trevor already told me as much—but at the implication she saw a lawyer. Something that's easy to verify. I don't need to be a detective to know how it makes me look—like I have a motive.

I snort. "That's convenient, isn't it?"

"What is?"

"The timing. Sabine disappears, pregnant with another man's child, right as she's about to file for divorce from a husband who once—and only once, so help me God—lost his temper. If I were the detective, I'd be calling me in for questioning, too." I twist on my seat, turning to face Ingrid. "Is that what this is? Is that why you came by the house, to haul me in for questioning? Did he send you to lure me to the station?"

"I'm pretty sure the detective can haul you in himself if he wants to." She gives me the same guilty side-eye Sabine does, right before she admits to having ruined my favorite sweater in the laundry. "But to be perfectly honest, I came to get you because I can't do this alone. Sit in some sterile room at the police station while the detective tells me something awful has happened to my sister. I'm terrified. And I couldn't bring Mom. She wouldn't understand, and even if she did, I can't deal with her and bad news at the same time. As much as I hate to admit it, I need you there."

"Why didn't you call Trevor?"

She presses her lips together.

"You did call him. He wouldn't come."

"He's a mess." She punches the gas to make it through a light, then merges into the far-left lane. "And he was right. Having him there would only make everything worse. At least I won't have to take care of you."

I'm not quite sure how to take that. Her mother would be too clueless, Trevor would be too emotional and I would be my usual asshole self. I choose to focus on the words she doesn't say: that I'm strong, solid, sensible. No matter what the detective has to tell us, at least I won't go apeshit.

But is she right? I think about what I'd do if the

detective tells me Sabine is dead, or asks to swab the inside of my cheek. What will my reaction be then? I look over at Ingrid, at her pointy features and shiny profile, and think I really don't want to do this alone, either.

"It's ironic," I say, turning back to the traffic.

"What is?"

"That it took Sabine disappearing to make us actually want to be in a room together."

BETH

For a boulevard named after a former peanut-farmer-turned-president, it's nothing like I expected. A magnolia-lined avenue, maybe, or a winding country road slicing through rolling green fields would be fitting, not this six-lane thoroughfare that packs the Buick Regal on all sides with bumper-to-bumper traffic. I cling to the far-right lane, keep a safe distance between my car and the guy riding the brakes in front of me and search the storefronts for Las Tortas Locas.

I spot it up ahead, a giant margarita glass jutting above the rooftops like a crown jewel. I swerve into the turn lane and head toward the building, a riot of flashing neon lights squeezed between a strip mall and a drive-through bank. I pull into the lot, and mariachi music rattles the Buick's tinted windows.

The inside is even worse. Music blares from the ceiling speakers, mixing with the din of a full house of diners and the hard chinks of porcelain and glass. The hostess has to cup a palm around her ear when

I yell at her who I'm here to see, and then she points me to a table at the far end of the restaurant.

"Are you sure?" I shout, squinting at the man across the room. Even from here, from clear across the room, the man doesn't match the name. "I'm here for Jorge. *Jorge*."

She leans on the hostess stand with an elbow, and I catch a slight roll of her eyes. "That's him. And I heard you the first time."

I wind my way through the tables to "Jorge," four hundred pounds of a milky-white man eating a burrito the size of his forearm. I hover at the edge of his table, waiting for him to stop shoveling food long enough to notice me. This Jorge guy may not be Latino, but he's no stranger to churros.

He looks up, and his eyes are thin slits, part genetics, part his cheeks squeezing them shut. It looks like he's glaring at me—and maybe that's exactly what he's doing. Martina said he was in a perpetually bad mood. He picks up a hard-shelled taco loaded with meat and cheese, and dunks it in salsa.

"Martina gave me your name," I say finally. I lean closer, across what looks to be a bucket of refried beans smothered with cheese. "She said you could help me get an ID."

"What kind?" His accent sounds Asian.

"A driver's license. For Georgia preferably. And maybe a social security card if you're able."

He gives me a look, and I don't know if it's to say he does or doesn't have one. "Four hundred dollar." He shoves the taco—the whole entire thing—into his mouth.

"For both?"

"Yup," he says around a mouthful of meat.

"But Martina told me three."

The slits all but disappear. I give him time to swallow some of the food bulging in his already-swollen cheeks. "Three hundred for license only. Four hundred for both."

Barter, you say in my head. For you haggling is a sport, a competition. You will hold up the grocery store line to bicker about the price for dented cans and boxes torn at the edges. *Say it like you mean it*, you tell me now. *There's always wiggle room in a price. Always.*

"Three hundred and fifty," I say.

"Three hundred seventy-five." A shard of ground beef flies from Jorge's mouth and ricochets off my leg. I make a face, edge backward until I am out of range. I will never eat Mexican again.

I nod. "Deal."

Jorge tells me to meet him in an hour, at a strip mall a few miles from here. He slides the beans closer, reaching for his spoon, and rattles off an address I commit to memory. That's it. Meeting over. I beat a semistraight path to the door before he changes his mind.

For the next forty-five minutes, I sit in my car in the restaurant's parking lot, listening to the radio and killing time. People come and go in a constant stream, construction workers and folks in business attire, moms with hair like mine emerging from a minivan full of kids. It's the weirdest combination of diners I've ever seen, and I think of Jorge, the way he shoveled in those tacos faster than he could chew. The food here must really be something.

My gaze sticks to a figure at the far edge of the lot. She's everything a woman in a neighborhood like this one is not supposed to be: alone, half-hidden behind a holly bush, completely oblivious to her surroundings. Her head is down, her thumbs flying across her phone, and even from all the way across the lot I can tell she's a perfect mark. Designer bag slung over her shoulder, a honker of a diamond on her finger. The stone winks in the afternoon sunlight, along with matching ones in each ear.

A car slows alongside her, and one by one, the hairs on the back of my neck soldier to a stand.

"Look up, lady. Look up look up look up," I say into my empty car. No way she can hear me, but still. I say it loud and with authority, like anyone who's ever taken a self-defense class would know to do. Straight punch to the throat, knee-kick to the groin, elbow in the nose. Basic moves, simple techniques every woman should have in her arsenal, both potent and effective.

But this woman doesn't look up, doesn't even glance at the car. Las Tortas Locas is apparently a hotbed for criminal activity, and she might as well have hung a sign over her head, advertising herself as easy prey.

"Shit, lady. Come *on*."

The car is completely stopped now, and I spot two shadowed figures behind the opaque windows who are not here for the taco special. I know it with everything inside me—my queasy stomach, my itchy skin, a cell-deep awareness that something is about to happen.

Something bad.

My fingers wander to my steering wheel, the heel of my hand hovering over the horn, while my brain shuffles through the scenarios. Leaning on the horn might scare off the bad guys and save the woman's jewels, but it might also get me noticed. It would mean her asking my name, noting my license plate, looking at me as a hero or worse: a witness. Beth Murphy's life would be over before it even began. This lady needs saving, but dammit, so do I.

The passenger's door swings open, and a man steps out. Pale skin, slouchy jeans, faded and ripped gray sweatshirt. No, not a man, a kid, tall and lanky, all shiny face and silly-putty limbs, probably no more than fourteen. He leaves the door open, and if that's not a getaway move, I don't know what is.

He stalks straight at her, and I scream into my car, "Put down the stupid phone!"

But as hard as I try, I can't make my hand press on the horn.

And so I sit, watching from fifty feet away while the kid whips out a gun and mugs her in broad daylight. Purse, phone, diamonds, watch, bracelets—she hands over everything with frantic, shaking hands. He forces her to the ground, his body language commanding her to hurry. She sputters and sobs but she obeys, lying flat with both hands shielding the back of her head. Behind him, the car's tires squeal and smoke, and the kid lunges with his loot through the still-open door. The entire episode takes all of sixty seconds.

As soon as the parking lot is quiet again, the woman clambers to her feet. "Help! Somebody help me. Help!"

I tell myself it's fine, that *she's* fine. Scared and shaken, maybe, her white jeans smudged where they made contact with the dirty asphalt. But otherwise, everybody is fine. Everybody but me, trapped here in this lot. The woman is standing between me and the only exit.

A gaggle of sorority types push out the restaurant's double doors, talking and laughing. They hear the woman's cries and stop on the concrete, their happy expressions falling into surprise.

"I was robbed!" the woman screams at them. "He pointed a gun at my head and he took my wedding ring. He took *everything*. Oh my God, don't just stand there. Somebody call the police!"

A tall blonde pulls out a cell phone, and I eyeball the curb height to the street, trying to judge if it's too high for the Buick to plow over without blowing out a tire. Would the women even notice? Would they jot down my license plate and hand it to the cops as a potential witness?

And what if I don't leave, then what? What will I say when the police find me sitting here, hiding in my car? I glance at the clock on the dash. Less than ten minutes until I'm supposed to meet Jorge. Even if I ditched my car and ran, I'd never make it on time.

The women are all babbling now, gesturing and talking over each other, their expressions tight with the near miss, and guilt pushes up from somewhere deep inside me. All my life, I've believed in karma, in the universal principle of cause and effect. Do good, and good comes to you. Do bad, and... Well, you better watch your back.

And today I stood by and watched a woman get mugged.

What does the universe have in store for me now?

The women storm inside, and I start the car and drive as fast as I dare, squealing into the strip mall Jorge directed me to a full six minutes late. I pray Jorge's not a punctual guy, the type who doesn't tolerate clients who show up later than promised. Then again, I am the client, and I'm guessing the black market ID business must by definition remain fluid. In the grand scope of things, six minutes isn't all that long.

I step out of my car and scan the half dozen storefronts. Jorge didn't give me anything other than an address, so which one? Discount stores and *carnicerías*, a cell phone shop, a smashed window covered in butcher paper. And then at the far end, I spot a single word: *fotográfico*. I slam the door and hurry to the store.

Inside, the place is tiny—a shoebox of a room with a camera on a tripod, a register counter and not much else. Jorge is waiting for me by the register, beside a man he introduces as Emmanuel, no last name. Emmanuel demands six dollars in cash, then points me to a grubby white wall. "Stand there. No smile."

Emmanuel is a man of few words, but he gets the

job done. There's a blinding flash, and by the time the spots have cleared from my vision, two passport-size pictures are rolling out of his printer.

While Emmanuel cuts them into tiny squares, Jorge hands me a piece of paper and a pen. "Write down name, birth date, height, weight and address. You can use fake ones if you want."

"Do your customers ever use real ones?"

He shrugs his linebacker shoulders. "Don't know. Don't care."

I write Beth's full name across the top of the paper, dredging up a middle name on the spot—Louise, a character from some book I just read. I give Beth two extra years, born on February 20, 1983. She's my height, five foot eight, but I tack on a few pounds. The best way to hide in plain sight, I've decided, is to put some more meat on my bones with a strict pizza, doughnut, hamburger and french fry diet. Her address is the one for Morgan House.

I hand the paper back to Jorge, and he holds out a meaty palm.

"Three-fifty, right?"

He grunts. "Funny."

I contemplate the wisdom of forking over the money now, before I've gotten my ID cards, but I'm not exactly in a position of power here. I slap the three hundred and seventy-five dollars I already peeled off my stash into his hand. Jorge counts it, then counts it again.

"What's your number?" he says, pulling out his phone.

I open my mouth, then stop myself just in time.

The only number I know by heart is my real number, for the phone sitting at the bottom of a trash can back in Arkansas. My new number, the one for the prepay phone in my back pocket, is a blank. I haven't memorized it yet.

"I… I don't remember."

Jorge heaves a sigh that reeks of cheese and jalapeño, and the look he gives me says "amateur." He rattles off a string of numbers that I realize too late is for his cell phone.

"Hang on, hang on." I fumble for my phone, and he repeats the numbers, this time slower while I type them in. I hit Send, and his cell phone lights up in his hand.

He flips it so I can see. "Your number. I call you when ready."

"How long?"

He lifts a meaty shoulder. "Thirty minute. Maybe more. Wait at Sonic up the road."

It is seventy-three eternal minutes before a shiny black SUV rolls into the Sonic parking lot. I watch from my table by the window as a man who is definitely not Jorge—too dark, much too skinny—slides out. He looks up and down the parking lot like a villain on an episode of *Cops*, then tucks a manila envelope under the Buick's windshield wiper and hustles back into his car. By the time I make it outside, the man is long gone.

I pluck the envelope from the windshield and drop into my car, my fingers shaking as I slide my nail under the flap. I jiggle the envelope upside down, and two small squares drop onto my lap. One is paper, a social security card with a bright yellow *sign here* sticker. The other is plastic, a driver's license that looks as real as any I've ever seen. I examine it, turning it back and forth in a shaft of sunlight, and the hologram Georgia seal brightens and fades. The signature is not mine, but it's generic enough that with a little practice, I can duplicate it. Other than that, it's perfect. Beth Louise Murphy is legit.

My cell phone rings with a number I recognize as Jorge's cell. I pick up to the sound of chewing.

"You get ID?"

"I did get ID, thank you." I toss the cards on the passenger's seat and start the car. "They look great. Totally real."

He grunts, a sound I take to mean *you're welcome.* "Listen, you have friends who need ID, you send them to Jorge. Fifty dollar every friend."

And there it is, I think as I ease the Buick into traffic. What Martina wanted from me.

MARCUS

The Pine Bluff Police Department is housed in a squat, one-story complex on East Eighth Avenue, blinding white stucco against a sprawling green lawn. The place is a dump, dingy walls and scuffed linoleum floors, but on a bright note, we're understaffed enough that the detectives get their own private rooms. They're cramped and stuffy, but they're a million times better than a desk in the bull pen they surround.

Jeffrey and Ingrid arrive a full twelve minutes late, and just like yesterday, the two are practically vibrating with animosity. He opens the door for her but only because I'm watching, prompting a *thanks* she doesn't want to give. These two people detest each other, and I want to know why.

I gesture for them to follow. "This way."

I usher them through the rowdy bull pen to the open door of my office. "Have a seat," I say, gesturing to the twin chairs across from my desk, but only Ingrid sinks into one. Jeffrey is frozen just outside the door. He pokes his head into the room, and his relief when he sees it's an office is palpable. The sucker thought this was going to be an interrogation room. I raise a brow, and reluctantly, he steps inside, sinks into a chair.

I round my desk and drop into mine. "We found Sabine's car."

"What?" the two say in unison, their voices high and wild.

"Omigod, where?" Ingrid says. "When? And that's good news, right? It means you have some idea which way she went."

I don't shake my head, but I don't nod, either. A car is not necessarily good news, especially one like Sabine's—undamaged and untouched. So far, the only DNA we've found on it is hers.

"The car was parked at the far end of the Super1 lot on East Harding. According to the security footage, she walked through the door yesterday at 1:49 p.m. Ten minutes later, she purchased a loaf of bread, some sliced turkey and cheese, and a lemonade. She paid with her ATM card and was out the door by 2:03 p.m. The cameras don't cover the entire parking lot, unfortunately, so we lost her soon after."

Ingrid scoots to the front edge of her seat. "I don't understand. You're saying she never made it back to her car?"

"It sure looks that way. We searched the lot and trash cans for the groceries, without any luck. Somebody could have picked them up, or maybe she took them with her."

"With her where?" Ingrid shakes her head. "What are you saying, exactly?"

"You both mentioned you talked to Sabine—" I flip through my notes, pausing to find the right page. "Ingrid at 10:45 a.m. and Jeffrey…" I look up, meeting his gaze. "You didn't actually tell me a time."

"I was at the Atlanta airport, boarding a flight."

"The DL 2088, I know."

Jeffrey told me he talked to Sabine as he was boarding his flight, but he didn't say which one. He didn't even mention the airline. I did a little digging.

"The flight left Atlanta at 11:30 a.m.," I say, "so boarding would have been what, a half hour earlier?"

He nods, shifting in his chair. "Yeah, eleven sounds about right. I can pull it up on my call log if you need the exact time and duration."

I ignore his offer, turning to Ingrid instead. "In either of these conversations with Sabine, did she mention where she was going?"

Jeffrey shakes his head, but Ingrid nods. "She was on her way to the office."

I frown. Not the answer I was expecting. "This particular Super1 is nowhere near her work. I checked with her office, and she didn't have any showings that morning. Only a staff training later in the afternoon at the office, which she missed."

"Oh, she had a showing, all right," Jeffrey says, his voice thick with sarcasm and something else. Anger, for sure. Disgust, too. And more than a little pain.

Ingrid looks over with a frown.

"Sabine was coming from the hospital." His lip curls into an ugly sneer. "Her lover told me she dropped by for a little conjugal visit."

I lean back in my chair. By now I know about the

affair. Dr. McAdams already told me, tripping all over himself in his hurry for a face-to-face, a million questions disguised as a statement. The poor guy is desperate for answers, almost too desperate to be believable. "Well, if she was coming from the hospital, the route makes more sense. She could have stopped to buy herself a late lunch."

"And then what?" Ingrid squirms on her chair, clutching her hands. "Where did she go next?"

"Well, it's certainly not out of the realm of possibility that Sabine left on her own accord, that she got into a car with a colleague or a friend, but my gut says no. For one thing, she wouldn't have left her cell phone behind. We found it in the car, charging in the cup holder. I was hoping one of you could identify it for us." I pull an evidence bag from my desk drawer, holding it up to show the Samsung smartphone inside.

Ingrid releases a loud, relieved breath. "That's not Sabine's. Are you sure the car you found is the right one? Maybe you made a mistake."

Again, not the answer I was expecting. The phone was found in Sabine's locked car. Who else's could it be? "Are you positive? We haven't been able to check it. Not without the code."

"One hundred percent," Ingrid says. "Sabine has an iPhone. A white one. The newest model."

I look to Jeffrey for confirmation. "It's true, she does have an iPhone." He stabs a finger at the Samsung. "But *that*'s probably her burner phone."

Ingrid's face whips to his. "What the hell are you talking about? Sabine doesn't have a burner phone. Don't be ridiculous."

"Yes, Ingrid. She does. The one that for the past five months, she's been using to talk to her lover." Ingrid twitches, and his smile is a mix of mean and condescending. "Looks like she doesn't quite tell you everything, does she?"

Ingrid slumps in the chair, and Jeffrey turns to me. "Dr. Trevor McAdams, Chief Obstetrician at Jefferson Regional Hospital. I believe you spoke with him last night. I'm guessing if you crack the code on that phone, every number on the call log will be his."

"Try 8-2-6–6-3-7," Ingrid mumbles. "It's the one she uses for her iPhone."

I pluck a plastic glove from the box on the sill, wriggle my hand inside, then shove it in the bag and tick in the code. The log-in dissolves into a colorful home screen with neat columns of apps. The icon for phone has a bright red number in the top right corner, twenty-three missed calls. I tap it, and they're all from the same number, which matches the one scribbled on my pad. "You were right. It's the number for Dr. McAdams's cell."

Ingrid shifts in her chair with a huff.

I reseal the bag, peel off the glove and drop both in my desk drawer. "This doesn't explain where the iPhone is, though. We've put out a trace on that number, but we're not finding anything. Looks like wherever it is, she's turned it off. And according to her bank, the transaction at the Super1 was the last purchase she made. She hasn't used her credit card or ATM card since. There were also no big withdrawals in the weeks before, which tells me she wasn't planning on making a run for it."

"Of course she wasn't," Ingrid says. "Sabine wouldn't run, not without telling me." Sometime in the past few minutes, she's started to cry. Her face is messy with it—red eyes; mottled cheeks; swollen, dripping nose. She sniffs and swipes at it with a sleeve. "So, what now? Where do we look next?"

"Well, we've begun questioning Super1 staff who were working Wednesday's shift. We're hopeful that one of them saw something out of the ordinary, or maybe some*one* out of the ordinary. I've also put out an APB for anyone matching Sabine's description, which means we've got a lot more than just our eyes looking for her. We're going through her bank records, her credit card usage, anything that will help us trace her movements. We'll be interviewing her friends, her colleagues, all the people in her life—and before you ask, that includes Dr. McAdams—and we'll be asking them the same question I'm asking you—where were you Wednesday afternoon, from 1:00 p.m. on?"

An alibi. I'm asking them for an alibi.

The two exchange a look.

Ingrid folds her arms across her chest, her expression a mixture of insult and concern. "I work at home. I'm a virtual assistant. People pay me to arrange their schedules, type up reports, handle their social media. Things like that."

"Was anyone there with you?" I ask.

"I live alone."

"Okay. Is there anyone who can verify your whereabouts? A neighbor, maybe, or a client who called on the house line."

"No," she says, then brightens. "But I was online all day. I can prove I was there with the IPs from websites I visited, and the emails in my Sent folder."

"You know how to do that?" Jeffrey sounds dubious, like he doesn't think she's that capable.

"Yes," she says, slow and satisfied. "I have a degree in computer science."

Mentally, I shuffle the sister to the bottom of my list. Ingrid is a spinster, the kind of woman who lives alone, works alone, stays alone, but so far, everything I've seen and heard from her seems sincere. As suspects go, she's not a strong one.

Jeffrey, on the other hand. He checks all the boxes. Every single one.

He clears his throat, folds his hands atop his lap. "Well, let's see. I landed at just after noon or so—"

I nod. "At 12:05 p.m."

Surprise flashes across his face, though it shouldn't. I already told him I looked up his flight number, which means I'll also know when he landed. I'm not a small-town cop, and I've done my homework.

"Your plane arrived at the gate at 12:11," I say without consulting my notes. "By 12:24, everyone but the crew had deplaned."

"Okay," he says, thinking. "But I was all the way in the back, so one of the last people off the plane, and then it took forever to get my bag. The Little Rock Airport is notoriously slow. After that I grabbed some lunch."

"At the airport?"

"No. At a little Italian place near the airport. I don't remember the name."

Ingrid makes a sound: *convenient.*

"What time was this?" I ask.

"I don't know. After one, for sure. Maybe closer to one thirty."

"Did you use a card?"

"I paid cash."

Ingrid gives up all pretense. She blows out a sigh, long and loud, and sits up straight in her chair. She's ready for me to arrest him, to slap some cuffs on him and cart him downstairs.

"What time did you get back to Pine Bluff?"

He shrugs. "I think it was around four or so."

"Your neighbor, a Mrs. Ashby, confirms it to be around four ten. She remembers because she was watching a rerun of *Ellen,* who'd just finished her dance. Mrs. Ashby was in the kitchen during the commercial break, making herself a snack."

He makes a noise deep in his throat. "More likely pouring herself a drink. Rita Ashby is a nosy old hag whose face is pressed to the kitchen window more often than not. She's also a drunk. In all those years we've lived there, I don't think I've ever seen her sober." He's trying to distract me, buy some time. He knows the question coming next.

"Why so late?" When he doesn't immediately answer, I add, "I mean, by my math, even accounting for the baggage delay and the lunch stop and afternoon traffic, which we all know can be a real bitch, you should have been home by 2:30 p.m. at the latest. How come you were so late? What were you doing for that hour and a half?"

His shrug is trying too hard, as is his tone, too high

and much too smooth. "It was a nice day, and I'd spent all week cooped up inside at a conference. Don't tell my boss, but I really didn't want to go back to the office. I stopped off at a park along the river to read."

"Which park?"

"Tar Camp."

A forested recreation area popular with families and fishermen, about halfway between Little Rock and Pine Bluff. Emma and I used to go camping there, back when we were newlyweds.

I scribble the name on my pad. "How long did you stay?"

"An hour and a half, maybe longer."

"What were you reading?"

"The CEO of one of our biggest competitors just came out with a book, *Stoking the Fire at Work* or some such nonsense. My boss is making everyone at the office read it. Honestly, it's not very good."

"Did you see anybody there?"

"It's a public park," he says, getting defensive. "I saw lots of people."

"What I meant was, did any of them notice you? A guy in business attire sitting by himself, on a park bench—"

"It was a picnic table. There's a cluster of them at the edge of the river." He pauses to glance at Ingrid, whose brows are bunched in a skeptical frown. "And I was in jeans and a polo. Travel attire."

"Still. A guy all alone at a picnic table, reading a book. I'd imagine you stood out."

"I'd imagine so, but tell me this, Detective—how am I supposed to find them?"

I dip my head, ceding the point. Not that it helps him any. Even if he had been at Tar Camp, it's not like any of the people there would remember him, and they certainly wouldn't have exchanged names and numbers.

But the bigger point is, he's lying. All the signs are there. The stare down across my desk, the way his breath comes quicker, the microscopic flashes of panic I keep catching on his face. Something about his story is not true.

"Help me out here, Jeffrey. I just want to make sure I'm not missing anything." I lean toward him, hands folded on top of a sloppy pile of papers. "According to what you just told me, you were alone all afternoon yesterday, either in your car, at an unnamed restaurant or in a public park, from around 12:30 p.m. until a little after four, when the neighbor confirms you pulled into your driveway."

He nods. "That's right. Yes." Add sweating to the list. His face has gone shiny, sprouting a million wet pinpricks.

"And at no point during those three and a half hours, the same hours your wife walked out of the Super1 on East Harding and disappeared, can anyone but you verify your whereabouts."

He's silent for long enough I almost feel sorry for him. He sucks a breath, then two more, thirteen brain-numbing seconds, and then the best he can do is: "Pretty much."

I try to hold my expression tight, but the smile sneaks out anyway.

Gotcha.

BETH

I pull to a stop in the middle of the two-lane drive, double-check the address on the Post-it note Martina handed me earlier this morning and gawk at the building before me.

A church. Martina works at a church. A neo-Gothic monstrosity of beige brick and stained glass, with crimson gables and scalloped finials and lancet arches. In the very center of the main tower, a rose window stares out like the eye of a cyclops. Above it, at the steepest point of the roofline, a wooden cross reaches with long arms into a pale blue sky.

The Church of Christ's Twelve Apostles.

Oh hell no.

My hand clenches around the gearshift, jiggling it into Reverse. The Church and I aren't exactly on the best of terms, not since I went to the leader of mine for guidance and he refused to unshackle me from a monster.

"It's perfectly normal to argue," Father Ian had told me. "All couples do. But the successful couples learn to forgive. They put the resentment behind them and move on."

I nodded my head in pious agreement. "I understand that, Father, but he...hurts me."

"Hurts you how?"

For a second or two, I considered pulling up my shirt and showing him my cracked ribs. In the end, I settled on, "With his hands."

"Closed or open?"

"I'm sorry?"

"His hands, when he hurts you. Are they closed or open?"

The logical part of me understands Father Ian's reluctance to believe you would be capable of such cruelty. He's known you most of your life, guided you through so many sacraments. And we were together for two years before you shoved me into that hotel wall. It was two more years before you punched me, and another year after that before you punched me again. The violence came on so gradually, and then so fast. To Father Ian, to everyone but you and me, my complaints came out of nowhere.

In the end, we compromised: Father Ian would counsel you on the proper ways to handle an argument, and I would pray to become a better wife.

A honk comes from behind me, two friendly, rapid-fire beeps. I look up to find a pretty blonde in my rearview mirror. She waves, diamonds winking on her wrist, and I try to remember what Martina called them, these wealthy women from the northern suburbs. Betty somethings. I gesture for this one to go around, but she doesn't move, and the road is too narrow for me to turn around. With a sigh, I put the car in Drive.

The two-lane road slices through a manicured lawn clotted with oakleaf hydrangeas and boxwoods sculpted into perfect circles. Before I can find a place to turn around, it dumps me into a parking garage, five-plus stories of stacked concrete. I swing the Buick into a visitor's space, finally shaking off the blonde on my tail. She motors past, rounding the corner to the next level.

The holy hush—that's what I've since learned it's called, this brushing of allegations like mine under the altar rug, though I suppose I should give Father Ian a little credit. He lived up to his end of the bargain and talked to you. But whatever he said only made things worse. You came home looking for a fight, one that ended with a concussion and a weeklong ringing in my ears. That Sunday, Father Ian pressed the communion wafer through my split lips like nothing had ever happened. As soon as I turned away, I spit the thing into my hand.

I realize that not every church operates this way. That ignorant and willfully blind priests like Father Ian are, for the most part, a dying breed. I once read an article about an abused woman who claimed church was the only thing that kept her going, the one hour each week she allowed herself a glimmer of hope. And yet I stare out my windshield at this one, and I feel nothing but dread.

Martina all but guaranteed they would hire me on the spot. She said she told them that I clean like she does, powering through six toilets in the time it takes others to scrub one, even though she's never seen me work so much as a sponge. I have no idea why she has taken up the role of my protector, but I'm not exactly in a position to turn her down. I do a mental count of the bills strapped to my stomach. After Jorge and groceries, it's a whole lot lighter than it was just yesterday. It would take me days to find another job, which means church or not, I can't afford to walk away from this one. I brace myself and climb out of the car.

The garage stairwell dumps me out at a side entrance, and I step into a hallway that smells like pine and incense. I follow it past a long line of double doors, then stop at an open one, gawking into a cavernous space three stories high. Rows and rows of plush crimson seats, thousands of them, are arranged in sections on a gentle slope around a podium hung with stage lights and two giant LED screens. And what's that—an orchestra pit?

Voices come from somewhere behind me, and I continue down the hallway, following the signs to the administrative offices. Colored light trickles down from stained glass windows high above my head, painting patterns across a freshly vacuumed carpet. I can't imagine why they need another person on their cleaning staff. So far, everything I've seen here has been spotless.

The executive offices are bright and spacious and, as far as I can tell, span the entire length of the church. There's a reception area straight ahead, with hallways dotted with doors on either side. A woman sits behind the receptionist's desk, one I recognize. Prim white blouse, understated pearls, diamonds at her wrists, blond hair teased into a helmet atop her head. Up close, she's not half as pretty as she was in my rearview mirror.

She greets me like she's never seen me before. "Welcome to the Church of Christ's Twelve Apostles. What brings you in today?"

"I'm here to see Father Andrews."

"It's *Reverend*," she corrects, turning to her computer. She punches a few buttons on the keyboard with a baby pink nail. "Do you have an appointment with the Reverend?"

"Yes, at ten." I arrange my face into a careful neutral. "My name is Beth Murphy."

She tells me the Reverend had a minor emergency in the music room and asked me to meet him there, then rattles off a series of convoluted directions for what is basically a trek to the basement. I thank her, then head in search of the stairwell.

A few minutes later, I step into a full-on recording studio. Modern and airy, furnished with sleek black chairs and leather couches arranged in clusters around a stage. Multiple rehearsal rooms each with their own mixing panel are lined up along the wall, across from a soundproof recording booth. Behind its smoky glass, a spongy microphone hovers like a spaceship from the ceiling.

"Hello?"

A thump, followed by a muffled curse, drifts up from somewhere behind me. I turn and that's when I see them, two stovepipes of dark denim ending in orange Nikes, poking out from under one of the mixing panels. He wriggles himself out and heaves to a stand, holding out a hand.

"Erwin Andrews," he says, smiling behind his clipped white beard. "And you must be Beth."

I shake his hand, swallowing a flutter of nerves. It's been years since I've been on a job interview, especially one for which I am so monumentally unqualified. I know how to scrub a toilet, yes, but what if he asks about prior experience? What if he asks for references?

"Why don't we sit?" The Reverend is fit despite his age, popping off the ground with surprising speed and agility. He leads me with long, nimble strides to a matching pair of couches to the right of the stage. He's a runner, judging by his shoes and his build.

He points me to the couch, then plucks a chair from the stage and swings it around, placing it so we're almost knee to knee. Not too close, but not far away, either. Relaxed and informal.

"I know what you're thinking," he says, clasping his hands. "Why would the pastor of a place this size want to interview every potential employee? Why not let someone else do it? The office manager, maybe, or the head of the cleaning crew."

It's almost word for word what I said to Martina last night, when she told me she'd set up the interview. She didn't know the answer, either.

"Martina says that you interview everybody." I tell my nerves to shut up, but they don't listen, and neither does my body. Sweaty hands, hammering heart, the works. I clear my throat, struggling to rein myself in.

"I do, Beth, and I'll tell you why. Because we are a community here at CCTA, and as its leader, it is my responsibility to keep people from harm. Everyone who walks through that door needs to know that they are sheltered. Regardless of where they came from or what brought them here. That is the promise I have made, to provide a secure, positive, healthy environment where everyone, from the worshippers to the volunteers to the janitors, know that they are safe."

In other words, he needs to ensure I'm not a criminal. He says it without rancor, but still. Reverend Andrews is the godlier version of Miss Sally. I wouldn't want to cross him, either.

I nod, plastering my most law-abiding look on my face. "That makes total sense."

"Good. Excellent." He slaps his thighs. "Now, I assume you know how to operate a mop, so we can skip the boring parts of this interview and get right to the part where I ask if you can sing."

"I…" I blink, frowning. "I'm sorry, what?"

He waves an arm at the setup along the edge of the stage, guitars and microphone stands and a drum set worthy of Charlie Watts. "Music is an essential part of worship at CCTA, an essential part of our culture. God has blessed me with parishioners who have the voices of angels, to make up for others who are… how shall I say this…not put on this earth to carry a tune. Sometimes the Lord works in mysterious ways, and other times He is painfully obvious." He sticks a finger in his ear, jiggles it around. "What I want to know is which one are you?"

"I fall in the second category, unfortunately."

Another lie. I *can* sing, and I can read music, too. But admitting to either would mean getting shoved onto this stage or worse, the one upstairs, in a cathedral that must seat thousands. The spotlight can feel too hot, too bright, even when you're not trying to hide. No way I'm letting them shine it on me.

"What about an instrument? Do you play anything?"

Piano—or I used to, until you mangled my left pinkie.

"No." I shake my head. "Sorry."

The Reverend looks mildly disappointed. "What about a beat? Can you carry one of those?" He taps his foot, snaps his fingers in a slow, rhythmic cadence.

I can't help but smile. "I can do that."

"Excellent! Then you can play the tambourine. We always have room for more tambourine players."

And here it comes. The invitation to attend Sunday services. Reverend Andrews wants to save my soul, and he wants me to play the tambourine while he does it. I picture me in a singing, swaying crowd, joyous faces tipped to the heavens, while he holds his healing hands above us all. There will be no tambourine playing in my future. No church service, either.

He swings an ankle over a knee, leaning back in the chair. "Do you have a favorite team?"

I dip my chin, raise my eyebrows. *Team?*

"You know, sports. Football, baseball, basketball. And don't be looking at me like it's a crazy question. More than half the hard-core Atlanta United fans I know are female. Fifteen-nine our first season. You like soccer?"

"I'm not really much of a sports fan."

For the next twenty minutes, the Reverend wanders topics like a drunken bumblebee, bobbing from bloom to bloom. We talk about movies (I haven't seen one in ages), books (I will read anything but horror), whether or not I thought the TV show did *The Handmaid's Tale* justice (yes, absolutely). He asks me my favorite color (what am I, twelve? Fine, yellow), and what do I think about when I'm alone in my car (how *not* to get pulled over). We touch on favorite foods (mine: french fries, his: pizza) and this place I absolutely must visit, the BeltLine, a walkable, bike-able trail that connects dozens of in-town neighborhoods, because I haven't lived until I've had the truffle fries at Biltong Bar (ask for extra mayonnaise). Our banter is more suited to a bar, or maybe a match.com chat group. I don't know what this conversation is, but it's definitely not an interview.

"Well, Beth," he says once the topics are exhausted, "sounds like you'd fit in just fine around here."

I blink in surprise. *That's it? Interview over?*

"You seem surprised."

"Not to be rude, but don't you want to ask me about my experience? Question me about cleaning skills or ask me about… I don't know, my relationship with God or something?"

"Your relationship with God is just that—yours. It's no business of mine unless you make it that way. And Martina already vouched for your cleaning skills. Everything I've seen and heard from you so far lives up to what she told me."

I don't ask what she told him, because I'm not sure I could keep a straight face when he rattled off what must have been a string of lies and fabrications. I've known Martina all of two days, and the longest conversation we've had was on that first night, when I bumped into her in the kitchen. She knows nothing about me other than what she's seen, and I've made sure she hasn't seen much. And yet she's told the Reverend all about me—yet another favor, yet another reason for me to question her motivations. What does that girl want from me?

"There's some paperwork that needs filling out upstairs," he says, standing. "The official application so we can process your paycheck, and another one so the USCIS doesn't come banging on my door with a big, fat fine. I assume Martina told you to bring some identification?"

Trotting out my new ID feels as precarious as walking the ledge of a cliff, but I pat my bag with a nod. "Not a problem."

"Then welcome to Church of Christ's Twelve Apostles, Beth." He sticks out a hand, and we shake, mine pressed between his two warm palms. "We're glad to have you join our ranks."

"Thank you, Reverend. Really, this means a lot to me." To my absolute horror, my eyes grow hot, the tears welling so quickly it's impossible to blink them away. I choke on a small but audible sob. "I can't even tell you how much."

The Reverend takes me in with a kind expression. "Are you all right, child?"

I wipe my cheeks with my fingers, but new tears tumble down before I can mop the old ones away. "Thank you, but I'm fine. Or I will be. I don't even know why I'm crying." I force up a throaty laugh. "I promise it won't be a regular occurrence."

I hate to cry. For the past seven years, my tears have been slapped, backhanded, punched, yanked, kicked, squeezed and one time, burned out of me. Tears are a sign of weakness, followed always by punishment. Only losers cry.

But this man doesn't taunt me for them, and he doesn't look away. "If you ever want to talk about anything," he says warmly, patiently, "you should know that I'm a good listener. Ask anyone. They'll tell you I take care of my flock."

I murmur another round of thanks, though the only thing I can focus on is getting out of here and into the restroom across the hall, where I can splash the splotches from my face and reapply the mascara I'm almost certainly crying down my cheeks. He lets me go, and I'm almost to the door when he stops me.

"Oh, and Beth?" His lips curve into a gentle smile, and I can see how it could melt a churchful of people, hanging on his every word. "What I said before, about taking care of my flock… That includes you. Whatever brought you here, whatever burdens you think you're carrying, you can lay them down. You're one of us now."

Forty-five minutes later, I'm back in the church basement, where Martina is busy attaching a battery-powered vacuum to my back.

"Did he ask you to be in the band?" Martina says, holding up the straps for my arms.

The two of us stand in the center of a room that does triple duty as a kitchen, break room and cleaning supply closet. An old television is pushed against a wall in front of mismatched sectionals, and to its right, a workstation with multiple sinks for rinsing buckets and rags. Two walls are lined with floor-to-ceiling shelves that belong in a grocery store cleaning aisle, or maybe an episode of *Extreme Couponing*. Sponges and mops, neatly stacked buckets, every cleaning product imaginable.

My uniform came from the giant Tupperware containers on the bottom shelf, khaki pants and a white T-shirt with the church logo and God Works Here embroidered in looping navy letters across the front. The getup looks ridiculous over the pleather Mary Janes I wore with my interview dress, but I didn't think to bring sneakers.

"He asked me if I could sing or play an instrument, yeah." I shove one arm through the loop, then another, and she settles the thing on my shoulders. For a piece of machinery, it's pretty light.

"I knew he would. He asks *everybody* to be in the band." She reaches around me from behind, snaking the harness around my waist, and I stiffen. Her fingers brush over the money belt but don't linger. She smells like bleach and peppermint gum. "What else did you talk about?"

"I don't know. Lots of stuff. TV shows and books and truffle fries. It was the weirdest job interview ever."

She grabs me by an arm, turns me around to face her. "Did he tell you the joke?" I shake my head, and she grins. "Knock knock."

"Who's there?"

"Jesus."

"Jesus who?"

"Jesus Christ, open the door."

I laugh, not because the joke is funny, but at the idea it originated from a man of God. What happened to not taking the Lord's name in vain? Father Ian would lose his shit.

Martina hands me the vacuum hose, shows me how to work the on and off button on the side. I flip it on, and the nozzle suctions itself to the carpet.

"Good gear is half the work," I say before I can stop myself, one of your favorite one-liners. I flip the switch, both on the machine and in my mind, and turn to Martina. "I still don't understand. He didn't ask me one single question that was relevant to the actual job. No personal questions, either, other than silly things like whether I put on both socks before my shoes, or do one foot at a time. The whole time I'm just sitting there, waiting for the bomb to drop."

"The Reverend says the past only defines us if we let it. He says you can let it hold you back, or you can be set free." Martina takes on that church-like expression I've come to know so well, a combination of holier-than-thou satisfaction and wondrous, drank-the-Kool-Aid joy, and *this* is what Father Ian could never explain to me about organized religion. You are invited into the flock because you are damaged goods, and then you are expected to transform into a righteous follower, to throw out your doubts with your sins and just *believe*. In the end, after all that happened while going to that church, I couldn't do it.

I lean in and lower my voice, even though we're the only two in the room. "He also said they needed my

IDs so they wouldn't get fined by the USCIS. That's the Citizenship and Immigration Services, Martina."

Her eyes narrow. "What would *you* know about the USCIS?"

The accusation in her words revives my doubt of her Grady-baby story, and what about that Spanish-tinged accent she tries to bury under a Southern drawl? If Martina were born here, in a hospital in the state of Georgia, like she said she was, what would *she* know about the USCIS?

"I know what the letters stand for," I say, "but I'm also assuming they have these things called computers, which will light up like a Vegas slot machine at my fake ID and social security numbers."

She chews her lip. "They won't," she mumbles, but I catch a flash of panic in her eyes. "Jorge recycles the numbers. He only uses ones that are real. Ours won't get flagged."

Whatever uncertainty I had is wiped away, just like that. Martina is a Jorge customer, too. A fugitive posing under a name she wasn't born with. Maybe I'm right to guard the cash strapped to my waist.

Suddenly, this room feels too crowded, too hot. I need to get away from here, away from *her*. I gesture to the machine strapped to my back. "So where do you want me to start with this thing?"

"Upstairs," she says, stepping to the shelves for a vacuum of her own. "We start at the top and work our way down. Like a team."

But I'm not blind, and I'm no fool. I caught her glance at my waistline. Whatever Martina is after here, I'm pretty sure it's not teamwork.

JEFFREY

When I wake up on Saturday morning, I shoot off a text to my boss explaining why I've been MIA for the past two days, then pull the pillow over my head. It smells like Sabine, like that sweet-spicy stuff in the overpriced bottles on our shower shelf, and I shove it to the floor.

I stare at the ceiling and tell myself to get up, but my limbs feel hulking and heavy, like those sandbags they pile everywhere when the National Weather Service issues a flood warning. I barely slept, thanks to the constant hum of the search boats in the waters behind my house. They're out there now, and I waver between worry and fury.

What kind of idiot do they think I am? Like I would be stupid enough to dump my wife's body in my own backyard. Like I would ever be that reckless. I watch *Dateline*. I know to not pollute my own property with evidence. They could give me a little credit and search farther downstream.

Then again, I haven't given them much reason not

to suspect me, not after my miserable performance in Detective Durand's office, my nonanswers about my whereabouts Wednesday afternoon. I'd blame it on being rattled, the knowledge he'd been checking up on me, unsettling me enough to stumble over my answers.

But the truth is, it was Ingrid. If she hadn't been sitting right there, weighting the air in the room with her huffed sighs and cheap perfume, then I might have told him the truth. The detective is a guy; he might have understood, but not Ingrid... No fucking way I was telling her.

It was like when you get a Trivial Pursuit question you know the answer to, that panicked, white-hot moment before the answer rolls off your tongue. I took some deep breaths, blew them all out, but the answer didn't come.

And now Detective Durand and his Keystone Cops are determined to pin Sabine's disappearance on me, instead of finding the person actually responsible. Because it doesn't take a genius to figure out that though they say they're looking for Sabine, what they're really searching for is her body.

By the time I wake again, it's well past noon, and the noise of the boats is muffled by a low rumble coming from my front yard. Reporters have descended on the house like a flock of starving vultures, pecking at me through the glass. It's not enough that they ruined my front lawn with their vans, they hurl questions at the house whenever I so much as walk by a window. Yesterday I pulled all the shades, but I can still feel their presence the way you feel a tornado bearing down outside, ominous and deadly.

I know from their questions that the police and their merry band of volunteers have searched everywhere there is to search. Pine Bluff's fields and patchy woods, the town's parks and hills and riverbanks. No bits of fabric to show for their efforts, no long strands of brown hair found stuck in a tree. If Sabine is anywhere close by, if she's on Pine Bluff soil or in her muddy waters, chances are good that she's dead.

Anger and grief, remorse and regret, the emotions churn in my empty stomach. There are a million things I want to say to Sabine, and now it looks like I'll never get the chance.

The light in the room has shifted, the afternoon sun finally climbing high enough to hit the bedroom windows. I stare up at the ceiling, listening to the camera crews on my front lawn, and a wave of anxiety drags me from bed. I need to run. To pump my legs until my heart wants to explode and my chest burns with the lack of oxygen. To abuse my body until I forget these past few days ever happened.

I pull on running shorts and a T-shirt and grab my phone from the nightstand. A hundred and twenty-seven messages. I scroll through the texts and emails, variations of the same message. OMG, so shocking. Anything I can do to help? Thoughts and prayers, thoughts and prayers. I'm pleased that the tide hasn't turned, but I'm not naive enough to know that it won't. Ingrid is probably out there right now, alerting the world of the two-hour hole in my day. It won't be long until she tells the press, too.

I peel the shade from an upstairs window and take a peek outside. Reporters stand in clumps on my front lawn, drinking coffee and shooting the shit like my life is a fucking happy hour. The Arkansas sun beats down on their heads and reflects off the pavement behind them like water. Good. I hope they're roasting out there.

Downstairs in the kitchen, I inspect the contents of the fridge, searching for breakfast. Leftover pizza, a half-empty pack of eggs, some fuzzy cheese and a gallon of spoiled milk. Sabine didn't spend any of the time I was out of town at the grocery store, and why would she? My trip to Florida was like a birthday, anniversary and Christmas rolled into one, four whole days of unmonitored time with her lover. They probably spent every free second together, especially since his wife moved out. No nagging spouses at home, asking what's for dinner.

I grab the eggs and slam the refrigerator door.

If I'm going to hide out here all weekend, I need to go to the store. Tension creeps into my shoulders at the thought of backing my car through the throng of reporters. Maybe I should talk to a lawyer. Get him to chase them off with the threat of a lawsuit, and while I've got him, ask what the implications might be now that Detective Durand knows about the unaccounted-for patch in my Wednesday. Then again, what is the detective going to do, arrest me? He can't do that without evidence, without a body. A two-hour window doesn't make me a murderer.

I'm cracking the last of the eggs into a pan when the doorbell rings, and I check the window by the garage. Somehow, my brother Derrick has managed to plow his Camaro past the reporters, and now he's out there, preening for their cameras.

Shit.

I drop the blinds and return to the eggs, watching them pop and hiss in the pan. To open or not to open, that is the question.

The doorbell rings again, four quick punches followed by a fist pounding on the door. "Come on, Jeffrey. I know you're in there. It's me, Derrick. Let me in."

I poke at the eggs with a fork.

Letting him in would mean uncorking a spiky, barbed ball of age-old grievances and passive-aggressive rage. Derrick resents me for my job, my house, my wife—ha! joke's on me—my car and my clothes, the inch-and-a-half height I have on him, even though he's the older brother. I resent him for the way he tortured me at school, bullying me with taunts and ridicule and once, a wedgie delivered in front of the entire football team. We are like Mentos and Coke—put us in a container together and it's not long before we explode.

I hear him clomping up the steps to the back door. He finds the spare key Sabine hid under the flowerpot and slides it in the lock. There's a whoosh of sliding glass, a roar of rushing water, and a few seconds later, he's standing in my kitchen.

"Didn't you hear me?" he says, tossing the key onto the kitchen counter. "I've been banging on your door."

My brother is his usual, slouchy self. Faded and ripped T-shirt, cutoff jeans, flip-flops. Derrick is the high school star quarterback who never made it off the bench in college. He flunked out sophomore year, and his life has been shit ever since.

"I heard you. What are you doing here?" Not the nicest greeting, but considering our relationship, not the worst one I could give him, either.

"I figured you could use the moral support, but I can just as soon go back home." He hikes a thumb over his shoulder, but it's all for show. His soles are superglued to the hardwood. "So I guess your wife finally had enough of you, huh?"

"You're a real dick, you know that, right?"

"Jesus, chill out, will you? I'm only kidding." He moves farther into the room, taking a look around—kind of like that detective did in my foyer. Like he's cataloging all the things he can't afford and silently judging me for them. He whips off his shades and hangs them from the collar of his shirt. "Seriously, man. What can I do?"

"Nothing." I turn back to the stove. "Though I really appreciate you coming over to gloat and all, but you can go now."

Derrick moves closer, his flip-flops slapping against his crusty heels. "I'm just trying to be helpful. Jeez. Why do you always have to be such a dickwad?"

"I don't know. I guess it runs in the family."

"I thought maybe we could drive around and look for her or something."

I toss the fork into the pan and flip off the gas. The eggs are burned, the edges brown and papery. I dump them, pan and all, into the sink. "What, do you think she's just hanging out on a street corner or something, waiting for a ride?"

"No, but maybe she drove that fancy car of hers into a ditch. Maybe she had a flat tire."

"Don't you watch the news, Derrick? They found her car at the Super1. It was abandoned."

His eyes go wide, and he leans a hip against the granite. "Holy shit, bro. That sounds serious. What do the cops think happened, that somebody took her?"

I yank open the refrigerator, pull out the pizza box from the night Sabine went missing. The crust is hard as dried dirt, the cheese an orange, rubbery blob. I pick up a piece and bite into it, and it tastes as disgusting as it looks.

"I'm pretty sure they think that *I* took her," I say around the pizza.

"You? Have they lost their minds? Why would they think you took her?"

I stuff my mouth with another bite in lieu of answering. Answering would mean telling him about the backhand, her affair with the doctor, the missing two hours in my day—none of which I plan to share with my brother, ever. Derrick likes to pocket my shortcomings and failures, store them in his basement-brain like dormant Molotov cocktails. Weeks or months or years from now, when the rest of the world and I have moved on, he'll toss one into a conversation just to see the fireworks.

"What about Ingrid?" He helps himself to a slice of pizza, which he shoves in the microwave for a minute, and pulls a beer from the fridge.

"What about her?"

"Come on, man. Stop being so difficult. What does she think happened?"

I sigh, sinking onto a counter stool. That heavy, sandbag feeling is back along with a knifepoint throbbing behind my eyes. "I'm pretty sure she thinks the same thing."

He pops open the beer and tosses the top on the counter. "Well, okay, who cares what that old hag thinks? The cops are the ones you need to convince."

I roll my eyes, toss the bottle top and the rest of my pizza slice into the trash. "You're a motherfucking genius, Derrick. You really are. Convince the cops I didn't do it. Why didn't I think of that?"

"I'm serious, J. I know a guy who works for Century 21, and he's always talking about the crazies who wander into his open houses. Mostly people come for the free snacks or to take a dump in the powder room, but just last month, some asshat pulled out a gun. Took my friend's wallet, his watch, the keys to his car. Sabine's hot. It's not unimaginable somebody saw her and got the wrong idea."

"I know. I've been telling her that for ages."

The microwave dings, and he reaches in for the pizza, then snatches his hand back with a hiss. He rips a paper towel from the roll and tries again. "And what about those gangs over on the east side? All those break-ins on Cherry Street aren't for nothing, you know. Those little shits are taking over the city. It's only a matter of time before they move their territory up this way. Maybe it was them."

"Maybe," I say, because for once my brother is not wrong. The gangs *are* taking over the city, and thanks to the soaring unemployment, the poverty, the crappy schools graduating illiterate halfwits without a single marketable skill, there are fewer and fewer people here to stop them. What used to be a hardworking American metropolis now has the dubious honor of being one of the most dangerous cities in America, second only to Detroit. The smart folks have all moved away. Maybe I should join them.

He folds the slice in half, and orange oil spurts onto his hand, dripping down his fingers and onto the floor. "I'm just saying there are a million people it could've been. Seems to me the cops are being lazy, focusing only on you. Don't let yourself be an easy target. Show 'em it's not always the husband."

He shoves half the pizza in his mouth in one giant bite. A long strand of melted cheese dangles from his chin like a worm, but for the first time in well, *ever*, I don't gripe at him for the mess. My idiot, dickhead brother has a point. I *have* let myself be the easy target.

I pluck my phone from the countertop, pull up a number I once knew by heart. After two rings, a familiar voice hits my ear. "It's about time," she says. "I've only been leaving you messages all over town."

Amanda Shephard steps through my front door, looking just like she did in high school. Blonde, thin, a complicated sort of pretty—big lashes and acrylic nails and long, heat-curled hair. Her face is caked under a layer of makeup I've never seen her without, not even the summer before senior year when our entire class spent every day bobbing in blow-up tubes on the river. All the other girls had shiny cheeks pink from the sun, but Amanda's makeup was like a mask, flawless and impenetrable.

She pulls me into a perfumed hug. "Oh, Jeffrey, you poor, poor thing."

Her voice echoes in my foyer, loud and consoling in a way that makes it feel exactly the opposite. It's her television voice, the one she's cultivated for her show, *Mandy in the Morning*, a local daily featuring all things mundane and ridiculous.

I extricate myself and give her a tight-lipped smile.

"How are you doing? How are you holding up? Are you eating at *all*?"

I think of the eggs in the sink, the pizza I shoved out the door along with my brother, right before she got here. "A little."

"If I had known, I would have made you a casserole." She waves a manicured hand through the air and laughs. "Oh, who am I kidding? We both know I can't cook. I would have ordered you some Chinese takeout or something. Anyway, I'm so glad you called."

"Thank you. And please," I say, gesturing toward the living room. "Make yourself at home."

In the sixty minutes it took her to get over here, I cleaned up the place. I dusted and fluffed all the pillows, and I exchanged my running shorts for a pair of khaki slacks and a navy polo over loafers. Nothing too fancy. I don't want her to think I'm trying too hard.

She steps into the room and gasps, making a beeline to the wall of windows. She stops just beyond the desk, standing before a sheet of glass lit up by the sun. It turns her hair iridescent and makes the fabric of her dress float like a wispy cloud around her body—a cloud that is more than a little see-through.

Well, well, well. Amanda Shephard is wearing a lacy red thong.

"You're so close to the river," she says without turning. "Like the house is floating on top of it or something."

"I know."

"The view is stunning."

Yes. It is.

She presses a hand into the glass, and the sun turns her skin to fire. Amanda is conventionally beautiful, but up to now, I've never found her all that attractive. Too processed, too high maintenance. But standing here, in my cheating wife's house, I'm beginning to see another side of Amanda. The side that would make a spectacular revenge fuck.

I clear my throat. "The view is what sold us on the house. Turns every window into a piece of artwork. Did you know the river changes colors, depending on the weather and time of day? I didn't know that until I got to look at it every day."

She smiles over her shoulder. "Well, Jeffrey Hardison, you sensitive old dog, you. Next thing I know, you'll be reading me poetry."

At the south end of the river, a black search boat motors upstream, and multiple people lean over the sides, staring into the water.

"Do you mind if we get started?" I say, pointing Amanda to the couch before she sees the boat. "When we're done here, I need to get over to the police station and see if there's any update about Sabine."

"I just came from there, actually." She wrinkles her nose, stepping away from the window. "They won't tell me anything other than that Sabine's car showed up at the Super1, which in all honesty tells me nothing. Who are the suspects? What are the clues? The people of Pine Bluff deserve to know the truth, Jeffrey."

"I agree."

She sinks onto one of the twin three-seaters, and I choose the one opposite her. The search boat has stopped in the middle of the river, the flashlights all trained to one spot. I watch as a man in full diving gear slips over the side.

"I really wish you'd have let me bring the cameras," Amanda says, dragging a voice recorder from her bag.

I shake my head. There's an orchid in the air between us, and I shove it to the opposite end of the table. "I already told you, I can't say or do anything that might get in the way of the police investigation."

She freezes, one arm stretched halfway to the coffee table. "So this is off-the-record then?" She straightens, holds up the recorder. "Can I even use this thing?"

I lean back in my chair and pretend to consider it.

Amanda loses patience after only a second or two. "You called me here for a reason, Jeffrey. Stop playing around and tell me what it is."

"Fine. I called you here because I want you to help me set the record straight. The thing is, I've seen this movie, and I know how it ends. With the husband serving twenty to life."

"Only the guilty ones." She says it teasingly, playfully, letting it hang with obvious implication.

"Come on, Amanda. We've known each other for what—fifteen, twenty years?"

She purses her glossed lips. "I won't tell if you don't."

Behind her crossed legs, a stealthy thumb presses down on the record button. I pretend that I don't notice.

"Long enough for you to know what I am and what I'm not capable of. I may be a dick at times, but I am not the kind of guy who makes his estranged wife go missing. I'm not a murderer."

She *tsks* at the word *estranged*. "Shelley McAdams is a friend of mine. Let's just say she's not taking it well."

The doctor's wife. At least I'm not the only sucker.

"Yeah, well, no offense to Shelley, but she's one of the reasons I called you here. The police seem to be assuming this was a crime of passion, but I'm not the only one with a motive. How do we know Shelley didn't... I don't know, seek out her own revenge?"

"Because Shelley is in Chicago, interviewing divorce attorneys." Amanda flashes a sorry-but-I'm-on-her-side smile. "Don't be surprised if she gets full custody of the kids."

"Okay, so other people, then. You know the statistics on crime in this town. Sabine has money, she's gorgeous and she's often alone in some empty house. There are plenty of sickos out there. How do we know it wasn't one of them?"

"I'm sure the police are looking into it."

"No, they're not—that's the whole point. As far as I can tell, the only person the police are sniffing around is me."

"Then why don't you look into a camera and tell the world you're innocent?" When I don't respond, she adds, "If you're nervous, if you need some media coaching, I can help you get some. It's not that hard."

"I'm not nervous. I just think what I have to say would mean so much more coming from someone who's not me."

"What do you have to say?"

"I have…information about my wife. Information that coming from me would sound…suspicious. Coming from you, however, it would be news."

Amanda straightens in importance at the last word, just like I knew she would. Amanda longs to be seen as a real journalist. She spends a lot of time online, promoting the newsworthiness of her show on social media, defending it from people who dismiss it as fluff. Calling her a journalist is like handing her a Pulitzer. It validates her.

"How about this?" I swing my ankle over a knee, sinking deeper into the couch. "You put that recorder of yours onto the table, and I'll talk into it and tell you what I know. When we're done, if you like what I have to say and want me to say it all over again into a camera, we can talk about that, too."

By now, Amanda is like a dog with a bone. I've given her one with just enough meat that there's no way she will let it loose. But she's always been a bit of a drama queen, and she takes her time pretending to decide. Arms crossed, eyes narrowed, glossed lip working between her teeth. I settle in and indulge her theater. After a few seconds, she places the recorder on the table.

Showtime.

I walk her through what I know. That Sabine was there, in the Super1 lot, before she disappeared. That she left without her car and her burner phone, but with her iPhone, which the police have not been able to locate. That I was the one to sound the alarm, a few short hours after she was expected home. That I've barely slept since.

"So what, then? Do you think someone took her?"

I shrug. "It's possible, I guess. But there was no sign of struggle near her car, no blood on the ground or tire marks. If she got into someone's car, I'm guessing it was someone she knew. Then again, I think it's much more possible she…" I wince, looking down at the sisal carpet.

Amanda scoots forward on the couch, leaning in. "You think it's more possible she what?"

I heave a full-body sigh. "I feel like I'm betraying Sabine by even bringing this up, but I also think if she were here, she'd understand. The thing is—and you're the first person I've ever told this to, so please forgive me if I stumble over my words—but a little over two years ago, Sabine was going through a rough patch. Her mother has Alzheimer's, and she'd stopped recognizing Sabine. Not every time, but that first time was pretty devastating. On top of that, we heard the baby Sabine was carrying, the one we'd spent a lot of money trying to conceive, didn't have a heartbeat. All that goes to say, things were really, really shitty."

Amanda makes a sound of sympathy, but she waits for me to continue.

"After she lost that baby, it's like she… I don't

know, went to a place I couldn't follow. She stopped eating. She stayed in bed for days at a time. She was self-medicating, with alcohol and leftover painkillers and whatever else she could get her hands on before I flushed it all down the toilet. Then one day, she was fine. She got up, got dressed and went back to work like nothing had happened. She sold three houses that week and listed two more. I remember thinking that's how good a broker my wife is, that she can end three comatose weeks with deals totaling more than a million dollars."

"How did she do it?" Amanda asks.

"I have no idea. It could have been a fluke, deals that she had been working on before the miscarriage that suddenly came through, I don't know. But the point is, I finally relaxed. I thought things were better, that *she* was better, and I stopped hovering so much." I pause, counting in my head to three. "I shouldn't have stopped hovering."

Amanda's forehead crumples between perfectly sculpted brows. "I don't understand. What does all of this have to do with what happened to Sabine? With wherever she is?"

"Maybe nothing, maybe everything." I fill my lungs with breath, blow it slowly out. The vapid Amanda holds hers. "What I'm trying to say is, Sabine has done this before."

Amanda's eyes go wide. "You're not suggesting…"

I nod. "Two years ago in November, the day after Thanksgiving, Sabine got on a bus and disappeared."

BETH

Early Monday morning, Martina shows up at my door fresh from the shower. "Good morning! You look pretty. Let's carpool."

Her face is bare, rosy cheeks and scrubbed skin, a fringe of dark lashes that doesn't need mascara. Two French braids snake around each ear and leave twin wet marks on her God Works Here T-shirt. The total effect is easy, youthful, adorable.

I smile and reach for my keys. "Good idea. I'll drive."

"But I've already got mine." She holds her car keys up, jingles them in the air beside her face.

"I'm a real backseat driver," I say, nudging her out of the way so I can step into the hall. "You don't want me in your passenger's seat, I promise. I'll only make you crazy, and besides, I like to drive."

What I really like is to stay in control. No way I'm strapping myself into somebody else's car and letting them steer me Lord knows where, not with every penny I own strapped to my middle. I'm not about to relinquish my cash or my shiny new command on life that easily. At least behind the wheel of my own car, I am the one in charge.

As long as things are on my terms, I wouldn't mind the company.

Martina opens her mouth to argue, then becomes distracted by a door opening at the far end of the hall. Tom, the red-faced, sweaty guy who lives in the room across from mine, steps out of the bathroom in a puff of steam. He's soaking from his three-minute session under the shower, water streaming in rivulets down his short, square body and onto the hallway runner. His hair, usually wrapped into a complicated comb-over that's not fooling anyone, hangs in thin strands onto his bare shoulders.

"Good morning, ladies," he says. "You two are looking awfully spiffy today. Matching outfits, I like it."

Better than his outfit, which is a tiny slip of ancient terry cloth slung low around his potbelly. It flaps open when he walks, providing intermittent views of something I'm trying hard not to notice.

Martina makes a face. "Put some clothes on, Tom."

"Gotta dry off first."

"I thought that's what the towel was for."

I make a sound in the back of my throat. "Towel" is a generous term.

"Nope. Towel's for modesty." He stops at his door, giving us his hairy back while he works in his key. "My body parts function best when they air-dry. You two have a good day, now." He steps inside and shuts the door.

Martina turns to me with a concerned frown. "Is that true? Am I supposed to be letting my parts air-dry?"

I laugh and head for the stairs. "Come on. I don't want to be late."

We run into Miss Sally in the hallway below, her hair wound around fat curlers the same hot pink as her silk robe, a floral kimono wrapped loosely around her body. It hangs open between her breasts, two jiggly mounds of flesh right at eye level. What is it with half-naked people in this place?

"Well, don't you two look like the Doublemint twins," she says, taking us in from head to toe. "I see our Martina got you a job, huh?"

I glance at Martina, flashing her a smile. "She did. For which I am forever grateful."

Martina grins and bumps me with a shoulder.

"I hear good things about that place. A friend of mine goes there every Sunday. Sits front and center, right in front of the big cross. He's been trying to get me to go, but I keep telling him not to bother." Miss Sally's gaze dips to my chest, and the text written across my shirt. "Unlike your souls, I'm pretty sure mine is doomed."

"Don't be fooled," I say, laughing. "I'm going to need more than a T-shirt to save my soul."

Miss Sally laughs like we're in on the same joke, even though all those things I used to believe about my inherent decency are no longer true. I've lied, I've cheated, and before this thing is through, I will have done much worse.

Some might say that makes me just as bad as you, but I don't believe that. This is nothing like the times you held me down and spit in my face, punched me in the stomach so hard I stopped breathing, held my neck and tried to make me swallow a whole bottle of Ambien. "I don't *want* to do these things," you told me after every instance. "It must be you. *You* are the one who brings this out in me. I wouldn't be like this if you were a different woman." What I'm doing is self-defense. For me, this is survival.

We say our goodbyes to Miss Sally and head out the door. Sometime during the night, clouds rolled in, bringing with them a humidity that makes it feel like we're walking through water, the air so thick it has a weight to it. The inside of the Buick is even worse. The dampness has seeped through the cracks in the windows and turned the upholstery clammy. We sink onto it, and it belches up a bouquet of scents I've not noticed before, none of them pleasant. Cigarettes and body odor and something sour and rotten, like spoiled milk. I start the engine and hit the buttons for the windows to air out the stink.

"Sweet ride," Martina says, sliding her hand up and down the armrest, and I wonder if she's messing with me. Either way, it doesn't make me any more eager to ride in her car.

I pull up the map app on my phone, and Martina waves it away, directing me out of the neighborhood. She chatters as we wind our way through streets that are already crowded with the morning rush, people like us going to work and school, and I wonder how we look to them. Normal, probably. Like one of them.

Once we're hurtling toward the highway—a route I recognize—she settles back into her seat, kicking off her sneakers and swinging her feet up onto the dash. Her toenails are painted a bright metallic blue. "So, what's the deal with you, anyway?"

The question is broad enough that it could refer to any number of things. I glance over, trying to judge which one, but Martina's profile doesn't give anything away. She points at the light and says, "Green."

I look both ways, then tentatively press on the gas. "What's the deal with me, how?"

"Well, you insist on driving, even though—and no offense—you're not very good at it. You have nightmares almost every night. Screaming nightmares, and yes, everybody at Morgan House hears you. They're all talking about it. And any time anyone asks you anything even remotely personal, you mumble something vague and change the subject. You won't even tell me where you're from."

"I'm from Oklahoma." It's a lie, but it matches the car's plates so what the hell.

"Where in Oklahoma?"

"A town nobody's ever heard of." That, at least, is the truth. Except when it comes to crime rates, Pine Bluff isn't exactly on anyone's radar. "A town I'm trying really hard to forget," I add, trying to shut down this line of questioning.

Martina shrugs. "We're all running from something, but if we're going to be friends, you've got to at least give me something. That's how this works, you know. You tell me something about yourself, and I tell you something about me."

She's right, of course. That is how friendship works, though I'm not sure friendship is the goal here—for either of us. It certainly wasn't Martina's goal when she pocketed Jorge's kickback without a word to me about it.

And yet…

God, what would it be like to make a friend in this place? In this city? Someone to laugh and share jokes with, a ride or die like the ones I used to have, before you drove a wedge into every single one of my friendships. I like Martina, and the truth is, I could really use a friend.

"I told you where I was from," she reminds me. "I even told you about my crack-whore mom, and I never tell *anybody* about her. The least you can do is share a truth about yourself."

Truth. The word strikes me as funny, and I bite down on a laugh, a big belly guffaw. What truth? So far, neither one of us has been willing to take that first leap and share something completely honest, and I'm sure as hell not going to be the first. This new life, for as long as it lasts, depends on me telling no one the details of my past.

I take a left up the ramp to I-75, which looks like a parking lot. A bumper-to-bumper sea of red brake lights. Exhaust shimmers in the air, undulating waves rising up like heat. I slow to a stop behind a souped-up truck and twist on my seat to face her.

"You told me you were born at Grady Hospital but in an accent that sounds like it came from Mexico. You basically admitted you were Jorge's client, too. To be perfectly honest, I'm not sure I believe half the stuff that comes out of your mouth. What does an American-born citizen need from a guy like Jorge other than kickbacks?"

She frowns. "What does that mean, 'kickback'?"

"Like when he paid you a commission for sending me to him. That's a kickback. And speaking of kickbacks, a real friend would have told me about it, or maybe even shared it. Friends don't use other friends to try to make a buck."

"What are you talking about? I didn't earn a commission from Jorge. Who told you I did?"

The truck in front of us rolls a few feet forward, and so do I, nudging the nose into traffic. "Jorge told me. He said he'd pay fifty bucks for anyone I sent him."

"What—? Fifty dollars…" Her cheeks flush and her eyes squeeze into a squint. "Per *person*?"

I nod.

"Oh no." She shakes her head, hiking up on a hip. "Oh *hell* no."

Spouting a steady stream of angry, staccato Spanish, she wriggles her phone from her back pocket and stabs at the screen with a finger. I pick up a few choice words—*puta, cojones, mierda*—while the speaker burps a rhythmic tone. A few seconds later, Jorge answers with a curt "Yeah?"

She switches to English, her words high and clipped. "Jorge, Martina. What's this I hear about a commission?"

His voice bursts from the phone speaker. "Who tell you that?"

"Beth. You offered *her* one when I've sent you what, ten people at least? Don't tell me, all those checks must have gotten lost in the mail. Is that right?"

Jorge's pause is two seconds too long. "Commission is new. Just started."

"Uh-huh." Martina looks at me, rolls her eyes. The first wave of guilt rolls through me, nibbling its way across my stomach. "This is some serious bullshit, Jorge. You owe me like three hundred bucks."

"Okay, okay. I pay you next time."

"No, you listen to me. There won't be a next time, not until I get that money you owe me. Do you understand what I'm telling you? Not one more person until you pay."

There's another long pause, then a sigh. "Fine."

"Fine," Martina barks back, then disconnects the call. She drops it on her lap with an angry squeal. "I can't believe he did that to me. What a snake. What a dirty, disgusting snake."

Guilt flares, heating me from the inside out. If anyone's a snake here, it's me. I wrap both hands around the wheel and wince. "I just assumed he offered you the same deal he did with me, Martina. I never even considered…" I shake my head, glancing over. "I feel like such a shit."

She brushes away my apology with a wave of her hand. "You're not the shit. Jorge is the shit. He's the one I'm mad at, not you."

"Still. I'm really, really sorry."

At my apology, her anger vanishes as quickly as it appeared. She turns to me, and her smile is big and real. "See? This is what friends do. We apologize. We forgive, and then we do better the next time. If you have a problem, you come to me and we'll talk about it, okay?"

I nod. "Okay."

"Great. So now it's my turn." She inhales, long and deep through her nose, then blows it out in one giant huff. "Okay. Fine. I don't like the way you look at me sometimes."

"How do I look at you?"

"Like you think I'm about to tackle you. Like you think I'm after however much is in that thing hanging at your waist. But I wouldn't do that to you." She points a finger at my face, wags it in the air between us. "You and I, we are friends, and I wouldn't hurt a friend that way, Beth. I *wouldn't*."

She says it just like that—like it's decided, like it's a fact. She is to be trusted. We are to be friends. She holds me in her brown stare for a few more seconds, and I can't deny her message tugs at something inside me. The thing is, I like Martina. Even though I haven't believed much of what she's told me so far, I think this might be the nugget of truth I was searching for. I was wrong about her dealings with Jorge. Maybe I was wrong to be suspicious of her, too.

"I believe you," I say, and God help me, I mean it. I believe Martina when she says she wouldn't take my money. I just pray it's not a mistake.

The car behind me leans on the horn, and I press the gas and slide forward, smiling.

The truth is, it's nice to have a friend.

Unexpected. But nice.

Martina tells me she's twenty-eight as we work our way through the nave of the church later that morning, stacking Bibles and hymnals in the cubbies between the seats, dropping in bulletins for the evening service. Her family has either died or moved away, all except for a younger half brother, Carlos, a boy half her age about to start high school at Grady—which I gather is a different place than the hospital where she claims to have been born. The two share a father, a deadbeat drifter who last she heard was playing drums in dives up and down the West Coast. Carlos's mother is kind of a bitch, but she doesn't drink or forget to buy groceries, and in Martina's mind, that more than makes up for any snarky remarks.

Martina talks and talks, a constant stream of words to plug the silence, and I don't interrupt. As long as she's the one talking, I don't have to do anything but listen.

As we're nearing the last row of a section, I step on something hard and lumpy. I reach down, pick up a baby's pacifier. It's grubby and cracked, the pink face missing its ring. "Should I throw this thing away?" I say, holding it up.

Martina takes it from my fingers, tosses it into an empty box. "We never throw away anything here, *ever.* We take it to lost and found. Not that anybody will ever come looking for an old piece of plastic, but it's not up to us. You never know what you'll find. Phones, keys, gum wrappers and Lord knows what else. Once I found a diamond earring. A real one, too."

"How do you know it was real?"

"Have you seen the people who come in this place?" She snorts. "It was definitely real."

I think of Charlene, the blonde receptionist I met my first day here, with her silky dress and sparkly jewelry, and I don't argue.

"Anyway, wait'll you see this place tomorrow morning, after the Reverend packs the house here tonight. There are eight thousand seats in this place, eight thousand bodies, and at least half of them drop crap out of their pockets for us to pick up."

I reach inside a box for a fresh stack of bulletins. "This place is nothing like the church I used to go to."

As soon as I say the words, I wish I could snatch them back. Not that Martina seems to notice my accidental sharing. She picks up a piece of trash from the floor, tosses it into the box and moves farther down the line.

"Have you ever gone to one of the Reverend's services?"

She nods.

"What's it like?"

"The services are cool. Very happy-clappy, if you know what I mean, but the music steals the show. It's like going to a concert or something. It makes the hour fly by. We can stay tonight if you want to, but I say we wait until Wednesday."

"Why, what happens on Wednesday?"

"The Reverend puts on a buffet dinner after the services. Fried chicken, lasagna, mashed potatoes, more food than you've ever seen. And you should see those hoity-toity types tear into that buffet like they haven't eaten for days. They hover around the tables with their plates while the Reverend blesses the food, and his Amen is like the shot of a starting pistol. They dive into that food like…like what are those people in the Bible with the famine?"

"Canaanites?"

"Yeah, them. Anyway, if we stay for the service

and then help clean up afterward, we get to eat as much as we want, and the Reverend pays overtime."

Overtime and a free meal, the two magic words.

I nod, decision made. "Let's wait till Wednesday then."

I look to Martina for confirmation, but she's looking over my shoulder. Her spine straightens, and her brows slam together. "What the hell are you doing here?"

I turn to see a woman—no, a *girl*—coming down the aisle toward us. She's somewhere around sixteen or seventeen, though she's helped along by her height, six feet and then some. Her skin is bronze and her hair is natural, a wild crown of curly ringlets over high cheekbones and big green eyes. She's dressed like us, in the same khaki pants and God Works Here T-shirt, only hers are skintight, her shirt knotted on the side to reveal a seductive slice of coppery skin. She moves closer, and I see that she's biting back a smirk.

"I work here. What're *you* doing here?"

Martina shakes her head, and her hands tighten into fists. "You can't work here. *I* work here."

"Well I do." The girl says it short and matter-of-fact. "Here I am."

"Where's the Reverend?" Martina pushes past, almost mowing me over in her hurry into the opposite aisle. "I need to find the Reverend."

The girl rolls her eyes. "What are you going to tell him, that you stole my money?"

At the accusation, Martina does an about-face, arms slinging in fury. I press myself to the chairs and get out of her way.

"I already told you," she shouts, "I didn't take your

goddamn money. I didn't even know you had any until you accused me of taking it. And it's not like it was your cash to begin with. That hooker you stole it from probably just came back to claim what was hers."

They're making a lot of noise, too much. I check behind us, scanning the rows of empty chairs, but as far as I can tell, there's nobody else here. Still. I wish they would stop yelling and cussing.

The girl purses her lips. "That hooker *did* come back, and so did her pimp. Do you know what they do to people who take their money? You're lucky they didn't kill me."

"What is that, some kind of threat? Because I didn't take your stupid money, and if you know what's good for you, you won't make me say it again." Martina's accent is full-on south of the border now, all rolling *R*s and short, staccato spurts.

The girl lifts a brow. "Your Mexican is showing."

With a squeal, Martina rears back an arm, her hand squeezed into a hard fist, and I hook my hand in her elbow right before she punches the girl in the face. The move is not entirely unselfish. I like to stay out of catfights as a general rule, but seeing as Martina is the one who got me this gig, I'm thinking it's better to stop this one before any blood is spilled. I'm too new to have established a good reputation yet. What reflects badly on Martina reflects badly on me, too.

I plant my body between the two women, holding up a hand in both directions. "Both of you, see that cross up there? Either shut up or take it outside." Martina opens her mouth to protest, but I beat her to it. "This isn't the time or the place."

She shuts up. The tall girl, too. They glare over my head at each other while Martina does a deep-breathing technique, less meditation and more trying not to explode. I open my mouth to speak, but it's the Reverend's voice that rings out.

"There you are," he says, and the three of us freeze. Footsteps sound to my left, and I turn to see him walking across the stage. He stops under a stage light, the skin of his forehead shining like wet glass. Particles of dust dance in the air above him, suspended in the beam of light. "Oh good, I see you've already met Ayana."

Martina tosses me a panicked glance. *How much did he hear?*

But the Reverend's a good fifty feet away, and he has to raise his voice to be heard. He watches us with a benevolent smile.

"If you don't mind, I'd like you to work upstairs today, in the administrative offices," he says, and I don't know which one of us he's talking to.

I nod, but Martina frowns. "What happened to Oscar?"

Oscar is the unofficial head of the cleaning crew, an ancient, gnome-like man who, according to his hunched back and knobby, arthritic fingers, is somewhere between eighty and a hundred and fifty. As far as I can tell, his sole responsibility is pushing a rag over the desks in the administrative offices and shooting the shit with anybody who wanders through. Any other person could do it in half the time, but in this place, seniority comes with the benefit of a cushy job.

"Oscar had to go to Florida, to visit his ailing mother. He's asked us to keep her in our prayers."

I make a sound of sympathy, even though I'm thinking, *Oscar's mother is still alive?*

"Do you think you could take over, just until Oscar returns from his trip?"

"Of course, Reverend," Martina says, volunteering in her best Southern Belle accent. "Beth and I will be happy to help."

The Reverend leans back on his heels, his gaze flitting to Ayana, looking at her like she's a child who wasn't chosen for the party. "Maybe you can take Ayana, too. Introduce her around. Show her the ropes."

Martina falls silent, and an angry flush climbs up her neck.

I smile up the stage at the Reverend. "Not a problem. We'd be glad to."

"Excellent. Well...see y'all upstairs, I guess. And thank you. I'm so happy that God brought the three of you to me. I am blessed beyond measure." He drops his hands in his pockets and wanders off, leaving the three of us standing in the aisle.

As soon as he's gone, Martina swirls to face Ayana. "Swear to God, if you so much as look at me wrong, I'm telling the Reverend what you did."

"What did she do?" I say. I can't help it. Now I want to know.

Ayana folds her arms across her chest, her gaze dipping to Martina's collarbones. "Pretty necklaces. How'd you pay for them?"

Martina's face blooms bright purple, two matching spots on each cheek. She sputters something that would make Jesus blush, then turns and stalks up the aisle.

I look at Ayana, and she's smiling.

JEFFREY

PDK Workforce Solutions is housed in the center of a shabby strip mall on Sheridan Road, sandwiched between a consignment shop and a serve-yourself yogurt place on the brink of bankruptcy. The parking lot is mostly empty. I'm one of the first ones here, thanks to the early bird reporters who dragged me from a dead sleep, rumbling up in their noisy vans and calling out greetings like miners punching in at the quarry. So far, they haven't followed me here, though I figure I've only got another day or two before they line up on the sidewalk outside. My boss, Eric, will lose his mind.

Inside the glass door, Florence is parked behind the receptionist's desk, slurping from a foam jug of Diet Coke she refills at the doughnut shop across the lot a couple of times a day. I have no idea what she does here. Up until a few years ago, she was more than happy being a housewife, and then her husband died and she "needed something to keep her busy." She actually used those words on her application; I know, because I've seen it. Eric is such a slouch that he hired her anyway.

She sees me and her eyes go wide. "Oh, Jeffrey, you poor, poor dear. I heard about Sabine on the evening news." She rushes around her desk to pull me into a hug.

What is the proper amount of time to stand here while a colleague holds you in her wrinkly arms? I count to three, then extricate myself.

"Thank you, Florence." She smells like cigarettes and Oil of Olay, and now so do I. "I appreciate your concern."

"I just can't believe it. She's really gone? Do the police have any leads at all?"

It's the question I tried to ignore all weekend— from the reporters swarming outside my windows, from friends and neighbors who blew up my phone, from my boss who texted me late last night suggesting I take the week off. Every time, the questions hit me like a brick. Are there any leads? I have no fucking idea.

The search for Sabine has fizzled, the volunteers have washed the mud off their shoes and returned home to their families and their lives. For police, the investigation has morphed from *find her* to *solve the case*, though they're holding developments tight against their Kevlar chests. If there are any leads, if Detective Durand has found so much as a hair from Sabine's head, he's not shared the information with me. I haven't spoken to him since Saturday afternoon, when he stopped by the house to pick up Sabine's computer.

Part of me wonders if he's keeping me in the dark because I am a suspect, and the other part already knows the answer.

And so I spent the weekend on the couch, monitoring news of the search on my laptop while a constant stream of Netflix blared on the TV. Most of what I found was a rehashing of old facts or tabloid hacks spinning rumors into conjecture, into motive. That Sabine was taken. That she was killed, by a stranger or her lover or me, in a fit of jealous rage. That she made a break for it, sneaked out of town on purpose.

That last rumor was the result of my calling Amanda, of parking her on my sofa for an uncensored airing of Sabine's dirty laundry. The reality of last year's disappearing act was only a little less dramatic than I made it sound. Sabine really did board a bus—headed west, I later learned—but she didn't make it very far. Halfway to the Oklahoma border, she received a call from the nursing home that her mother had suffered a fall. She was home before any of us noticed she was gone.

But the point is, she *intended* to leave. She *tried* to sneak off, and for once without telling her sister. If her mother hadn't tripped over her own two feet, who knows how long she would have stayed gone.

So now the seed has been planted. Sabine is unstable. She has a history of running off. The husband is innocent. All I can do now is sit back and watch it grow.

I sneak a quick glance at my watch. *Mandy in the Morning* starts in less than an hour.

"I'm starting to think the police are not very competent," I say to Florence, shaking my head.

She makes a face, and she swats my bicep with a crepey hand. "Well, of course they're not. My house was broken into last year, and they did nothing. They didn't even come by to see the busted-up door or dust for prints. I had to go all the way over to the station just to file a police report. Their excuse was that the gangs on the east side were keeping them too busy for common house thieves, but I was like, 'well, who the hell do you think did this?' Of course it was the gangs."

I make a sympathetic sound, even though she's spouting nonsense. The gangs are a problem, yes, but they're slinging dope, not breaking into old ladies' houses to steal their tchotchkes. But Florence has always been brilliant at this, at flipping any conversation back to her and her own piddling problems.

I mumble some excuse about a conference call and head down the hall.

The office is quiet for a Monday morning, a few minutes before opening time. No phones ringing, no clacking keyboards, no voices muffled behind cubbies and walls. Eric must not be here yet, otherwise he'd be shouting out orders from his office at the end of the hall. "Make some calls!" he'll yell whenever the office gets too quiet, "Send out some emails!" As if selling his crappy software is as easy as making first contact, but I guess he's right to complain. A silent sales office is not a productive one.

I slip into my office and shut the door, going through my normal morning routine. Power up the computer, plow through my email inbox. Delete, delete, delete, ignore.

A knuckle raps against wood, and a second later, the door pops open. Eric's head pokes around the corner. "What are you doing here?"

I lean back in my chair, eyeing him over the top of the computer screen. Eric is dressed in his usual gear—pastel button-down, lightly rumpled khakis, suede saddle bucks. He looks like a frat boy playing boss man.

"Working."

His brows slide into a frown. "I thought I told you not to come in."

"No, you told me to take however much time I need, but I don't need time. I need to work. That mailing I did last month is finally starting to bear fruit, and I have a million things to do."

This place is set up for a roving sales department, with company-issued laptops and a VPN that can be accessed from the road. Both of us know I could just as easily work from home as from here. Easier, probably, because I could do it without ever leaving my bed.

He glances into the hallway, and I catch a flash of something in his expression—surprise? annoyance?—before he looks back at me and steps inside.

He shuts the door behind him. "Jeffrey, people are starting to talk…"

"What people?"

He makes an *are-you-kidding-me* face, a minuscule lifting of his shoulders. "The point is—"

"Who, Eric? What are they saying?"

I know what they're saying. *Sabine cheated. She was in love with another man. Jeffrey Hardison is a fool. A stooge. A sucker.*

My desk phone buzzes, and I tap the Do Not Disturb button. The system flips the call through to voice mail.

"People are worried about your wife, Jeffrey," Eric says evenly. "They're worried about you." His words toss yet another coal onto my belly-fire.

I slam both fists onto my desk and lean in. "*They're* worried? How do you think *I* feel? Today is day six. Six days since Sabine went wherever she went, and there's still no sign of her. The police think—" I stop myself just in time. I inhale long and slow, trying to put a damper on my tone, on my temper. "This whole situation is crazy intense. I've barely slept. I've lost my appetite. You can't even imagine the stress I'm under."

"I *can* imagine. Which is why I suggested you take some time off. Nobody expects you to be here, least of all me."

I choke up a chuckle, an attempt to laugh it off. "I gotta tell you, Eric, I never thought I'd hear you tell me I'd done enough work. I thought your motto was 'more is more.' I barely know what to do with this laid-back version of you."

He doesn't share my joviality, not even a little bit. The silence stretches, long and painful. He leans a shoulder against the door. "Are you really going to make me say it?"

I cross my arms, lean back in my chair. Wait.

He sighs, stepping to the edge of my desk. "Look,

if it was just the staff talking, that'd be one thing, but the clients are starting to ask questions, and not just of me. They're talking to each other, and already the gossip is swirling out of control. I can't have potential customers getting wind of this. Business is already bad enough."

I clear my throat. "So this suggestion of yours for me to take some time off. It wasn't a suggestion, really? More like an order?"

"Both."

"Are you firing me?"

He lifts both hands into the air, frustrated. "Come on, you know I can't do that. We work in HR, for crap's sake." There's a knock at the door, which we both ignore. "I'm placing you on paid leave so you can go home and worry about your wife in private. Just until this thing blows over."

I take a deep breath. Sit here calmly, at my desk across from him, while his words boil under my skin. *Until this blows over.* Meaning what, until Sabine is found safe and sound, and I'm proven innocent? Or that I'm carted out of here in handcuffs and he has reasonable grounds to fire me? Which one?

There's another knock, this time louder. More forceful. Florence's voice works its way through the wood. "Jeffrey? I tried to call but your phone is on DND."

I roll my eyes, but Eric's gaze doesn't waver. "Are we agreed?" he says, his voice low and filled with meaning. I give him a brisk nod: *fine.* In fact, fuck this place. A paid vacation sounds like just what the doctor— Nope, not going there. Fuck Trevor, and fuck Eric, too.

Eric steps back and opens the door, and Florence swipes the air with a knobby fist. She sees him, and her arm falls to her side. "Oh." Her gaze bounces from Eric to mine. "I didn't mean to interrupt. Sorry."

My jaw aches from the pressure creeping up my neck and shoulders, from keeping my molars clamped together. Of *course* she meant to interrupt, every time she banged on my door as well as however many times she tried to call. The Do Not Disturb button exists for a reason.

"It's fine, Florence," Eric says. "Jeffrey and I were done."

Florence's gaze cuts me like a knife fresh from the freezer. "There's a detective here to see you."

MARCUS

Jeffrey's office smells like coffee and expensive cologne, but it can't disguise the stink of his panic when I step through his door. I thank the receptionist and his boss, close the door in their faces. I picture them standing on the other side, pressing their ears to the wood. A detective dropping by an office for an unexpected visit is always a showstopper. They were equal parts captivated and horrified.

He watches me sink into one of the chairs across from his desk, trying to read my expression, but I don't give anything away. Let him sweat. I toss my bag and keys on the chair next to me, settling in like I'm planning to stay awhile.

"Thanks for squeezing me in. I'm sure you must be very busy..." I take in the PDK poster on the wall, his whiteboard messy with sales numbers and scribbled reminders, the *Every day I'm hustlin'* desk plaque on the edge of his desk. "What is it you do here exactly?"

"PDK Workforce Solutions provides an interactive human resources management software that helps grow your business. Recruitment, performance management, workflow, things like that. Honestly?" He lowers his voice to a stage whisper. "Don't buy it, it's a little buggy."

I watch him without even a shadow of amusement.

"Do I need a lawyer?" he blurts out before he can stop himself. His nerves are making him restless and blunt.

"Do you want one?" Now I'm amused. A smile sneaks out before I can stop it.

"That depends on what you're here to ask me."

"You want to see my list of questions?" I point to the pad balanced on a thigh. "Not sure you can read my handwriting, though. My wife seems to be about the only one on the planet who can." He doesn't respond, and I drop my hand. "How about I just read 'em off to you one by one, and you tell me when I hit the magic button."

Whatever remnants of the smile from his mocking of PDK's buggy software disappears. "Why don't you just tell me what I can do for you, Detective."

I flip through the pages of my notebook. "As you know, we've been combing through the files on Sabine's laptop, and we found a couple of things I'm hoping you can clear up for us. Like her bank accounts, for example."

His shoulders drop a good inch in relief. This is a question he thinks he knows the answer to.

"I assume you're not asking about our joint accounts."

I dip my chin in a nod. "Correct."

"Which one? She has three in her name only. The

mortgage account, a checking and a debit Mastercard. Those last two are business accounts, by the way. I don't really have much knowledge of them, other than to help her file her taxes."

"I'm referring to her savings accounts, actually. The two money markets, and the investment account."

Jeffrey goes completely still. He gave me Sabine's computer, but not before combing through it. He would have been a fool not to. But these accounts weren't on that Excel file she maintained. They weren't anywhere. I only know of their existence because Ingrid told me.

"You look surprised," I say, trying not to sound satisfied.

His answer comes through gritted teeth. "Since when?"

I consult the papers on my lap. "Well, let's see. The money markets are from early January and end of March, 2013. The investment account is more recent, December of last year. Together the accounts add up to a grand total of $379,385.29, give or take, but you know how those investment portfolios go. The value changes faster than you can add up the numbers."

He doesn't respond, but I see the thoughts rolling through his mind as clearly as if they were written in the air. Sabine has almost $400K squirreled away in accounts she never told him about. In accounts she *hid* from him. For *years*.

"I can see you need a minute to process this, so let's come back to it in a little bit. In February of last year, you transferred your share of ownership at 4538

Belmont Drive to your wife, and over the course of the next sixteen months, the monthly mortgage payment has been coming from her salary, not yours."

He shrugs as nonchalantly as he can. "Sabine makes a lot more money than I do. If you've been through the accounts, you know how much more. It only seemed fair."

"Was this her idea or yours?"

"I don't remember who suggested it, but Sabine was picking up the slack most months anyway. I didn't want it to become an issue between us."

"Was it ever?"

"Was it ever, what?"

"An issue. Because my wife and I, we just throw everything into one pot. But believe me, I get how money can become an issue, because she *used* to draw a salary. When she stopped working, she felt guilty spending the money in our account since I was the one who put it there. It took me a while to convince her that what's mine is hers and what's hers is mine. She contributes in other ways, you know? But to each his own, I guess."

This is me playing good cop. The witty and let's-be-buddies cop. Judging from the way his eyes go dark and squinty, Jeffrey doesn't believe it for a second.

"Sabine and I went in another direction, but believe me when I say there are no hard feelings between us. I may live in our house rent free, but I pay the utilities and buy most of the groceries, as I'm sure you've seen on the joint household account. That's my contribution."

"Sounds like a good deal."

"Yes," he says, nodding. "A good deal for *both* of us."

I scribble some bullshit on the pad, then flip to the next page. "Since Sabine's disappearance, you've discovered she was having an affair. That must have been rough."

He barks a sarcastic laugh. "*Rough* is one way of putting it, I guess. Finding out about the affair was difficult, yes, it was hurtful, but was it surprising? Maybe not so much. The truth is, Sabine and I have been moving further and further apart for some time now. I'm sure her sister, Ingrid, has told you as much."

"According to Dr. McAdams, it wasn't just an affair. He says the two are very much in love. That they've been making plans to reorganize their lives so that they can be together."

"By planning to ditch their spouses, you mean. Yes, I know about that, too. Ingrid and Dr. McAdams both told me."

"According to the doctor, Sabine was also pregnant."

"Yeah, he told me the joyful news." He says it through curled lips, and with a tone like he'd just stepped in dog shit.

"How'd that go over?"

"I punched him, if that's what you're asking. But I'd also caution him, before he gets too excited, to take a look at Sabine's medical records."

"You think she's lying?"

"I think he should take a look at her medical records. Out of respect for Sabine's privacy, I don't want to say more."

"You weren't respecting her all that much when you punched her in the face."

His face goes white, then beet red, fury firing through his veins. He knows that little tidbit came from Ingrid. It's the same expression he used with her in my office.

He stabs a finger on his desk. "Okay, first of all, I did *not* punch her. Not even close. It was a light slap with the back of my hand, one I regretted as soon as it happened. That's all it was."

"That must have been one hell of a slap."

"We were arguing. Things got heated. She shoved me. I slapped her. Afterward, we apologized, and that was that. We moved on."

"What were you arguing about?"

He lifts both hands in the air. "I don't know, Detective. What does any married couple argue about? Taking out the trash, dirty clothes on the floor, using the last of the shampoo. Take your pick."

"Would you say you're a jealous man?"

He narrows his eyes. "My wife is cheating on me, Detective. I think I'm allowed to be jealous. But again, I didn't find this out until *after* she went missing."

I shrug. "Still. Your wife certainly had her secrets. Secret bank accounts, secret lover. I wonder what else she was keeping from you."

I leave the question dangling, and he doesn't pick it up. It's something he's probably wondered a million times since finding out about the doctor, but what is it they say? Never ask a question you don't want the answer to.

"According to Ingrid, Sabine had consulted an attorney," I say, consulting my notepad. "She was going to ask you—"

"For a divorce, I know. This past weekend, apparently." He leans back in his chair. "Ingrid and Trevor told me that, too."

I scratch at a cheek, watching him. Waiting. For the span of a good three breaths, maybe four.

Jeffrey is the first to lose patience. "What?"

"I'm just wondering what would happen. If she'd gotten the chance to ask you for a divorce, I mean. Who would get the house? How would you split up your assets?"

"Come on, Detective. We both know I'd get the shitty end of the stick. But okay, I'll play this game. If Sabine and I got a divorce, I'd probably move away. This is a dead-end job in a dead-end town. I'd have better opportunities elsewhere."

I nod, satisfied for now. "Let's go back to the fight. After Sabine shoved you and you punched her—"

"Slapped," he says, his voice clipped. "I *slapped* her. Not punched. There's a big difference."

"After you slapped her, then what did you do?"

"I apologized, of course. So did she. We put it behind us and moved on."

"But not before you had another heated exchange via text."

He pales, his body twitching before he can stop it.

"What happened, did she lock herself in a bathroom and refuse to let you in? My wife does that sometimes, drives me up a tree. I can see how that might make you do things you might not otherwise do. Say things you might not otherwise say. A smart guy wouldn't have put it in writing, though." I pause, two seconds of silence that add weight to my next words. Give them extra meaning. "Unless, of course, you meant what you said."

A smart guy wouldn't have put it in writing, but hey, maybe he's that much of an idiot. I take in his expression, all slack chin and wide, wild eyes, and I'm pretty sure he thinks he's that much of an idiot, too.

I flip through my notepad until I find the single sheet of paper I tucked there, and then I slide it out and slap it to the desk. A printout of a text exchange, his and Sabine's. I flip it around so he can see, but he doesn't glance down. He doesn't need to. He already knows what it says. He's the chump who wrote the damn thing.

Come out of there or I will fucking kill you.

"Mr. Hardison, do you own a weapon?"

Jeffrey owns a .357 Magnum, licensed and registered in his name. If he lies now, I'll have a warrant by the end of the day.

He looks sick, like he might actually throw up, and my chest goes tingly and hot.

Victory.

"I think it's time I get an attorney."

BETH

Like the rest of the church, the administrative offices were designed to impress—solid and thick walls, generous molding, banks of ornate windows hung with gleaming, double glass—but they were furnished with the donors in mind. The decor is straight out of an IKEA catalog: functional, minimalist, Scandinavian sleek. As out of place in this neo-Gothic house of worship as a prostitute, which I'm pretty sure Ayana is. Or at the very least, *was*. Despite the bucket of cleaning supplies dangling from her finger and the vacuum strapped to her back, her hips wag in invitation, her head swinging back and forth like she's scrounging up clients on Fulton Industrial Boulevard.

A hooker, a thief and a fugitive walk into a church—except this is a joke without a punch line.

"Would you stop?" Martina hisses.

Ayana's spine straightens, and she frowns over her shoulder. "Stop what? I'm not doing nothing."

"The hell you're not. Show some respect for this place. You're not going to find any customers here."

Ayana snorts. "Right. 'Cause church people ain't freaks."

Martina rolls her eyes, but she doesn't argue, and neither do I. With the exception of the Reverend, the people I've met in this place might be freaks. As far as I can tell, he's the only normal one here, the leader of the Land of Misfit Toys.

The hallway dead-ends into a spare but bright kitchen, and Martina starts doling out orders. "Every single inch in this place needs to be either dusted, wiped down or vacuumed. Give extra care to the things people touch most—the telephone, computer mouse, keyboard, drawer pulls—and don't be stingy with the cleaning products. If one person gets the stomach flu, we all get the stomach flu." She nudges Ayana into an open doorway. "You start in the kitchen."

Ayana tries to strike a contrary, hands-on-hips pose, but the vacuum hose gets in the way. She settles for a scowl and a jutted hip. "What're *you* gonna do?"

"Not that it's any of your business, but Beth and I are gonna start in the Reverend's offices."

"How come y'all get to work together and I have to do everything on my own?" Ayana says it in a way that makes me subtract a couple of years from the age I'd originally guessed. If this girl is legal, it's barely.

"Stop bitching and get to work, will you?" Martina says. "Work your way down the hallway, and we'll meet where we meet."

We leave Ayana pouting in the hallway and backtrack to the Reverend's offices at the opposite end, which is a mini complex unto itself. A private work space overlooking an English-inspired garden, a conference room with a projection screen and a table that seats fourteen, a living area with kitchenette and twin three-seater sofas arranged on either side of a low table. The flat-screen television on the wall is tuned to Fox News on mute, bronzed and powdered journalists lined up on a couch in bright ties and floral dresses, their lips moving without sound.

"I call dibs on the living room," Martina says, plunking her bucket onto the coffee table.

"Really? You're not even going to explain?"

"Explain what?" She leans down to pull a spray bottle from the bucket, and the gold discs swing on their chain around her neck. Bought with Ayana's money, if I'm to believe it—and I just might. I try to make out the letters on the engraving, but the charms won't stop dancing around.

"What's up with you and Ayana, of course. You clearly hate each other. Why?"

Martina lurches upright, her eyes flashing with anger, with accusation. "I didn't steal her money, okay? I didn't know anything about it, and who tapes money to their toilet tank, anyway? Like, isn't that the first place a thief would think to look? If anyone's a thief here, it's *her*. She just admitted to taking that other hooker's money. You heard that part, right?"

I nod. "Right, but that's not what—"

"And excuse me for trying to help a bitch." She slings an arm through the air. "I mean, who wouldn't feel sorry for a girl her age, out there all on her own? I met her when she was *fourteen*. I fed her, I found her a place to stay. I thought I was some kind of mentor to her, though silly, stupid me, all that time she was taking my money, and she was also taking money from all those men she was spreading her legs for. And never once did she say thanks." She whirls around and douses a side table with cleaning solution. "Not that I needed a thank-you card, but it woulda been a hell of a lot better than accusing me of being a thief, because I'm not. I'm not a thief."

I watch her wipe down the table with sharp, angry strokes and wonder what to say. The thing is, I'm pretty sure Martina *is* a thief. Ayana never said that the money was taped to the toilet tank. How else would Martina have known that little fact, unless she was the one who found it?

And what does this mean for our newly formed truce? Was I wrong to believe she wouldn't steal my money, too?

A rapping on the door frame saves me from my thoughts, and the table from Martina's overeager scrubbing.

The man standing in the doorway is a stranger, and yet I know exactly who he is. Same runner's build as the Reverend, same hazel eyes that seem to be smiling even when he's not, same clipped beard, though his is a rusty brown instead of white. He is dressed like his father, too, in jeans and a pressed shirt, but his clothes are more modern, more youthful, cut in a way that make me think they might be designer. He even has his father's haircut, clipped closely on the sides with a longer hank on top, swept off his forehead with an identical cowlick.

"What do you want?" Martina says, emphasis on

the *you*. She stands like a statue in the middle of the carpet, the spray bottle and rag hanging from a hand.

"Hi," I say, smiling to soften her snub.

He takes it as an invitation, moving farther into the room, his cologne mixing with the other smells: bleach, lemon polish and spicy sandalwood. He extends a hand in my direction. "Erwin Jackson Andrews IV, otherwise known around this place as Erwin Four. The esteemed Reverend's firstborn and only son and last living carrier of the family name. The pressure is enormous."

I laugh and shake his hand. "Beth Murphy, and this is—"

"Martina and I have met, many times. Haven't we, Martina?" He gives her a good-natured smile she doesn't return. She doesn't answer, either. He turns to me with a shrug. "Have you s—"

"Your dad's not here," Martina says.

He looks at her, goading. "What if I was about to say Oscar?"

"Oscar's in Florida," I offer, at the same time Martina asks, "Were you?"

Erwin aims his smile at me, then Martina. *No, he was not.* It's a lighthearted teasing, but Martina isn't having it.

She gives him her back, attacking the console on the far wall. "I don't know where the Reverend is. Last I saw him, he was onstage in the church, but that was a half hour ago. He could be anywhere by now." On the other side of her body, the television flickers a Cialis commercial, an older couple holding hands before a setting sun.

Erwin drops his hands in his jeans pockets, and a platinum watchband gleams on his wrist. "If you see him, tell him I fixed his email issue. The last update messed up the syncing between his computer and his phone, but it's working now. I run the IT in this place." That last sentence he delivers to me, though I can't decide whether it's meant to inform or impress.

His gaze bounces between us, waiting for one of us to respond. He doesn't seem eager to leave.

I don't know what to say to this guy, the son of a holy man. The clothes, the watch, the impish half grin on his face. The result is anything but holy. The silence stretches, long and uncomfortable. Martina ignores us both.

"Okay, well…" Erwin takes the hint, backing out of the room. "Nice to meet you, Beth. Martina, you have a nice day. See y'all around." And with that, he saunters back into the hall.

"What is wrong with you?" I say as soon as we're alone. "Why were you being so rude to him?"

"Because Erwin Four is a creep, that's why." She sprays down the television screen with Windex, and I don't tell her she shouldn't. Something about how the chemicals eat away at the delicate film and distort the pixels. You told me so, right before you backhanded me in the temple for doing it to yours.

"He's your boss's son. It wouldn't hurt you to be nice."

She exchanges the Windex for a fresh rag, begins wiping down the screen. "I tried that once. It didn't work out that great. If you know what's good for you,

you'll stay far, far away from him. I mean it, Beth. He's bad news."

Whatever she says next fades into a pounding in my head, blood rushing in my ears because a national news alert is flashing across the television on the other side of her body. A face fills the screen, and dread, like warm bile, bubbles up my throat. I step to the side, bobbing my head to see around Martina's feverish scrubbing. A banner crawls across the bottom, white text shining on a bright red background.

MISSING: SABINE STANFIELD HARDISON.

A chill skitters up my spine, hollowing out my stomach and my lungs. I stare at the screen as the photograph grows smaller, shifting to a lopsided square in the upper right-hand corner. A journalist's face takes her place, and I focus on her brows like twin commas squeezed together in concern. Her shiny pink lips are moving, exaggerated, like a silent movie star. I want to search for the remote, but I can't tear my eyes away from the screen.

All this time I've been hunkered down, hiding and watching the news for reports of a missing Pine Bluff woman, and now here it is, and I can't breathe. The room spins, the words dancing in spots across my vision.

Martina steps away from the screen, pausing at the look on my face. She frowns at the TV over her shoulder. "What's wrong? Who is that?"

"Her name's Sabine Hardison." My voice is high and wild. It echoes in my ears like a scream.

Martina turns to face the television, shifting so

we're side by side. She tilts her head and studies the screen. "She's so pretty. Do you know her?"

Do I know *her.* I try to cough up an answer, but my lungs are hardened concrete. It's all I can do to shake my head.

"Then why are you looking at her picture like that?"

My thoughts careen and slide around, searching for purchase, for an acceptable excuse for the silence that I've already let stretch far too long. "Like how?"

"Like you want to throw up or something."

New words flash across the bottom banner: Pine Bluff, Arkansas. Martina doesn't read them out loud, but she sees them and turns to study me. Her gaze crawls across my profile, over my wide eyes and cheeks that are burning like I've been in the sun too long. Martina is neither blind nor stupid, and I don't like the way she's looking at me, like she's trying to solve a puzzle.

And now my breath is coming too hard, too fast. I need Martina to forget she ever saw Sabine's face, ever saw her name and those awful words that crawled across the bottom of the screen, and the only way to do that is to keep moving and stuff my feelings down. I peel myself away from the screen, pick up my bucket and carry it into the next room, casting one last glance back at the TV. The reporter has moved on to the next subject, and Sabine's picture has been replaced with that of a politician, some old guy with beady eyes and a smarmy smile.

Still. Just because the image of Sabine's face has been erased from the screen doesn't mean it's not still burned across my vision. I won't forget, and I'm not naive enough to think Martina will, either. One false move, one dubious answer, and she'll start up with the questions again. Already her questions are circling the outer rings of a bull's-eye. It's only a matter of time before she flings one that hits dead center.

People don't just fall off the face of the planet. They run, they hide or they are taken.

I should know, because I am one of them.

MARCUS

"Uncle Marcus!" The voice comes from somewhere behind me, a couple octaves higher than the racket of the other ten people crammed into Ma's tiny brick house. From my niece, Annabelle, the birthday girl. She's the reason for this get-together, and why we've all gathered here when normal people are supposed to be working. If Annabelle wants her birthday supper at three in the afternoon, Annabelle gets her birthday supper at three.

I scoop her up right before she tackles me at the knees. "Happy birthday, Anna-banana-Belle. How does it feel to be eight today?"

Her eyes go comically big. "I'm *nine*."

"You are?" I smack myself on the forehead with a palm. "Silly me."

Annabelle giggles. My niece may be nine, but she weighs practically nothing, the aftereffects of a scary bout with leukemia that left my sister traumatized and dropped Annabelle off the bottom of the growth charts.

I grab her by the waist, flip her upside down and carry her by her skinny ankles to the kitchen. We pass my mother on the way, and I drop a kiss on her cheek.

"Stop flinging her around like that," Ma calls out after us. "You're going to pop something out of its socket."

I swing Annabelle around in the air and deposit her feetfirst onto the kitchen linoleum. Her eyes are shining, her cheeks pink with happiness, and maybe the blood rush that comes with being flipped ass over heels. She's smiling with her mouth closed, which is a shame because that hole where her two front teeth used to be is the cutest goddamn thing I've ever seen.

"Did I pop something out of its socket?"

She shakes her head, bouncing her pigtails around on either side of her ears. Annabelle's hair used to be brown and straight as a pin. After the chemo it grew back in spiral curls the color of Flamin' Hot Cheetos. She plants her sneakers and holds up her arms. "Again."

I grab her by the wrists and she climbs me like a monkey, popping me in the chin as she executes a flailing back flip. I catch her before she can hit the ground and carry her under my arm like a giggling sack of potatoes.

"She has you wrapped around her little finger. You know that, right?" my sister, Camille, says watching from the other side of the breakfast bar. She's leaning on the kitchen counter, with an ever-present glass of chardonnay in a hand—another holdover from Annabelle's illness—even though it's the middle of the afternoon.

"I'm the only one in this family who doesn't treat her like a piece of glass." I put Annabelle down and point her in the direction of the other kids, her two older brothers and their cousins, currently tearing up the den. "Kids are supposed to roughhouse, Cam. Let her be a kid."

Camille makes a sound in the back of her throat, examining me over the rim of her glass. "You look tired."

I *am* tired. Fucking exhausted, actually. A week of nonstop work on the Sabine Hardison case will do that to you. I step to the fridge and pull out a beer.

"That bad, huh?" She digs through a drawer for the bottle opener, passes it to me. "Still no leads?"

"Nothing I can tell you about." Nothing I can tell *anybody* about.

Like every other person in this town, Camille knows what she's seen on the news—that there has been no trace of Sabine since she walked out the Super1 door and disappeared into thin air. No bank transactions, no check-ins on Sabine's Facebook or Instagram, no emails or texts. By now the media has poked enough holes in Jeffrey's story to turn it to Swiss cheese, turning the tide of public opinion about him from sympathetic husband to primary suspect, and it doesn't help that the guy's an ass. Plenty of people are coming forward with tales of times he ran over their dog or reneged on a handshake deal, and together their stories have swirled into something bigger, something dark and nefarious.

And then there's that stunt he pulled with *Mandy in the Morning*. What kind of tool bad-talks their missing wife on network television, then starts up an affair with the TV reporter? Neither move won him any points with the stay-at-home mom crowd—women like Camille, blue-ribbon, class-A gossips who wile away the hours their kids are at school at coffee shops and the gym, spreading rumors and stoking speculation. If Jeffrey were smart—which he's not—he'd have kept his paws off Mandy and blubbered into her camera like that lovesick doctor has been doing on other shows, begging for whomever took Sabine to send her back home. Thanks to Trevor's tears and Ingrid's tenacity, the national news caught wind of the story last week.

Camille refills her glass with a bottle from the fridge door and drops in two fresh ice cubes. "I still think it's the husband. I met him once, ages ago. Some party at the Magillicutty's, a housewarming or birthday or I don't remember what. But the point is, I walked into the kitchen and there they were, arguing about something. Well, *he* was arguing. She was mostly crying."

"Is that so?" I pop the top and take a long pull from the bottle.

Camille rolls her eyes at my nonanswer. As the detective assigned to the case, I'm walking a delicate balance here: releasing enough tidbits to keep the public invested, but not enough to make them lose hope. Feeding them enough information to fuel the investigation, but not enough to trip me up. I'm looking for leads, not vigilantes or armchair detectives.

"Oh for God's sake, Marcus. Everybody knows they were on the brink of divorce. Stop acting like I'm revealing some top secret detail about her life. She was having an affair, and honestly, who wouldn't in her place? Her husband is a real douche."

Camille isn't wrong. It's no secret their marriage was on the rocks. My sister is not the only one floating the theory he had a hand in Sabine's disappearance. Nobody's buying his reading-a-book-by-the-river bullshit, including me. Chasing down what he was really up to the afternoon his wife disappeared has eaten up the bulk of my investigation hours.

"Fine, you keep your secrets, but at least tell your favorite sister this—"

"You're my only sister."

"Whatever. Just tell me, second favorite brother of mine." A burst of laughter comes from the next room, and she leans her head around the counter to make sure we're still alone. Her concern is not about privacy, but about getting the scoop. Camille hates not being in the know. "What're your spidey senses telling you? Do you think you'll ever find Sabine?"

"No."

Her eyes go wide. "Really? What do you think happened to her? What does your gut say?"

"Honestly, Cam?" I drain the beer bottle, chuck it into the recycling bin. "My gut says that she's dead."

My younger brother, Duke, settles a steaming platter of pot roast swimming on a bed of vegetables onto a table already groaning under the weight of our mother's food. As usual, she's cooked for an army, enough to send all of us home with Ziploc baggies of leftovers that will last us well into next week. I can still hear her, banging around in the kitchen, rattling off a one-sided conversation with herself. *That needs more dressing. Now where did I put the butter? Don't forget the garlic bread.*

"Ma, come on," I shout. The smells are overpowering, meat and potatoes and vegetables plucked from the garden out back. "You're killing us here!"

I wink across the table at Annabelle, who's sneaked a slice of sausage from the tray and tucked it in a fist. Only Annabelle dares to sneak food because ever since her illness she's Ma's unofficial favorite, the only one besides me who can get away with breaking the house rules—rules that for everyone else are ironclad but for us a little fuzzy. (1) No cussing or talking back. (2) Nobody eats until everyone's seated and the food blessed. (3) Turn off the lights—what do you think, that we own the electricity company?

Ma barrels into the dining room in her apron, a frilly, floral thing she's had as long as I can remember. "Did everybody get themselves something to drink?"

Nods and yeses all around, including my own, even though my new beer bottle is already empty. Ma would only hold up dinner for me to go get another, and the Durand clan is a ravenous bunch. Best not to get in their way.

She sits, then registers the empty place setting at the far end, and her expression shifts from surprised to offended. Her gaze scans the faces at the table, ticking them off one by one in her head. Her three adult kids and their spouses. Duke and Joanie's twins. Camille and Shawn's two hellions and Annabelle. It's only a matter of time before Ma's gaze lands on me.

"Marcus, where's Emma?"

My absent wife. Her beloved daughter-in-law. The

same person she last Christmas referred to as the daughter she never had. "Uh, hello, Mom," Camille had said at the time, "I'm standing right here." Ma just patted her hand. "You know what I mean." She's been so busy she didn't notice when I walked in without Emma, not until now.

I slide the napkin from under my silverware, drape it over my lap. "Home in bed. She said to tell you she's sorry to miss this."

Like everybody else here, my mother is well aware of my wife's delicate constitution. Emma's always got something, a headache or stomachache or earache or dizzy spell she can't quite shake. Usually, I'm cool with her bowing out of family dinners and kids' soccer games, but today's different. Nobody misses a Durand birthday celebration, not even Camille, who once waited until everybody was finished with dessert to tell us she was in labor.

"Was," I say. "Emma *was* sick. She picked up that stomach bug that's going around."

"What stomach bug?" Camille says, looking up and down the table. "I haven't heard anything about a stomach bug. Since when? What kind?" She frowns at Duke, then at her husband, Shawn. "Do y'all know anything about a stomach bug?"

Ma frowns. "Well, if she *was* sick, then why isn't she here?"

"Give her a break, will you? Em's better, but still she's not a hundred percent yet. She just wanted to sleep it off, and honestly, both of us were a little worried she might still be contagious. We didn't want to risk it, not with a houseful of kids." I follow up my words with a meaningful glance at Annabelle, whose immune system is still wonky.

For Ma that does the trick. She lets it go, pushing back her chair. "I think I have some homemade chicken soup from the freezer."

"Later."

She ignores me, pressing to a stand. "I'll just get it out so it can defrost. It'll only take a second."

Someone groans—Camille's oldest, I think, down at the kids' end of the table. My mother's freezer is a black hole. Food that gets shoved into its icy belly rarely ever makes it out, except for the one day every year Ma loads everything into shopping bags and takes it to the homeless shelter downtown. If there's chicken soup in there, it'll take her weeks to dig it out.

Camille widens her eyes at me, a not-so-subtle sign to stop this train before it runs off the tracks. To her right, the kids clutch their forks and throw wild, panicked glances—all but Annabelle, who's leaning back in her chair and chewing. She looks like a red-pigtailed Snoopy, one cheek fat with sausage.

"Ma." She stops at the door to the kitchen, and I soften my tone. "Emma would love some of your chicken soup, but please, for the love of all that's holy, get it later, will you? The kids down there are about to start a riot."

"Yeah," someone whispers. Shawn, I think, from the way Camille elbows him in the ribs.

Ma looks at the kids, and they bob their heads. "Nana, we're *starving*," one of them says.

She presses a palm to her bosom, then bustles back over to her chair, reciting a rapid-fire blessing over the food like one of those disclaimers at the end of a radio commercial. Then, finally, come the words we've all been waiting to hear: "All right, y'all. Dig in."

There's an explosion of movement and voices, of passing plates and scooping spoons, of people tearing into the heaping platters like they haven't eaten since last week. The Durand version of a food fight, Emma calls it, a complete free-for-all. So much commotion that I almost miss the buzzing at my hip.

I see the name, and a shot of adrenaline hits my veins like liquid fire. There were a dozen reasons for me to become a cop—my firstborn's need for order and control; our jailbird father, who dropped dead halfway through his fourteen-year sentence; the way I had to work two jobs to supplement his nonexistent life insurance. But this feeling when something breaks, punch-drunk with energy and a pulsing in my chest, that's the reason I stay. It's a high as addictive as a pull from a crack pipe.

I pull my cell phone from the holder, wave it in the air by my ear, and Ma shoos me off with a flick of her fingers. Some mothers dream of their sons becoming priests; for mine, there is no more honorable profession than cop.

In three strides I'm in the kitchen.

"I got something," Charlie says in that gruff smoker's voice that sounds like he could keel over at any minute.

Thank fuck.

Charlie is an ex-cop, a freelance detective specialized in finding the unfindable, and my go-to secret weapon. His methods may be a little questionable—

according to the Chief, a *lot* questionable—but he's discreet, and he always gets the job done. I pay him under the table and from my own pocket. So far he's been worth every hard-earned penny.

I unlock the sliding glass door and step out, onto the tiny deck overlooking Ma's backyard. The late afternoon sun slants through the trees, lighting up Ma's beds of Early Girl tomatoes and E-Z Pick beans and whatever the hell else she's got sprouting in the greenhouse at the very back.

"I found an application for an apartment in Tulsa," Charlie says. "Some place called…" Papers rustle in the background. "The District at River Bend. I checked it out, more hipsters there than you can beat with a stick, which is exactly what I wanted to do, beat 'em with a stick. Anyway, the leasing manager conducted a background check that went nowhere. Your gal disappeared before she could sign the lease."

Charlie's message hits me, and I clench my jaw so hard something pops in my temple. My "gal" knew what she was doing when she filled in that application. She knew that as soon as she forked over her license and social security number and whatever else needed for the background check, they would act as beacons, lighting up her location on a map. An electronic trail leading the police straight to her.

"It's a bait and switch," I say. "She's on the run."

Charlie's grunt says he agrees. "I called the numbers she gave the leasing manager as references. Both took me to QuikTrip, one for the corporate offices in Tulsa, the other for a gas station south of Oklahoma City. That's two places of employment a hundred and twenty miles away from each other. I thought that was kind of funny. Don't you think that's kind of funny?"

"Fucking hilarious."

"Both of them were dead ends, of course."

Of course. I suck in enough air to pop a lung, then I blow it out long and slow while I count to ten. A ridiculous technique I learned from the department psychologist, and just like when Chief Eubanks sent me to the shrink under threat of administrative leave, it doesn't do anything other than piss me off.

"If she laid a trail to the west, that means she probably went east," I say. "She'd stay in the South so her accent wouldn't stick out."

"Memphis?"

"Nah, too close. I'm guessing she'd put at least a day or two's drive between us. Start with the cities."

"Got it."

"And Charlie?"

"Yeah."

"She'll have dropped some balls by now. I don't know what yet. But find them."

"Roger that."

He hangs up, and I slide the phone into my pocket and stand there for a long minute, white-knuckling the railing and watching a bird tug a worm from the dirt. The worm is flailing about, struggling to keep itself tethered to the earth, but the bird claws the ground and holds fast.

"Uncle Marcus?"

I turn, and there's Annabelle, her pretty face crinkled with worry. Behind her the sliding door stands open, just enough space for her tiny body to slip through.

"Hi, princess." I smile down at her, trying to assess from her expression how long she's been standing there, listening. How much she's heard.

She tips her head back, squinting into the sun. "You said a bad word."

I flip back through the phone conversation, trying to remember what I said. *Which bad word?* It could be one of many. I crouch down, putting us face-to-face. "I did?"

She nods. "You said f—"

"Don't you dare." I clap a hand over her mouth. "Your mother will string both of us up if she hears you say that. Speaking of your mother, didn't she ever tell you not to eavesdrop on important police business?"

Annabelle wriggles away from my hand, and she's grinning. "She's the one who told me to come out here and find out what you were talking about."

I laugh, the muscles relaxing in my neck, releasing the tight lines across my back. "Is there any food left on the table, or did you savages eat it all?"

She smiles. "Nana made you a plate. A really big one."

I snatch Annabelle off her feet, swing her around and carry my squealing niece to the door. "Good, 'cause I'm starving."

BETH

I spend the rest of the day obsessing about the missing-person report on the TV and thinking about the first time I tried to leave. We'd been married a handful of years by then—long enough for me to know your apologies and promises to change would turn up empty again, but short enough I still thought I had some sliver of control. In a moment of daring recklessness, I threw some things into a bag, shoved it in the trunk of my car and drove across town to my sister's house. The week prior, after seeing the bruises across my back and ribs, she'd pressed her house key into my hand and told me to use it anytime, day or night.

My freedom lasted for all of four hours.

Just thinking about my sister stirs up a wave of fresh sorrow, a bittersweet churning in my chest. I remember her face when you showed up on her doorstep, with flowers and that diamond necklace I still don't know how you paid for, the disappointment that curled on her lips when I followed you out to the car.

Do you remember what you said to make me go with you? Do you? Because I remember every single thing. Your hands gripping my arm. Your hot breath in my ear. My sister hollering at me to come back inside.

"Either get in the motherfucking car," you said as calm as could be, "or I will slice your sister into a million bloody pieces, and I will make you watch."

I got in the motherfucking car.

After that my sister and I didn't speak for months, because I couldn't tell her the truth of what you said, and she couldn't understand why I would go back to someone who kept breaking my bones and my heart. She accused me of being too proud, too blinded by love, and I couldn't tell her that love had nothing to do with it. I went with you that day because I believed you. Unlike all your other promises—that you were sorry, that you would get help, that you'd never, ever raise a hand to me like that again—the threat to my sister, I knew, was not an empty one. You'd slice her to pieces, and you'd do it without blinking an eye.

I learned another lesson that day, one that in the end, was much more sinister: my leaving was not just about me. You would mow down anyone who got in your way.

"Hello, Beth?" The Reverend's voice comes from right behind me, but it takes two more attempts before I realize he's talking to me. That I'm Beth.

I startle, and my head whacks against the upper shelf of the cabinet I'm hunched under. Stars burst across my vision. I slap a hand to the throbbing spot and back out of the cabinet on my knees.

The Reverend presses his hands in prayer and

gives a little bow. "'Whatever you do, work at it with all your heart, as working for the Lord, not for human masters.' Colossians 3:23."

I don't know how to respond to this, what to say to this godly man who I've put in danger by the simple act of accepting a job. He's one of the people you'd mow down to get to me—collateral damage, that's what you would call it. I try to focus on the Reverend's smile, not the spiky ball of dread gathering in my gut.

"Can I borrow you for a little bit?" he says. "I could use your help upstairs with the bookshelves in my office."

I push to a stand, brushing crumbs and dirt off my pants. "Of course. What's wrong with them?"

"Well, for one thing, the books are just shoved in there, willy-nilly. There's no rhyme or reason to them, and I can never seem to find the one I'm looking for. I need somebody to organize them, come up with some kind of a system. It's a big job. It will probably take you the rest of the day."

I don't understand. Up to now, Martina, Ayana and I have been a team, scrubbing our way through the church like locusts through a field, and now the Reverend seems to be singling me out. I flick a glance at Martina, frozen on the other side of the day care room. She frowns, and the look she gives me makes me tense.

I wave a casual hand in her direction. "Should I bring some reinforcements?"

"That's an excellent idea, but this room needs to be ready for the kids tonight." The Reverend turns to them with a smile. "Why don't you ladies finish up down here, then join Beth when you're done. In the meantime, I'll walk her up and explain what's what."

Martina's brows dip even farther, but I have no choice other than to snag my bucket and follow the Reverend up the stairs, trying to tamp down my heightened sense of paranoia. Why has he called me upstairs alone? Does he know about the fake ID, the fake social security card, the fake everything?

Judging from his friendly chatter, he doesn't. We wind our way through the church while the Reverend talks nonstop about his book collection—instructional manuals on expository preaching, a collection of antique Bibles, an entire shelfful of *Sermons for Dummies* some jokester puts in his stocking every year at Christmas.

"The problem is, my parishioners are always forgetting to return whatever they borrow. Last year my wife put those *From the library of* stickers inside every book, but it's still a fifty-fifty shot if I'll ever see it again."

"You could create a sign-out sheet," I suggest as we approach the double doors to the executive offices. "You know, like libraries have. After two weeks, their time is up. They have to bring the book back or risk… I don't know, eternal damnation or something."

He laughs and opens the door. "I'm not beyond an infernal threat or two, if it means books stop disappearing from my shelf."

Charlene is perched behind the receptionist's desk, a phone pressed to her ear. She smiles as we come inside.

"But the sign-out sheet is a great idea," he says, ushering me down the hall. "Do you think you could make me one?"

I look over to see if he's serious, why he's asking me, a cleaner, and not his secretary. I study his profile, searching for whatever motivation fueled his question, but I can't find anything beyond a request for help. I tell myself to chill and keep my expression steady and warm. "Sure. I'd just need a computer and a printer."

"You can use mine. My password's ErwinGrace2." His kids. He smiles, obviously proud. "Just don't tell Erwin Four or he'll get a big head."

In his office, we spend a few minutes in front of his shelves, floor-to-ceiling slabs of glossy wood stuffed with religious books and icons. The Reverend wasn't joking when he said they were a mess. Bibles mixed in with devotionals and sacred texts and history books and evangelical tomes, spread across multiple volumes. There's no order as far as I can tell, no reasoning for the way some shelves are half-empty, and others crammed to bursting.

"Look at this one," he says, pulling a raggedy book off a middle shelf. "This is the Andrews family Bible, purchased by my great-great-grandmother and given to her son, Erwin Jackson Andrews the first, on his wedding day." He peels the leather cover open, flipping carefully through the yellowed pages to a colorful one at the back. A family tree, the branches reaching out like leafy fingers, ending in handwritten names and dates. Births, deaths, marriages. He taps two at the bottom. "Erwin's sister, Grace, and

Erwin Four. One day, God willing, they'll pass this down to their kids."

"They're lucky to have such a beautiful heirloom," I say. "This one deserves its own shelf. A middle one. With maybe a spotlight shining on it."

"See? I knew I had the right person for the job." A muffled melody sounds from somewhere deep in his pocket, and he hands me the Bible. "That's my wife. Excuse me a minute, will you?"

He ducks into the hallway, and I carry the book to his desk, setting it gingerly next to his computer. I'm not entirely sure I believe in God, but maybe I believe in a greater power, in some sort of order to the chaos. That there might be a reason why the Reverend brought me up here, to a room armed with a computer and no one to look over my shoulder. Maybe this is the universe laying out the pieces I need to survive, fate pointing me the way.

All day long, I've been smuggling snippets of time in the bathroom, scrolling through news on the tiny screen of my phone, fretting about how the searches are eating up expensive data I can't afford. And now here I stand, next to a computer I know the password to. The sneakier part of my brain kicks into gear, and my whole body tingles.

Or then again, maybe this is a test. Maybe the Reverend suspects me of violating his trust, and this is a chance to prove to him I'm worthy.

The Reverend's voice is gone now, faded down the hall. I check my watch, think of Martina and Ayana downstairs, wiping germs off a million plastic toys. They'll be busy for another hour or more, but how long do I have before the Reverend wraps up his call? Seconds, maybe; minutes if I'm lucky.

I fall into his chair, and my insides thrum, my heart beating on overdrive. I tell myself I'm doing nothing wrong, that popping onto the internet is not a crime. The Reverend is a kind, accommodating man. If I'd asked him for a few minutes to check the news from home, I'm almost certain he would have said yes.

I jiggle the mouse, type in the Reverend's password, and the lock screen dissolves into a crisp image of the Church of Christ's Apostles taken from above by a helicopter, maybe, or a drone. At its tallest peak, a golden cross gleaming in a cloudless blue sky.

I listen for the sound of people in the hall—footsteps, the clattering of keyboards, voices calling out or talking into a phone. Someone sneezes, but otherwise it's quiet. Like everyone disappeared for lunch.

I pull up the internet and type in the words that have been playing all day in my head on repeat: *Sabine Hardison missing.*

I'm rewarded with thousands of hits, and I suppose I shouldn't be surprised. News travels fastest over the internet. If the story has bled across state lines, if it's spread far enough to become a national news item on a major television network, then of course there's plenty more online. CNN, Fox News, all the major networks have picked up on the story.

I scroll through the links, and a familiar title catches my eye. *Mandy in the Morning.* A taped episode promising dirt from Sabine's sister and a lover— as usual, Mandy doesn't mind speculating, and like the promos for her shows, the title on this one is complete clickbait. People in Pine Bluff love her, but I've never been a fan. I click instead on a link to the *Pine Bluff Commercial*, the local hometown newspaper. The article's title, Police Search for Clues in Case of Missing Pine Bluff Woman, swims on the page.

A wave of nausea pushes up from the deepest part of me, and I breathe slow and steady and wait for the sensation to pass.

I surf around a little more, casting panicked glances at the empty doorway. As far as I can tell, the news sites are all reporting the same meager facts: last seen on Wednesday, car abandoned and unharmed, no clues, zero evidence or leads. After a few more articles, I realize I'm getting nowhere, learning nothing new. I need to go straight to the source.

With shaking fingers, I type in the address for Facebook, and the Reverend's personal wall fills the screen. Inspirational Bible memes, pictures of food and vacation snapshots, an ad for an expensive pair of running shoes. I lean back in his chair, chewing at a thumbnail that reeks of bleach, chastising myself for prying into his private business. Maybe I should sign out of his profile, create a new, fake one for Beth, but I shove the idea aside as soon as I think of it. I don't know the Reverend's Facebook password, which means there's no way I could sign him back in. No, better to leave the computer just like I found it, and with no trace I've ever been here.

"I am so going to hell for this," I whisper.

On the Reverend's Facebook profile, I pull up the page for the Pine Bluff Police Department.

Pinned to the top, a call for information pertaining to Sabine's disappearance, another reference to the tip line. I scan the post, but it tells me nothing new. If the police have any evidence or leads, they're not revealing them here.

I scroll farther down the page, past staff announcements and PSAs for the dangers of texting while driving, then pause on a post at the bottom of the page. Another call for information about Sabine, alongside a photograph and four little words, bursting like a bomb across my brain.

Missing woman feared dead.

Movement sounds in the hall, footsteps and a door banging against a wall, and the Reverend's voice calls out. "Charlene, get Father Pete at Christ the King on the line for me, will you? I'll be at my desk."

Shit.

I fumble for the mouse and back frantically out of the site, closing down Explorer and returning to the desktop image of the church. The footsteps are moving closer, closer still, and I glance at the bookshelves, still full and unchanged, and realize I need a reasonable cover. I double click the icon for Microsoft Word, and underneath the desk, the computer churns and whirrs.

Shit.

I spring up from the chair, pluck a spray bottle and rag from the bucket, and give the desk a dousing, right as the Reverend walks in.

"You make any progress?" he says, glancing around at an office that is just as he left it. The bookshelves still stuffed with books. The printer still quiet. The answer, I'm thinking, is obvious.

I point at the screen with the bottle. "I think your computer's stuck. It's been trying to open Word since you left, and—oh, look, there it is. It's working now."

His smile bubbles up something unpleasant in my belly. "Good. But can I ask you to start on the shelves, so I can get behind my desk? I'm expecting a call any second now, and I need a file on my computer."

Just then, right on cue, his desk phone rings.

With one last flourish of the rag, I step away from the desk. "All yours."

He sinks into his chair and I move to the shelves, my heart banging in my chest like a war drum. I stare at the books and pretend to come up with a plan, trying not to eavesdrop on his conversation, something about a joint day of service at a downtown soup kitchen. I concentrate on the sound of his voice, the way it rises and falls when he talks, so I don't have to think about my guilt for betraying his trust.

"I've still got the notes from last year somewhere," he says as I'm emptying the first shelf, piling the books in neat but lopsided stacks across the floor. "I'll dig them up and send them to you. Just give me a minute."

Behind me, his fingers click across the keyboard, and that's when it occurs to me.

I didn't clear the browser history.

MARCUS

The Pine Bluff PD's computer forensics unit is crammed in the lower back end of the building, in a windowless room that could do double duty as a broom closet. Jade, the unit's sole employee, can barely move around the computers and monitors and the giant industrial-strength air conditioner shoved in one corner, blowing icy air over the overheated electronics. If Jade minds the cramped quarters or the frigid temps, she doesn't complain. This job is a million times better than prison, which is where she was headed after she hacked her way into a national security program run out of Little Rock.

I rap a knuckle on the door frame, and Jade swivels in her chair. "Move some shit around and have a seat," she says, gesturing to a chair piled three feet high, with files and unopened mail and a ratty pair of rain boots covered in mud. "I'm almost done here."

Jade's dishwater hair is shoved into a neat ponytail I've never seen her go without, her bangs hanging in frizzy chunks over glasses that were purchased last century. She's wearing her usual uniform, a holdover from the eighties—mom jeans, an oversize sweater and giant neon earrings made of plastic. If I stopped her on the street, I'd think she was a schoolteacher or maybe a librarian, until she said something. She has the mouth of a sailor and the speech patterns of someone half her age.

I dump the junk on the floor and pull the chair closer to the desk. Six monitors are stacked up the wall on the other side of Jade's head, and I try to make sense of what I'm seeing. Long lines of computer code crawling across the screens. Jade called me down here with promises of news of Jeffrey, but now that I'm here, I'm going to need a little additional help.

"What the hell is all this?"

"Magic," Jade says, tapping the enter key. Somewhere under her desk, a printer whirrs to life.

She spins around, and her lips, coated in an unflattering coral, widen into a smile. "Okay, so first of all, we totally lucked out that Jeffrey's cell phone account is with Verizon. Compared to all the others, they're a breeze to get into."

"Legally, I assume."

"Well, *duh*. Arkansas, remember? No warrant necessary, especially once the folks at Verizon heard Sabine's name. They didn't push back, not even a little bit."

There's a *but* coming. I wait.

"Before you get too jazzed, I want to warn you that geographic location isn't always one hundred percent accurate. Like, if we see your guy in a strip mall, for example, we won't know if he's in the coffee shop on one end or the dollar store on the other, or maybe even in the apartment complex next door."

I think about the scenario Jeffrey stitched together for the afternoon his wife disappeared. Lunch at an Italian restaurant in Little Rock, followed by an hour, maybe more of alone time on the river. I don't need Jade's pings to be exact, only close enough to verify he was where he said he was—or not, and I'm betting on not. Jeffrey doesn't strike me as the introspective type. A hundred bucks says he was somewhere else entirely.

"How close can you get?"

Jade shrugs. "Depends on the phone. Not all GPS chips are created equal, if you know what I mean. But even with an older model phone with a crappy chip, if your guy was, say, reading a book on a park bench by the river, we might get a ping that makes it look like he was standing knee-deep in the water, but at least we'd know he was where he said he was."

"Was he?"

She grins. "No, he was not."

That little shit. A familiar heat pulses in my chest, and my hands tighten into fists. This case might turn out to be a hell of a lot easier than I thought it would be.

"Are you familiar with microcells?" she asks, and I shake my head. "A microcell is a little box the cell phone companies install in order to augment service in busy places. Places like parking garages and shopping malls and office high-rises. Think of it like a mini cellular tower inside a building where you otherwise wouldn't have the best reception. Microcells record highly precise location data. As long as your phone is on, I can see where you are, down sometimes to a few feet."

"Are you saying what I think you are?"

"I don't know. Do you think I'm suggesting he was in a building with a microcell?" She gives me a saucy smile. "Because he was."

I want to reach across the desk, grab her by the ears and plant one on her. That two-hour hole in Jeffrey's day? History.

She whips a paper from the printer, slaps it to the desk and flips it around so I can see. A map of Little Rock, covered in time stamps. She taps a finger to one, smack in the middle of the airport.

"I started at twelve o'clock, right before his plane landed in Little Rock, and tracked him until 6:00 p.m., two hours after the neighbor said she spotted him pulling into his driveway in Pine Bluff. The time stamps on this map are every ten minutes, but if you need me to narrow the time gap, I can do that. It'll just take me a few minutes to print you a new one."

"Walk me through this one first, and then I'll decide." I scan the paper, taking in the time stamps. "Looks like he was at the airport until quarter to one."

"Correct—12:48 p.m., to be precise. He gets into a car, then heads west on 440 to 30 North. Just over the river, he takes exit 141B." She taps the spot with a short-clipped nail.

The next ping is a block away. I squint at the letters on the page. "What's on Olive Street?"

"Vinny's Little Italy. This isn't the microcell yet, by the way. These are all pings from a cell tower."

I nod, studying the map. So lunch at an Italian restaurant, at least, was true. "Vinny's must be a pretty special place, seeing as he went all the way across the river. That's what, twenty minutes out of the way?"

"Something like that, but it's a dive. A 76 on the latest health inspection, which is basically like putting your life into their hands. A one-way ticket to a twenty-four-hour puke fest. He was there until just before two."

"Don't tell me that's where he went next, clutching a toilet all that time."

"Possible." She locates the 2:00 p.m. dot on the map, then follows the pings south, back across the river then due west. At 2:10 p.m. he veers off another exit, heading north on University Avenue. Her finger stops at another cluster of time stamps, all within a square block.

"What's this?" I say, looking up. "Why are these dots so spread out?"

"Bigger building. That whole block is CHI St. Vincent, a hospital with a microcell. He walks through the doors at 2:23 and heads to the southwest corner of the building. This is where things get dicey. The hospital is ten stories, including the basement. I can see where he is, but not which floor. I had to do a bit of sleuthing."

"Again, legal sleuthing?"

She rolls her eyes. "Do you want to know where he was, or not?"

"Just tell me."

"I held the pings up against the building plans, and then used process of elimination. Four stories I could cross off right away—supply closets, bathrooms, the morgue. I crossed off the floors with patient rooms next. The rooms are too small, and the time stamps would've meant he was moving through the walls. It had to be a larger space, and there was only one floor that had one big enough, the second. Suite 203, specifically."

"Which is?"

"The urology unit. A Dr. Patrick R. Lee."

"And you know this for sure."

"One hundred percent." Jade pauses, and she chews her bottom lip. "But maybe don't tell anybody I said that. Maybe just take my word for it."

I puff a laugh. "You hacked into the cameras, didn't you?"

She doesn't respond, and I take her silence as a yes.

To tell the truth, I could give a shit how she got the information. The point is, Jeffrey has an alibi, and it's not food poisoning but a problem with his plumbing. So why lie? He had to know I'd track down the truth eventually. And didn't he stop to consider that every minute I've spent chasing him down the rabbit hole of this reading-by-the-river bullshit, I could have been out there looking for his wife?

"Have you checked his finances?" Jade says, blowing back a chunk of bang. "Could have used a hired gun."

"That's what I'm thinking. I'll take another look, but the accounts are mostly hers. Her salary is more than double his, and she's squirreled a lot of it away.

With her out of the picture, he'll be a very wealthy man. Even the house is in her name."

Jade raises an eyebrow. "Want me to keep digging? I could track his movements since Sabine went missing, see if there's anything out of the ordinary."

"There won't be. He's been careful, stuck close to home."

"What about his emails, texts, things like that?"

"I'm going to forget you even suggested it, since we don't have a warrant. Not yet anyway." I drum my fingers on the desk, considering my next move. "Actually, I do have something I'd like you to do, and that's keep a watch on the police department sites for me. The website, Facebook and Twitter pages, log-ins on the scanner and whatever else we've got out there. I want to know about any strange hits."

"Define *strange*."

"Clusters of IPs coming from somewhere outside of Pine Bluff, most likely a city in the South."

She gives me a skeptical look. "You think Sabine is on the run?"

"Maybe. Jeffrey said some things that made her seem like she might be unstable, and—"

"Oh, come on. You don't believe that bullshit story he fed to *Mandy in the Morning*, do you?"

"Not necessarily. But the sister confirmed Sabine has tried to leave before, and I have reason to believe she had some medical issues that may have been in play here, as well."

I don't mention that last little tip came from Jeffrey, and his carefully placed suggestion that Sabine might not have been pregnant. I found some old medical records on her laptop that indicate a string of failed pregnancies, along with correspondence with a local pharmacy about some prescriptions. All leads I'm still chasing down.

I push up out of the chair. "Just keep a watch on the sites, will you? Let me know if you see a bunch of hits coming from the same location. Call me the second you find something."

"You got it." Jade scribbles something on a sticky note, then turns back to the monitors. "Now, get out of here, will you? I got shit to do."

I slide the map from her desk and duck into the hall, my cell phone buzzing with a message from Charlie. I swipe and read the text, which is terse and to the point: Bingo. Charlie is a man of few words, but it's one I want to hear. I step into the stairwell and give him a call.

"I found a bank account," he says by way of hello. "Wells Fargo, opened a little over three weeks ago at a branch in Texarkana. Her first deposit was a thousand dollars, which it looks like she made in cash. Since then, no more money flowing in."

My throat clenches in excitement, followed by a surge of something a lot less pleasant. A thousand dollars is a hell of a lot of cash. An amount that doesn't just go missing overnight, not without raising some red flags. An amount she would have to have been squirreling away for months in order to not get noticed.

"And the withdrawals?" I say from between clenched teeth, because for fucking sure there are withdrawals.

"A five hundred withdrawal last week, followed by withdrawals of twenty or thirty bucks a pop, and they're all over the place. North Platte, Nebraska. Lexington, Kentucky. Amarillo, Texas. Boise, Phoenix, Charlotte, Pittsburgh, Colum—"

"She's trying to throw us off."

"Sure looks that way," Charlie confirms. "At this pace, she's got another three and a half weeks before the account runs dry. You want me to keep following the transactions?"

I drop my head and stare at the stairwell floor, grimy linoleum that looks like it hasn't been cleaned since the last century, and try not to scream. My pulse jumps, ticking away in my temples. Charlie can follow the transactions, but no way in hell it's her at the ATM machines. This is a ploy to throw me off, to send me scurrying down an opposite road, in an opposite direction.

Good thing I'm not that stupid.

"Keep an eye on the account," I tell Charlie, "but don't get excited until there's a deposit, and then I want eyes on that camera footage. In the meantime, focus on what else she's got up her sleeve. Because there's more coming, that's for damn sure. Call me when you find it."

"Roger that," he says, and the line goes dead.

I spend the rest of the day chasing leads.

From a search of the prescription drug database, which the Arkansas Department of Health tells me I don't need a warrant for as long as I have a case number and probable cause. From Sabine's doctors, her general practitioner and ob-gyn, neither of whom were as forthcoming. Both demanded a warrant before saying the first word. And from Dr. Lee, the urologist from Suite 203, where Jeffrey was pissing in a cup when fifty-one miles away, his wife walked out of a Super1 and disappeared. Dr. Lee wouldn't tell me anything, either.

Which leaves me with Jeffrey. I pull to a stop at the curb and take in the stone and cedar siding, the neatly manicured lawn, the decorative woodwork around the dormers on the upstairs windows. What is this place—four thousand square feet? Five? Even before Sabine went missing, it was more house than two people could ever need. Soon, this big fancy house and everything in it will be all his.

I ring the bell, and his pleasant expression clouds over when he sees it's me.

"Good thing the reporters have packed up and gone." I hike a thumb over my shoulder, in the general direction of the trampled grass at the edge of his lawn. "Pine Bluff Detective questions Jeffrey Hardison in broad daylight, news at nine."

"Talk to my attorney."

He moves to shut the door, but he doesn't get far. I put out a foot, stop it with my boot.

"Riddle me this," I say, leaning against the door frame with a shoulder. "Why would a guy give the detective investigating his wife's disappearance a bogus alibi, when he already *has* an alibi—a real one that's easily verified. I just can't figure it out. Not unless he has something to hide."

I catch a flash of *oh shit* pass over his face before

he blinks it away. "Are you always this cryptic, Detective?" he says, but his sarcasm falls a little flat. "This would go a lot faster if you just say what you came here to say."

"Dr. Lee." Jeffrey pales at the name, and I know I hit the bull's-eye. "I know you were at his office in Little Rock on the afternoon Sabine disappeared. How come? Got problems with the plumbing?"

A red flush rises up his face like a rash. "That's none of your goddamn business."

"I can get a warrant, you know. Take a little look-see at your medical chart."

"A warrant is the only way you're going to get your hands on my records. And unless you happen to have one in your back pocket for this address, I suggest you move your foot from my doorway and back the hell off my porch. In fact, get the hell off my property."

The *or else* hangs in the air between us like a bad smell. I inhale it long and slow, letting the silence stretch. The truth is, I don't care what his medical issue is, other than its ability to get him good and riled up. A cornered rat makes mistakes.

"There are lots of ways to skin a cat." I step back, planting my soles at the edge of the porch. "Just because you weren't there to wrap your hands around her neck doesn't mean you weren't the one to kill her. Who'd you pay? How much did you pay him to kill Sabine?"

His face is purple and shiny now, like an overripe plum. He slams the door in my face.

BETH

The work at Church of Christ's Apostles is hard, the hours long, mostly because this place is always bustling. A rolling program of worship services and holy get-togethers, Bible studies and prayer breakfasts and marital counseling and kidz clubs and child care and wee worship for kids two to three—*reel the little punks in before they know they're bait*, you would say.

And then there are all the people it takes to make this place run. The Reverend and his slew of church-lady assistants. His pastors and ministry staff. An army of volunteers. And everywhere these people go, they leave traces of themselves, fingerprints and shoe prints and keys that tumble from their pockets. We spend the day picking up and wiping away.

But in the short time I've been here, the faces have become familiar, their smiles as we pass in the hallways more relaxed and instant. The Reverend was right; I am one of them now.

The realization pushes a new worry up from the pile: that I will become too comfortable here. Or maybe that I already am. When I walked through the doors, I was so scared, so worn down from running that this place felt like something of a relief, a much-needed calm after the shitstorm.

But already the relentless peacefulness of this place is getting to me, lulling me into a sense of security I can't afford. Now that Sabine's story has crept across state lines, now that it's stretched from a tiny Arkansas town to Georgia and beyond, I know what it means.

It means you're closing in.

The fear comes on strong and out of nowhere, and I sit back on my heels and swallow. Take a deep breath. Tell my heart to settle. I can't afford to be lazy because you are stealthy and cunning. I won't see you coming until you're already here.

I drop my sponge in the bucket and whirl around, feeling ungrounded even though the carpet is grinding into my knees. Sleep has been hard to come by the last few nights, and my exhaustion is doing a number on my head—too much up there to sort through. I can't get a grip on any one solid thought.

There's nobody here. I'm alone. The Reverend's office is an oasis of quiet.

I spend all day up here now, ever since Oscar called to say he was staying in Florida and the Reverend gave me his job. Martina rolls her eyes whenever he brags about the brilliant job I did with his bookshelves, the way I grouped the books by subject, alphabetized them by author and created a checkout system that any idiot can monitor. She thinks there's something else going on, some other reason he's taken me under his wing, and I don't disagree. Maybe it was my tears that first day, or my internet search history on his computer. Maybe he feels protective and wants to keep me close, or maybe he's suspicious, I don't know. I study his face for clues when he thinks I'm not looking, but I can't find anything but kindness.

Martina accused me of abandoning her, and she's not wrong about that, either. Without me running interference between her and Ayana, the two in the same room are like a pressure cooker. The tiff I witnessed that first day only scratched the surface of the animosity between them, and eight hours of scrubbing the same floors each day has not improved the situation. I try to stay out of it, but Martina is like a middle schooler, badgering me to choose a side on the car rides to and from Morgan House.

"Yours," I told her just this morning behind the wheel of the Buick. "Of course I'm on your side."

And I am, mostly. Probably. Even though we haven't had any heart-to-hearts, she still feels like someone who has my back. The least I can do is return the favor.

So now I spend my days much like Oscar did, wiping down desks that are already spotless and shooting the shit with Charlene and the six other church ladies in the offices lining the hall. I haul drinks and snacks to staff meetings and the late afternoon huddle in the kitchen. I empty their trash cans and pick up the bits of paper that flutter from their pockets. The women are a chatty bunch, and in the dull patches of the day, when they're not blabbing into their phones or clacking away at their keyboards, their questions come like gunfire.

Where are you from? *Out west.*

Are you single? *Very.*

What brings you to Atlanta? *It seemed like a nice place to settle.*

I don't detect any agenda to their questions other than curiosity, but I always shift the conversation back to one of them. I'd much rather hear some long-winded discussion about a sister's money troubles or how to choose the right private school for the twin four-year-olds. I feign shock when they tell me that Atlanta's public schools are not godly places, nor are the people who let their children go there. I shake my head in dismay when they say the standardized test scores from the students who attend public school are barely high enough to squeak out an acceptance letter to DeVry. What I don't do is bring up Martina's half brother at Grady High, or tell them that even if he has the grades to get into private school, he probably couldn't afford it anyway.

But I'm not fooled by their friendly get-to-know-you inquiries and watercooler conversations. When lunchtime rolls around, they hook their bags over an arm and file out the door, arguing about whose turn it is to drive or whether they want salads or sandwiches, but not one of them ever thinks to ask me to join. There's still a hierarchy to this place, and I'm still the maid.

Or maybe they wonder if I'm not who I claim to be.

It's Thursday afternoon, and I'm standing in the doorway of the Reverend's office, looking for something to clean. I've scrubbed all the floorboards and organized his desk. Color-coded the file cabinets and polished all the picture frames. Unknotted every paper clip and thrown away every empty pen. How did Oscar do this job? Unlike him, I was not made to piddle the day away, scrubbing at spots that are already spotless. I need somebody to turn a briefcase upside down, or dump a full pot of coffee onto the Reverend's carpet. Until something falls or spills, there's nothing left to do.

A commotion comes from behind me, from somewhere down the hall. Hurried footsteps and voices talking all at once, frantic words tumbling over each other in urgency, in alarm. One word sticks to the air like glue: *money.*

I turn and collide into a cluster of church ladies, a knot of panicked women gathered around a pink-faced Charlene. I take in her wide, worried eyes, the two red spots that glow on the apples of her cheeks like a rash.

"Where's the Reverend?" she says, her voice breathy and taut. "I need to speak to the Reverend this instant."

"He had a meeting, but he should be back any minute. What's wrong? What happened?"

"It's gone!" she wails. "The collection money is *gone.*"

"Are you sure?" one of the church ladies says. "Maybe you just misplaced it."

"Well, of course I didn't misplace it." Charlene punches a fist into her bony hip. "It was there, in my top desk drawer, and now it's gone. Somebody took it. Somebody *stole* it."

The words fall into the hallway like a dirty bomb, and two things flash through my mind at once. First, that I've never seen the normally perfect Charlene like this, all wild hair and smeared lipstick, not even when two birds flew into the chapel and began dive-bombing the women's Bible study group. Charlene had calmly fetched a couple of oven mitts from the kitchen, plucked the birds out of the air and released them outside without ruffling a feather—theirs or hers.

And second, that I'm surprised it took this long. What kind of idiot keeps a wad of cash in their desk drawer? Even in a church, even surrounded by all these godly people, it was only a matter of time before somebody swiped it. There were thieves in the Bible, too.

The ladies gathered around Charlene clutch at their pearls. They may hold titles more impressive than Charlene's—head of youth programming, volunteer coordinator, manager of a whole squad of counselors—but Charlene runs this place. When she says the money was stolen from her desk drawer, the money was stolen.

"Maybe whoever took it… I don't know, moved it to a safer location." *Like a bank*, I think but don't say.

Behind them, at the other end of the hall, the Reverend steps through the double doors. He's wearing a suit today, and a paisley tie so tightly knotted I wonder how he can breathe. He waves at me, cordial and cheerful as ever, and I hate what this is going to do to him.

"My desk drawer is perfectly safe," Charlene says to me. Her back is to the Reverend, so she hasn't seen him yet, doesn't know he's sped up at the cluster of church ladies. "It's locked, and only two people have a key—me and the Reverend."

"What about me?" he says, and the church ladies suck in a breath. Any other day, any other situation, I would laugh at how their eyes go wide, how they pivot to him as one. He takes in their expressions, and his friendly grin disappears. "Good gracious, what's wrong?"

Charlene fills him in on the missing money. The more agitated she becomes, the more the Reverend remains calm. He cups his chin in a hand and listens.

"How much are we talking about?" he says when she's done.

Charlene turns a pale shade of green, grimacing like she might throw up. "Somewhere around two thousand dollars. A little more."

The Reverend takes it like a champ, barely even wincing. "Okay. Well, that's…that's a lot of money, isn't it? When is the last time you saw it?"

Charlene presses a finger to her lips and thinks for a moment. "Well, I added Monday night's collection money to the bag this morning, along with the two twenties you borrowed from petty cash. The bag was still in there, closed and zipped, when I checked after lunch, but I didn't look inside. I just assumed… But just now, when I went to get it ready for the bank deposit, it was all gone. The bag was empty."

"So if I'm understanding you correctly," the Reverend says, "the last time you know for sure the money was still there was this morning. Is that right?"

"Well...yes. When I added in the twenties."

"And you're sure you locked the drawer afterward?"

"I *always* lock the drawer. It's as much a habit as brushing my teeth in the morning. I don't even think about it, I just do it. There's no way I would have forgotten." Charlene's answer is immediate, but her tone doesn't sound all that certain.

The Reverend turns to me. "Is Charlene's key still in my desk drawer?"

"I..." I glance at Charlene, who's crying for real now, and shrug. "There are a lot of keys in your desk drawer. Which one is it?"

"The blue one, on a ring with a plastic running shoe and a pompom. Nike, I believe."

"Then yes. I was at your desk just this morning. I saw it."

Charlene flashes me a frown. "What now?" she says to the Reverend. "Shouldn't we call the police?"

At the last word, my heart stutters, and the skin of my face goes hot. If the Reverend says yes, I will be in my car before he can even pick up the phone. The instant his chin even dips in the direction of a nod, I'm out the door.

What, you thought leaving me would be easy? Your voice whispers in my ear. *You're not just running from me. You're running from the police now, too. How far do you think you'll get now that every-*

one is hunting for you? Who do you think will find you first—them or me?

As much as I hate to admit it, you're right. If I run now, if anybody here decides I'm worth chasing down, one problem turns into two, and this becomes a whole different paradigm. And what about the money belt strapped to my waist? What would they think if they found it? What would the Reverend think? I wait for his response, and a trickle of sweat runs down my back.

"'People do not despise a thief if he steals to satisfy his hunger when he is starving.' Proverbs 6:30. Let us assume that whoever took that money has a hungry soul."

Charlene nods, then frowns. "You're just going to let them keep it?"

"Not exactly. What I'd like to do is for you to stay away from your desk for the next day or two, and to leave the top drawer open. That'll give the thief time to rethink his or her actions and opportunity to return the money where they found it. If the money is back in the envelope by close of business tomorrow, we'll forget this ever happened."

"But what if it's not?" Charlene says, the question on everybody's tongue. "What if they don't put back the money?"

The Reverend looks around at the people gathered in the hall, his gaze pausing on each woman's eyes. When he gets to mine, my heart explodes. "Let's just pray that they do."

MARCUS

Dr. Trevor McAdams lives in one of those houses on Country Club Lane that's trying too hard. Four sides of brick crawling with ivy. Sprawling rooms topped with slate roof tiles. A view of the golf course, where men in prissy shorts whack balls and slap each other on the shoulder as they discuss where to outsource Pine Bluff's jobs next—Mexico or Asia. At least they'll never be able to outsource mine. The more this city gets steered into the gutter, the more bad guys there are for me to catch.

Not that Trevor McAdams is a bad guy. As far as I can tell, he's only a heartsick puppy mooning over his missing lover. If those tears are an act, then give the man a golden statue.

I ring the doorbell, one of those sleek high-tech devices with a camera picking up every pore on my skin. Inside, a dog goes ballistic.

Along with Sabine's sister, Trevor has grabbed hold of the search for Sabine like a single-minded pit bull, transforming the story into a prime-time media shit show. It's got all the right ingredients for tabloid fare: a local heroine who's young, attractive and mon-eyed; a handsome lover pitted against a brooding and unpopular husband; enough mystery to fuel a Twitter following of amateur detectives, all of them chatty and opinionated, filling his social media feeds with a million unanswered questions. The bloodsucking, schadenfreude-loving people of America are capti-vated.

But I don't like it, and neither does my boss. The Chief thinks the constant media attention is fucking with the investigation, and I don't disagree. Before Sabine went missing, the Pine Bluff police force was already overworked and understaffed. Her case is not the only thing on my plate. I've got better things to do than pander to the press.

The door opens, and there he is, our story's hero, though standing here in rumpled scrubs and bare feet, he doesn't look the part. He looks dingy, like he hasn't slept in days. Hasn't showered, either. His face is pale and thick with scruff, and his hair is flat, stuck to his head in greasy clumps.

"Good morning, Detective. Please, come in." He gestures with his arm that's not holding the dog, a white, fluffy thing baring its fangs.

I step inside. "Thanks for seeing me. I know you're very busy."

He shuts the door, then puts the dog down, and it scurries off into a bright, modern kitchen over-looking the seventh green. Remainders of breakfast are spread across the granite countertops—a loaf of bread, a half-empty package of eggs, butter and two types of organic jam. The doctor pulls a couple of glasses from the cabinet and pours from a giant jug of orange juice. "Can I offer you something to drink?"

"No, thanks. This shouldn't take long."

"Please tell me you're here to share some news."

"I've got some news to share. But not the news you're hoping for, unfortunately."

"It's been eight days, Detective."

Like I don't know that. The doctor has only been phoning me daily, halting my work to hound me for information. *Have you put a trace on her phone? Have you dusted for prints? Have you questioned her clients, her colleagues?* What does he think, that I'm new at this? That I'm incompetent? Of course I've traced and dusted and questioned. This isn't the movies, and I'm not some dumb ass small-town cop.

He picks up the glasses and motions for me to follow.

We pause at the door to the den, a room along the back of the house with a flat-screen as big as the wall. Two kids are parked on an overstuffed leather couch, a boy and a girl with the doctor's face, two miniature doll-eyed yuppies. He settles the drinks on the coffee table.

"Guys, I'm going to be out in the sunroom, talking to the detective. I need you both to stay here until we're done. Okay?"

The kids nod in unison. The boy returns his attention to the television screen, but the girl's gaze sticks to me, wandering down my frame, zeroing in on my holster. Her eyes go wide, and she sinks deeper into the cushions. Great. The doctor is one of *those* parents, teaching their kids to be scared, not respectful of guns.

We end up on a screened porch, where the sun beats down on the slate roof and turns the room into a furnace. The doctor digs through a giant clam filled with remotes until he finds the one he's looking for, then points it at the wicker fan above our heads. From out on the green comes an occasional *whop* of metal whacking a ball.

"Sorry about the heat, but this is the only room the kids can't sneak into and hear us. They're having a really tough time with this—the separation, I mean. I'm sure you've heard that their mother and I are divorcing. She wants to move them to Salt Lake City, where her parents live. Things are about to get ugly."

"I'm sorry to hear that." The fan stirs the air, sending down a breeze that feels like Emma's hair dryer after she's just come out of the shower, hot and humid. Already a steady line of sweat is dripping down my back. "Your daughter looks a lot like my niece, Annabelle. Well, like she used to look, before the chemo. Her hair grew back in red and curly."

He nods, sinking into the chair across from me. "It's called chemo curls. The color change isn't uncommon, either, though I don't think I've ever heard of it coming back red. But hair often picks up pigment as it grows back in so I suppose it's possible. Who's her doc?"

"Annie Capelouto."

"Annie's the best in town, but Pine Bluff isn't exactly the center of the medical universe, you know. If your niece ever needs anything, give me a call. I did my residency at Northwestern and still have some pull there. Chicago's not all that far."

And that right there is the problem with outsiders like Dr. McAdams, people who swoop into town with their money and their fancy degrees, acting like the people of Pine Bluff should be grateful they've come to this podunk town. I never asked for his help. Dr. Capelouto already saved Annabelle once; who's to say she can't do it again if the worst happens, and the cancer returns?

He swipes his palms down his thighs. "I'll move to Salt Lake City if I have to, but not yet. I can't leave this place. Not until you find Sabine." He makes a sound, somewhere between a cough and a sob.

I search for a fresh page in my notebook, giving him a moment to pull himself together.

"What about Jeffrey?" He spits the name, his voice hard and hateful.

"What about him?"

"Please tell me he's your lead suspect. He's violent and he's angry and he's got a two-hour gap in his day, at the exact time Sabine went missing. I *told* her to change the locks and take out a restraining order, but she wouldn't listen. She was scared of him—you know that, right?"

"We're looking into Mr. Hardison, but I'm afraid I can't discuss the details. What I'd really like to talk with you about is you and Sabine."

This is what I meant when I said he's a pit bull. It's like I didn't even speak. Excitement is piling up Trevor's words, and he barely pauses to take a breath.

"And it's just all too convenient Sabine disappears right before she can file for divorce. Now he's living in *her* house, spending *her* money. Have you checked his emails, searched the files on his computer? Have you looked into his internet history? I mean, I know it's cliché but maybe he forgot to clear out his cache. You read all the time about how some idiot gets caught because they used Google to help them figure out the best place to bury a…"

He swallows the last word, and his face crumples. "Is that what happened here? If it is, just tell me, Detective. For God's sake, put me out of my misery. Because I'm trying to be hopeful but people simply don't disappear into thin air and show up eight days later, alive and well. I mean, somebody must have seen something, right?"

"If that person exists, they haven't stepped forward."

A tear nosedives into the scruff on his cheek, and he drops his head in his hands, shoulders quaking. I should have known this would happen. It's the same stunt he pulls every time a reporter points a camera at his face, blubbering for all the world to see. If he's faking it, he's a natural, I'll give him that. Sabine's disappearance has made national news, mostly thanks to this guy's bawling.

"Did you know Sabine was on Lexapro?"

The doctor's head pops up, and his expression is almost comical. Bugged eyes, unhinged jaw. "Lexapro is an SSRI, a selective serotonin reuptake inhibitor. A very potent one. It's used to treat anxiety and depression. Since when? Who prescribed it?"

"I'm afraid I can't tell you the details. But according to the Prescription Drug Monitoring Program, she took it for years."

"Okay." Trevor says it without conviction, like he's bracing for what comes next. Like he suspects the prescription is not the only thing I'm about to drop on him. "But Sabine wasn't depressed. I would have known. And I was with her a lot of the time. I never saw her taking any pills."

"She went off it last year..." I flip back a page or two in my notes. "In February. She was pregnant, and she was worried it would hurt the baby."

The doctor nods. "It's a valid worry. SSRIs have been associated with increased risk for persistent pulmonary hypertension of the newborn. Her doctor would have helped wean her off it, and probably would have switched her to some kind of bupropion like Wellbutrin."

"That might be so, but she didn't run it by her doctor. The pharmacy filled it, then reached out to her when she didn't pick it up." This part, at least, is true, at least according to the email correspondence I found on her laptop. The pharmacist warned her about going off it too quickly.

But the doctor in him picks up on my point, and his eyebrows shoot up. "Please don't tell me she quit cold turkey."

"She quit cold turkey."

Initially, when I'd gleaned this from the emails on Sabine's laptop, I didn't understand the implications, but the doctor does. He jumps up from the chair with a curse, pacing the length of the room. "And nobody told her what to expect? Nobody told her to, I don't know, maybe check WebMD before deciding to go off her meds? She could have died!"

I don't respond. There's a reason the FDA requires warning labels on drugs like Lexapro, because of too many links between the pills and people like Sabine slitting their wrists in a bathtub.

But again, the doctor knows this.

He stops pacing, turning to me with a frown. "Why are you telling me this? What does this have to do with whatever happened to Sabine?"

"I don't know yet. Maybe nothing. Maybe everything."

"It sounds to me like you're blaming the victim. Trying to make it seem like she was unhinged. Unstable."

"I'm just trying to get a clear and complete picture of Sabine."

"Does this have something to do with the bullshit Jeffrey was spouting off to *Mandy in the Morning*? Because Ingrid told me what happened back then. Sabine was leaving him, but she wasn't running away. Ingrid knew where she was the whole time."

"Yes, she told me the same." Twice, actually. First in a voice mail after Mandy's show, then again when she stopped by the station.

The doctor's eyes go squinty. "Why do you say it like that?"

"Like what?"

"Like you don't believe her. Like you think Sabine might have been a little unstable."

"We just determined that she was on Lexapro."

I might as well have slugged him in the gut. His

shoulders hunch, and he falls back into his chair. "So she was going through a rough time. She lost her baby, got some shitty medical advice—or maybe none at all. But that was a long time ago, and the Sabine I know is not depressed. She doesn't have mood swings. Her energy is normal, and so are her sleep patterns. The only symptom I've seen started a couple weeks ago." His eyes tear up all over again, and I know he's referring to her pregnancy.

"I'm glad you brought that up, because—"

"But the nausea never lasts long. She vomits, and then ten minutes later she's digging through the pantry for food. Not like when—" He stops himself, grimacing, and I know he was about to compare his lover's pregnancy to his wife's. "The point is, Sabine's appetite is fine."

"You know for certain that Sabine is pregnant." I don't phrase it as a question, even though it is one. The same one I asked her general practitioner and the ob-gyn who'd handled her last pregnancy. Both refused to give me an answer.

The doctor looks properly insulted. "What? Of course Sabine is pregnant."

"Did you conduct the pregnancy test yourself?"

"She peed on a stick. Those tests are ninety-nine percent accurate, you know."

"Did you see with your own eyes that the stick read positive?"

"What are you implying here?" He's getting riled up. His voice rises and his muscles tense, coiled for attack. "That Sabine lied? That she wasn't pregnant?"

I keep my own voice low and even. "I'm not implying anything. I'm just trying to dig up the truth."

"By implying she wasn't pregnant."

"According to her husband, Sabine had trouble both getting pregnant and staying that way. Over the course of their nine-year marriage, she lost some seven pregnancies, and that's only after going through multiple rounds of IVF."

"Maybe the problem was with him, with *his* sperm."

"Or maybe she's had enough false starts to know how this pregnancy will end. If she's pregnant, chances are high that she'll miscarry, and if the past is any indication, somewhere between ten and fourteen weeks."

"*If* she's pregnant? Why would she lie about something like that?"

"That's what I'm trying to figure out."

He leans forward, elbows on his knees. "Let me get this straight. You don't want to ask me about my relationship with Sabine, when it started or what our plans are or to talk about any one of the million messages Sabine and I exchanged over these past five months. Instead you want to put doubts in my head as to her sanity and fertility. It's almost like you're trying to make me think that the woman I know and love is someone else entirely."

"All I'm doing is trying to fill in some blanks. In order to find a person, I need to know who she was."

He pales, his cheeks draining of blood. "Was?"

"Is," I say with all the conviction I can muster. It's a blunder I won't make again. "I am working under the assumption that Sabine is still alive, but in order to find her, I need a complete picture."

"You want a complete picture? Well, then, here it is. Sabine Hardison is a kind, loving, funny, honest, loyal, caring woman, and I love her with everything inside of me. No, she didn't tell me about the Lexapro or the miscarriages, but that doesn't make her a liar. It makes her a human with a past."

"Okay then. Let's talk about your wife."

His spine straightens. "Shelley? What about her?"

"I understand she's in Chicago. Since when?"

"Since last We—" He stops himself, shakes his head. Grows an inch in his chair. He was about to say Wednesday, the day Sabine disappeared. "No. She wouldn't. She *couldn't*. Shelley may be hurt and angry, but she's not a monster. She is the mother of my children. No way."

"Still. I'd love to talk to her in person, hear her say those words to me herself. When is she back?"

"I don't know."

"I've been leaving messages on her cell. Maybe you could give her a little nudge, ask her to call me back."

He blasts me with a cold, sharp stare. "Look elsewhere, Detective. My wife has been through enough."

My wife. I let the words linger in the steamy air long enough that the doctor looks sheepish. He's the possessive type, another strike against him.

And if he thinks I'm going to overlook his wife just because he wants me to, he's crazy.

The door behind him opens, and a gust of cooler air sweeps across my sweaty skin. Not enough, but still, a relief, and for both of us. The doctor looks beyond grateful for the interruption.

"Daddy, I'm hungry," his daughter says, but she's looking at me.

He stands and moves to the door, reaching for his daughter's hand, but his gaze never leaves mine. "Detective, what are you currently doing to find Sabine? What steps are you taking? What leads are you exploring?"

"I'm sorry, sir, but I—"

"Can't discuss the details. I know. Fine." He picks up his daughter, hoisting her onto a hip in one smooth move. "How about instead of sitting here, wasting my time with this baloney line of questioning, you get out there and find Sabine?"

He stops there, but his words, his tone—they both carry the unmistakable weight of a threat. "I hope you're not implying what I think you are. Did you just threaten an officer of the law?"

"Do your job, Detective. Do your job, or else I will find someone who will."

BETH

For the rest of the day, all anyone can talk about is the missing money. Where it is. When it went missing. Whether or not it's going to magically reappear in Charlene's desk drawer before the deadline tomorrow. But mostly, which one of us took it.

It doesn't take a genius to know I am the main suspect. Sure, people float in and out of the executive offices during the day, but I'm the only one besides the church ladies who's here all day long, from 8:00 a.m. until closing time, and the only one besides the Reverend with access to the keys in his drawer. They all look at me differently now. Their formerly friendly smiles have turned pinched around the edges, and they've closed ranks, stopped being so nice. They wouldn't put it past me.

Everybody steers clear of Charlene's desk, presumably to give the thief (me) opportunity to repent her (my) sins and return the money to the bag, but they haven't thought their strategy through. All afternoon, they linger in the offices lining the hall, pretending to discuss church business while one of them keeps an eagle eye on the reception area. Any time anybody comes within a twenty-foot radius of Charlene's desk drawer, they drop the pretense and come running. It's probably the most excitement this place has seen in ages, maybe ever.

The news has spread through the church like a deadly virus, infecting the staff with a *Hunger Games* kind of fear, the sinking knowledge that one person will take us all down. I know because Martina has been texting me all afternoon, saying that things downstairs have turned ugly. The rest of the cleaning staff is pointing fingers, and their fingers all seem to be pointing to me.

They're convinced that you took it. Well, everybody but Ayana, but she's never been the brightest votive in the chapel. They want me to tell you to put it back before you get us all fired.

I try not to be hurt by their easy assumption of my guilt. I tell myself the only opinion I care about is Martina's. The others don't know me, don't know my situation or my thoughts, but the accusation still stings.

And you? I type back. What do you think?

Her answer lights up my screen.

IDK I'm still trying to decide.

A thunk comes from the double doors, and a foot kicks one of them open. The Reverend shoulders his way through carrying a cardboard box half his size, concealing his upper body, his face, all but the tips of his hair. But I know it's him from the shoes, the well-loved sneakers he changed into earlier, under his navy suit pants. I slip my phone in my back pocket and rush to hold the door.

"Oh, thank you, Beth," he says, flashing me a smile around the side of the box. "That's very kind of you."

If the Reverend suspects me of anything—of whatever he saw or didn't see in his computer's history files, of swiping the cash from Charlene's drawer, of not being who I claim to be—I can't detect it in the way he looks at me. It's the same way he looks at the men and women who stand before his altar when he pats their shoulders or folds his hands in prayer. Like I am a sheep to be saved.

Which will make it all the more awkward when I sneak out the back door tomorrow afternoon, right before he makes good on his promise to call the cops. Jorge's good, but he's not that good. One look at my license, and the cops will slap on the cuffs.

But the Reverend is not stupid. He'll know the reason for my vanishing act, just like how everybody else in this place will be making their own assumptions.

Guilty.

And then what? I've heard those sermons the Reverend practices in his office, the ones about uncertainty and grace and turning the other cheek. Will he do the same with me? Will he let me go, or will he dispatch the police to the address on file, the one I listed on my application—stupid, *stupid* mistake—

the one for Morgan House. And next week is payday. I picture my paycheck languishing in the bottom of Charlene's drawer like catnip. A whole week's worth of salary, down the drain. I need that money, every cent.

"Come with me, will you?" the Reverend asks. "I'm putting together welcome bags for the newcomers, and I could use some help."

I follow him down the hall into his office, where he settles the cardboard box on the conference table. Printed papers and shiny, colorful brochures are spread across the table in neat stacks. He points them out one by one. "Pastor's letter, church brochure, invitation cards to various clubs and groups, a Bible booklet and a feedback form. What I need you to do is clip them together and drop them into an envelope." He pulls a pile of envelopes from the box and hands them to me.

I smile. "Sounds simple enough."

"Once you're done, the packets go into one of these." He drags a white canvas bag from the box and shakes it out for me to see. The logo is a variation of the one on my T-shirt, a sketch of the church skyline with God Lives Here underneath. "Every tote also gets a coffee mug, personalized pen and refrigerator magnet, all of which are in the box. If you run out of anything or need help, just give one of the office ladies a holler. I have to dash to visit a sick parishioner on the other side of town."

While the Reverend gathers up his things, I sink onto a chair and get started. Pile, fold, clip, stuff. The work is slow and monotonous, but it beats scrubbing floors, and at least I can do it sitting down. I think of Martina and Ayana downstairs, sterilizing toys and bonding over their shared distrust of me, and I wince. I'd hate me, too, if I were them.

"See you tomorrow," the Reverend says.

I look up, and he's standing at the door, his suit coat folded over an arm, his leather wingtips dangling from his fingers. He smiles, and it's all I can do to return it.

"See you tomorrow."

I'm working my way through the piles when Martina sneaks into the Reverend's conference room without making a sound. I look up and there she is, watching me from the doorway. I smile, but she doesn't return the greeting.

I ignore the snub, working with the papers in my hand, fastening them with a paper clip. "Don't tell me. They sent you up here to talk to me, didn't they?" I picture the cleaning crew cornering her in the break room, demanding she march up here and… Do what? Confront me? Pat me down? I keep my eyes on the papers and Martina in my peripheral vision.

She shuts the door behind her. "Can you blame them? They have pretty much all done business with a guy like Jorge, if you know what I mean. They're nervous as hell, just like I am. Just like you should be."

I look up at her with a frown. "Who says I'm not? And if you came up here to lecture or accuse me, you can go ahead and leave now. The church ladies have been giving me the side-eye all afternoon, and I already feel shitty enough."

"This isn't some kind of game, Beth. I got you this job. I vouched for you. If the Reverend finds the two thousand dollars in that thing strapped to your waist, what do you think is going to happen to me?"

"So you think I took it, too. Great." I lift both hands, let them fall to the table with a smack.

"The church ladies had Bible study this morning."

"So?"

"So the offices would have been empty. You would have had an opportunity. And we both know how you like to hoard money." Her eyes stray to my waistline. "How much is in there anyway?"

I push to a stand, make myself loose at the knees. One wrong move, and I'll mow her down on my way to the door. "None of your business, that's how much. And what about you and Ayana? Y'all were up here, too, bickering about which one of you was the bigger thief. I saw both of you go by Charlene's desk more than once."

"Yeah, but we don't have access to the Reverend's keys." She pauses, and I brace for what I know is coming next: "You do."

I shake my head to hide that I'm squirming inside. "I'm not going to stand here and defend myself when I haven't done anything wrong. Especially when it sure looks like you're the one who took Ayana's money. Well, did you?"

Martina squints. "I already told you. I'm not a thief."

"Then who took it?"

She tosses up her hands. "Who the hell knows? There were always a million people going in and out of her apartment. And her hiding place wasn't exactly subtle. If I found it, others would have, too."

I reach for a stack of envelopes and think about Martina's answer. Her tone is sincere, but that still doesn't explain why she was searching behind Ayana's toilet. Who goes looking for money they're not planning to steal?

Martina sighs and slumps against the wall, looking around. "What is it you do up here all day, anyway?"

"Die of boredom, mostly."

"Why does the Reverend want you up here? What made him ask you?"

"I don't know. The bookshelves, I guess. And you know how the Reverend is. He likes to take care of people." I think of my sudden tears that first day, the way he told me I was safe here. In the days since, he's certainly made good on that promise.

"He's never taken care of me like that."

A question lingers in the air between us, but I don't touch it. Martina wants to know what makes me special, and to answer is to acknowledge she's right. The Reverend has singled me out, and for reasons I don't understand and would rather not think about. *Why me? Why not her?*

She pushes off the wall, stalking straight at me. Automatically, my hands move to the belt at my waist. My palms spread out, my fingers curling around the edges.

"Tell me you didn't take the money, Beth. Look me in the eye and tell me it wasn't you."

"I can't believe you're even asking me that."

"Say it."

Panic flutters like a swarm of bats in my chest, but I park my expression in neutral. "I'll tell you, if you tell me who Rosa and Stefan are."

The names—the ones written in complicated, curly script on the silver discs hanging from her neck. Her face pales at the accidental bull's-eye. My heart kicks, then stops completely, as does my breathing. If she looks me in the eyes and answers me honestly— if she trusts me enough to tell me this truth—then I will do the same with her. I will sit her down and tell her mine, the whole sad, sordid story.

She leans in so close that her features go out of focus. "Put it back, Beth. You're not the only one who's going to pay if you don't. Put the money back."

MARCUS

There are a few dozen authorized cell phone retailers in Pine Bluff proper, wireless franchises like AT&T and Sprint, along with a couple of big-box stores like Walmart. Places lawful people go when they're shopping for a cell phone, the kind that have customer service departments and surveillance cameras.

And then there are the unauthorized outlets, repair shops and minimarts where cell phones are bought and sold on the sly. I start there, on the north side of town and work my way south.

And every time, it goes a little something like this:

Me, flashing badge: *Detective Marcus Durand, Pine Bluff PD. I'm looking for a female, early thirties, brown hair and eyes, five-eight, slim build.*

Store manager: *I'd love to help you, Detective, but that's half the women who come in this place.*

Me, holding up a photograph: *I'm thinking you'd remember this one.*

Manager, whistling: *She's pretty, all right.*

Me: *She would have purchased multiple prepaid*

cell phones, and she would have paid in cash. The transaction would have been in the past month or so.

Manager: *Sorry, Detective, we have dozens/fifty/ hundreds of transactions a day. It's impossible for me to remember every one.*

Me, slapping down a fifty: *How about you check your computer? If her transaction is in there, it won't take you that long to find it. It would have been bigger than usual, and all cash.*

Him, pocketing the fifty and slinking off to the back.

Sometimes it takes him a couple of minutes to search, sometimes longer. But every time, when he returns from whatever back office he disappeared into, he's shaking his head, and every time, I leave the store empty-handed.

Except for this time.

This time, the manager walks out, grinning like a fool. "May 24 at 10:24 a.m. She bought four. Two new LG K8s, and two refurbished Motorolas. Total, including tax and minutes, was $407.73."

I breathe through the white-hot rage, waiting for the flames to cool, but the anger doesn't subside. Four hundred dollars is a lot of money to have spent in a place like this one, a total dump. The kind of store that has a gun under the register and bars on the windows to tamp down on the drive-bys. The kind that trades stolen goods for stolen cash.

"I'm going to need the numbers," I say through clenched lips. My jaw is like a boulder, bearing down on my molars hard enough to crack them in two.

The manager frowns, his face scrunching into a

heinous mess. "I just gave you the numbers." He looks at the paper in his hand, where he'd scribbled the basics in messy blue pen. "Here—$407.73."

"The *phone* numbers." My hands curl into fists, my muscles vibrating with the force of holding them still. I want to punch this idiot in his ugly face for fucking with me.

Especially when he drops his hands in his pockets and leans back on his heels, squinting in a way that doesn't look the least bit thoughtful. "I'd love to help you, Detective. Really I would. But I can't be handing out a private citizen's telephone number to just anybody."

"How about to an officer of the law? Can you hand it out to him?"

He shrugs. "With proper motivation, I can."

In other words, another fifty.

"You really want to go down this route? Because I can arrest you for soliciting a bribe, or I can go get a warrant not for just one transaction, but for *all* of them. Which one would you prefer?"

His smug expression disappears. "I'll be right back with those numbers."

"That's what I thought."

I drum my fingers on the counter and fume while at the end of an aisle, a teenager slips a pair of Bluetooth earphones into his pocket. As shoplifters go, he's not very good. Too obvious, and way too oblivious that a cop is standing twenty feet away at the counter. But he's fast, I'll give him that, in and out the door in thirty seconds flat.

My phone buzzes against my hip, and I'm checking the screen when the manager returns from the back office. It's Ma, and I push her to voice mail. With a grunt, the manager shoves two sheets of paper my way, still warm from the copy machine. I smile at what I find there: four receipts, each with a cell phone number. By now she'll have burned through two, maybe three of them, but if I'm lucky, one of them will still be trackable. I only need one to lead me to her.

I spread the papers on the counter and take a picture of each. I'm attaching them to an email when my mother calls again. She's not going to like it when I push her to voice mail for a second time, but I'll call her back as soon as I send the images to Jade to start tracking. I hit Send, then gather up the papers, carry them to my car and pull up my mother's number on the screen.

She picks up on the first ring, and she's pissed. "Marcus, what the hell is going on here?"

I stifle a sigh. Tough to feel self-righteous when you're getting scolded by your mother. "What's going on is I'm in the middle of a missing-person case. I'm a little busy."

I fall into the car, where it's easily a hundred degrees, even though I parked in the shade. I crank the engine and aim the vents at my face.

"I realize that," she says, "but—"

I lose her when the call flips to the hands-free system, a two-or three-second spot of dead silence.

"Ma. You still there?"

"What? I'm here. I've been here all along."

"What were you saying?"

She sighs, an annoyed sound. "I was talking about your house."

"What about it?"

"Why does it look like a hobo lives here?"

My skin ices over despite the heat. She's at the house. I shove the gear in Reverse and punch the gas, lurching backward into the lot. "Where are you exactly?"

"I just told you. I'm at your house."

"*Where* at the house? Where are your feet right now?" I work the gearshift into Drive. "Be specific."

"Specifically, my feet are parked on your living room carpet, though I can barely see the thing for all the papers. When's the last time you picked up?"

I floor the gas, and whatever my mother says next gets lost in the squeal of my tires, peeling across the pavement. At the end of the lot I take a hard right, pulling into traffic to a chorus of beeps and tire screeches. Just in case, I lay on the horn.

Her voice crackles over the squad car speakers. "And Marcus. Where's Emma?"

Mistake number one: giving my mother a house key, though for the record, that was all Emma's doing. But what was I going to do when I found out, ask for the key back? Ma would've had a fit, and I would've had to hear it every holiday and birthday for the rest of my life. I let her keep the key, but if I had any sense at all, I would have changed the locks.

Mistake number two: leaving the house in such a state—though again, it couldn't be helped. Police work is messy at times, and I'm a visual kind of guy.

I like to spread my files across tables and floors, tape notes and pictures to the walls. I picture my mother walking through the kitchen and living room, piecing everything together and shaking her head, and I lean on my horn.

"Move it!" I scream at the driver in front of me, flashing my lights, and he flips me off over his shoulder. I swerve onto the shoulder, slam the gas and fly past.

Thirteen eternal minutes later, I screech into my driveway, coming to a hard stop behind my mother's white Honda. The front door pops open, and she comes out slinging—her arms, her words, that expression she always used on me when I was a kid, the one that still to this day can give me phantom pains of an almost-constant childhood bellyache. Even now, all these years later, trying to please this woman is a full-time job. She's fussing at me before I've even clambered out.

"…looks like somebody tossed the place. Now I know you've been busy, but I didn't raise my son to live in a pigsty. Did a tornado blow through town and no one thought to tell me?"

I jog up the walkway, boots tearing up the concrete. "Ma, what are you doing here?"

She gives me an insulted frown. "What do you mean, what am I doing here? I made another batch of chicken soup for Emma. That's what people do when one of their loved ones is sick. They bring them chicken soup."

"That key was for emergencies only."

She points a finger over her shoulder. "Have you

seen your house? This *is* an emergency. And I'll have you know I rang the bell for at least fifteen minutes, just ask that nosy Ms. Delaney next door. I went around the side and saw Emma's car in the garage. I thought something happened to her. I thought maybe she'd fainted, or fell down the stairs." She pauses to take me in, shaking her head. "You look awful. When's the last time you've eaten?"

For Ma, every bad or busy day, every sickness or heartache or worry—it all boils down to food. What kind, and when you'd last had some, and if it was prepared with loving care and the correct amount of salt. I don't dare tell her the truth—that for the past three days I've been living off the leftovers from Annabelle's birthday dinner: standing over the counter, shoveling cold bites straight from the container, barely tasting any of it. But only when I remember to eat, which isn't often.

Then again, if she's looked in my kitchen, which she most definitely has, she already knows. The dirty Tupperware is piled high, smelling up the sink.

"I just came from Leon's," I lie, knowing the restaurant name will make her back off from this portion of the argument, at least. Leon's is known for their fried catfish, fried shrimp, fried everything, the kind of fare that'll keep you full for days. "Look, I appreciate you coming all the way over here, but—"

"Marcus Robert Durand, you tell me what's going on right this second." She stabs a fist into her hip and scowls. "Where is Emma? I thought she was sick. Why isn't she here?"

Mistake number three: I should have had a story

ready, a believable excuse I could pull from my sleeve without stumbling over my words. Both of us know Emma would have called to thank Ma for the chicken soup. She would have texted or sent a note. My mother coming over here now isn't about seeing to the health of her favorite daughter-in-law, or bringing her some more soup. It's about snagging the thank-you she should have gotten days ago.

I sigh, nudging my mother inside. "She didn't want you to know, okay? She didn't want anyone to know." I shut the door, leaning against the cool wood. Ma's right. This place is a pigsty, and it smells like a barnyard. "If I tell you where she is, you can't tell a soul. Not Camille, not Duke, not anybody."

Ma is already nodding, quick and manic like a bobblehead. "Of course, of course. My lips are sealed. You have my word."

I look my mother in the eye, and somehow manage to hold her gaze. "She's at a retreat."

She frowns. "What kind of retreat?"

"The kind that makes her better. Less…depressed." My mother squints, folding her arms across her chest, closing herself off. She always knew when I was lying as a kid, and she knows it now. I kick things up a notch. "The thing is…it's just… Em cries all the time, Ma. She… You know what? I don't want to get into the ugly details. What? Why are you looking at me like that?"

"Because this story makes no sense. If your wife is depressed, the last thing you do is send her away. You definitely don't send her off with a bunch of strangers.

You keep her here, under your own roof, and you fix things. Above all else, you hold your family together."

For my mother, there's no other option. Family is why her kids haven't moved more than five miles away, why she summons us to her house every Sunday and on birthdays and holidays, why we haul our asses over there without complaint. Camille and Duke might not remember how Ma practically killed herself providing for three kids on a minimum-wage, single-mother salary, but I do. I remember her constant exhaustion, the way her worries—about money, about what people were saying about our jailbird father, about how the gossip would affect me and Camille and Duke—filled my stomach with something sour and itchy. I remember the sound of her tears when she thought I wasn't listening, how they boiled inside me into a white-hot rage. When Dad died in prison, she lined us up along the grave site and ordered me to look sad, even though I detested the man, even though I'm pretty sure by then she detested him herself. "He's your father," Ma said, smacking me on the back of the head. *Family.*

"I *am* holding us together," I tell her now. "Or at least, I'm trying to. But I can't do that when I'm standing here, arguing with you."

"Does this 'retreat'—" she uses air quotes and pursed lips to let me know what she thinks of the word "—have anything to do with what happened at Easter?"

I wince, wishing to all hell that she hadn't brought it up. I don't know how else to explain that it was nothing, the product of too many of us crammed into her tiny kitchen. I tossed Emma a pack of napkins, but all she saw was something coming at her head. She let out a scream so bloodcurdling, it froze everybody's shoes to the linoleum.

We all tried really hard to laugh it off, especially Emma, but I saw the way Ma looked at us after that. Like she was worried.

Like she's looking at me now.

"Ma, I told you, that was nothing. Em just… thought she saw something that wasn't there. That's all."

She watches me carefully, her expression hard. "And what were all those papers on the kitchen table?"

"Work. I'm in the middle of a missing-person investigation, remember? I've been working 24-7."

"What do hundreds of Emma's emails have to do with the search for Sabine Hardison?"

Her question tightens around my chest, pushing into my lungs and expanding, sucking up all the air. I need to get Ma out of here. I need her to leave. The last thing I need is for my mother to be butting into my case.

"Maybe nothing, but maybe everything. Sabine showed us a house last year, and she sent Emma a list of people to work with. Inspectors, lenders, things like that. I need to find that list, and I need to talk to those people. They might know something about Sabine."

"Why don't you ask Emma where the list is?"

"Because I'm not allowed to talk to her. The doctors won't let me. Not until she's done with the whole program."

"And when will that be?"

"I don't know yet."

Ma doesn't say anything for a really long time. She looks at me, and I look at her, and the longer this staredown drags on, the more my skin turns cold and clammy. Emma has a good life. She lives in a nice house, drives a nice car, goes to nice restaurants and parties, all things I provide for her. It's more than my deadbeat father ever did for Ma and us kids, and yet there's a hurricane whipping up in my gut at the look on Ma's face. I turned thirty-six last month, and my mother can still do this to me.

"I'll take care of it, Ma. I swear to God. I'm taking care of it."

She presses her palms to either side of my face and shakes her head. "You go. Clean up this mess you made. I'll clean up the one here."

BETH

"Hey."

I jump at the man's voice, and the papers slip from the stack between my fingers, hitting the table and scattering. First Martina, now Erwin Four. It's like visiting hour in here, a revolving door of people coming and going. He stands in the same spot his father did less than an hour ago, looking like he just came from the mall, or maybe a visit with his tailor. The creases in his shirt are knife-sharp, his belt buckle so shiny I can see my own reflection.

"You scared me."

"I noticed." He comes into the room uninvited, dipping his chin at the piles on the table. "New-member bags, huh? Looks like fun."

I gather up the papers I dropped, shuffle them into a neat pile. "Are you looking for your father? Because he went to visit a sick parishioner."

"Mrs. McPherson, I know. Charlene told me." He wanders over, looking over the stacks of papers and brochures on the table. He picks up one of the Bible booklets, flips through it with a thumb. "I hear somebody got into her drawers. Probably the most action she's seen in decades." He gives me a sly grin. "How much did they get away with?"

"Two thousand dollars is the number I heard."

He whistles between his teeth. "That's a pile of cash. Who do you think took it?"

I push to a stand, digging through the box for a handful of tote bags and draping the straps over an arm. "I'm trying not to think about it too much, to be honest." It's a lie, of course. Like everybody else in this place, I've thought of little else.

He tosses the pamphlet back on the stack with a shrug. "I just figured since you're up here all day, you might see things others don't. Like somebody sniffing around Charlene's drawers."

Ha ha, snicker snicker. As much as I like and respect the Reverend, I'm not getting the same upstanding vibe from his son.

"I didn't see anybody sniffing around anywhere," I say as casually as I can, "but I also wasn't looking. I've been too busy working."

He nods like he doesn't quite buy it. "What do you think about my father giving the thief time to return it? I mean, this isn't preschool, and two thousand dollars is not nothing. If it were me they stole from, I'd have called the cops hours ago."

I shrug. "I don't know. I like to think I'd be as compassionate and forgiving as your father, but there are few people on this planet as softhearted as he is."

Erwin snorts, sinking into a chair and stretching

out his legs. "Is that what you kids are calling it these days—softhearted?"

"What, you don't think so?" As soon as I pose the question, I wish I hadn't. I don't much care what Erwin Four thinks about his father or the money or anything else for that matter. I just want him to leave. The skin on the back of my neck is tingling, the hairs rising up one by one.

"Home by ten. Straight As or else. Don't just read but memorize the Bible, so you're able to chastise sinners with apt verses at all times. Thus is the life of a preacher's son." He sighs, watching me fill the bags on my arm but not lifting a finger to help. "I never see him, not unless I come here. I can't tell you the last time we've had a family dinner."

If Erwin Four wants me to feel sorry for him, he's going to have to give me something better than some daddy issues. So his father didn't spend enough time tossing baseballs with him in the front yard. *My husband beat me*, I want to scream in his face. *He put a gun in my mouth and pressed his finger to the trigger, and he's looking for me right now so he can finish the job.* I think all these things, but I press my lips together and move down the table, dropping coffee mugs in the bags when what I'd really like to do is bean Erwin Four in the head with one.

"Hey, I have a question for you," he says, almost conversationally. "What did you do to get Oscar's job?"

My hands freeze midreach, and my head whips in his direction. "Excuse me?"

"Like, do you stroke my dad's ego? Tell him how

kind and wise he is? Convince him to do you favors? Oddly enough that's a confirmed technique to make a person like you, you know. The person who *does* the favor actually ends up liking the other person more. Weird, I know, but true." He laughs in a way that is the opposite of funny. "Or maybe you're the one doing *him* favors."

It's not just his words but the way he's looking at me—like I'm some sort of puzzle to be put together. Like I'm slightly dirty. A phone rings out in the hallway, but distant, at the far end. Martina's warning floats through my mind: *Erwin Four is a creep. Stay far, far away.*

"I hope you're not implying what I think you are."

"I'm not implying anything. I'm trying to figure you out. What my dad sees that the rest of us can't. And while we're at it, if you have any tips on how to win some affection for me and my sister, I'm all ears."

How about stop acting like a spoiled brat? Maybe don't be an asshole? I get that the pressure on a preacher's kid must be enormous, but Erwin Four should be able to see the bigger picture—that he has a father who cares enough to hold him to a higher moral standard than others in his flock. That should count for something.

"You and your sister are hardly unloved," I say. "Your father talks about you all the time. You're even his computer password." The Reverend asked me not to mention it, but I'm pretty sure if he heard this conversation, he'd say something similar.

"ErwinGrace2, I know. What, you don't think IT has access to the computer passwords around here?"

I don't answer. If Erwin Four runs the IT, if he knows how to log on to his father's computer, he'll know how to pluck Sabine's story from the history files. I study him for clues, but then again, maybe him cornering me here is the biggest clue of all. The first pinpricks of understanding burn like hot ice on my skin.

He raises both hands, lets them fall back to his lap. "Do you believe what my dad preaches, that marriage is a holy covenant between three people—a man, a woman and God?"

I almost laugh. Almost. Not just because this conversation is ridiculous, but also because if God had been anywhere near my marriage, He wouldn't have just stood by and watched you slap and punch and kick me. He would have shielded me. He would have taken one for the team.

"Another thing I've never really given much thought," I say carefully.

"Well, I have, and let me tell you, it's yet another reason for me to never tie the knot. That is a threesome I am not the least bit interested in."

He stands, and at that moment, right there and then, is when I feel it. Something stark and obvious. Something not right. I put some space between us, scooping items from the table into the bags, hurrying farther down the line.

"What about sin? What are your feelings on that?"

"Why are you asking me? I'm hardly an expert on anything Biblical."

"Because you're not one of Dad's mindless sheep. You're not going to parrot his words back at me. I get enough of that at home. I'd like to hear an honest answer from someone like me, someone who's bitten into more than a few apples." His gaze wanders south. Alarm zips up my spine.

I turn away, tugging on my T-shirt. "I've made mistakes. Hasn't everybody?"

"Yes, but according to my dad, sin is preordained. The Bible tells us not to sin at the same time it tells us we're destined to lie and cheat and steal. If you ask me, that's the whole problem with Christianity. It takes away an individual's free will. It renders us powerless."

Leave, a voice screams in my head. *Don't stay here alone with this man.*

I eye the distance between Erwin Four and the door, the way he's standing there like a roadblock.

"I don't think it's about taking power away," I say slowly, buying myself some time. I drop the bags in the box and edge around to the opposite side of the table. "But to give it back. Choose God and go to heaven. Isn't that the point?"

"You didn't answer my question." He steps to the right, and I ease to the left.

"I'm pretty sure I did."

Get out, get out, get out.

In three lightning steps, Erwin Four is in front of me, smelling of aftershave and astringent and—beer? Or maybe that's my memory, playing tricks on me.

"No. I'm pretty sure you didn't. The question still stands. How do you feel about original sin? Good?" He runs a finger down my forearm, his touch so light

I have to actually look down to make sure it was real. "Or bad?"

I don't move because I can't. A wave of disgust, so intense I'm paralyzed, sticks my sneakers to the floor. The air between us shimmers, and I'm transported to another time, another place. A dusty field at last year's annual barbecue.

I remember everything about that day. How the afternoon air was muggy and hot, the official start of what would be a sweltering summer. How the beer was flowing faster than the river behind the bandstand, and how you chugged it from a red Solo cup. How when I made a joke, saying you might want to switch to water, you laughed and ran your finger down my forearm, soft and light as a feather, like Erwin Four did just now.

But only because people were watching.

Your laugh was for them, but the words you whispered in my ear were for me. You leaned in, stinking of beer and fury. "If you ever, and I mean *ever* embarrass me like that again, I will kill you and dump your body somewhere no one will ever find it."

It's your face I see now when Erwin Four leans in, your breath heating up my cheek. "I think you took the money, Beth," he says, low and deadly, "and if you're nice I might just let you keep it."

There's only one thing to do here, really. Only one way to satisfy both my temper and my terror.

I look Erwin Four in the face and knee him hard in the balls. And then I'm off at a dead run.

MARCUS

Ma starts upstairs while I gather up the files I'd spread across the living room and kitchen, unpin the papers from the wall and toss everything in a basket I fetch from the laundry room. I can't stay in the house, not with Ma's weighted sighs and worried stares. I haul the basket to the car, dump it in the trunk and drive to the station.

The place is changing shifts by the time I arrive, beat-weary cops trudging out the door, nodding to their fresh-faced replacements like an unspoken passing of batons. I don't want to think too hard about how long I've been on the job, or how little I slept last night. I'm running on fumes and adrenaline, like I do every time I'm nearing a break on a case. Something big is about to happen—I can feel it. The papers with the four phone numbers are burning a hole in my pocket, excitement vibrating in the deepest part of my bones.

I park at the edge of the lot and head to the door.

"Hey, Marcus," another detective says, nodding at

the basket in my arms. "Rick's gym clothes are stinking up the office, if you're doing a load."

"Har. Get the door for me, will you?"

He backtracks a couple steps, pulls on the handle. "Oh, and Chief was looking for you earlier. Watch your six, he's on the warpath."

Great. A grilling from Chief Eubanks is the very last thing on my agenda. He's the kind of cop who was born to wear a uniform, an eternally grumpy guy who barks out orders in a tone that makes grown men shake in their buffed boots. I take the long way to my desk, sneaking up the back staircase and looping around.

I don't relax until I step into my office, where the Chief is sitting in my chair, looking through a pile of papers I really wish he wasn't reading.

"Oh. Hey, Chief." He doesn't look up. I settle the laundry basket on the floor, kick it so it's half-hidden under the desk. "Can I help you find something?"

He stabs a finger to the top page. "Yeah, you can tell me what this means: 'Charlotte, Louisville, Jacksonville, Raleigh, Atlanta.'" He looks up over his half-moon reading glasses. "You have some reason to believe Sabine Hardison is on the run?"

It's the assumption Jade made, as well. I sink into the chair across from the Chief, the one I normally offer to guests, and swing my ankle over a knee, relaxed and casual. "Just covering all the bases, sir. The husband said it wouldn't have been the first time. She has a history of antidepressants and wasn't exactly stable."

Chief peels off the glasses and tosses them on the

desk. "Yeah, well, funny you should mention the husband. I received a call from Olivia Spinella. I'm sure you know who that is."

I shake my head, the name squirming in my belly. I don't know who Olivia Spinella is, but the fact Chief's bringing her up can't be good. "Not familiar, no."

"Ms. Spinella is Jeffrey Hardison's attorney. She claims Jeffrey has an alibi for the window of time his wife went missing, and she also claims you knew about it when you showed up at her client's house two days ago to harass him."

"I wasn't harassing him. I was questioning him. There's something fishy about his alibi. Why not be straight about where he was? Why not just say what he was doing in Little Rock?"

"At 2:30 p.m., Mr. Hardison checked in at the offices of a Dr. Lee, a urologist at CHI St. Vincent in Little Rock. His appointment took about forty minutes, after which he got his prescription filled at the hospital pharmacy downstairs. The prescription was for Viagra, and his attorney has offered up the still-full bottle as evidence. It seems Mr. Hardison had plans to reinvigorate his marital relationship with Mrs. Hardison that night, but he never got the chance."

His words are like a punch to the gut, and I try my damnedest not to wince. "Oh."

"Yeah. 'Oh.'" He heaves a heavy sigh, never a good sign. "Ms. Spinella and Mr. Hardison would like to know what we're doing to find his wife, and to tell you the truth, I'd like to hear the answer, too. Where are you looking? What leads are you exploring?"

Chief Eubanks knows better than anybody here the limitations I'm working under. There are sixteen detectives under this leaky roof, and we've shared 357 case files so far this year. All of us have more work than we can handle, and the city won't grant us pay raises or overtime. We're the most necessary work force in a city that doesn't appreciate us. It's no wonder that every year our rank shrinks.

And yet it sure feels like the Chief here is accusing me of not doing the legwork.

"Come on, Chief, you know I work harder than anybody in this place. Everything I've done has been by the book. I interviewed her friends and family. I combed her computer and tracked her phone. I looked at her bank accounts, even found a couple her husband didn't know about."

He gives me a slow nod, and a pounding starts up in the base of my skull.

"I also received a complaint from Trevor McAdams," he says.

I take a deep breath, blow it out long and slow. "Is that so?"

"He claims you came to his house with all sorts of accusations about Sabine, that she's unstable, that she faked a pregnancy test. You want to explain yourself?"

"She *was* unstable. The pharmacy confirmed an ongoing prescription for antidepressants *and* that she had an adverse reaction when she went off them cold turkey last year. She has a history of difficulty getting pregnant as well as a long string of miscarriages. I haven't been able to confirm she was actually pregnant, or if she had some sort of irregularity that made it impossible to stay that way."

"So you think what, that she had some kind of breakdown and took off?"

I lift both hands like, *maybe*. "Like I said, sir, I'm just covering all the bases. And Shelley McAdams skipped town the day her husband's lover disappeared. There's definitely motive there, maybe opportunity, as well."

"The doctor wants you to stay away from her, too."

I puff a laugh. "I'll bet he does."

"Did you question her?"

"She's in Chicago through the weekend."

"Do you have enough to haul her back?"

"I'm working on it."

In other words, no. Chief shakes his head. "This McAdams guy is a doctor, Marcus. He's smart, respected. Determined as hell. He's not some guy off the street."

I bite down on a scowl, clear my expression. "I'm aware of that, sir."

"He knows his rights, and he's not playing around. He's got a shitload of folks on Twitter who think you're incompetent or at the very least, dragging your feet. I don't know if you've seen his feed, but they're killing you over there."

Oh, I've seen his feed, all right. It's just as infuriating as the guy is in real life, a constantly rolling wall of melodramatic wails into the void. One second he's pissed, then next he's blubbering like a baby. His emotions bounce around like a dented Ping-Pong ball, with no clue where it's going to land next. The tweets have a constant theme, though, and that's me. I'm obstinate, thickheaded, on the wrong path. Last time I scrolled through it, I punched my fist through a wall.

"He wants you off the case. He's threatening to sue, and he's got the money and the pull to make good on his threats."

"Is that what this is about? You want me off the case?"

There's a long beat of silence—too long—and I try not to squirm like a two-bit criminal brought in for questioning, even though that's exactly how I feel. That's *my* chair he's sitting in, *my* desk he's plunked his Popeye forearms on. *My* case he's grilling me on. I can't have him take it away.

My desk phone lights up, the ring shrill in the silent room, and a burst of electricity surges under my skin. Jade, calling me from downstairs.

Chief Eubanks ignores the phone. "If you want to pass this case to another detective—"

"I don't."

"If you've got other things you need to deal with or need some cooling-down time—"

"I *don't*," I say through gritted teeth because one time, just once, I lose my shit with some asshole pointing a cell phone camera at my head, and the Chief is still bringing it up, two years later.

The phone rings for a third time, and he reaches for his glasses, folding them up and slipping them into a pocket on his shirt.

"I want a report. I want to know what leads you are following, what people you are talking to, what you are doing with my hard-earned tax dollars to find Sabine Hardison. And I want it on my desk by the end of the day."

The Chief leaves, and I sit here, breathing through my rage. Fucking Jeffrey Hardison and his fucking attorney. Fucking Doctor McAsshole. The footsteps fade into silence in the hall, and I punch in the number for Jade. "*Please* tell me you have good news."

"That depends. Atlanta's kind of a hike, and I hear it's really hot this time of year." She snorts, but I'm in no mood for joking around.

I shove the door closed with a foot and edge around my desk, holding the cord high so it doesn't snag. "Tell me."

"Okay, so I found a cluster of check-ins, and from a whole slew of IP addresses. They're kind of all over the place, which means they're most likely coming from a cell phone."

"Any of the burner numbers?"

"I can't see the cell phone numbers, only the IP of the carrier. And a carrier's IP address changes all the time, depending on the cell phone tower it's pinging. The only exception is when the cell hops onto a Wi-Fi network, and then it becomes static."

My head is pounding. I yank open my top drawer, reach in for the bottle of Excedrin—industrial-sized, because of all the moments like this one. I don't give a shit about IPs and cell phone towers, only where they point. "So, did you find her or not?"

"Hold your horses, Sparky, I'm getting there. I've got two addresses for you, each of them with dozens of hits, both of them coming from inside Atlanta city limits. One for a boardinghouse on English Street, and the other for a church."

She rattles off the addresses, and I scribble them onto the pad.

"And the burner numbers?" The manager gave me four, all of which I passed on to Jade less than an hour ago.

"Those are up next. I'll call you as soon as I've got something. Now go out there and get her."

I'm already on my feet, already thinking about the fastest route to the airport. "On my way."

BETH

I am packed and banging on Miss Sally's door in record time, by my calculations a mere twenty-seven
minutes after kneeing Erwin Four in the balls. The
whole time I was hurtling through rush hour traffic
to Morgan House and stuffing my belongings into a
bag, I was doing the math. Four minutes, maybe five
for the little shit to pull himself off the floor, double
that for him to sound the alarm… He'll spew lies
and false accusations, which means I need to hurry.

I lift my fist and bang on the door again.

"Hang on, hang on, I'm coming," Miss Sally's
voice says through the wood. She pulls the door open
with a smile. "Hey, sugar, what are you—uh-oh. Why
are you so sweaty?"

I don't really wait for her to invite me in; I wriggle my way past.

"And how come you're panting? Did you run all
the way here?" She shuts the door behind me, flipping the lock with a metallic clunk, and the noise
sends a sliver of panic up my chest. My gaze flicks

to the windows, two paned sheets of glass plenty big enough for an escape.

And then I see the rest of the room and I freeze.

"What's wrong?" she says, taking in my expression. "What happened?"

I don't answer because I can't. I am rigid with shock, my entire body frozen at the spectacle that is Miss Sally's room. It looks like something out of a movie set. Dark and blood red, with sculpted molding and carved furniture, Victorian behemoths with stubby clawed feet. There's velvet everywhere, rich maroon and burgundy lined in fringe and hung with tassels. Even the walls are papered in it, lit up with an occasional filigreed brass lamp.

And on every horizontal surface, on the tables and cabinets and elaborately carved stands, are sculptures of very large, very erect penises. It's like *Moulin Rouge* meets gay porn, an orgy of Belle Epoque with homosexual brothel.

I turn in a slow circle, taking it all in. "What is this place? Where am I?"

"You like it, huh?" Miss Sally sinks onto an overstuffed love seat, patting the cushion beside her. "Now come on. You sit down and tell Miss Sally what happened. What's got you all in a tizzy?"

I tear my gaze off a ruby dildo lamp, telling her the two-second version: "I kneed the pastor's son in the balls, and now I have to leave."

Disappointment flashes across her face. "Wait a minute. You don't just knee some poor sucker in the balls, not without a reason. There's got to be more to the story than that. Miss Sally wants to know what it is."

"As much as I'd love to tell you everything, I don't have time. I used this address on my job application."

"So, you're leaving." Miss Sally is a lot of things, but stupid is not one of them.

I nod, acknowledging an unexpected pang. I didn't realize until now how much I'll miss Morgan House, how much I've come to think of it as home, even if only a temporary one. I sink onto the couch next to her, brushing away the sadness. The police will be here any minute. It's past time to go.

"How much do I owe you?"

"Well, it's past noon," she says, crossing her long legs. Under her white eyelet skirt, they're lotioned into a high shine, reflecting in the room's dim light like glass. "I'll have to charge you through tomorrow."

"That's fine. How much?"

I expect her to check a list, to pull up some file on her computer or at the very least, reach for a calculator, but she rattles off a number without the slightest hesitation, like Rain Man. "One hundred and twenty dollars."

I peel off the bills and hand them to her. "Can I borrow a piece of paper and a pen?"

She stands, fetching some from a sideboard on the opposite wall. Perfumed stationery and a fountain pen, of course. I kneel, scribbling my message on a glass-topped side table. When I'm done, I fold it twice, write Martina's name on the outside and hand it to Miss Sally.

"Do you know where you're going?" she says, pocketing the note.

"I will when I get there."

Miss Sally gives me a sad smile. "You take care of yourself, you hear?"

"You bet. And thanks for everything. I'm really going to miss this place."

She grabs me by a shoulder and yanks me in for a hug. I wasn't expecting it, and for the first few seconds, stand stiff as a board in her arms, but she smells so good and her breasts are like two giant, soft pillows against my cheek, so I relax and give in to the embrace even though the clock is ticking. She pats me on the back with a giant paw, murmurs into my hair, "Poor, sweet girl. It gets easier, you know."

"What does?"

She cranes back her head to look down, arching her back, and something unexpected presses into my leg. "Running. Starting over. But you're smart, and you're stronger than you know. You'll find your place."

It's all I can do to nod.

She releases me, waving a rose-scented hand through the air. "Now get out of here. I've got shit to do."

A few seconds later, I'm racing down the back-streets to where I parked my car, a couple blocks away, thinking that's one mystery solved, at least. Miss Sally's boobs might be bigger than mine, but she definitely wasn't born female.

Dear Martina,
Sorry I ditched you today, and sorrier still that I lied. As usual, you were right. I'm the one who

took the money from Charlene's desk. I know, I know—stealing from a church is pretty much a one-way ticket to hell, but I had my reasons. Valid ones, I promise. Tell the Reverend it was me, will you? Make him point the police away from you and the cleaning crew. And tell everybody, too, that I'm really, truly sorry.

Thanks for everything—for Jorge, for the job, for your friendship. Especially the last one. One day, when all of this is behind me, I hope I can come back to thank you in person.

Be safe.

XO,

Beth

When it comes to finding a new place to stay, the two thousand dollars from Charlene's top desk drawer and the Georgia ID in my pocket have certainly broadened my search parameters. I don't dare to turn on my phone, which I powered down as I was running out the church door, so I drive to a new part of town and putter up and down random streets until I spot a motel advertising rooms for the bargain-basement price of twenty-two dollars a night. It's an ancient three-story building wedged into the downtown connector, one wing literally hanging over the overpass, which probably explains the price. One semi too many rumbling by its shabby walls, and they'll come crumbling down.

The lot is packed, but I find a vacant spot between two rusted-out heaps that make the Regal look like a late-model Cadillac. Two men lean against the railing on an upper floor catwalk, watching me make the trek to the office. I acknowledge them, but I don't wave or smile.

The office is tiny, a windowless room with a couple of ratty chairs and a desk behind bulletproof Plexiglas. The woman sitting behind it is nondescript—drab hair dragged into a low ponytail, an unlined and makeup-free face, a lumpy body under shapeless clothes. A boring slice of white bread compared to the smorgasbord of color that is Miss Sally.

She waves off my ID. "You don't need that here. You alone?"

I nod.

"Then you'll want a room upstairs. Fewer stray bullets up there."

An upstairs room would mean a more difficult escape route should the need arise—and it will. Without my cell to guide them to me, Erwin Four and the police might not find me here, but you will. I can maybe fight you off—if I'm prepared, if I take you by surprise—but I can't fight off a bullet. I take the upstairs room.

"Do you happen to know if there's a Best Buy nearby?"

She rattles off directions to one a couple of miles away, then slides the keycard under the screen along with the Wi-Fi code. I thank her and head back to the car.

After a few wrong turns, the Regal and I make it to the Best Buy, where I select a midpriced laptop, another piece-of-crap smartphone with a stockpile of prepaid minutes and a pretty pink phone case with butterflies swimming in golden glitter on the back, just because. The grand total comes to $846.23.

"Whoa," the salesclerk says when I start peeling bills off a wad of cash. "This is Atlanta, girl. Put that away."

I speed up the counting, even though I know it makes me look suspicious or at the very least, memorable. I also know there are two little cameras mounted to the ceiling on either side of my head, capturing my face in full-color high definition— and that those are only the two that I've seen. How many others did I miss on my jaunt around the store? Dozens, I'm betting. I push the thick mound of cash across the counter.

The clerk counts it, then counts it again. It takes him longer than it should. I'm paying in mostly fives and ones, crumpled and wrinkly from the church collection basket.

To be clear, I wouldn't have taken the money if I didn't need it, and I won't be keeping it, not even a penny. Every single cent will make its way back into the Reverend's collection basket at some point, even if it takes me years to repay it. I close my eyes, press a palm to what's left in my money belt and remind myself that this is who I am now. Beth Louise Murphy, a runner. A thief.

The clerk passes me my change and a plastic bag bulging with electronics I could have never otherwise afforded. I'm back in the Buick a few seconds later, steering the car down the street to my next stop—a CVS I passed on the way. I pluck a basket from the stack by the door and stroll the aisles, dropping in items from my mental list: black liquid eyeliner, burgundy lipstick, enough groceries to tide me over for a day or two, toothpaste, a box of Miss Clairol. I pay cash and console myself with the only bright spot I can find in this shitty, shameful day: I've always wanted to be a redhead.

I'm pulling into traffic when the skies open up, the rain forming a shimmering silver curtain on the other side of my windshield. I flip the wipers as high as they'll go, but they can't clear the glass fast enough. I squint into traffic and think maybe the flash flood is a sign, an omen of things to come.

You. You are coming for me.

And I will be ready.

MARCUS

By the time I pick up my rental car at the Atlanta airport and point it north to the city, it's almost ten, and the highway is dark and slick with rain. It floods the streets and beats on the roof and windows, jamming the lanes with the remnants of one hell of a rush hour. The road in front of me is basically a parking lot of taillights, flashing bright red. I hit the hazard lights, nudge my way onto the shoulder and punch through the gridlock.

The GPS spits me out at 1071 English Street, one of the addresses Jade said had a cluster of IP check-ins to the department website and Facebook page. I ease to the curb and squint through the rain, clocking the fresh coat of paint, the picket fencing, the light spilling from windows lined with frilly curtains. This place is too nice to be a boardinghouse. Way too nice. How the hell does she afford it?

I jog through the rain to the door.

On the covered porch, I lean my face into one of the windows and peer into a living room. Three men are lined up on a navy couch, beer bottles resting on their bellies, faces tipped to a Braves game on a flat-screen. I study their profiles, their clothing, the size of their feet propped up on the coffee table. The middle one. Long and lean and still in possession of most of his hair. He looks like the type to hit on another man's wife. Is he staring at the TV and thinking about her? Is she in one of the rooms upstairs, thinking about him? Thunder rumbles overhead, and I rub a fist over my breastbone instead of what I really want to do: punch it through the glass.

I take deep breaths until I get myself under control, then ring the doorbell with a thumb.

It's not one of the men but a woman, tall and curvy in a hot pink robe and hair curlers, who opens the door. She flips on the porch light, and *whoa*. I stumble backward on the porch planks and look again. That ain't no woman. Nope. No way in hell.

He looks down his powdered nose. "Can I help you?"

Okay, so the voice belongs to a man, but those breasts. They look—well, if not *real*, then definitely expensive. I raise my gaze and—oh shit, he caught me.

I gesture over my shoulder, at the rain clattering to the asphalt in sheets behind me. "Some weather, huh?"

He doesn't seem the least bit amused.

I clear my throat and turn up the charm. "I'm new to town. Just got in, actually. I heard this place has really nice rooms."

"Sorry. We're full."

He starts to close the door, but I stop it with a boot.

"What's your rate?" I say, giving him a chummy smile. "Because I'll pay double."

"I already told you. We're full." He looks down at my foot, planted in the open doorway. "Now please don't make me tell you to remove your boot from my door."

"Or else what—you'll call the cops?"

His glossy lips curl in a smile. "Come on, honey. We both know you *are* a cop. Why don't we just drop the charade? You tell me why you're standing here, dripping all over my welcome mat, and I'll tell you if I can help you or not."

"I'm looking for somebody."

He rolls his eyes. "You don't say."

"Five foot eight, long, dark hair. Though she may have cut it since this was taken." I pull up a picture on my phone, flip it around so he can see.

He leans down to take a closer look at the screen, and I get a partial view of a woman standing behind him—a knockout Latina in khakis and a T-shirt. Her eyes are wide, her expression frozen in surprise, or maybe fear. I lift my chin, and she steps out of sight.

"Sorry." The man in the pink robe straightens. He shakes his head, and a curler bobs behind a pierced earlobe. "I've never seen that woman before."

He's lying. I've been a cop long enough to recognize all the signs. The tightening of the skin around his eyes, the way the sarcasm disappears from his tone. He knows.

"Okay, well, I appreciate your time," I say, stepping back. I flip up my collar, and water runs down the back of my neck. "Y'all have a good night."

He shuts the door without a word, and I return to my car, sidestepping puddles and grinning like a fool. If she's not here, then I know where to find her. It was written on the pretty girl's face, across her generous chest in big, black letters.

God Works Here.

My eyes pop open at five the next morning, and I'm instantly awake. I flip on the lamp on the nightstand and unhook my phone from the charger, wishing this crappy hotel had room service or a coffee machine because I slept for shit.

The Chief didn't like my report. He claims it was half-assed, stitched together in a quarter of the time it should have taken me. He told me this in a long, shouty voice mail that ended with him taking me off the case. He's passing the search for Sabine on to Detective Phillips, and if I weren't so pissed I'd be insulted. Detective Phillips is a hack, a lazy investigator with questionable tactics and a fifty-fifty success rate. I need to get my ass back to Pine Bluff, like *yesterday*, to make sure Sabine's case lands on the right side.

An alert sounds on my phone, and I watch the emails roll in. Junk, mostly, but between the Facebook notifications and ads for penis implants and energy efficient windows, I spot the one I've been waiting for, from Jade. I tap it with a thumb.

Three of the burners are a bust, but one's still live,
the 607 number. No calls yet, but plenty of activity,
including loads of check-ins from a hotel on the highway in Atlanta. And jackpot! They have a microcell.
When you're ready to go after her, give me a call,
and I'll help you track her in real time.-J

I toss the phone on the bed and head for the shower.

I'm dressed and behind the wheel of my rental
thirty minutes later, a cup of coffee steaming in the
holder. The streets are filling with early morning traffic, slowing the drive to the boardinghouse to a crawl.
On English Street, I do a quick reconnaissance loop
around the block, then park under a dogwood at the
far end of the street.

By now the rain has moved on. The sky is cloudless and bright, giving me a clear view of the front
door. I drink my coffee and watch the residents file
out. The three men from the couch, now in construction gear; folks in kitchen attire, an apron slung over a
shoulder; the pretty Latina in a ponytail and the same
T-shirt she wore last night. She makes a beeline to
an ancient clunker on the street, looking around as if
she's searching for someone. She falls in the car and
cranks the engine, and after three tries it catches in
a burst of black smoke. I start the rental and follow.

The girl winds her way through the neighborhood
and onto the interstate while I stay out of sight a couple of cars back. I already know where she's going,
have already staked out the route from the boardinghouse to the church, and she follows it to a tee.
The only thing I'm a little surprised about, and sure,

also a little disappointed to see, is that she's doing it alone. The way she looked at me last night… She knows something. I'm certain of it.

She takes a right onto the church driveway, and I go straight, gawking out the side window. The building is massive, a monster of brick and beige stone built to impress. A megachurch to beat all megachurches. It fills my rearview mirror as I hang a U-turn and pull into a parking lot across the street. I find a spot by the road, kill the engine and reach for my phone.

After striking out with the drag queen, I'm trying a different tactic today. I poked around last night on the church's website long enough to find a cover—a church mission trip to build a school in Guatemala this fall, and a call for skilled volunteers. I don't know shit about construction, but I know how to sling a hammer and a nail and some bullshit.

As soon as the clock rounds nine, I start the car and peel across five lanes of traffic.

The blonde seated behind the receptionist desk has an accent as sweet as her pink blouse and fat white pears. A fancy kind of drawl that belongs in a plantation town strung up with Spanish moss. Her name, she tells me, is Charlene.

I lean an elbow on her counter, and she blushes under my gaze. "Nice to meet you, Charlene. My name's Marcus. I saw on the website y'all were looking for some skilled volunteers for a trip you've got planned to Central America. Where was it, Costa Rica?"

"Guatemala."

I snap, pointing at her with a finger. "That's right. Guatemala. It just so happens that I run a construction company down in Macon, with a group of skilled and enthusiastic guys who are looking to give back. I was thinking, you give 'em the opportunity, I give 'em a few days off and we make everybody happy."

She clasps her hands on the desk and leans across it. "Oh my gosh. That's…that's amazin'. The Reverend is definitely gonna want to talk to you."

Batting eyelashes. Lingering gazes. That glimmer of hope when she smiles up at me. This woman wants something from me, she's making it very clear, but I'm not at all interested—not when I'm this close to my target.

I point down the long hallway to my right. "Is the Reverend in?"

"Oh." She springs up from her chair, comes around the side. "It's the other way, but yes. Come with me, I'll take you right back."

Charlene leads me down a shorter hallway, stopping before a door at the end. "Reverend, there's someone here to see you about the Guatemala trip."

"Send him in," a voice calls out from inside the room. "And bring us some coffee, if you would, please."

She turns to me with a flirty smile. "Coming right up."

The man behind the desk is long and lean, with the sunken cheeks of a marathon runner. He stands, extending a lanky arm. "Reverend Erwin Andrews. How are you with a hammer?"

"Marcus Durand of Durand Construction. And

I can drive a nail in three slams flat. So can all my men. Seven of us, including myself."

"Do any of y'all speak Spanish?"

I laugh. "I don't know how familiar you are with the construction business in this country, Reverend, but *all* of us speak Spanish."

"Excelente," he says, slapping his thighs. "What about music?"

"What about it?"

"Do you sing? Play any instruments? We could use somebody on bass guitar, banjo would be even better. And we're always looking to add to the choir."

This guy's a trip, in his pressed polo and salon haircut—nothing like the solemn Father Ian. I'm guessing the Reverend didn't take a vow of poverty.

I shake my head. "Nope, sorry. But my wife is pretty decent on the piano. Or at least, she used to be."

"Well, bring her along. I'm sure we can get our hands on a keyboard."

We spend the next half hour going over the details of the trip, dates and costs and required immunizations, all of which I tell him won't be a problem. The guy's a talker, and I nod and smile and pretend to listen, when really I'm just waiting for the right moment. It comes as he's walking me out.

"Oh, I almost forgot," I say, almost as an afterthought. "I think I passed somebody I know in the hallway earlier, but she disappeared before I could chase her down. She's the neighbor of a friend of mine who lives in one of those houses on English Street. About yay high, real pretty. Latina."

The Reverend brightens. "You must be talking

about Martina. Yes, she's been with us for six months now. She's a lovely, lovely girl."

I nod, smiling. "That's her. Please tell her I said hi. Oh, and tell that friend of hers, too. I can't remember her name."

"Do you mean Beth? She and Martina are attached at the hip. Or at least they were, until just a few days ago. I'm afraid I can't talk about the circumstances."

I raise both brows, try not to let on that my pulse just surged. "I hope everything's okay."

He makes a face I take as a no. "I'm certainly praying it is. Include her in yours tonight, if you don't mind."

"Consider it done." I shake the Reverend's hand for a second time, rattle off another round of thanks, and promise to email him the list of names and passport numbers in the next few days. Then I hurry to my car, one word roaring like a train horn through my head.

Beth.

The bitch is calling herself Beth.

BETH

Room 313 of the Atlanta Motel is as bad as I thought it would be, a dark, damp space that reeks of cigarette smoke and body odor. The bedspread is a throwback to the '80s, a threadbare, floral thing covered in stains I don't want to think too much about, which is why I slept fully clothed and curled up under a scratchy bath towel I spread across the sheets. The air-conditioning unit under the window rattled and wheezed all night long, but on a bright note, it drowned out the shouting coming from the room next door.

I haul my body off the bed and turn off the air. The room falls into silence, my neighbors on either side still sleeping off whatever they shoved up their veins. I peek out the curtains onto the catwalk—empty. Beyond it the sun is blazing, beating down on the parking lot with an almost-hostile brightness. People call this place Hotlanta for a reason.

In the tiny bathroom, the remnants of last night's makeover are lined up on a narrow glass shelf and in smudged lines on my face. My emo makeup, black-lined eyes and dark-stained lips that no amount of soap could scrub off, and hair a color God could never have intended. The box promised me a rich reddish-brown, but the chemicals on my short, overprocessed locks came out less Radiant Auburn and more Bozo the Clown. I look ridiculous, but also completely un-recognizable.

I brush my teeth and return to the bed, pulling my new computer from the box and firing it up for the first time. The screen shuttles me through the setup, and I pause at the prompts. Name. Email address. Geographic location. Every one of them feels like a trap, each answer a potential land mine. I think of all the people who are looking for me—the Reverend, Erwin Four, Martina, you—and remind myself to be careful.

Once the computer is activated, I hop online with the code I got at check-in. Say what you will about this shithole motel, but its Wi-Fi is top-notch. The World Wide Web at my fingertips, and at lightning speed.

I enter the address for the local Pine Bluff newspaper in the search bar. The screen loads, and there she is. Sabine, the top story. And then I read the letters above her head, and the room in the air turns solid.

Missing Pine Bluff woman found dead.

A wave of nausea pushes up from the pit of my stomach, catching and swelling in my throat. I hold it back with a hand pressed hard to my lips, but the effort breaks me into a cold sweat.

Sabine is not missing.

She's not in hiding.

She's *dead.*

The knowledge hits me in a cold, horrible, horrifying rush, and I feel weightless. Not quite falling, not quite steady on the bed. I see Sabine's face on the Reverend's television screen and each of those times I went searching for more news, hoping, praying she was safe somewhere, hiding. I double over, hugging myself and fighting a sudden pressure in my chest. Is this what a heart attack feels like?

The truth is, I should have expected this. Since I first heard Sabine was missing, I've been frantic for some sort of update. The dread has been building for days, trembling in the hollows of my bones during the day, poke-poke-poking me awake at night with a worry that was too big, too terrifying to sleep through. This news has been coming all along. On some level, I've always known.

Outside on the catwalk, two men are negotiating a drug deal. They're arguing about price, debating quality of product, but their voices are muffled by the roaring in my ears. All I catch are broken words, fragments of sentences, like the ones swimming on my computer screen.

Body. Badly decomposed. Autopsy.

I spring to my feet and pace in front of the bed. How stupid was I to think this was only about me? About me running from my past, from you. I was prepared to fight for my freedom, to pay for it with blood and broken bones, but I never stopped to consider that I might not be your only victim.

I sink onto the bed, my eyes growing hot. Poor, sweet Sabine.

I read the rest of the article in chunks, digesting the details with a rising horror.

Sabine was strangled, her neck broken in two places, the bones and windpipe crushed. Her body was weighted and dumped into a pond off Highway 133, where it rotted for at least a week, maybe more. Something—a boat, the wildlife—worked her free from her underwater grave, and she bobbed and floated until a hunter and his dog found her facedown in the reeds. She'd been picked apart by buzzards.

Buzzards, oh my God.

I picture Sabine's body decaying away at the bottom of some unnamed pond, and the image knocks the breath out of me. For a second or two I can't move, can't even *think*, and then my brain kicks into overdrive, flashing the faces of people I've seen splashed across the news. That heartsick doctor. Sabine's twin sister. Her husband. People who loved her, who prayed for her and wanted her back. My heart breaks at the idea they're picturing the same thing.

I drop my face in my hands and give in to my tears, crying for Sabine, for her friends and family, for me. For my own grief and fury and horror and rage and guilt.

Most of all, for my guilt.

Because I know Jeffrey is not the one who wrapped his fingers around her throat. He's not the one who squeezed until two bones snapped, not the one who left her for the buzzards.

I know it was you.

BETH

Ten days prior

I crouched behind a juniper hedge, watching balloons bob above the open house sign, and waited until everybody left. A gaggle of blonde brokers in teetering heels, an older couple I recognized from church, a straggler with his pockets full of food. Sabine had once told me there were always moochers. She'd laughed as she said it, as if she couldn't care less that strangers stopped by with the sole motivation of snagging some snacks, and I remember thinking she was so nice, so understanding and generous, and that was even before she offered to help me. But the point is, I waited until everybody was gone.

When it was all quiet, I craned my head around the branches, searched up and down the street. No cars, no pedestrians out walking their dog in this heat. Only the sounds of traffic on Hazel Street, humming in the distance. Still, I waited and I watched and I listened. Seven years with you had taught me I could never be too careful. When I was certain it was safe, I burst out of the shrubs to the side door.

Sabine was stacking leftover cookies into a plastic container when I came into the kitchen. She saw me, and she sucked in a breath. "What are you doing here? Is everything okay? Omigod, don't move. And get away from that window."

She shooed me out of sight and rushed past, her heels clicking on the marble. I heard the metallic *clunk* of the front door lock sliding into place, and two seconds later, she was back. She looked me over for cuts and bruises.

"Are you okay? Are you hurt?"

"Only my ribs," I say, cradling my right side with a palm, "but nothing's broken."

Anyone else would have asked how I knew, but not Sabine. Sabine knew what you did to me. All those times you threw me down the stairs, the punches and the kicks and the bites, the concussions and broken ribs. She knew what you were capable of, and she helped me anyway.

Do you even remember meeting her? I bet you don't, do you? Sabine was the broker on that house on Hillcroft Street, the one we looked at last year. It was more house than we could afford, but you wanted it, and I knew better than to point out the obvious. The mortgage bank did it for me, two weeks later. When they turned us down, you got so mad you kicked me in the head.

But you probably don't remember Sabine because you were so busy strutting around the house, taking in the twelve-foot ceilings and granite countertops, the kitchen filled with shiny appliances we'd never use. But I noticed. I noticed the way her smile was too big but her eyes were sad, the way her makeup was thicker on one side, the way she kept touching her cheek like she had a toothache.

She's like me, I remember thinking. *Her husband is like mine.*

And so, while you were up in the attic, banging on the rafters and inspecting the wiring, I asked if she was okay.

"I'm fine," she said, but her eyes didn't quite meet mine and she smiled way too bright, the way I did when people asked me. "Honestly, I'm fine."

I could hear your footsteps overhead, stomping around up there in self-importance even though you didn't have the slightest clue what you were looking at, and I knew I didn't have much time.

I wrapped my hand around her wrist and whispered, "My husband does it, too." Sabine's eyes went wide with understanding, with acknowledgment. "He hurts me, too."

Swear to God, I don't even know why I said it. Up till then I hadn't said those words to a single soul, not even to my sister, but that day the words just came right out. Finally, I'd dared to push open that heavy metal door that I thought was protecting me and told someone our dirty little secret. My knees went wobbly with relief.

It was months before I ran into her again, in the shampoo aisle at the drugstore. She told me her husband had become a new man. Bringing her coffee in the mornings, tucking sweet notes in her work bag, calling her just because. He was trying so hard, she said around a stiff, synthetic smile, and my blood turned to ice and my fingers tingled. I looked at Sabine and I saw me, all those years ago. Before I understood that a backhand was the beginning, not the end, of a cycle.

I took her hand, squeezed it until the bones slid under her skin. "This is what they do, Sabine. They create perfect, perfectly happy moments so that when the bad ones come again, and they will, we will remember those perfect moments and stay."

The understanding that crept up her face was identical to the one that was blooming in my chest. No woman wants to admit their marriage is over. We want to keep loving the person we once loved. We want the dream, the fairy tale of forever and ever after. To leave is to admit defeat.

But it was that moment in the drugstore, warning a stranger off going down my path, when I knew I had to do the same. I needed to get off this path, too. I needed to break this cycle of tenderness and brutality. Even if parts of me got broken in the process.

Sabine is the one who helped me come up with a plan—to skim off the grocery money, to make you think I've gone one way and then go another, to change my name and my hair, to hide in plain sight. She started volunteering at shelters, both for herself and for me. She interviewed the women there, researched what worked and what got women killed. She was like a graduate student with a thesis, single-minded and thorough.

She fed her findings to me in bite-size chunks—

in the locker room at the gym, at the water fountains at the park, in whispers while pumping our gas. We never chose the same place twice, and we never put anything in writing.

We were so careful, and yet you found her anyway.

But that day at the open house, I came to say goodbye.

"You're leaving? You're really going through with it?" Her eyes widened like they did when she first saw me, only this time not with surprise but with pride. As much as she encouraged me to leave you, as many times as she told me I could, I think a bigger part of her never thought I'd do it. I'd been with you for so long, she didn't think that I dared.

I nodded. "I am."

"Do you know where you're going?"

I nodded again. Tulsa, then a roundabout route to Atlanta, but I kept that part to myself. Sabine wouldn't want to know, and I wouldn't want to tell her. She already knew too much.

"And what about his friends? Those cops you thought might be watching you. How do you know they won't follow?"

"I don't. But the whole department is at a training in Little Rock today. Anger management, if you can believe the irony. Anyway, they're all there until four. If you've ever thought of robbing a bank, today would be a good day to do it."

She laughed. "Speaking of banks, how much money do you have?"

"Not quite four thousand, including what's on Nick's card." Sabine knew Nick because he was her idea. She was the one who told me how to set up the account, the one who dug him up from God knows where. She didn't tell me, and I didn't ask, though by then she was volunteering at that battered women's shelter so I had my suspicions. But it was an unspoken agreement between us, to share only the most essential information, nothing more, a need-to-know basis. She'd lived here all her life, too, and she was all too aware of how much power you had in this town, how many people were watching. The less we knew about each other, the better.

She fumbled through her bag on the island, pulling out a wad of cash crumpled from her wallet. "Here. This is all I have on me, but I want you to have it." When I didn't immediately reach for the money, she wagged the bills in the air. "Please. It'll make me worry a whole lot less if you take it."

I pocketed the cash, because the truth was, I needed it. Four thousand dollars wouldn't last me long.

And yet when it came to my interactions with Sabine, the money was the very last thing to be thankful for. Not only did she hand me the road map to a life away from you, she told me I was strong enough to go down it. She said not only that I should, but that I *could*. It wasn't one thing she said but a million encouraging words piled on top of each other. Sabine believed in me, and she taught me to believe in myself. It's because of her that I took back my power.

"I'm going to pay you back," I said, standing. "Not just for the money, but for everything. I don't know how yet, but I swear to you, one day I'll repay all your kindness."

"Oh, hush." She smiled, her eyes going bright. "You know, when we first started talking about this, I didn't think you'd go through with it. I thought it would take a tidal wave to get you away from him, but look at you now. I'm so stinking proud of you."

There were so many things I should have said. That she was the strong one for stepping out of her marriage before the violence could become a cycle. That when she supported me, she gave me some of her strength. That her pride and friendship made me so much braver than I ever thought I could be. That I owed her everything.

But I thought I had plenty of time.

"Thank you," I said instead. "I'll never forget everything you've done for me."

"Just be safe, okay? And be happy again. That's the best thanks you could ever give me."

We hugged and then she pushed me out the door, and I made my escape through the side yard. Right before I slipped into the bushes, I turned one last time, and I spotted her, proud and hopeful, in the kitchen window.

It was the last time I ever saw Sabine.

BETH

I don't mean to fall asleep, but the news of Sabine so exhausts me, so drains me of energy and emotion and tears, that it's all I can do to peel off my jeans and brush my teeth. I collapse on the bed in yesterday's T-shirt, and I'm out the second my head hits the grubby pillow.

Shouting on the catwalk pops my eyes wide. A jumble of angry voices, right outside my room. I bolt upright in bed, springing onto the floor before I'm even aware of being awake. A woman's voice hollers, something about money. A lower rumble answers, muffled and slurred, but the woman isn't having it. Her words escalate in volume and urgency, her shrieks rattling the glass in the window.

I check the time on my phone. Just before 4:00 a.m.

"Shut the fuck up!" a third voice yells through the wall. My neighbor, the skinny black man in the next room, but it doesn't do him any good. The people outside are still slinging curse words, still threatening each other with bodily harm. There's forty dollars on the line, and both of them are convinced that it's theirs.

The argument swells into a sharp *pop*, followed by a quick burst of three more—*popopop*—and I hit the floor. The commotion soon fades into footsteps, a heavy body making a noisy run for it, and the catwalk falls into silence. I peel myself off the grimy carpet, lift up a corner of the curtains and peek outside.

A light flickers outside my door, a short in the system that should come with a warning for epileptics. But there are no bodies as far as I can see, no blood on the concrete.

I drop the curtains and skirt past the window to the door, pressing myself to the cinder block wall. The silence stretches for three minutes, then five. I push off the wall and step into my jeans with the efficiency of a firefighter.

The silence lingers, but the adrenaline in my veins says I'll never get back to sleep, so I fire up the laptop and navigate to the internet. Might as well get to work.

Work. Funny how I've come to think of my internet check-ins as work. Scouring the Pine Bluff police department's website and Facebook page, monitoring the news and police scanner. Ever since finding out about Sabine, I've been pinging back and forth between the two sites, watching for news and waiting.

Sabine's funeral is later today, a service at First Baptist that's expected to be standing room only, followed by a private burial at Memorial Park featuring her husband, her lover and her sister, none of whom are getting along. Ingrid is suing Jeffrey for the money in Sabine's bank accounts, and Jeffrey is countersuing to keep it. Trevor doesn't want the money but a couple of personal effects—the photographs off her computer, a ring she was wearing when she died, an antique vase they bought on a clandestine weekend getaway. In response, Jeffrey sued him for $1.5 million in damages, blaming him for ruining their marriage. My heart pinches for Sabine, who would be horrified at their ridiculous bickering.

I pause at an uptick in chatter on the scanner, a break in the drone of the mundane shoplifting and suspicious person sightings, suddenly shifting to something much more frenetic. Another body found, a man shot in the head in a downtown alleyway, according to one of the voices a drug deal gone bad. I relax somewhat, carrying the laptop into the bathroom, balancing it on the edge of the sink and turn on the shower.

I'm smearing conditioner through my overprocessed hair when I hear it, your name and badge number, the dispatcher calling you to the scene, and my hands pause on my hair. I swipe the curtain aside and stick my head out, listening for your voice, but it's another one that crackles on the scanner. That cop buddy of yours, jumping in on your call.

I rinse and towel off in a hurry.

I knew when I left Pine Bluff you would find me eventually. Finding people is what you do, and I've left enough clues to make it—well, if not easy, then definitely enjoyable. I picture you speeding in your car east to Atlanta, congratulating yourself on hunting me down like I knew you would. As long as I'm alive, you'll never let me go.

I sling my bag over a shoulder and take a peek outside. All clear.

You told me I was stupid, that I was helpless without you, and for a long time, I believed you. But I'm a lot smarter than you think I am. Sabine taught me that. I know that every check-in to a website leaves a ping for Jade to find. I know as kind and forgiving as the Reverend is, he has reported the stolen money by now. Police reports mean clues, charges involving a woman with a fake name, a fake ID with a picture of me, yet another ping. And I suspect you're no longer in Pine Bluff, at least according to the scanner. You might even be here already. If I close my eyes, I can feel your breath on my neck and your teeth snapping at my back.

And when you get here, I'll be ready.

With my new phone, I navigate eighteen miles to the north, to a park overlooking a bend in the Chattahoochee River. I walk to the edge and stare out over the water, and the sight is both familiar and disappointing. The river you and I grew up on is a wild thing, with dangerous, unpredictable currents and banks that encroach on yards and farms at the slightest hint of rain. Unlike that one, this river is lazy, a gentle stretch of brown water trickling across rocks and lapping at the red clay shores. A fallen tree angles across the stones, stretching almost to the other side.

I slide my old cell, the last of the burners I bought in Pine Bluff, from my bag, look down at the dark screen. I didn't have to come all this way. I could have tossed it in a dumpster on the opposite side of town, or handed it over to a bum like I did with the other three. I kind of liked the thought of sending whoever's tracking it on a wild-goose chase, but just like insisting on a McDonald's for my meeting with Nick, it seemed fitting to give it a watery grave. This chase started along the banks of a river, and it will end at one. Symmetry.

I rear back with an arm, but an unexpected wave of nostalgia sticks my cell to my fingers. This device is the last thing tying me to the people I've met here, Miss Sally and the Reverend and Martina. If they've tried to reach me, it will have been on this device.

I power it up one last time, my heart kicking when it catches a cell tower, even though by the time anyone tracks it here, I'll be long gone. The phone beeps, and the messages roll in. Missed calls, unanswered texts from the church, from the Reverend, from a bunch of numbers I don't recognize. I spot the one I'm looking for, tap it with a thumb.

Two unread messages from Martina, plus a photo.

The picture comes first, and the sight of it catches in my throat. It's you, back to the camera, walking down the steps of the church. She took it from an awkward angle, through a window in the executive offices, but I recognize your hair, the shape of your ear, the shirt I got you last Christmas. The sight of you rattles my heart.

You're here.

I scroll down, find the following message:

Is this who you're running from? Because he was here, looking for you.

And then:

Rosa and Stefan are my babies. Twins I left with my mother back in Mexico. Now you.

Not all that long ago, you told your brother Duke that I was the worst shot to ever pull a trigger. We'd just come from one of our monthly sessions at the gun range, which I always pretended to hate even though they filled me with hope. With power.

"No, the bull's-eye," you'd say, berating me for my shaking hands and shoddy aim. "You're supposed to aim for the bull's-eye."

I'd nod and clip an upper corner, folding the paper like a dog ear.

Sometimes, the guys at the range took pity on me. "Keep your body balanced across both feet," they'd suggest, encouraging my improved stance with a nod. "Keep both eyes focused on the target, and try not to blink at the recoil."

I'd smile and tell them thanks, my eyes stinging with the stink of gunpowder and disapproval—for the record, yours, not theirs. The more you criticized, the more my shots went wild.

"You are the wife of a police detective," you'd say after I squeezed out yet another bullet that missed the target entirely. "That paper's just hanging there. It's not even moving. How hard can it be?"

I hear your words as clearly as I did all those times

you hissed them in my ear, and I wonder what you would say if you were standing beside me now, on this street pocked with potholes on the south side of Atlanta. With a man who calls himself Clyde and a van full of weapons, laid out like prime merchandise across the ratty carpet. A tip from the owner of a downtown pawnshop, after I convinced him I was serious about getting armed.

"That one," I say to Clyde, pointing to a compact Sig P320.

He picks it up, hands it to me like it's not a deadly hunk of metal.

I look down the barrel, curl my finger around the trigger, check the slide. The weapon could use a thorough cleaning, but it feels good in my hands. Nice and light. Sturdy. "How much?"

Clyde shrugs. "Two hundred bucks."

It's way less than I'd pay in a gun store, not that I could do that with a fake ID. "Do you have another one?"

"Another gun?" He says it like *duh*, cutting his gaze to the ones spread across the back of his van.

"Another Sig P320." I hold up the one in my hand. "I'm shopping for twins."

"You want two Sigs."

I nod. I want two Sigs.

With another shrug, Clyde leans across the merchandise, digging through a cardboard box by the wheel well. The Sig he pulls out is not identical to the one in my hand; one is black, the other black and silver, but they're the same model. "Three fifty for both."

I could bargain, but considering I'm buying two unregistered weapons out of the back of a van, from a guy who is for sure not named Clyde, I peel off three hundred and fifty from my stash and pass it over.

"Do you need some ammo?"

I nod. And then say, "Just one."

"One box?"

"One bullet."

Clyde's eyes go big and wide, and he looks at me like I'm crazy. "You know those magazines hold fifteen rounds each, right?"

I smile at that, resist telling him that I know how to work the gun. "I only need one. A hollow tip." The kind of bullet that will tear a man in two.

With a shrug, he pulls a box of nine-millimeter bullets from the van and hands one to me. "On the house," he says, and I drop it in my pocket.

The thing is, after all those years of ridicule at the shooting range, I learned a few things. I learned that the Sig has a much smoother trigger than the .357 you made me practice on, and the compact model fits much better in my hand and the pocket of my bag. That if I focus on the target, not the din of the other shooters at the range or the feel of your hot breath on my neck, I have almost-perfect aim. That my hands don't shake and my eyes don't blink, not unless I want them to.

Do you get what I'm telling you?

I know how to shoot, Marcus.

You taught me.

BETH

I'm back in room 313 at the Atlanta Motel, listening to the drone of the police scanner when the phone rings. The sound is sharp, an old-school ring that practically levitates the ancient beige rotary phone on the nightstand. I lean across the bed and pick up the receiver, keeping one eye on the door. "Hello?"

"Yo, this is Terry, down at the front desk. The maroon Buick with Arkansas plates in the lot. Is that your ride?"

I scoot off the bed and scoop up the phone with two fingers, stretching the cord as far as it will go toward the window. The curtains are pulled wide, ugly paisley polyester shiny with age, but the sheers are still tucked tight. I can see out, but as long as I don't turn on the lights, the only thing anybody outside can see is shadows. The Regal is exactly where I left it, squeezed between two sedans at the edge of the lot.

"Yes. Why?"

"'Cause somebody just busted in the window."

It's a trap, your voice whispers in my other ear,

and I flinch. I don't want to hear it, hate that it's your voice in my head, especially because you're right.

This is definitely a trap.

"Thanks," I say into the phone, then drop the phone on the cradle.

I move to the dresser, where the guns lie side by side. The first gun I tuck into the front of my jeans. The barrel is not long, but it's too obvious, and the metal digs into my hip bone. I slide it around until I find a semicomfortable spot, at the small of my back, and then pull my T-shirt over to conceal it. The other I drop into the pocket of my crossbody bag, which I strap across a shoulder. It hangs heavy and deadly at my hip.

"Never point a weapon at another person," you once told me, "not unless you're prepared to pull the trigger."

I've thought about this a lot, Marcus, and I am not you. Anger wouldn't make me shove my gun in another person's mouth any more than it would drive me to wrap my hands around another person's neck and squeeze until the bones break. I can't so casually take another human's life, but these past ten months of planning have been anything but casual. This is do-or-die time, you or me. I am more than prepared to pull the trigger.

"Okay," I tell myself, stepping to the door. "Okay."

Outside, the catwalk is quiet, nothing but a long, empty walkway littered with cigarette butts and trash. I peer over the railing onto the lot, and I see what I missed through the sheers—glass, glittering like a million diamonds tossed across the asphalt. I study the cars, a dozen at best, looking for one that's out of place. A generic rental, or your unmarked sedan. Not that you would be reckless enough to park where I could see, but still. I look for it, and then I study the parked cars, searching for movement inside. A pedestrian wanders by on the sidewalk beyond, but otherwise the lot is still.

I move to the stairwell, leaning my head around the bend, half expecting you to jump out and shout *boo*. But you don't, and the stairwell is empty. I hold my breath and rush down it, hugging the railing. The bums use the corners as a toilet, and no amount of soapy water can wash away the stink.

At the bottom, I ease across the pavement to my car, glass crunching underneath my sneakers. The heat out here is oppressive, the sun beating down on black asphalt, hot, humid air thick with exhaust from the highway on the other side of the building. Even today, a Saturday, traffic is a constant roar.

I arrive at the Buick, and there's a hole where the driver's window used to be. I lean my face into it, and there it is: further proof you're here. It sits in the middle of the cracked dash, a bright yellow Hot Wheels car. The same toy I held across the aisle at a McDonald's all those years ago. The one I gave you for your nephew. It sits atop a pink Post-it, the edges wilting in the heat. I reach inside and snatch it from the dash, my heart free-falling at the words slashed across it in dark blue ink.

Dear wife, I found you.

I drop the note and whirl around, my breath coming in raspy gulps, my gaze searching out all the places in the lot you could be hiding. By now I've walked this lot a dozen times, and I know where they are. The shadowy openings of the two stairwells, the dark corners by the shrubs, that narrow slit between the dumpsters and the wall. If you're here, which you are, you're well hidden. Watching. Waiting.

A door opens at the far end of the building, and I turn toward the sound. Terry, poking her head out of the office. "Want me to call somebody?" she yells.

We both know that by "somebody," Terry means the police—an offensive word in a place like this one. But my fake ID and lack of valid driver's license puts me in the same boat as my drug-dealer and hooker neighbors, who skitter into the bushes at the first sign of the law. I shake my head. Terry shrugs like she doesn't care either way, then disappears back inside.

I stand here for another minute, considering my options. I could go back up to my room, but one way in means one way out, and for me there is no scarier sound than the clunk of a lock sliding into place and you standing in front of the door. I could get into my car and drive somewhere, but that would be only delaying the inevitable, moving the confrontation to a place where I don't know the layout, haven't walked the property and picked out all the shadowy corners. I could scream bloody murder, pray Terry makes good on her offer to call the police, and then what? Seven years with you has taught me not to trust someone just because they carry a badge.

I lean a hip against my car. "You can come out now, Marcus." My voice sounds surprisingly normal, calm even, despite how I'm shaking inside. The fear is visceral and intense, and so is the anger.

Good. Anger is good. I think of Sabine, of my broken bones and heart, of the seven years you stole from me, all while claiming to love me. Anger will give me the strength to do what I need to do.

I hear you before I see you. The dull thud of your shoes on the pavement, that low chuckle I'd recognize anywhere. Last time I heard it was right before you pushed me down the stairs.

You step out from behind a white van, and I'm glad there's a car behind me, supporting my weight, because I'm not sure my legs would hold me up. You're just as handsome as ever. Scruffy cheeks, square jaw, dark hair just the right amount of tousled. And just like when I caught sight of you the very first time, something deep inside my head pounds. You've brought me so much pain over the last seven years that it actually hurts to look at you.

You come across the asphalt, stalking me like prey. I read once that abusers can pick out their victims by the way they walk. After that I spent more time than I'd like to admit walking toward myself in the mirror, analyzing my own gait. Was it the slump of my shoulders? A telling bounce in my step? What was it that made you pick me? How did you know I would be a willing victim?

I don't have to pretend to be afraid of you, because I am. A scream builds in my head, but there's no way I'm giving you that pleasure. You relish my fear. You feed on it like a vampire.

"Your hair," you say, taking me in. You don't sound angry but surprised, and maybe a little disappointed. "What did you do to it?"

I run my fingers down the strands behind an ear. "You like it?"

"It's…different." You smile, but it's at odds with your tone. You hate everything about my hair, I can tell, but mostly you hate why I did it—to spite you.

"How did you find me?"

"What, you thought you could fool me with a bunch of twenty-dollar withdrawals? A background check for an apartment you never followed through on? This is what I do, Emma. I find people. I find criminals. You're not half as smart as you think you are."

This is the way it always starts, with insults. With a barbed putdown, with your lips curled in revulsion. You say you love me, but this isn't love. This is you, pushing me down in order to build yourself up. You need my approval; you crave it. You think it will give you back your power.

I press my lips together and don't say a word.

"Were you listening? Did you hear a word I said? I found the burner cell phones. I traced the check-ins to the boardinghouse, to the church, to here. You made this way too easy."

"I thought…"

You cock your head and look at me. "You thought what?"

I thought you were a good guy. I thought you really loved me.

"I thought you'd find me eventually."

It's not the accolades you were fishing for, but my admission has the intended effect. You step closer, within an easy arm's reach, and your expression doesn't change, but your body language does. You shift forward on your toes, the stance a lot more aggressive. This is the part you like best, the part where you're flexing your muscles and I'm shaking with fear.

Except it's not fear that has me shaking.

It's fury. Righteous and determined rage. The gun tingles against my hip, cradled in my lower back, and my fingers itch to grab for one, but you're armed, too. Your service weapon hangs in your shoulder harness, and that's only the one I can see. There are more, probably, in your pockets, at your ankle. And I'm not crazy enough to think that I could beat you at quick-draw.

"You shouldn't have run, Em. You shouldn't have left."

I shake my head, because what other choice did I have? Staying would have gotten me killed eventually. Leaving, too. I didn't see any other way.

"What did you tell everybody? Where does your mom think I am right now?"

"I told her you were at a retreat. That you were mental and needed to get away."

"And she *believed* you?"

You shrug, a gesture that's not quite a yes. "You haven't been gone all that long. I would've come up with something."

"And Sabine?"

"Sabine." You spit the word, and your lip curls in disgust. "That bitch was butting into something she had no business with. I did some research on her, you know. She was a board member at the women's shelter in town. She bragged all over town about how she's some kind of victim's advocate, about how she was helping women get away from their husbands. I bet she made you think you were one of them, didn't she? A victim."

Did you do it? Did you kill her? The questions bubble up, but I can't make myself force them out. I see your face, hear the fury fueling your words, and deep in my gut I already know the answer.

"Stop looking at me like that," you say. "This isn't my fault, it's yours. You're the one who left. This is on you."

I imagine Sabine's face when you came up on her in the Super1 parking lot, how scared she must have been. She would have known what was coming, and she would have been terrified.

"So now what?" I don't sound scared. I sound genuinely curious. "What do we do now?"

How do you plan to kill me? Because I'm not stupid enough to think there's any other option for you. You can't cart me back to Pine Bluff like nothing ever happened. Surely by now someone besides your mother has noticed I'm gone. Your friends and family, the ever-watchful Ms. Delaney next door. What have you told them about where I've been? Or maybe I'm like that wife of the Scientology leader who's not been seen in public for more than a decade. If my husband doesn't report me missing, am I really gone?

Then again, your mother knows what you've done to me, and so, I suspect, does your sister. For the longest time, I hated them for looking the other way, for studiously ignoring my bruises and pretending not to see, for not lifting a finger to try to save me. "Why?" I wanted to beat on their chests and demand. "Why do you not tell him to stop hurting me? Maybe he'd listen to you."

And then I saw your mother's face at Easter, after I mistook a pack of napkins for your fist and let out that terrible scream, and I realized why she didn't.

Just like me, your mother has been laboring under the delusion that I could save *you*.

I tried. God knows I tried. I thought if I was nice enough, agreeable enough, competent enough, I could return you to the man you were when we met, the one who took out the trash for the wheelchair-bound man in the apartment under us or who helped put down wood floors in the church nursery. But that was the fake Marcus, the sweet and helpful Marcus, the guy you are when you know people are watching. No one can save you, and I've paid with bruises and broken bones to come to that understanding.

You wrap a hand around my head and yank me forward so fast I screw up my eyes, expecting an explosion of pain, my nose connecting with your forehead. But nothing happens. I crack open an eye, and your face is an inch from mine.

Your fingers press into the base of my skull, not painful but uncomfortable, a hint of what's to come. "Now you and I go to your shithole room upstairs. We have a pleasurable—me—and tearful—you—reunion. After that, after we are thoroughly spent—again, mostly me—we take a nap. You will wait for me to doze off, and then you will slip out of bed, write a sad note begging for forgiveness from me and God, and shoot yourself in the head with this."

In one swift move, you snatch the gun from my waistband. I blink, and it's gone.

"A Sig. Nice choice." You check the safety, eject

the magazine, look up with a laugh. "You didn't even load it? Jesus, Em, have I taught you nothing?"

My heart pumps hard and fast, beating against my ribs. If you pat me down, if you reach a hand into my bag, I'm done. I arrange my expression into something scared and defeated, and I do a good-enough job of it that you look pleased. After all, I've had plenty of practice.

You heave a disappointed sigh, your breath hot on my cheeks, and slide the gun into your waistband. "I'm going to have to confiscate this thing, as I'm guessing you don't have a permit. I'm sure you understand."

Oh yes, I do. I understand perfectly. I understand that no matter what happens next, I will not go into that hotel room. As soon as I cross that threshold, I'm dead.

"Let's go." You tilt your head across the pavement, gesturing in the direction of the stairwell. I don't budge, and you lift your brows. "The sooner we get upstairs, the sooner we can get this over with."

Despite your words, my heart thrills with excitement. You haven't reached for the bag hanging at my hip. I'm not even sure you've noticed it.

You shove me across the broken glass toward the stairs, and my thoughts are a jumble of desperate Hail Mary pleas. I search the lot for people, scanning the windows for anyone, for a hooker or her pimp or Terry, her face pressed to the glass. But the folks here can sense danger like a dog sniffing out a bomb, and they know when to barricade the doors and stay away from the windows. If anyone is up there peeking out of theirs, watching you force me across the lot, they're not going to help.

You make me go first, pushing me into the stairwell, and I begin the slow climb. You stay close to my heels, and I drag my feet on purpose. The gun bounces in the bag at my hip, but I won't win in a shoot-out. I need a distraction, a junkie with a needle in his arm, a bum crouched in a corner, his pants around his ankles. I just need a second, just one, to catch you off guard.

We're almost to the second-story landing when it happens. The giant brown pile I passed on the way down, one that was definitely not left there by a dog.

You crook an arm, press your elbow over your nose at the unholy smell. "Jesus, how do you stand living here?"

Now.

Gripping the railing in a fist, I lurch backward, throwing my upper body into yours with everything I've got. I feel the flash of pain as we butt heads, hear the crunch of your nose connecting with my skull. Blood explodes and you stagger backward on the stairs, but my arm works like a bungee cord. I give a hard tug on the railing and it pulls me forward. The momentum flings me right past the landing and around to face the stairs.

I don't look back. I hit the ground running.

BETH

I shake off the pain and sprint up the stairs, taking them by twos and threes to the second-story catwalk. I'm rounding the corner when the ground beneath me shakes, your body lumbering up behind me. Your heavy footsteps, the swish of your jeans, the low growl of your voice—*bitch bitch bitch*. You're fast, but I have a decent head start, and I know where I'm going.

What, you thought I wouldn't have a plan? That I would come all this way, lie and cheat and steal, and not be prepared? There you go again, underestimating me.

I tear down the catwalk, screaming and banging on doors. "Help! Somebody help me. *Help!*"

Nobody's going to help. This place is a revolving door of drug deals and armed robberies, of tussles in the parking lot and gunshots right outside my door. People stay inside for a reason, to get away from the discarded syringes and avoid stray bullets.

But you'll think I'm counting on them to save me.

I reach the stairwell on the opposite end and fly up the stairs. The only way away from you is up. My only advantage, the element of surprise.

At the top of the stairwell, I scale the metal rungs on the wall to the door in the ceiling, a heavy metal plate that opens to the rooftop. It's supposed to be locked, and it was, until I took the lug wrench I found in the trunk of the Buick to the rusted metal loop on the padlock. I give the door a shove, and I'm greeted with sunlight and a blast of heat. I hoist myself out, then flip the door shut, right as you come around the corner.

There's nothing up here to weight the door down, no air-conditioning units or piles of junk I can haul over. No fire escapes or balconies I can lower myself onto, either, just a sudden, steep drop to the highway, three stories down. Nothing up here but bird shit and a giant billboard, looming above six lanes of traffic.

Whether I am ready for it or not, I am officially done running.

I hear you just below me, metallic dings as you scale the ladder. I edge around the door to the opposite side, step back so I'll be out of sight. By the time you turn around and see me, it'll be too late. I'll already have a gun pointed at your head.

The door explodes, metal clanging against asphalt, sending up a puff of dust and dirt. Your hands clasp either side of the opening, pulling your body up with a lot less effort than it took me. You pop up like a spring, landing on the rooftop with both feet. You look around, realizing too late that I'm behind you.

I widen my stance and aim.

When you see the gun, you laugh. You actually laugh, and your eyes gleam in the sunshine. So does the blood on your face, streaming from your nose, leaving dark red trails down your shirt. You don't look scared. You look entertained.

"This one's loaded." I jut my chin at the gun in your holster. "Put yours on the ground."

You roll your eyes. "You're not a good enough shot to use that thing. You'll miss me by a mile."

"I can hit you between the eyes, through the center of your heart or I can take out a kidney. Just tell me which one, left or right?"

You quirk your head at the confidence in my tone, but your cocky smile doesn't fade.

"Put your weapon down," I say again.

You don't move. "You're really starting to piss me off, Emma."

My finger presses harder on the trigger. "You have exactly three seconds to unclip your gun and put it on the ground. One. Two—"

"Okay, fine. *Fine.*" You unclip the one in your holster and place it carefully on the ground. The Sig is next, the unloaded one you took from my waistband. You don't try anything, don't take your chance and shoot me, and that is another mistake. You think you'll get another chance. You're underestimating me still.

"The one at your ankle, too."

You puff a laugh, then put that one down, too.

"Good. Now empty your pockets."

"Come on, Em—"

"Empty them."

With a theatrical sigh, you toss everything to the ground. Your wallet, a set of cuffs, your badge, some papers and loose change. When you're done, you hold your hands high in the air, humoring me, but your expression is anything but humorous. "Happy now?"

Not even close. I point the Sig at your face and nudge you backward, putting some distance between you and the weapons. When I get close enough, I kick them away.

"So, what—you shoot me in the head and leave me for the rats? Take out my kneecaps then roll me over the side?" He glances behind him to the edge, some fifteen feet away and closing fast. "What's the plan here?"

The plan is to *not* do any of those things.

You take another step back, then another. The look you give me is the same as always, firm and fierce, but the fire I saw in your eyes before is gone.

I'm in control now.

"How did you know?" I have to shout over the roar of the traffic below us. "About Sabine, I mean. How did you know she was the one helping me?"

"I saw you together in the park."

You pause to let that one soak in, and I do the math. The park was what—two, three weeks ago? That's when Sabine told me about Nick, made me memorize his phone number. I wonder what else you know, what else you saw when I didn't realize you were watching.

"I know a guilty person when I see one, and I saw the look on your face. You were terrified somebody would see you together, so I did some research. As soon as I found out she was working at the shelter, I knew what the two of you were planning. And then I came home early from that training, and I couldn't find you, but I found her at that Super1. I was waiting at her car when she came out."

"But Sabine didn't know where I was. I didn't tell her on purpose."

You shrug. "That explains why she wasn't very helpful."

"So you *killed* her?"

Despite everything, I'm still praying you'll deny it. It's one thing for you to enjoy hurting me, but to hurt a stranger for helping me? I'm praying you're not that evil.

"What else was I supposed to do? She looked me in the eyes and lied about that day in the park. She said it was a chance meeting, that you only talked for a minute or two when really it was sixteen. Sixteen whole minutes. I know because I timed it. When I told her that I knew she was helping you make a run for it, she got loud. She went for her phone. I shoved her in the back of my car and got out of there before anybody came over to see what the fuss was about. And what do you think would have happened if I'd let her get away? I'll tell you what. She would have gone running to my boss. She would have told him lies about us. About me. I couldn't have her doing that. I have a reputation to uphold."

Yes, your precious reputation, more important to you than how you actually treat your wife. Something you fabricated to deflect from what you really are, a coddled mama's boy with the same hot head as his convict father. Everything you do is an attempt to prove you're nothing like him. Becoming a cop. Taking care of your mother. Shoving your gun down my throat so I wouldn't leave. Anything to project this big, happy family.

I hate you with a burning, blazing fury. "I did this on purpose, you know."

"Did what?"

A truck rumbles by, shaking the rooftop like an earthquake, and I wait for it to pass.

"Brought you here."

Your brow crumples. "What do you mean, you brought me here? You didn't bring me here. I am trained for this. This is what I do. You tried to throw me off your trail but I *found* you."

"You think I didn't know you'd be clocking all the Wi-Fi check-ins to the Facebook page? That you wouldn't notice all those long listens on the scanner website? Those were all huge Bat Signals in the sky. I knew they would be."

You tilt your head, and the look you give me is dubious. "No, you didn't. You couldn't even install the new printer. I had to come home on my lunch hour to do it for you."

Your heels are inches from the edge of the roof now. One more step backward and you'll be hanging over air.

"Pay attention, Marcus. I knew that Jade would be working her magic down in the basement, plotting all the IP check-ins onto a map, and I knew they would lead you straight to me. Did you see my friend

Nick on all the ATM cameras? I am not as stupid as you think."

You don't say a word, but your expression is cussing me out.

"And how about those phones from that skeevy minimart? Did you find those?" I catch the flash of surprise in your eyes, the way your jaw goes slack, and I laugh, a harsh, bitter sound. "I gave three of them away to random people I met on the street. The fourth one I used for *days*. I stole money from a *church*, and then I spent it in a place just up the road, one with dozens of surveillance cameras. Are you getting what I'm telling you? I *planned* this. I sent up flares that would lead you here. I *wanted* you to find me."

I see the moment the quarter drops, the way your brow clears in understanding, in shock. Your voice is both incredulous and enraged. "You fucking bitch."

"Why, because after all these years I'm finally standing up for myself? That doesn't make me a bitch, it makes me brave. Now apologize."

"No." Even now, backed into a literal corner with nowhere to go but through a bullet, you won't say the words. You can't get them over your tongue.

I wag the gun, pointing in the air at your face. "Repeat after me, Marcus. I am a sorry excuse for a human and I apologize for ever hurting you."

"No." This time you shout it. You shake your head, your expression bitter. "You're the one who should apologize, because this is all on you. I would have stayed with you forever. I would have died for you.

You fucked this up, not me. I loved you, and you fucked us up."

I shake my head. "You didn't love me. You only loved what I could give you—control."

"What? That's the dumbest thing I've ever heard. You don't give me control. I take it."

And that right there is the crux of the problem. The one thing you did right. For too long, I allowed you to take my power. I was complicit in my own victimization. It took an outsider, another woman— Sabine—to make me see that in order to end this, I had to demand my power back.

I give the gun another wag—*hello? I'm in control now*—and it works. The fury drops off your face, and your eyes get glassy.

"You were wrong before, you know. I really do love you. You are the best thing in my life. The only part that makes it worth living. If I live to be a hundred, I'll never love anyone the way I love you."

I shake my head. There is literally nothing you can say to make me lower this gun.

"Come on, babe. We still have good times. I can still make you laugh, and remember all those days last summer on the river? You, drinking wine and sitting between my legs while I rowed? Let's go home and do that again. Let's pack a picnic and take out the boat."

Your words are as manipulative as your apologies, the fake tears and grand romantic gestures that always come after a beating. A year ago, I might have said okay. I might have said you are not well, you have a problem—I won't let you work through it alone. But I'm not the same person I was ten months ago, when

I started planning this. Not the person I was ten days ago, either, when I told Sabine goodbye.

I'm Beth Murphy now, and Beth Murphy knows what you're about to do.

I know it from the way your weight shifts and your eyes get squinty at the corners. The way your hands tense into tight, white fists, how your muscles vibrate but your knees get loose and liquid. You are a predator, ready to pounce.

At the first sign of a lunge, I tilt the barrel a half inch to the right and squeeze the trigger. Even though I was prepared for it, the *pop* reverberates up my arm and through my bones, a shock to my system.

But it's nothing like the shock on your face. The bullet whizzes past your ear, and I bet it makes a whistling sound, doesn't it? I bet it feels like fire where it nicks your skin—only a millimeter or two but hot enough to send you staggering. One foot lurches back, but there's nowhere for it to go. Your other boot connects with the rooftop's rim, and your weight tumbles backward. Your ass hangs over the highway.

You teeter on the edge for what feels like forever. Long enough for you to lift a hand to your ear and come away with blood. Long enough for me to lower the weapon and step back. Long enough for you to open your goddamn mouth and tell me you're sorry.

And then, just like that, you're gone.

BETH

Four months later

I arrive twenty-seven minutes into the Sunday service, halfway through a hymn that sounds more like a rock ballad. A good forty singers are lined up across the back of the stage in bright purple robes, their expressions glorious on the twin LED screens above their heads. The Reverend sings along at the far end, tapping a tambourine in time on his knee. Their faces, their entire bodily beings radiate joy, as do those of the people around me, a full house of people swaying to the music. What did Martina call it? *Happy-clappy*, though now that I've seen it for myself, I'd sooner call it *euphoric*. Enough that nobody notices when I slip into an upper row seat.

Not that anyone here would recognize me, now that my hair is back to its original color, the deep mahogany God originally intended. A couple more months and it'll touch my shoulders. Then again, maybe I'll leave it like this, in a bob just long enough

I can tuck a curl behind my ears. Now that I've gotten used to it being short, I rather like the freedom of fresh air on my neck. Sure beats the weight of hair, or the feel of Marcus's hand on it. And a woman at the airport yesterday said the haircut suited me, that it was sassy. I don't feel sassy quite yet, but I'm getting there.

Is it weird that I still hear his voice? It's annoying, certainly, and maybe a little crazy, but sometimes I'll be going about my day, heating up a can of soup for lunch or brushing my teeth before bed, and he'll bitch about how I'm doing it all wrong. "Put the cap on the tube. You're making a mess. And lay off the ice cream. You're looking a little hippy."

You you you. Bad bad bad.

But I'm not the same Emma he pushed around for all those years. Now I do what I couldn't when he was still here: I ignore him. I let him go on and on and I act like I don't hear a thing. I read a book, take a long bubble bath, bake brownies and eat half the pan. This will not be his lasting legacy, this ability to take up space rent-free in my head, making me feel shitty about myself. If Marcus talks and I pretend not to hear, is he really there?

The music fades, and the congregation sinks into their seats.

The Reverend steps to the podium, and I wish I could say his sermon was about something relevant. Forgiveness or new beginnings, maybe, or the many reasons why good people do bad things and still get to go to Heaven. But I suppose that would be too convenient, much too serendipitous, and real life doesn't come tied up with a pretty bow. He preaches about the greatness of God, and I listen for a while before my mind starts to wander.

It's been four months since Marcus tumbled off that rooftop, four months since the police slapped handcuffs on my wrists and carted me downtown. I told them everything, and still they threw the book at me. They charged me with falsifying my identity, with fraud, with unlawful possession of not one but two stolen weapons. They even threatened me with second-degree murder for a while, until my attorney pointed out both guns were empty. The bullet Clyde gave me was never found, but the residue was, up both of my arms, my shirt, my face and Bozo-the-Clown hair.

And then the Atlanta police received a call from Chief Eubanks. He told them that when Sabine's body floated up from the darkness, she brought along an unequivocal clue: strapped to her wrist was a sports watch, one of those devices that monitors heart rate and tracks workouts. Running. Biking. Swimming. This model was waterproof, and once they recharged the battery, they discovered she'd turned on the GPS function, which tracked her all the way into the lake. Unsurprisingly, it matched the GPS on Marcus's patrol car at the time of her death.

They also found a basket of papers in his trunk, printed emails and scribbled notes and lists, all of them painting the picture of a man obsessed, not with finding Sabine, but with locating me. All of a sudden, my pleas of self-defense were looking more and more credible, my reasons for possessing the fake ID and firearms perfectly reasonable. The Atlanta police let me go, but not without a hefty fine. One they offered to waive if I gave them the name of the person who supplied such a fine counterfeit Georgia driver's license. I paid the hefty fine.

But the whole time I was sitting there, sweating buckets behind the locked metal door of an interrogation room downtown, I kept waiting for someone to charge me with theft. To bring up the money that went missing from Charlene's desk drawer, to ask me if I took it. But no one ever did. These past four months, I've given a lot of thought as to why the Reverend didn't turn me in. Maybe Martina didn't show him the note I wrote her, or maybe he really did mean all those sermons he preached about forgiveness and helping others in need. I hope that one day I'll work up the courage to ask.

The lady next to me nudges me with an elbow, then drops a basket on my lap, a square wicker container filled with crumpled bills and folded checks. I retrieve the envelope from my bag and drop it in. Inside is a cashier's check for the two thousand dollars I liberated from Charlene's drawer, plus 20 percent interest. I would have given more, but death is expensive, and I'm still waiting for Marcus's benefits to kick in. Chief Eubanks gave me everything I'd be entitled to if Marcus had died in the line of duty—a generous gesture I probably don't deserve. Any day now, I should be receiving a hefty lump sum, a full pension and restitution for the funeral expenses I paid from our savings.

But Chief Eubanks ended up giving me something

even better. When I sat at his desk and told him the whole, sordid story, he held my hand between both of his and said the words my own husband couldn't. He told me he was sorry, both for what Marcus did and what the department didn't, and my heart broke right then and there. If I had gone to Chief all those months ago, maybe Marcus would still be alive. In jail, but alive. But the past seven years had taught me to trust no one, not even a cop. *Especially* not a cop. Of all the reasons I have to resent Marcus, that is the one I think of most. He robbed me of the ability to trust in others, made me forget so many of them come from a place of kindness.

I'm not really the praying kind, but this seems as good a place as any to say one. I pray for Ingrid, who can barely stop crying long enough to tell her sister's story to anyone who will listen, including a true crime writer from Netflix for a six-figure sum. I pray for Trevor, who's packed up and followed his family to Salt Lake City, the only way he could talk his wife into shared custody. I pray for Jeffrey, who's trapped in a house he can't sell, living off money he didn't earn in a town that wants nothing to do with him. He's a hermit, a recluse, the town pariah, a creep who slept with Mandy while his wife decomposed in a pond fifty miles away. The only time he ever goes outside is to chase vandals off his lawn.

But mostly, I pray for Sabine. That she knew she was loved, that Marcus didn't make her suffer for long. That wherever she is, she's found peace.

The Reverend starts to wrap up the sermon, and

I scoot past my neighbors and out of the row. I've done what I came here to do, and now it's time to go.

"Not every question has an answer," he says as I'm climbing the stairs. "Not every problem has a solution. But if you're open for it, there is grace in uncertainty."

Grace in uncertainty.

The words stick my sneakers to the carpet, and I turn. The Reverend's head is tipped back, his face raised to mine, and my skin prickles. I wonder if he recognizes me, if he can see my face this far away, all the way on the very top step. I study his expression in the LED screens, and I think I see recognition.

He smiles and lifts his arms on either side of his body like wings. "Uncertainty leaves us open to doubt, yes, but it also opens us up to splendor and joy and wondrous surprise. To the beauty of hope. Nothing is certain, nothing is known, but it is in those moments of our greatest uncertainty that miracles happen."

These past four months, I've shed a shitload of tears. More than I'd like to think about. But I stand here, in the middle of the church aisle and bawl, and for the first time I don't feel ashamed of my tears or wipe them away with a sleeve. I let them fall because these are the good kind of tears. The—well, if not *happy* kind, at least the everything's-going-to-be-okay kind. I tell myself the Reverend is right. There is grace in uncertainty, and everything's going to be okay.

Down in the pit, the band starts up a melody, and the notes chase me up the stairs and out the doors, into the bright October sunshine. Autumn makes Atlanta a much more pleasant place, the air dry and crisp and glorious under a bright blue sky. I tilt my face to the sun, letting the rays warm my skin. Maybe this is why people come to church, to feel lighter, to relinquish their fears and be calm, if only for an hour.

I check my watch. Three more hours until a plane carries me back to Pine Bluff, where I will pack up the house and leave for… Somewhere. I haven't decided yet. But after what happened on that rooftop, I have some karma to set right, and I plan to start here.

I pull out my phone and thumb in the number I memorized on the banks of the Chattahoochee. She may be a thief, but who am I to judge? I know better than anyone that people will do all sorts of things in order to survive.

The line connects, and I recognize the husky hello, that twinge of Spanish inflection she tries so hard to hide.

"Hello, Martina? It's me. Emma Durand."

* * * * *

ACKNOWLEDGEMENTS

Writers write alone, but bringing a book into the world takes a village. I am incredibly blessed to have a team of people—talented people, brilliant and funny people—who helped me with this one.

To Nikki Terpilowski, thanks for rolling with it when I came to you with this idea at the eleventh hour, and then taking both the concept and early drafts to the next level. To Liz Stein, who connected with the concept enough to green-light it, and to Laura Brown, who swooped in and filled Liz's shoes and then some. Thanks for your unwavering enthusiasm for this story, and for pushing me to make it the very best it could be. To Emer Flounders and all the talented folks working behind the scenes at Harlequin and Harper Collins, thank you will never be enough. I am so grateful to be part of the Park Row Books family.

To my critique partner, Laura Drake, and the best early readers a girl could ask for: Kristy Barrett, Tonni Callan, Andrea Peskind Katz, Bob and Diane Maleski, Laura Rash, Jen Robinson, Missy Robinson.

Thanks for suffering through early drafts and finding encouraging words to keep me going. To Emily Carpenter and Kate Moretti, for all the belly laughs and talking me off many a ledge. Where are the Calamity Dames going next?

To all the bloggers and online readers groups: Great Thoughts Great Readers and their Ninjas, A Novel Bee, Readers Coffeehouse (come join us!), Sue's Booking Agency, Tall Poppies, Women Writers Women's Books, and a million more I can't list here. Thank you for the conversations and the shout-outs and the friendship. You make this writing gig feel a lot less lonely.

To Lisa O'Brien, who paid good money for the dubious honor of having her name appear in this book, and to the Kingsport Literacy Council on the receiving end of Lisa's generous contribution. I can't think of a more worthy beneficiary.

To my girl squad: Elizabeth Baxendale, Christy Brown, Lisa Camp, Nancy Davis, Marquette Dreesch, Angelique Kilkelly, Jen Robinson, Amanda Sapra, Raquel Souza, and Tracy Willoughby. Thanks for being my cheerleaders, my secret keepers, my sisters in crime. Y'all complete me.

To Ewoud, who when I'm in the throes of writing is always happy to take over mealtimes or help brainstorm the best ways to murder a person. Thanks for knowing when I need a hand, and when I need to be left alone. If I ever get arrested, please delete my search history.

Last, but certainly not least, to Evan and Isabella. Of all my works of art, you two are my favorite.

*Read on for a sneak peek at Kimberly Belle's
gripping new psychological thriller,*
Stranger in the Lake.

CHAPTER ONE

I untie the dock cleats and shove the boat into water as gray as the sky. Sometime in the past few hours, gunmetal clouds have rolled over the mountaintops, shooting down icy gusts that froth the surface of Lake Crosby into a million white peaks. My stomach churns, and not from the water's chop.

Maybe morning sickness, maybe nerves at the words I need to say to my new husband out loud.

Surprise! I'm pregnant.

I sink onto the helm seat and shove my hands into the pockets of my new down jacket. A gift from Paul, who has impeccable taste—the kind that comes from good breeding and a big bank account. We've only ever spoken about children in the vaguest of terms. Things like "this room would make a good nursery" or "we would make pretty babies," the "one day" silent but implied. He and his first wife had never tried for a baby before she died, a little over four years ago. I haven't known him a year. This wasn't exactly the plan.

But neither was falling for a man eleven years older than me, a man who always claimed he'd never marry again. The thirty-seven-year-old wealthy widower falls for a gas station clerk from the muddy side of the mountain, both of us touched by tragedy. A combination that everybody from our town said would never work.

"I don't give a damn what people think," Paul is constantly telling me. "I love you and you love me, and that's all that matters."

But now… My hand feels under the jacket to my still-flat stomach. What will he think about this little surprise blooming inside my belly? I have no idea.

His mother, the people in town, friends who've known him all his life. I know exactly what they'll say.

They'll say that this baby was no accident. That the littlest Keller will cement my place at the family dinner table in a way the three carats on my ring finger can't. That marriages are temporary, but children are until the end of time. That now he's *really* trapped.

Sugar daddy, sugar baby, baby daddy.

By now the wind has pushed me away from the dock, and I start the engine and swing the boat around. Paul and I live on a cove, but the currents here are swift, the water dangerously deep. The hill his house is perched on doesn't stop at the shoreline, but plunges to depths of up to three hundred feet. There's a whole town buried down there, tucked in the hills of what was once a thriving valley. Homes, roads, farms, schools. Graveyards. Whenever anything manages to wriggle loose—a battered shingle, an algae-covered shoe, a slimy dog collar—it ends up here, in Skeleton Cove.

Halfway to the town's center, I ease up on the throttle, going around the point to Buck Knob Cove, and look westward, over the water and mountains and endless smoky skies. I've never lived anywhere else but Lake Crosby, North Carolina—have never even considered it—and still the raw beauty of this place can take my breath away. These mountains are as much a part of me as my own skin and bones, the connection as real as the cells multiplying in my belly. If I close my eyes, I can feel the plates shifting under my feet. I am the mountains and the mountains are me. I couldn't live anyplace else if I tried.

It's the one thing I can't resent my mother for, I suppose, choosing this place to have a family—not that she was much of a parent. I mostly raised myself, and then I raised my brother, Chet, which is how I know love can only go so far. Love doesn't put food on the table. Love doesn't pay the rent or the creditors who come banging at the door. A baby needs so much more than love.

People say I married Paul for the money, but that's just not true. I married him because I love him, and I love him for all the things he provides. A mortgage-free roof over my head and a belly stuffed with nutritious, organic food. Health insurance and car insurance and cell phone and internet. The freedom of never having to choose between going cold or going hungry again. A life that is safe and stable and secure.

And really, when you think about it, isn't *security* just another word for *love*?

CHAPTER TWO

The town of Lake Crosby isn't much, just three square blocks and some change, but it's the only town in the southern Appalachians perched at the edge of the water, which makes it a popular tourist spot. Paul's office is at the far end of the first block, tucked between a fudge shop and Stuart's Craft Cocktails, which as far as I can tell is just another way to say "pretentious bar." Most of the businesses here are pretentious farm-to-table restaurants and specialty boutiques selling all things overpriced and unnecessary.

For people like Paul, town is a place to socialize and make money—in his case, by selling custom house designs for the million-dollar lots that sit high on the hills or line the lakeshores. My old friends serve his drinks and wait his tables—but only the lucky ones. There are ten times more locals than there are jobs.

The covered terrace for the cocktail lounge is quiet, a result of the off-season and the incoming weather, the sign on the door still flipped to Closed.

I'm passing the empty hostess stand when I notice movement at the very back, a tattered shadow peeling away from the wall. Jax—the town loon, the crazy old man who lives in the woods. Most people turn away from him, either out of pity or fear, but not me. For some reason I can't put into words, I've never been afraid to look him straight on.

He takes a couple of halting steps, like he doesn't want to be seen—and he probably doesn't. Jax is like a deer you come up on in a meadow, one blink and he's gone. But this time he doesn't move.

His gaze flicks around, searching the street behind me. "Where's Paul." A statement, not a question.

Slowly, so not to spook him, I point to the sleek double doors on the next building, golden light spilling out the windows of Keller Architecture. "Did you check inside?"

Jax shakes his head. "I need to talk to him. It's important."

Like every time he emerges from out of the woods, curiosity bubbles in my chest. Once upon a time, Jax had everything going for him. High school prom king and star quarterback, the golden boy with a golden future, and one of Paul's two best friends. Their picture still sits atop his desk in the study, Paul and Jax and Micah, all tanned chests and straightened smiles, three teenage boys with the world at their feet.

Now he's Batty Jax, the raggedy, bearded boogeyman parents use as a warning. Do your homework, stay out of trouble and don't end up like Jax.

He clings to the murky back of the terrace, sticking to the shaded spots where it's too dark for me to make out much more than a halo of matted hair, the jutting edges of an oversize jacket, long, lean thighs. His face is dark, too, the combination of dirt and a life outdoors and dirt.

"Do you want me to give Paul a message? Or if you stay right there, I can send him out. I know he'll want to see you."

Actually, I don't know; I only assume. Jax is the source of a slew of rumors and petty gossip, but for Paul he's a painful subject, one he doesn't like to talk about. As far as I know, the two haven't spoken since high school graduation—not an easy thing to do in a town where everybody knows everybody.

Jax glances up the street, in the direction of far-off voices floating on the icy wind. I don't follow his gaze, but I can tell from the way his body turns skittish that someone is coming this way, moving closer.

"Do you need anything? Some money maybe?"

Good thing those people aren't within earshot, because they would laugh at the absurdity of the trailer park girl turned married-up wifey offering the son of an insurance tycoon some cash. Not that Jax's father didn't disown him ages ago or that I have more than a couple bucks in my pocket, but still.

Jax shakes his head again. "Tell Paul I need to talk to him. Tell him to hurry."

Before I can ask what for, he's off, planting a palm on the railing and springing over in one easy leap, his body light as a pole vaulter. He hits the cement and takes off up the alley. I dash forward until I'm flush with the railing, peering down the long passage between Paul's building and the cocktail lounge, but it's empty. Jax is already gone.

I push through the doors of Keller Architecture, an open space with cleared desks and darkened computer screens. The whiteboard on the back wall has already been wiped clean, too, one of the many tasks Paul requires his staff to do daily. It's nearing five, and other than his lead designer, Gwen, hunched over a drawing at her drafting table, the office is empty.

She nods at my desk. "Perfect timing. I just finished the Curtis Cottage drawings."

Calling a seven-thousand-square-foot house a "cottage" is ridiculous, as are whatever reasons Tom Curtis and his wife, a couple well into their seventies, gave Paul for wanting six bedrooms and two kitchens in what is essentially a weekend home. But the Curtises are typical Keller Architecture clients—privileged, demanding and more than a little entitled. They like Paul because he's one of them. Having a desk is probably ridiculous, too, since I only work twenty hours a week, and for most of them I'm anywhere but here. My role is client relations, which consists mainly of hauling my ass to wherever the clients are so I can put out fires and talk them off the latest ledge. The job and the desk are one of the many perks of being married to a Keller.

"Thanks." I tuck the Curtis designs under an arm and move toward the hallway to my left, a sleek tunnel of wood and steel that ends in Paul's glass-walled office. "I'm here to pick up Paul. There's something wrong with his car."

When he called earlier to tell me his car was dead

in the lot, I thought he was joking. Engine trouble is what happens to my ancient Civic, not Paul's fancy Range Rover, a brand-new supercharged machine with a dashboard that belongs in a cockpit. *More money than sense*, my mother would say about Paul if she were here, and now, I guess, about me.

Gwen leans back in her chair, wagging a mechanical pencil between two slim fingers. "Yeah, the dealer is sending a tow truck and a replacement car, but they just called to say they're delayed. He said he had a couple of errands to run."

I frown. "Who, the tow truck driver?"

"No, Paul." She swivels in her chair, reaching across the desk behind her for a straightedge. "He should be back any sec."

I thank her and head for the door.

On the sidewalk, I fire off a quick text to Paul. I'm here, where are you?

I wait for a reply that doesn't come. The screen goes dark, then black. I slip the phone into my jacket pocket and start walking.

In a town like Lake Crosby, there are only so many places Paul could be. The market, the pharmacy, the shop where he buys his ties and socks. I pop into all of them, but no one's seen him since this morning. Back on the sidewalk, I pull out my phone and give him a call. It rings once, then shoots me to voice mail. I hit End and look up and down the mostly deserted street.

"Hey, Charlie," somebody calls from across the road, two single lanes separated by a parking strip, and I whirl around, spotting Wade's familiar face over the cars and SUVs. One of my brother's former classmates, a known troublemaker who dropped out sophomore year because he was too busy cooking meth and raising hell. He leans against the ivory siding of the bed-and-breakfast, holding what I sincerely hope is a hand-rolled cigarette.

"It's Charlotte," I say, but I don't know why I bother.

On my sixteenth birthday, I had plunked down more than a hundred hard-earned dollars at the courthouse to change my name. But no matter how many times I correct the people who knew me back when—people who populate the trailer parks and shacks along the mountain range, people like Wade and me—no matter how many times I tell them I'm not that person anymore, to them I'll always be Charlie.

He flicks the cigarette butt into the gutter and tilts his head up the street. "I just saw your old man coming out of the coffee shop." Emphasis on the *old man*. "If you hurry, you can probably catch him."

I mumble a thanks, then head in that direction.

Just past the market, I spot Paul at the far end of a side street, a paper cup clutched in his hand. He's wearing the clothes I watched him pull on this morning—a North Face fleece, a navy cashmere sweater, dark jeans, leather lace-up boots, but no coat. No hat or scarf or gloves. Paul always dresses like this, without a second thought as to the elements. That fleece might be fine for the quick jogs from the house to his car to the office door, but with the wind skimming up the lake, he must be freezing.

The woman he's talking to is more properly dressed. Boots and a black wool coat, the big buttons fastened all the way to a neck cloaked in a double-wrapped scarf. A knitted hat is pulled low over her ears and hair, leaving only a slice of her face—from this angle, her profile—exposed.

"There you are," I say, and they both turn.

A short but awkward silence. If I didn't know better, I'd think he looks surprised to see me.

"Charlotte, hi. I was just…" He glances at the woman, then back to me. "What are you doing here?"

"You asked me to pick you up. Didn't you get my texts?"

With his free hand, he wriggles his cell from his pocket and checks the screen. "Oh. Sorry, I must have had it on Silent. I was on my way back to the office, but then I got to talking and…well, you know how that goes." He gives me a sheepish smile. It's a known fact that Paul is a talker, and like in most small towns, there's always someone to talk to.

But I don't know this woman.

I take in her milky skin and sky blue eyes, the light smattering of freckles across her nose and high cheekbones, and I'm positive I've never seen her before. She's the kind of pretty a person would remember, almost beautiful even, though she's nothing like his type. Paul likes his women curvy and exotic, with dark hair and ambiguous coloring. This woman is bony, her skin so pale it's almost translucent.

I step closer, holding up my hand in a wave. "Hi, I'm Charlotte Keller. Paul's wife."

The woman gives me a polite smile, but her gaze flits to Paul. She murmurs something, and I'm pretty sure it's "Keller."

The hairs soldier on the back of my neck, even though I've never been the jealous type. It's always seemed like such a waste of energy to me, being possessive and suspicious of a man who claims to love you. Either you believe him or you don't—or so I've always thought. Paul tells me he loves me all the time, and I believe him.

But this woman wouldn't be the first around these parts to try to snag herself a Keller.

"Are you ready?" I say, looking at Paul. "Because I came in the boat, and we need to get home before this weather blows in."

The talk of rain does the trick, and Paul snaps out of whatever I walked into here. He gives me that smile he saves only for me, and a rush of something warm hits me hard, right behind the knees.

People who say Paul and I are wrong together don't get that we've been waiting for each other all our lives. His first wife's death, my convict father and meth-head mother, they broke us for a reason, so all these years later our jagged edges would fit together perfectly, like two pieces of the same fractured puzzle. The first time Paul took my hand, the world just…started making sense.

And now there's a baby, a perfect little piece of Paul and me, an accidental miracle that somehow busted through the birth control. Maybe it's not a fluke but a sign, the universe's way of telling me something good is coming. A new life. A new chance to get things right.

All of a sudden and out of nowhere I feel it, this burning in my chest, an overwhelming, desperate fire for this baby that's taken root in my belly. I want it to grow and kick and thrive. I want it with everything inside me.

"Let's go home." Without so much as a backward glance at the woman, Paul takes my hand and leads me to the boat.

We're smack in the middle of Lake Crosby when it starts to snow, lazy fat flakes dancing down from a canopy of white. Flurries, but there's more coming. Those are snow clouds spilling over the mountaintops.

Paul has the bow pointed to home and the throttle buried, and I don't blame him. His fleece was bad enough in town, where there were warm shops to duck in and brick buildings to huddle behind. Out here on the open water the wind is fierce, and he might as well be shirtless.

He's hunched low behind the windshield, steering the boat with his knees, his hands shoved deep in his pits for warmth. I take in his blue lips, his chattering teeth, and wince. I should have brought his coat.

Tell him. Just open your mouth and say I'm pregnant. *Do it now.*

"Hey, Paul?" The words get lost in the roar of the engine, but there's no stopping now. Not when I've finally summoned my courage. I tap him on the shoulder and try again. "*Paul.*"

He pulls back on the throttle, slowing the boat to a crawl. "What's wrong? Did you forget something?"

I shake my head. An hour ago, I left the house with exactly two items, the boat keys and my cell phone, both of which are here with me now. The keys dangle from the ignition, and I tucked my cell in the cubby by my seat, along with the Curtis Cottage drawings.

"You know how I've been feeling kinda out of sorts?" I don't have to tick off my symptoms—the bouts of nausea, the bone tiredness I can't seem to shake. Paul had brought me chicken soup from the market in town, covered me with blankets whenever I'd nap on the couch.

"You had the flu."

"That's what I thought, too. But who has the flu for three whole weeks?"

I stare at him hard, waiting for the realization to hit, but Paul's face is a complete blank. I can't tell if it's because he doesn't understand where I'm going with this, or if he's trying to contain his panic—or worse, suspicion. Will he accuse me of flicking my pills into the toilet, of forgetting to take them on purpose? His mother certainly will.

I look away. "Anyway, it wasn't the flu."

He reaches up and kills the engine. All around us, the air goes quiet the way it can only here, in the middle of a lake cradled between mountains and trees. A strange kind of muffled silence punctuated by the far-off cry of a hawk.

Paul swivels on his seat to face me, his voice laced with worry. "What is it? Are you sick?"

"No." My answer is swift, and I make sure to look him in the eyes. Paul's already lost one wife. Of course his mind would go there. I probably should have led with my good health. "No, I'm fine. Better than fine. Healthy as can be."

My heart is pounding now, but that's to be expected. I think of the matching pink lines on the sticks, wrapped in toilet paper and buried at the bottom of the wastebasket. The instructions said one line may come out lighter than the other, but any hint of a second line meant I was pregnant. All three times I pulled a new one from the wrapper and peed on it just in case the ones before it were defective, the lines were so pink they were almost purple.

I see the second the quarter drops. Paul huffs out a breath, and the twin lines between his eyebrows smooth out. "Are you saying what I think you're saying?" He sounds stunned, not angry. In fact, he kind of sounds the opposite, happy and hopeful—but maybe that's just me.

Still. I bite down on a smile. "That depends. What do you think I'm saying?"

"Charlotte McCreedy Keller, don't play games with me. My brittle old heart can't take it." He stands, reaching for me with icy hands, pulling me out of my chair. "Are you going to make me the happiest man on the planet? Are you going to make me a father?" He wraps his hands around my biceps and gives them a little jiggle. His eyes are gleaming, his smile stretched clear to his sideburns. "Are you?"

After a second or two, I nod.

Paul whoops, and a flock of swallows bursts from a bush on the shore, birds and batting wings swirling in the air. Suddenly I'm in the air, too, my legs wrapped around Paul's waist, his hands firm on my backside. He twirls me around in the tiny space between the seats, and I laugh, from relief and at Paul's reaction—a stunned but unapologetic joy.

"You're pretty strong for an old man."

"I'm not an old man, I am *the* man. My swimmers are bad*ass*. They are fucking *fierce*." I laugh, and he puts me down. "How do you feel? Any other symptoms?"

"A little tired still, and kinda pukey in the mornings. Once I eat something, I'm usually fine."

"This is…this is amazing. I can't wait to tell everybody. Let's go home and make some calls."

"Paul, can we just… I don't know, keep this quiet for a little while longer? At least until I see the doctor and she gives us the green light. I want to know everything's okay before we go telling the whole world."

Worry flits across his brow. "What, you think this baby might not stick?"

"No, but it's still so early. I want to see this baby with my own two eyes and be sure. Let's just wait until after the first ultrasound, okay?"

"Okay, but so you know, I have a good feeling about this little guy. He's going to be fine."

I lift a brow. "Little *guy*?"

"Well, yeah. An adorable baby Keller to carry on the name." He presses a hand over my lower stomach and smiles. "Paul Junior."

Now *that* his mother would approve of, a carbon copy of her precious son. I think back to Diana's reaction when we told her we were getting married, the fake smile that tried to crack open her cheeks when Chet walked me down the aisle. I am not what she pictured for Paul—I'm too young, too unpolished, too poor and crass. She thinks that some time very soon, her son will snap to his senses.

But a baby… A baby changes everything.

"What if it's a Paulette?"

Paul makes a face. "*God*, no. I can't saddle my daughter with a name like Paulette. She'll grow up and go on *Dr. Phil*, talking about how we ruined her life. She'll never speak to us again."

Neglect, alcoholism, a felon father and a mother who had no business ever pushing out kids—now those are some things to bellyache about on national television. This baby will have everything Chet and I didn't: a real house with real walls to keep out of the cold, a fridge filled with food, clothes that don't come from a church basement bin. Two parents who stick around, who don't disappear for days at a time or get carted off to jail.

And as corny as it sounds, love.

I smile over our hands at my husband. "I do have one more request."

"For the love of my life? The mother of my child?" He lifts my hand to his lips, presses a frosty kiss to my knuckle. "Absolutely anything."

"When it's time, you get to tell your mother."